To Bill

Watching Jeopardy

Watching Jeopardy

Norm Foster

Library of Congress Control Number: 2011908129
ISBN: Hardcover   978-1-4628-7449-1
                    Softcover   978-1-4628-7448-4
                    Ebook   978-1-4628-7450-7

This book was printed in the United States of America.

To order additional copies of this book, contact:
Xlibris Corporation
1-888-795-4274
www.Xlibris.com
Orders@Xlibris.com
99631

-1-

The body was discovered the same night that Mickey Welton made his appearance on Jeopardy. As a singular event, the discovery of a dead body was prodigious news in a town which boasted only nine thousand citizens, especially if foul play was suspected, but when coupled with a local man's appearance on a nationwide television game show, it grew to gargantuan news, and it made September the twenty-first, nineteen ninety-nine, the biggest night ever in the history of Rainbow, New Brunswick.

*

Pete Golliger sat on the third stool in from the front door of The Frying Dutchman, Rainbow's number one greasy spoon, and the home of the finest raspberry pie in the entire world, at least that's what the hand-written sign in the window said. Behind the counter, Henry Van Etten, the Frying Dutchman himself, was using the remote control to adjust the color on the twenty inch Magnavox that sat on a jerry-rigged shelf above the microwave. Henry found 'The Frying Dutchman' a clever name, he being of Dutch descent and a restaurateur on top of that. It probably hadn't crossed his mind that the other three thousand owners of establishments in North America called 'The Frying Dutchman' had mistakenly found it clever as well.

"That was a helluva rain shower we had," said Pete looking out the window onto Main Street. A storm had blown into Rainbow about an hour earlier and had dropped an inordinate amount of precipitation on the small town in less than fifteen minutes.

"Is that too green?" Henry wasn't paying attention to Pete. He was looking up at the Magnavox.

Pete looked up at the aged television set. "No, but I think it needs more red."

"Well, then it's too green."

"What?"

"You've got two hues on a color t.v., Pete. You've got your green hue and your red hue. If it needs more red then that means that it's too green, so, you turn the green down."

"Why can't you just turn the red up?"

"No, you can't do that, no. You start turning the hues up and before you know it you have to roll off some of the contrast, and then some of the sharpness and then you're really up shit creek. No, best to pull back on the hues. It makes for a more even and subtle tone on the set. It's easier on the eyes."

"Two hues, huh?"

"Two hues."

"I didn't know that."

"Well, you should start watching more television."

"Yeah, I guess maybe I should."

Pete didn't have time for television these days, being one of the only two policemen left in Rainbow, but, before long he was going to have more time on his hands than he would know what to do with. The Royal Canadian Mounted Police were swallowing up most of the local forces in the province – Moncton, Bathurst and Campbellton had already fallen to the Mounties – and the Rainbow force would be absorbed next. September the twenty-eighth was the target date. One week away. After that, Pete and the other remaining cop in town, Wood Lynch, would be cut loose with a modest stipend and a firm handshake as parting gifts.

The Rainbow police force used to be five strong, but, when they heard about the takeover six months ago, the other three members of the force, including Police Chief Walt Steeves, found employment elsewhere. Walt took a position fairly high up in the Halifax-Dartmouth Police Force in the neighbouring province of Nova Scotia, and at last report was doing very well there. In fact, his first week on the job, he talked a jumper down off the bridge to Dartmouth. As luck would have it, the jumper shot himself in the head the next day, but, Walt reasoned that he couldn't be everywhere. So, Pete Golliger and Wood Lynch were now enforcing Rainbow's laws all by themselves. They hadn't really talked about which one of them was the ranking officer. Pete was nine years older at forty-four, but Wood had been a member of the Rainbow force for a year longer than Pete, having joined just after he turned twenty-three. It wasn't that important who was in charge anyway, seeing as how the biggest threat to the community was Duffy Higgenson, the Parkinson's Disease-afflicted dentist on Main Street. Duffy's unsteady hand had wreaked enough havoc on the local citizenry to qualify as a minor crime spree.

Pete Golliger was not a native of Rainbow. Pete was raised in Toronto, but had always had a curiosity about places that he had never seen, and every so often that curiosity developed into a wanderlust. When Pete finished high school, he took a year off and backpacked his way west to Vancouver, then south down the west coast of the United States into Mexico.

It was in Acapulco that Pete realized his money was just about gone, and with it, his wanderlust. That was when he afforded himself the luxury of a bus ticket and headed home. This time up through Texas, Louisiana, Mississippi, and Tennessee, where he and a woman passenger from Cincinnati talked the bus driver into taking a detour in Memphis so they could get a photograph of themselves in front of the gates at Graceland. Then on through Kentucky to Ohio, where the woman from Cincinnati said goodbye to Pete by planting a big kiss right on his nineteen year-old mouth. He and the woman were not romantically involved at all. She had to be at least thirty, Pete estimated. In fact, the only thing they had going on between them was that photograph in front of Graceland, and a couple of thousand miles worth of friendly conversation. Maybe she just felt like doing something outrageous. Maybe that was why she kissed him. Maybe she felt a fondness for this good looking nineteen year-old. After all, his was the first face she saw when she boarded the bus back in Shreveport, and he had smiled at her. She welcomed this after the solemn visit she had just had with her sister. Her sister had found a lump in her breast and the woman had taken the bus down to be with her only sibling when she got the test results back. The news was not good. Mastectomy. Double. Maybe this was why the woman gave Pete the big kiss. Maybe she figured, "What the hell? You only live once, and in some cases not long enough." Pete wished that he had returned her kiss to show her that he felt a fondness for her too, and so she wouldn't feel alone in her outrageousness, but he was so surprised by her action that he didn't have time to gather himself, and before he knew it, the kiss was over, she said "See ya, Pete," and she disappeared into the bus station. That night, his bus passed through Michigan, across the border into Ontario and back to Toronto.

After his year of travel, Pete bounced around at a few jobs and eventually wound up working for a moving company. He had worked his way up to assistant manager of the outfit by the time he was twenty-eight. This was when he met a real estate agent named Heather Walsh. They were married when Pete was thirty-one and divorced when he was thirty-two. Pete used to say "It was a marriage made in heaven that went straight to hell."

Heather and Pete had been married only six months when she announced that she had fallen in love with an American real estate agent and she was moving down to Buffalo to live with him, leaving Pete to file for divorce. Now, it wasn't the fact that he lost Heather that stuck in Pete's craw. He wasn't even too annoyed that it was, in his opinion, the uncomely city of Buffalo that she was moving to. It was the swiftness of Heather's fall for this American fellow that Pete could not quite comprehend. When Pete was courting Heather, it took him two months just to get a date with her, then another three years to get her to marry him. How could she meet, fall for, and run off with another man in only six months?

"Six months," Pete said to his lawyer when he went in to file the divorce papers. "And that's assuming she met him on our honeymoon! It was probably only four or five months. And he was an American for chrissake. He didn't even live in the same city as us! How in the hell could it possibly happen?"

"It's the real estate business, Pete," his lawyer told him. "I deal with real estate people all the time and believe me, the pressure is so intense–the competition so fierce – that sometimes two agents are forced into one another's arms as a comfort more than anything else. They find solace in someone who is going through the same hell that they are."

"They're selling bungalows!" countered Pete. "They're not invading goddamned Normandy!"

It was right after his marriage ended that Pete got another case of wanderlust, and made the decision to leave Toronto and go east. He had never been to the Maritimes and he thought maybe this would be a good place to start fresh, so, he put what furniture he had into storage, threw a few things into his Pontiac Grand Am, and headed east on the Trans-Canada Highway.

Pete had not planned on stopping in Rainbow, New Brunswick. In fact, he was speeding right by it at about one hundred and thirty kilometers an hour, when officer Walt Steeves pulled him over.

"Damn it," thought Pete. "Shit, shit, shit."

The officer approached the car as Pete watched him in his side view mirror. Pete thought the man looked a little overweight to be a cop, but maybe the qualifications were a little more relaxed out here, or maybe things appeared larger in the side view mirror than they actually were.

"Afternoon", said Walt. "License and registration please."

Pete had his wallet at the ready and he reached in and pulled out both pieces of information and handed them to the officer.

"Where you headed?" Whenever he wrote out tickets, Walt liked to make small talk.

"East," replied Pete.

"Well, you're going in the right direction. How far east?"

"I'll probably stop in Prince Edward Island."

"That'd be a good idea. Otherwise you'll be in the friggin' ocean." Walt walked around to the rear of Pete's car to get the license number, then he approached the car window again. "I see you're an Upper Canadian."

"I'm a what?"

"An Upper Canadian. You're from Ontario."

"Oh, yes. Yes, I am."

"I also see your inspection sticker's expired." Walt tapped the little blue sticker on Pete's front windshield with his pen.

"Shit," Pete thought. He hadn't even noticed that his safety inspection was three months overdue. He had been preoccupied with the divorce. "I'm sorry, Officer. I forgot all about it. I'll get it renewed as soon as I get to where I'm going."

"Oh, you'll get it renewed a lot sooner than that, Jim," Walt said, tearing the ticket off and handing it to Pete. "Follow me. There's a service station bout' a mile from here."

"But, I'm . . . ." Pete didn't finish his sentence. He was going to say he was in a hurry. He had to be somewhere. But, he wasn't, and he didn't. Why not get the car inspected here? What the hell else did he have to do? He followed Officer Steeves to an exit that said 'Rainbow Business District.' The fact is, this was the only exit to Rainbow, so whether you were going to the business district or the suburbs or the Rainbow Golf and Country Club, this was the exit you took. The exit turned onto Nylander Street, where they passed a small park with a large gazebo in the center of it. Moran Park, named after the town's first mayor, Lowell Moran.

At the first stop sign they turned left onto Main Street and about five hundred yards down the road, Pete saw what he assumed must be the business district. They passed Proctor's Electric, a Sobey's grocery store, a medical center housing the offices of an optometrist, two general practitioners, and a dentist, Doctor Duffy Higgenson. There was a Tim Horton's Donuts, Ingersoll's Hardware, The Frying Dutchman, Doug Petty's La-Z-Boy Furniture Store, and a wealth of trees. Pete was impressed with how the town seemed to have taken the care to leave plenty of trees on their main thoroughfare. He knew they weren't newly planted because they were big elm trees. Had to be a hundred years old, these trees. And they seemed to separate the businesses from one another. Tim Horton's, elm tree, hardware store, elm tree, furniture store, elm tree.

"Nice," thought Pete.

At the end of the business district where Main Street ended and split into two different streets, Holly Street and Koonary Road, was Glen Makarides' Esso Station. It was situated right smack in the middle of the fork, with entrances off both Holly and Koonary. A prime location for a gas station.

Walt Steeves climbed out of his cruiser and was greeted by Glen Makarides himself. Glen was in his fifties but looked seventy. He wore coveralls, and had a cigarette in is mouth with an ash that was a good inch long.

"Got an inspection for you, Glen. Can you fit me in?"

"Sure thing", said Glen. "Put him into the second bay." He didn't remove his cigarette when he spoke and the ash didn't drop.

Walt waved to Pete and pointed to the second bay of the garage where Glen was opening the door. Glen turned and directed Pete in until his car was perfectly situated over the hoist. Pete got out of the Grand Am and walked to the rear end where he found Glen staring at his license plate.

"From Upper Canada, huh?"

"Yeah. Toronto," said Pete.

"Well, I won't hold that against you," Glen smiled and hit the lever that raised the hoist. "This'll take bout' a half hour." The ash dropped onto his coveralls and Glen brushed it away casually, as if it was a common occurrence.

"Might as well have a seat," came Walt Steeves' voice from the other bay.

Pete turned around to find the officer sitting in a green and white checkered lawn chair just inside the number one service bay door. This was Pete's introduction to a quaint Rainbow custom. For some reason, as Pete was to find out, many Rainbow citizens liked to sit on lawn chairs in their garages and watch the traffic pass by out on the street. It was as if they wanted to go outside, but not all the way outside. So, Pete sat himself down in the lawn chair next to Walt Steeves and they passed the wait with some small talk. Every once in a while, Walt would wave to somebody driving by out on Holly Street and they would honk their horn and wave back. One of them even waved to Pete and Pete obligingly waved back.

"Who was that?" Pete asked.

"Laura Pooley's girl, Rachel. Been out west for a few years. Probably thinks you're somebody she should know."

Pete had just been introduced to his second quaint Rainbow custom. Everybody in Rainbow was referred to as their parent's children. "Bob Trimble's boy, Charlie", "Harry Kirk's boy, Gordie", etc.. And so, even though Rachel Pooley was thirty-five years old and had three children of her own, she was still "Laura Pooley's girl, Rachel", and she would remain so until Laura passed away, at which time Rachel would acquire her own identity.

As the half hour inspection turned into an hour, Pete discovered that Walt was very easy to talk to, as Walt would prove years later by talking that jumper down off the bridge to Dartmouth. Pete began to wonder if everybody in this town was as easy going and friendly as this forty-something police officer with the sizeable girth. "Wouldn't hurt to find out," he thought.

By the time the inspection was finished, Pete had decided to stay overnight in Rainbow. That one night turned into the next eleven years of his life.

*

"Tell me this, Pete," said The Frying Dutchman, still fiddling with the hue situation on the Magnavox. "How in the hell does a kid growing up in the family that he grew up in, turn out to be so smart?"

"Beats me. He just got lucky I guess."

"Of course, he is adopted. Probably helps that he didn't inherit his old man's brain matter."

"Couldn't hurt."

"And now he's going to be on Jeopardy. Gonna be right up there on my television set. Right there. Unbelievable." Henry paused for a moment, as he stared up at a car commercial out of Bangor. "He's Canadian, you know. The host? Alex Trebek?"

"Yes, I knew that," said Pete. He stared up at the car commercial too. A man wearing what appeared to be a Superman's cape over a grey double-breasted suit was shouting into the camera.

"We'll take anything for a trade-in!! Anything!! Drag it in!! Push it in!! Pull it in!! Just get it down here to Super Manny Kerwin's Ford today! That's Super Manny Kerwin's Ford, where we put the satisfy in satisfaction!!"

Henry paused again. He wasn't one to speak without thinking. "There is no satisfy in satisfaction."

"No, there isn't," agreed Pete.

"What a stupid fuck."

Pete checked his watch. Seven-twenty. He would be off duty at eight o'clock. He and Wood had been working in eight hour shifts since the rest of the force moved away. Wood had come on duty at four a.m. today, then Pete took over at noon. Wood was scheduled to work from eight p.m. until four a.m., and then it would be Pete's turn for the early morning shift. This system seemed fair to both men. Besides, things were slow in Rainbow on most days, and there were plenty of opportunities to grab an hour's nap on the cot at the police station, so the men were never overtaxed by the schedule.

"Slow tonight, Henry," said Pete, looking around the empty diner.

"Well, sure it is. Everybody's home watching Mickey."

Pete sipped his coffee. "Good," he thought to himself. "This will be a slow night even by Rainbow's standards. Maybe Wood can make use of that cot tonight."

He had no idea how wrong he was.

-2-

It was eleven months ago that twenty-five year old Mickey Welton had heard that the television game show, Jeopardy, was going to be holding a contestant search in Bangor, Maine, which is about two hours south of Rainbow. Mickey decided that he would like to try out for the show because he had always done well at the game while sitting in front of the television at home, and after all, how different could it be with millions of people watching you, and two socially-stunted eggheads trying to buzz in ahead of you? So, without telling his parents, Jack and Myrna, and under the pretense of driving his younger sister, Peggy, down to the Bangor Mall to buy some shoes for the upcoming Teens Against Tuberculosis charity dance – a title which would indicate that there were some teens out there who were pro tuberculosis – Mickey headed south with Peggy to take part in the auditions. The reason for not telling his parents was simple; If his father knew that Mickey was going down there, and if Mickey didn't win a spot on the show, then Jack would ridicule the boy. It wasn't that Jack Welton was mean-spirited. He simply didn't know any better. Ridicule was a big part of his growing up and he was just passing it on.

"I'm nervous, Peg," Mickey said as he wheeled the family's blue Toyota four-door into the parking lot of the Superior Bangor Hotel. The Superior was where the contestant search was being held, and prominently displayed over the front entrance of the hotel was a banner that read "Welcome Jeopardy Hopefuls."

"You're gonna do good, Mickey," said Peggy. "I mean, Jesus, you're the smartest guy in Rainbow."

"Yeah, well being the smartest guy in Rainbow is like being the prettiest girl in Rainbow. It isn't saying much."

It took Peggy a good fifteen seconds before a light went on and she said, "Hey! I am the prettiest girl in Rainbow." And she was too.

They walked into the hotel lobby, Mickey, wearing his only suit, the one he would be wearing on television if he made the cut, and Peggy wearing tight jeans and a tight orange top that emphasized her splendid physical gifts and made her bright red hair seem almost fluorescent. Mickey was feeling very much like Gomer Pyle must have felt the first time he left the filling station in Mayberry and headed up to Mount Pilot. Peggy didn't feel that way at all. Peggy felt as if she belonged anywhere and everywhere. They say that it's not unusual for siblings to be as different as night and day the way Mickey and Peggy were. In this case though, there was a simple explanation for it. Both Mickey and Peggy were adopted. Mickey, when he was two years old, and Peggy, three years later when she was one

The two Welton children looked around the hotel lobby. They were about to ask the desk clerk for directions to the Jeopardy room, when Peggy noticed a sign over by a set of stairs on the other side of the lobby. The sign read simply, 'Jeopardy', and a red arrow pointed up the staircase. Mickey and Peggy climbed to the top of the stairs where they saw a smaller 'Jeopardy' sign with another arrow pointing down a hallway. This sign led them to a large meeting room, outside of which they found a skinny man with thick, black-rimmed glasses seated at a fold-up table. It was the kind of flimsy table that Mickey and Peggy's parents and their friends used to play Hearts on up at the camp every summer. The sign on the desk said 'Jeopardy contestants sign up here.'

"Is this where you sign up to become a Jeopardy contestant?" Mickey asked.

The man looked at Mickey for a moment, then down at the sign on his desk, and then back at Mickey.

"Are you sure you want Jeopardy? Wheel of Fortune's gonna be here next month. Why don't you wait for them?"

The man's sarcasm was not lost on Peggy. "He wants Jeopardy, thank you."

"If you say so."

The skinny man looked at Peggy. She had seen that look before. It was usually followed by drool. Still looking at Peggy, the man spoke to Mickey. "What's your name, Sport?"

"Mickey Welton."

The man took his eyes off Peggy's chest long enough to write Mickey's name down on a master list and then handed Mickey a booklet measuring eight by ten.

"This is your test. You've got twenty-five minutes. Right through there. Pencils are inside." The man pointed to the door behind him. He was looking at Peggy again.

"Thanks," said Mickey, and he took two measured steps toward the door.

As Peggy moved to follow her brother, the skinny man held his hand up to her.

"Hang on, Rosemary. Only people taking the test are allowed inside."

"Oh." Peggy looked at Mickey and gave him a thumbs up sign. "Good luck. I'll wait for you down in the lobby."

Mickey tried to force a confident grin, but failed miserably and then disappeared into the 'Jeopardy' suite.

The skinny man had not taken his eyes off Peggy. He looked at the attractive young redhead like a shark looking at a bucket of chum. "You can wait out here with me if you like," he said.

"I'd rather crap glass," said Peggy, and with those parting words, she retired to the lobby.

The two basic steps to qualify as a Jeopardy contestant are 1) taking a fifty question test, and for those that pass the test, 2) playing a mock game. If you pass the test and do well in the mock game, you are put in the active file for the current tape year. Being put in the active file, however, does not guarantee that you will be invited to appear on the show. That day at the Superior Bangor Hotel, Mickey passed the test with flying colors, and he did very well in the mock game too. He won it, in fact. But, he was still surprised when, in March of the following year, he received a telephone call from a member of the Jeopardy staff asking if he could be in Los Angeles for a taping in June. He had made it! He was going to be on Jeopardy!!

"I don't understand", said Myrna, when Mickey gave his mother the news. "You're going to be on Jeopardy?"

"That's right," said Mickey.

"Well, when did you audition for this show?"

"In October, when I drove Peggy down to Bangor to get some shoes."

"Oh?" Myrna was puzzled. She looked at Mickey and then at Peggy. "Well, did you get the shoes?"

"Yes, mum," replied Peggy.

"Oh, good."

Mickey's father was equally dismayed by the news that his son was going to be on nationwide television.

"Are you sure they got the right Mickey Welton?" Jack said over dinner that night. The Welton family dinners were never eaten at the dining room table, but on t.v. trays in the living room.

"Dad, it's me. They got the right one."

"Well, how do you like that? Gawd-damn. So, this test was pretty easy then, was it?"

"Not really."

"For Mickey it was," said Peggy. "Because he's the smartest guy in this whole town."

"He certainly is," added Myrna, and she reached out and rubbed Mickey's arm lovingly.

"Yeah, well let's not forget one fact," said Jack. "Population nine-thousand."

And so with that brand of encouragement from his father, twenty-four year old Mickey Welton headed off to Los Angeles for the taping. He had never traveled this far in his young life. The occasional trip to Bangor and one excursion to Montreal to see the Canadiens play were the extent of Mickey's worldliness. He had a chance to go to the University of Toronto when he finished high school, but with his family living on only Jack's salary as a cable installer for the local cable t.v. outlet, Mickey decided it was best to get a job and pitch in. He had been working selling furniture at Doug Petty's La-Z-Boy for the past three years.

Mickey had prepared well for Jeopardy. He read every trivia book he could get his hands on. He even enlisted the services of Bonnie Hoyt, a local high school teacher, to help him get ready. Bonnie helped Mickey in the areas of English Literature and American History. Mickey had watched a lot of Jeopardy and he knew that those two categories came up quite a bit in one form or another. Mickey's own specialties were sports, television, and geography, so he figured between the two of them, he and Bonnie had all the bases covered. Mickey was determined not to humiliate himself on national television, so he and Bonnie worked together three times a week for three straight months to make sure that would not happen.

When Mickey returned from Los Angeles that June, Jack and Myrna and Peggy were waiting for him at the Bangor airport. (It was much cheaper to fly out of Bangor than Fredericton or Saint John.) Mickey gave his mom and Peggy hugs, and said hi to Jack, and of course they all wanted to know how he did on the show, but he couldn't tell them. He was not allowed to tell anybody the outcome of the match. This was one of the stipulations outlined in the Jeopardy agreement that Mickey had to sign before he taped the show.

"What the hell do you mean you can't tell us?" said Jack as they waited by the luggage carousel.

"I can't. It's the Jeopardy rules."

"Jeopardy rules? Screw the Jeopardy rules. Did you bring any money back or not?"

"I can't tell you."

"Aw, for chrissake."

A woman standing beside the Welton's at the carousel became interested in the conversation. "I'm sorry. I couldn't help overhearing. Were you on Jeopardy?"

"Yes. I just got back from taping in Los Angeles," replied Mickey.

"Oh, isn't that exciting? Well, congratulations. Did you have a good time?"

"Yes, very nice, thank you."

"When is the show going to be broadcast?"

"September the twenty-first."

"Oh, well, I'll have to tune it in."

"You do that, Mrs. Buttinsky," Jack said. "Now, do you mind if I continue my conversation with my son?"

Mickey, Peggy and Myrna all looked away, as if this action would disassociate them from the man who was embarrassing them in public once again. Mrs. Buttinsky moved to the other side of the carousel. Mickey, Peggy and Myrna watched as the luggage began to drop. Jack was saying something about the ineptitude of the airport baggage handlers, but his family members blocked out his words. They just wanted to get away from there as quickly as they could. More luggage dropped, and with each piece that wasn't Mickey's, Mickey, Peggy and Myrna died a little inside.

*

When the evening of September the twenty-first rolled around, the Welton family was gathered in the living room of their modest two storey home on Bagnell Street. Mickey, Peggy, Jack, Myrna and Gran Welton, the family matriarch sat staring at the television, and in the den, just off the living room, sat Buster, the dementia-ridden patriarch of the Welton tribe. Buster, approaching his seventy-seventh birthday, preferred the comfort of his big old La-Z-Boy chair and the reassurance of his black and white t.v. set. In Buster's mind, he was still living in an age before the advent of color television, and certainly no one would begrudge him the solace that he found in his memories of the old days.

So, there they sat, with only fifteen minutes to go before Mickey's name would be etched into the Rainbow history books for all eternity. Jeopardy would be coming on at seven-thirty on WLBZ-TV, the NBC affiliate in Bangor, Maine.

"Come on, Mickey," Jack implored, "Surely to God you can tell us how you did now."

"It'll be on in fifteen minutes, Dad," said Mickey stubbornly. "You can't wait fifteen minutes to find out?"

"Well, I don't know why you can't tell us. What are they going to do, send the game show police up here to arrest you?" Jack took a defiant pull on his bottle of beer as if to say, "I'll bet you don't have an answer for that one, Mr. Smartest Man In The Whole Friggin' Town."

"Jack, don't start a fight, please." Myrna was probably the most fragile of the entire Welton clan, a clan that was considered to be the most eccentric group of individuals assembled under one roof since that gathering in Waco a few years ago.

"They're very strict about the rules, Dad. If they were to find out that I told anybody, they could take my winnings away."

"Ah-hah!!" cried Jack, as if he had just cracked the Jimmy Hoffa case, "Then you did win something!! How much?"

"Oh, leave him alone, Dad," Peggy chimed in from her place on the sofa. "I don't want to know who wins anyway. I want to be surprised."

"I don't believe I was talking to you Miss 'Wear-my-skirts-above-my-ass-so-all-the – boys-can-see-my-equipment'". Jack had strange pet names for his offspring. He turned his attention to Mickey again, like a hound dog who wouldn't let go of an old bone. "All right, just tell us how you did in the first round. Were you leading after the first round?"

"Oh, for godssake, Jackie, shut your goddamned mouth," said Gran. "I'm missing the goddamned weather forecast." Gran was watching the television for tomorrow's weather. She always had to know what the weather was going to be, even though she rarely got to experience it first hand.

"What in the name of Jesus H. Christ do you care about the weather for, Mother?" said Jack. "Goddamn it, you haven't been out of the house in three years. God almighty!" Jack had inherited Gran's fondness for taking the Lord's name in vain, and they often went at it tooth and nail, tossing derivations of the Holy Father's John Henry back and forth like a couple of circus jugglers with bowling pins.

"Dampness. That's what I want to know for," replied Gran. "I want to know how much my arthritis is going to hurt tomorrow. Any more stupid goddamned questions?"

"Well, I don't know why you don't go out. You're not disabled for chrissake."

"Jack, please, this is a special night. Let's not spoil it." Myrna would be ignored a second time.

"I'll tell you why I don't go out," Gran shot back, "Because at my age, you goddamned twit, I'm a sitting duck for the elements, that's why. Rain makes me ache, sunshine could give me heat stroke, and when it snows . . . well, a person my age would have to be a bloody idiot to go outside in the snow. I could slip and break my goddamned hip and that'd be the last of me.

"Aw horse shit," said Jack. "You'll outlive us all, just for spite."

"I'll outlive you just so I can get some peace after you're gone, you hump-backed moron. You hurt me when I delivered you and you've been a pain every day since."

Jack had been a breach birth, and was born with a spinal deformity which caused him to walk slightly hunched over.

"Hey, I'll gladly go first just to get the hell away from you!" Jack said.

In the den, Buster sat upright in his La-Z-Boy. His hearing hadn't faltered one bit in seventy-seven years, and he called out to the living room. "Don't you talk to your mother that way, boy, or I'll come downstairs and lay a whipping on you!"

"Dad, you are downstairs," answered Jack. "We're all downstairs! Christ, Mother, we have got to get him into a home."

"No! Not as long as I've got a breath left in me," Gran said, blowing on her cup of Red Rose tea. "I will do no such thing to that man. After all he's done for me? Why, that man in there made me what I am today."

"Right. A foul-mouthed, bitter old hermit. Thanks a lot, Dad!"

Buster, having just leaned back after his last contribution to the ever-deteriorating conversation, sat upright in the La-Z-Boy again. "That's it! I warned you, and now I'm coming down there with a belt."

Buster struggled to get to his feet, but, the La-Z-Boy was in the reclining position, and kick and squirm as he might, it soon became apparent that the old man was trapped there for the evening. After a spirited five minute campaign, he fell, exhausted, into a deep sleep.

-3-

Wood Lynch turned his squad car onto Poole Street and headed north towards the cul-de-sac. In the passenger seat sat his six year-old son, Evan. Wood had taken Evan to the Dairy Delight for dessert, as he did quite often on a whim. It was a good arrangement that Wood had with his estranged wife Jeannie, that's if any separation arrangement can be termed 'good'. Jeannie realized that Evan needed to see his Dad as much as possible, and by the same token, that Wood needed very badly to be in contact with his son, so, even though the legal agreement said that Wood only had Evan every other weekend and three weeks in the summer, Jeannie pretty much let Wood have access to the boy whenever he wanted, provided he called first to set it up.

Wood Lynch and Jeannie Dupont were married twelve years ago, just after Wood was accepted as a member of the Rainbow Police Force. They were high school sweethearts, both having attended Rainbow High, which was where Wood got his nickname. His given name was Robert, or 'Bobby' as everybody called him, but during his senior year at Rainbow High, he was talked into going out for the school football team by coach John 'Tudder' Halliwell. Tudder got his nickname from his father who always referred to him and John's older brother Dewey as 'That one and tudder one'. Bobby Lynch was a tall, solidly built boy, and coach Halliwell thought he might just be the tight end that the Rainbow football team needed that year, so Bobby was installed as the starter at that position without even having to try out. The thing was, Rainbow High was a small high school, and Coach Halliwell, who was a history teacher first, a music theory teacher second, and a football coach third, didn't really have a large pool of talent to draw from. That being the case, any kid who was over five-ten and had any meat on his bones whatsoever, was coerced into playing football. The shorter, scrawnier ones were put into the school band. The problem that Bobby Lynch had though, was that a tight end was expected to block and catch. Bobby could block all right. He had no problem throwing his body in front of an opponent to clear a path for the runner coming around the outside on a sweep, or coming through his 'hole' on a counter play, but he never did get the hang of catching that damned ball. He would run a slant over the middle for about seven to ten yards and then turn to find the ball already delivered by the quarterback, headed for his waiting arms – and he would drop it. Or he would run the 'quick out', which is a much easier route to the outside away from traffic, again turning to find the pigskin in flight – and he would drop it.

It was in the second game of the season, against the dreaded Fredericton High School team – the largest student body in the commonwealth, they liked to boast, as if having a grossly overcrowded school was something to be proud of – that Bobby Lynch acquired his nickname. Now, a good receiver is said to have 'soft hands', meaning the ball just seems to sink into his palms like a traveling salesman into a Holiday Inn sofa. Bobby Lynch did not have soft hands. Thus, when he trotted off the field after dropping a pass that would have gained a sure first down for the Rainbow High Golden Beetles, Coach Halliwell grabbed him by the facemask, pulled his helmeted head in close to his own, and said in a gentle, almost forgiving voice, "Lynch, you've got hands of wood." He then released Bobby's helmet and turned his attention back to his team's losing effort on the gridiron. Bobby though, unfamiliar with the term 'hands of wood', did not leave the coach's side as a wiser player might have at that moment. Instead, he moved a step closer and said, in an equally gentle voice as if the two were sharing a deep dark secret, "What does that mean, Coach?"

"It means that before the season's out, you'll be playing second trombone."

And so, the name stuck.

Wood had known Jeannie Dupont since the two were in grade school together. They had both grown up in Rainbow on opposite ends of the town's main street. Jeannie's family was fairly well-to-do, her father, Gerald Dupont being a bank manager, and her mother, Teresa, a chartered accountant. Jeannie was their only child. Wood's family, on the other hand, was not what one would call well-to-do. His father, Frank Lynch, deserted the family when Wood was only five, so Wood had no memory of him at all. Wood's mother, Deborah, raised him and his older brother Donnie all by herself, working mainly as a waitress/housekeeper at The Allemane, a local inn.

Wood and Jeannie had always been friends, but they didn't become romantically involved until the annual Sadie Hawkins dance in grade ten. This was the dance in October where the female students invited the male students to be their dates, mimicking the ritual event in L'il Abner's Dogpatch, where the women proposed marriage to the men on Sadie Hawkins Day. That year, though, Jeannie didn't have a boy that she wanted to ask to the dance and she had decided that she wasn't going to go. Her best friend Glenda Brewer though, had already invited someone and insisted that Jeannie find a date so they could all go together.

"Why don't you just ask Bobby?" Glenda said. "You like him, don't you?"

"Sure," said Jeannie. "but not as a boyfriend."

"It's just for one night," Glenda persisted. "Come on. Just tell him you need someone to go with so we can hang around together. Pleeease."

That seemed fine to Jeannie. As long as she told Bobby the truth, there was no way he could get the wrong idea, right? That way, nobody – meaning Bobby – gets hurt.

"Hey, Bobby, wait up!!" Jeannie called to the boy as he left school on the Monday before the dance.

"Oh, hi, Jeannie."

"Bobby, has anyone asked you to the Sadie Hawkins dance yet?" Jeannie didn't waste any time with small talk. She still didn't to this day.

"Nope," replied Bobby, feeling slightly embarrassed by, a) the suddenness of the question and, b) his loser-like response.

"Well, you wanna go with me?"

"You??" The instant the word was out of his mouth, Bobby sensed that he had insulted Jeannie in some way, but being an insensitive clod as most males are at that age, he didn't quite know how he had insulted her.

"Yeah me! Whaddya mean me?"

"Oh. That was how," he surmised.

"Forget it then. Forget I even asked you. Shit! I was only asking you because Glenda wanted me to ask you so her and I could hang around together. I didn't even want to ask you. Shit!"

Jeannie turned and took two steps that appeared to be in full storm mode, but Bobby caught her before she stormed too far.

"Jeannie, wait! That's not how I meant it."

Jeannie stopped and turned loaded for bear. She was going to give him one chance to explain his "You?", and by God, it had better be good. Bad enough a girl has to get up the nerve to ask a boy out in the first place, but to be blind-sided by a "You?", well, that was more than she was going to put up with.

"No? Then how did you mean it?"

"I meant . . . ."

There was a pause. A very small, barely noticeable pause, as Wood prepared to throw up a grappling hook of words and pull himself out of the abyss that he had innocently plummeted into ". . . . You can have any guy in the whole school," he continued. "Why would you ask me?"

Jeannie's scowl melted. It left her face like a depression sharecropper leaving Oklahoma, and it was replaced by a glow that Bobby was sure he could have warmed his hands on. This was probably the very moment in which the 'friendly' relationship became more than that. After the Sadie Hawkins Dance, Jeannie and Wood dated regularly through the rest of their high school days, and when they graduated Jeannie went to work in her father's bank as a teller, and Wood took a job at Pinelli's Sporting Goods. Wood figured he would work there for a year or two until he decided what to do with his life. He never did decide, however, and finally, his brother Donnie got him into Holland College, the police officer's training school on Prince Edward Island, and then eventually onto the Rainbow police force. Ironically, when September the twenty-eighth rolled around, and the Rainbow police force disbanded, Wood, once again, would be trying to figure out what to do with his life.

*

Officer Lynch pulled his cruiser into the driveway at forty-seven Poole Street. At the end of the driveway sat the three bedroom red brick house that he had shared with Jeannie for four years. He and Jeannie bought this house when they found out that she was pregnant with Evan. Her father pulled a few strings at the bank and got them enough of a loan so they could make the down payment, but they were still mortgaged up real good. Mr. Dupont offered to make them a loan of his own money, interest-free, for the down payment, but Wood felt uncomfortable about that, coming from a family where every dollar was hard-earned and nothing was ever handed to you. Looking back, Wood saw his turning down of his father-in-law's magnanimous offer as the second crack in the foundation of his marriage. The first crack was that Gerald Dupont didn't think Wood was good enough for his daughter to begin with.

"You've got an ice-cream face there, Ev," Wood said as he shifted the cruiser into park. "What's the matter with you? Forget where your mouth is?"

Evan reached up with his free hand and wiped the misplaced dessert off of his chin with his sleeve.

Wood smiled. "Oh, yeah, that's better. Mummy'll like that," he said. "Come on, let's go. Everybody out."

Evan pushed the cruiser door open and climbed out the passenger side, taking another lick of his ice cream cone as he did so. Wood reached over and held his hand out to make sure the door didn't come back and close on the boy before he was clear. The boy wouldn't have noticed if he was in danger. His mind was occupied by the cone right now, and nothing else.

Wood pulled the passenger door closed and then climbed out of the cruiser and waved to Karl Vasser who was putting two green garbage bags out on the curb in front of his house next door.

"Hey, Karl," Wood said in his usual friendly manner.

"Hi there, Wood," Karl replied. "Some rain we had, huh?"

"Yeah, she came down all right," replied Wood. "You're uh . . . you're putting your garbage out a little early, aren't you? Garbage day isn't for three days yet."

"Got to." Karl dropped the bags on the curb. "Nina says it's stinkin' up the house."

"Well, then it's probably best that you stink up the neighbourhood instead," said Wood with a friendly policeman's smile. "Sure, let the raccoons have a couple of extra days to chew through the bags. I mean, the way they're making those hefty bags these days, a raccoon can't get through them in one night. Not like the old days. No sir. These days with that new and improved thick plastic, an animal needs a couple of sittings to tear into one."

Karl stared at Wood as if staring might help him to figure out if Wood was joking or being dead serious.

"You could always put it in your garage until garbage day, Karl," Wood offered, trying not to sound like someone in a position of authority.

"Can't do that either," said Karl.

"Why not?"

Karl pointed towards his garage. Wood looked over, and there in a lawn chair in the yawning mouth of the garage next door, sat Karl's wife Nina.

"Evening, Wood," Nina called.

"Nina," Wood said with a resigning wave.

Karl looked up at the setting sun. "It's almost time for Jeopardy," he said. Karl Vasser never wore a watch. He always looked up at the sun to tell the time. He said he learned it when he was a Boy Scout, and he always bragged about the money he was saving on timepieces. Cloudy days, however, were the big fly in this money-saver's ointment. "You gonna watch Mickey?" Karl was now moving back up the driveway towards his house.

"Yeah, I'll probably turn it on back at the station, Karl. You have a good night now."

The front door to the brick house opened and Jeannie stepped outside onto the porch. Jeannie Lynch was a pretty, pert woman with short blond hair. Lorraine Finney, who owned a pewter shop on Main Street, always said that "Teresa Dupont's girl, Jeannie, looks like that woman who was in that Harry Met Sally movie a while back." She was right. Jeannie did bear a strong resemblance to Meg Ryan.

"Hi, Angel," Jeannie smiled as Evan ran up the walk towards her. "Ya' have fun?"

"Mm-hmm", Evan mumbled through his ice cream.

"He's a little messy. Sorry," said Wood as he moved up the walk behind Evan.

"That's okay. I've gotta do a laundry tomorrow anyway. You getting any sleep these days?"

"Oh, yeah," said Wood. "I'm gettin' used to the shifts now. Besides, there's only one more week to go."

"Figured out what you're going to do yet?" Jeannie played with Evan's hair as he leaned against her legs and finished the last of his ice cream.

"Not yet. But, I'll find something."

Wood could have applied to the Charlottetown Police Force. He knew they were looking for people, but that was a four and a half hour drive from Rainbow and he didn't want to be that far away from Evan. That would mean only seeing his son on weekends. And what if something happened and Jeannie or Evan needed him in a hurry? Wood felt that even though he and Jeannie had been separated for two years, he still had to look out for her. The fact was, he still loved her.

"Well, I think you should consider Charlottetown," said Jeannie.

"Naw. Somethin'll turn up."

There was a pause. Jeannie knew why he wouldn't take a job with the Charlottetown Force and it bothered her that Wood thought he had to stay around because she might need him. She didn't need him. She had told him that. She was a big girl now. Thirty-four years old. But, Wood always felt like he had to look out for her. Always. This was one of the reasons the marriage fell apart. Jeannie was a strong, independent woman, and yet Wood smothered her with his care. When she finished work, Wood would be there to walk or drive her home. One time when she was pregnant with Evan, Jeannie ate some shellfish that didn't agree with her and she became nauseous in the middle of the night. Wood drove over to Doctor Lalonde's house in his cruiser, sirens blaring, and brought the doctor back to look Jeannie over.

"She ate some bad shellfish," said Wood when the Doctor was about half way through his examination.

"That's right, she did," replied the Doctor, indignantly. "Is that why you dragged me over here? To confirm your diagnosis?"

Jeannie could not function in that kind of environment, even though in her heart, she loved Wood too. She knew he was a good man with a beautiful soul. The kind of man that most women would be happy to have as a husband.

"Well, I'd better get going," Wood said.

"Think about it, Bobby," Jeannie said. "Charlottetown wouldn't be too bad. I mean, Evan and I could drive out there to visit once in a while or . . ."

"No. I don't want you driving all that way. It's not safe with just you and Evan."

"Bobby . . . ."

"No, I mean it. What if Evan distracts you and you take your eye off the road for a second?"

"Bobby, I know how to drive for God's sake."

"No, well, I don't think it's a good idea."

There was another pause. They both realized that this discussion was another example of why their marriage didn't work. Wood changed the topic. "So, how's work with you?"

"Fine. Pretty busy," said Jeannie. She had quit her job as a teller at the bank three years ago to take a position at the local Howard Johnson's, and in those three short years, she had worked her way up to assistant manager. She left the bank, not because she didn't like the job, but because leaving got her out from under the watchful eye of her father, Gerald, the bank manager. Again, this was a case of Jeannie seeking a more independent lifestyle.

"You gonna watch Mickey on the t.v.?" asked Wood.

"I suppose," replied Jeannie. "You wanna stay and watch it with us? It's coming on in a couple of minutes."

"No, thanks. I've gotta meet Pete at the office at eight for the shift change."

"Oh, okay."

"Gotta go, Ev!" Wood picked his son up and flung him onto his hip so that Evan's butt was cradled in Wood's forearm. "Gimme a kiss, Bud."

Evan gave his father a kiss on the cheek.

"Attaboy. How much does Daddy love ya', Ev?"

"Bigger than a . . . . rhinoceros?"

"Way bigger." Wood kissed Evan and set the boy down in front of his mother.

"Bobby, can we talk sometime?" Jeannie asked.

"Sure. What about?"

"Not now," said Jeannie, and she looked down at Evan and then back to Wood. "Maybe you could call me later."

"Yeah, okay. I'll call you in a while." Wood wanted to know what it was about right now, but obviously Jeannie did not want to talk about it in front of Evan. "See you later, Ev." Wood brushed his forefinger along his son's cheek, and then looked back at Jeannie. "I'll call you."

"Good," said Jeannie.

Wood climbed into the squad car, backed it out the driveway, and headed back the way he came. He took the first right off of Poole which was Yarbro Street. Two blocks later he turned left onto Fairlawn Street. He would be on Fairlawn Street for another four blocks before he turned onto Lilac Road.

-4-

Grace Downey had never been in an eighteen wheeler before. She didn't particularly want to be in one now, but here she sat, higher off the road than she had ever been in her life. She stared straight ahead watching Interstate Ninety-Five disappear under the massive front end of the Kenworth vehicle. Beside her, at the controls of the 'big rig', as she had heard them referred to, was Dan. She didn't ask his last name and he didn't offer it.

Four hours earlier, Grace had gotten out of a cab with her suitcase and walked into Shiner's Truck Stop on the outskirts of Bangor. She was there to hitch a ride. She didn't care to where, just so long as it was away. Away from him. And Grace was angry, not at him, but at herself. How could she have lived with this man for ten years and not realized what kind of a person he was? How does a smart woman like Grace Downey get fooled like that? And now, here was this 'smart' woman having to sneak away with little more than the clothes on her back, just to get free of the man. She was angry and just a little ashamed at the same time.

When Grace walked into Shiner's at two-thirty that afternoon, it seemed to her that everybody's head had taken a simultaneous turn to look at her. Maybe she was just imagining it. Maybe she was just feeling a little paranoid at the moment. It would be ridiculous to think that that many people – there must have been thirty customers in the place – would all turn to look at her at the same time. She slid her brown leather suitcase into the booth closest to the front door of the establishment and then she slid in after it, not with her back to the rest of the patrons as one would expect from someone feeling a little intimidated, but facing everyone. When Grace had settled in, and after placing her purse on the suitcase beside her, she looked up again, and she realized that she was not imagining that feeling she had when she first walked in. Everybody *was* staring at her. And why not? Aside from being an attractive woman, Grace wasn't really dressed for a truck stop. She wore a cream-colored wool blend pant suit over a white Gap t-shirt, and she had on a pair of diamond earrings set in cloverleaves. Not exactly the kind of outfit you wear when you're ordering a hot beef sandwich and a cup of 'Joe'.

"What can I get you, dear?" The waitress was beside Grace before she saw her coming.

"Uh . . . . just a coffee please."

"Coffee it is." The waitress moved away as quickly as she had approached.

Grace tugged self-consciously on her right ear, feeling the diamond as she did so. Grace took the diamond earrings because she had earned them. Entertaining his friends all those years, preparing guest lists, hiring 'people' to do catering, gardening, decorating, and all of the other 'ing' things that hired people do. She was the 'woman behind the man' that you always hear about. She was by his side as he climbed the ladder of success, eventually landing on a rung high up in the district attorney's office. And she had given up her own career in a reputable public relations firm to do so. She had also put aside her desire to have children. He felt they should concentrate on achieving his lofty ambitions first, and then they would talk about a family, and Grace's career. Grace agreed. She knew that it would take all of their energies to stake out a place on the political landscape for her husband. And then she found the earrings.

It was two days before the Governor's Ball. Bryden Downey was in the running for District Attorney of Penobscot County, and he had received an invitation for himself and his wife, Grace, to attend the ball. This was a real feather in Bryden's cap. This meant that the Governor himself was throwing his support behind Bryden. His being elected as the new District Attorney was almost assured. His superior, who would retire at the end of this term, had also recommended him as his successor, and the invitation to the Governor's soiree was, in a way, Bryden's coming out party.

That night, two days before the ball, Grace was picking up after Bryden as she usually did. His suit jacket had been thrown over the divan in the master bedroom. His suit pants, folded, but not hung up, lay on the end of the bed. She took a wooden hanger from the closet and put the pants over it, but when she went to hang up the jacket, she noticed a spot on the pocket flap. It looked to be dried ketchup. Grace smelled it. There was no discernable smell. She scratched it a little with the nail of her left index finger and smelled again. Yes. Yes, the distinct odor of ketchup. Obviously, Bryden had glopped it on himself during lunch and hadn't noticed, leaving it to dry there. She would take the suit to the cleaners first thing in the morning. It was Bryden's favorite suit, a dark blue one, and he would surely want to wear it again before too long. Grace emptied the pockets. On the inside breast pocket, a package of matches from the Squire's Roost, a downtown bar where lawyers sometimes gathered at the end of the day. Bryden didn't smoke cigarettes, but he did have the occasional cigar, so there was nothing unusual about finding a pack of matches. In the same pocket, an inscribed pen which had been given to Bryden by a church group after he had prosecuted two men who broke into the church hall one night, beat the pastor senseless and took over four hundred dollars from the church children's fund. The inscription read "And He sent a messenger." In the left jacket pocket, there was a receipt, probably from that same lunch at which the ketchup was spilled, and in the right jacket pocket . . . . felt? It was a felt-covered box. Grace removed the object from the pocket. A ring box.

"Why would Bryden have a ring box in his pocket?" she wondered. She opened the box. Inside she found, not a ring, but a pair of diamond earrings set in cloverleaves. "Oh, my God." The words came from her throat in a whisper.

Bryden must have bought them for her to wear to the Governor's Ball and he was going to surprise her with them. Grace suddenly felt terrible. She had found the earrings and ruined the surprise.

"No, wait. Maybe not."

He didn't have to know she found them. She could act surprised. She had played Annie Sullivan in a community production of The Miracle Worker ten years ago and many in the audience stood up when the show was finished, so, yes, she could fake it. She put the box back into the pocket. She put the receipt back and the pen and the matches. Then she laid the coat down on the divan.

"No, that's not how it was," she muttered, and she picked it up and laid it down again. "Still not right," and she repeated the process. "Oh, what am I doing? Is he going to notice how his jacket was laying? He didn't notice the ketchup spill, did he? No. Leave it."

Grace walked out of the room quickly. Seconds later she returned to the room, picked up the jacket and laid it down again. "That's better. That's how it was." She quickly left the room.

The night of the Governor's Ball arrived. The time was six oh five. They were to leave in ten minutes . . . and Bryden had still not surprised Grace with the earrings. Grace chalked it up to Bryden's lawyer training. He was waiting until very the last minute. More dramatic that way.

Grace sat in front of her make-up mirror in the bedroom. She was wearing a black strapless gown that covered her body like milk. Even she thought she looked good in this dress and she was hard to please where her own looks were concerned. In the large bathroom just off the master bedroom, Bryden had finished getting into his tuxedo and was pulling a comb through his prematurely grey-flecked hair one final time.

"You just about ready?" Bryden called from the bathroom.

"Just about," Grace called back.

In front of her on the dressing table, sat Grace's jewelry box. She had opened it and taken out two pair of earrings. One black pearl, and the other, teardrop shaped. "There's one problem, Bryden. Can you help me?"

Bryden entered from the bathroom. He was pulling his shirt cuff out from under his jacket sleeve. A good-looking man, Bryden could have played one of those multi-millionaire business magnates you see on the soap operas all the time. "What is it?"

Grace held a black pearl earring up to her left ear and a teardrop to her right. "I can't decide. Which do you like? Black pearl, or teardrop?"

Bryden looked for a second. He yanked down the other cuff.

"Uhhhh . . . ."

"Well?"

Bryden continued to look at the left ear, then the right. "Boy, you know what?

"What?"

"I'm not crazy about either one."

"No?"

"No."

Grace was sure this was it. Bryden would reach into his tuxedo jacket pocket and out would come the felt-covered box and the diamond earrings. And she thought *she* could act. He was drawing this out right until the very last second!

Bryden moved toward Grace and she saw him move his hand up to his jacket pocket. He grabbed the pocket flap and straightened it, making sure it wasn't tucked in. With the other hand he reached over Grace's shoulder and pulled a pair of gold earrings out of her jewelry box.

"I like these. I've always liked these." He handed the earrings to Grace.

" . . . . These?" Grace said as Bryden put the earrings into her hand.

"Yeah."

"Oh."

"What's the matter, you don't like them?"

"No, they're . . . . they're fine," said Grace. "And they match the dress too."

"Good. So, we're all set. I'll be downstairs."

Bryden left the room. Grace looked at the gold earrings in her hand. She put them on and went down to meet her waiting husband.

At the Governor's Ball that night, Grace was introduced to a lot of new faces, plus she saw a few familiar faces that she knew from Bryden's work. There was Thomas Antonetti, the current District Attorney of Penobscot County, and his wife Jocelyn; Judge Lewis Harvey whom Bryden had argued cases before many times; Pam Carpenter, a capable defense attorney that Bryden had faced off against on more than one occasion; and Senator Kathleen Drakeford, Bryden's nemesis from the state legislature. Bryden had always complained that the felons he put behind bars were back on the street in no time because the Senate kept sending back bills that would protect the rights of the victim. Senator Drakeford countered that Maine citizens would rather not see their tax dollars wasted feeding and nurturing a bunch of check forgers and purse snatchers.

On this night though, the politics had been checked at the door and everyone was on friendly terms. There was wonderful food, music provided by an orchestra from Portland in the southern part of the state, plenty of dancing, and fortunately, only a minimum of speech making. Grace hated listening to speeches. She had been a speech writer early on in her public relations career and she always found herself getting angry when the writer beat around the bush with a lot of flowery padding instead of getting to the point of the speech.

Tonight there would be very little of that. Tonight she would dance with her husband for the first time in over a year. Grace loved to dance and Bryden was a very good dancer. He held a woman with a gentle strength, so that she knew she was being held, but so softly that she felt she could be carried off by a gossamer breeze at any moment. The dance floor was crowded as they moved about. Grace recognized the song the orchestra was playing as an instrumental version of The Beatles "Ob-La-Di Ob-La-Da".

"Are you happy?" Grace asked Bryden, knowing full well what the answer would be.

"I have never been happier. This is where I belong, Grace. This is what we've worked for all these years. I mean, do you have any idea the number of influential people there are in this room tonight? The things I could accomplish, the wrongs that I could right with these people on my side . . . well, it's just over-whelming."

And he was right. The most influential people in the state were dancing right along side them at this minute. Mayors, judges, senators, leaders of industry . . . .

and a woman with diamond earrings set in cloverleaves. The image went by with a blur. As she danced past, Grace was being turned in the opposite direction by Bryden, but she knew what she saw. She was not mistaken. She turned her head back and saw Senator Kathleen Drakeford. Was it her? Her ears. What did she have on her ears? Grace couldn't see. She was being spun again. Where did she go? It's so crowded on this dance floor. She must . . . . there! There she is. And she's wearing . . . . long earrings. Pearl, it looks like. Damn! Where did they go? Where did the diamond earrings go? Who's nearby? Off to her left, Grace saw John and Doris MacDonald. John was with the forest industry. Grace had written him a speech once. He delivered it poorly. Doris was wearing green earrings.

"Jesus, Doris, what can you be thinking? Green with that dress?" Grace's thoughts were only momentarily distracted from the task at hand.

She looked to the couple on her right. Who were they? She didn't recognize them. An older man and a younger woman. Pretty woman. As she craned to see the woman's ears, Grace silently hoped that they weren't a couple because if they were, it would mean that he had power and money and she wanted some of it and Grace hated to think that a woman would humiliate herself like that just for money. Besides, she couldn't stomach the mental picture of the two of them in bed together. Him sweating and grunting, and her counting the seconds until it was over. There it is!! Her left ear, and . . . . a diamond stud. Very nice. Very tasteful. Just then, Grace felt a bump from behind.

"Oh, I'm sorry," came a man's voice.

Grace turned around.

"Oh. Judge Harvey."

"Sorry, Judge," said Bryden. "My fault."

"No, I think it's these two left feet of mine," replied the judge. "Sorry, Grace."

Before she could say, "Think nothing of it," the Judge spun around to continue his dance, and when he did, a diamond earring set in a cloverleaf was placed directly in Grace's line of vision.

"Sorry," came the woman's voice, and she and the Judge danced away into the crowd.

*

"Here's your coffee, hon," the waitress said, setting the white mug down on the table in front of Grace.

"Oh, thank you," said Grace.

Grace wasn't paying attention. She was watching the room. Watching for that one driver that she thought she would be able to trust. After all, a woman can't be too careful at the best of times, but to ask a strange truck driver for a ride out of town, well, who knows what kind of trouble she could get into?

She watched each driver carefully. What expressions did their faces carry? Were they somber, happy-go-lucky, tired? How did they interact with the waitresses? Did they call them 'Honey', 'Sweetheart', or did they use their given names? Details. Very important.

There were three men seated at the counter to Grace's left. When the waitress walked by, two of them watched her ass. One poked the other in the ribs with his elbow and they both smiled. They were summarily dismissed by Grace. The third man who was with the other two did not look at the waitress' ass and he did not smile either, but Grace eliminated him because of the company he was keeping.

Seated by himself at a table for two near the window was a man about fifty years-old. He was reading a magazine. Grace strained to see the magazine's title. 'Home Renovations' it said. She liked this. He was probably a family man. Nice guy. Looking to do some sort of fix-up job around the house. Maybe he's building a deck for his wife. As she watched him, the man looked up and caught Grace staring. Grace looked away quickly. Her eyes roamed the room nonchalantly. She looked at the clock behind the counter and compared it's time to the time on her wristwatch. She found an imaginary crumb on her table and brushed it away. She straightened the napkin in front of her. Finally, after about thirty seconds of casual indifference, Grace cautiously brought her gaze back to Mr. Home Renovation. He was still looking at her. He winked and was immediately dismissed as an asshole.

Grace and Bryden sat down at their table. Seated across from them was a couple from the town of Houlton near the Canadian border. They had introduced themselves as Ron and Judy Winkley, and explained that they had won their invitations to the Governor's Ball via a phone-in contest at a local radio station. The Governor wanted some 'ordinary folks' at his ball and he thought this was a fair way to do it. The Winkleys were one of four couples who had won invitations from all over the state.

"I feel like Cinderella," Judy said giddily at one point.

Grace watched as Judge Harvey walked Pam Carpenter back to her table on the other side of the room.

"So, what do you two do?" asked Judy.

"Well," said Bryden, "Grace used to work in the public relations field, and I'm with the District Attorney's office in Bangor."

"Oh. We watch Law and Order every week, don't we, Ron?"

"Never miss it," said Ron. "Or if we do miss it, we record it. That's why we never miss it."

There was a pause. This portion of the conversation had obviously run it's course. Judy tried another tack.

"Ron and I work for the government too."

"Really?" Bryden looked at Grace hoping that she would spell him, but Grace was distracted, looking off towards another part of the room.

"Yes. Just a couple of civil servants. That's us."

"In what branch?"

"We're customs inspectors. At the crossing in Houlton."

"You don't say? Well, I'll bet you've got some interesting stories to tell."

"Oh, we do that. We do that. In fact, those stories are going to pay for our retirement. Isn't that right, Ron?"

"That's the plan."

"How's that?" asked Bryden.

"We're going to write a book," replied Ron. "We've already got the title. 'Strange Customs.'" Ron paused here to let the full effect of the title wash over Bryden. "Pretty good, huh? You see, it's going to be about all the strange things we've seen as customs inspectors. 'Strange Customs.'" Ron said it again hoping it would get a rise the second time. It didn't. He persevered. "What do you think, Grace? You used to be in the public relations game. Does that sound like a title that'll sell?"

"Yes. Yes, it does." Grace turned long enough to answer the question with a smile and then turned away again.

On the other side of the room, Pam Carpenter rose and headed in the direction of the ladies room.

"Excuse me," said Grace, standing in such a hurry that she bumped the tops of her legs against the table and gave everyone's drink a good shake. "I have to use the ladies room."

"I'll come with you," said Judy sprightly. She even made a trip to the washroom sound like fun.

Grace strode towards the ladies room purposefully, while Judy, in a much tighter dress, was taking three steps to every one of Grace's, just to keep up.

"Honestly, Grace, I'll remember this night for as long as I live. I mean, I don't want to sound like some hick who's never been off the farm, but to think that I'm here rubbing elbows with the Governor himself, well that's one for the books. Do you think he'd pose for a picture with Ron and I? The Governor? I brought the Instamatic just in case. Oh, and I want to get one of you and Bryden too. Bryden is such a distinguished name. It suits him very well."

Grace didn't hear Judy. At this moment she heard nothing. It was as if she had suddenly slipped underwater, blocking out any noise from the fancy gala on the surface. She pushed open the door to the ladies room vigorously, nearly hitting an older woman who was just reaching for the door on the other side. The older woman let out a short, crisp "Oh!" in surprise and watched as Grace breezed past her. As she started to leave again, the older woman was met head on by Judy, walking like a Geisha.

"Oh, I'm sorry," said Judy, stepping aside.

"Excuse me," the woman said, and she made good her exit.

"Isn't this a lovely affair?" Judy called after her.

The woman didn't answer.

"We're having such a . . . wonderful time." Judy's sentence tailed off as she realized the woman was not going to acknowledge her.

Inside, the plush ladies room was adorned with bouquets of fresh flowers. A row of seven sinks and mirrors lined one wall. Seven stalls lined another wall, and on a third wall were four paper towel dispensers, but instead of the usual thin paper towels, these were filled with scented, super absorbent, two-ply paper towels.

Pam Carpenter stood at the mirror situated nearest the paper towel dispensers. She rubbed her pinky finger over her eyebrows, and then she rubbed it underneath her lower lip. Pam was a striking woman, with deep auburn hair and full lips that glistened like dew drops. Her chocolate brown eyes were the perfect compliment to her tan complexion.

Grace moved to the mirror next to Pam and began flouncing her hair lightly and without purpose. Judy moved to the mirror next to Grace and removed a lipstick from her silver clutch purse.

"Oh, hi, Grace," said Pam, looking at Grace in the mirror.

"Pam." Grace's head didn't turn but her eyes shifted to Pam's reflection in the mirror.

"This is quite a night, isn't it?" said Pam.

"Mmm, yes."

"Yes, our Governor sure knows how to throw a party at the taxpayer's expense."

"I love your earrings," Grace said, now smoothing a crease from the front of her dress.

"Hmmm? Oh, thank you." Pam touched her left ear, admiring the shiny adornment there.

"Oh, my yes, they're beautiful!" said Judy, looking towards Pam in the mirror. "Absolutely gorgeous." She turned back to her own reflection and began carefully applying her red lipstick.

"Thank you," said Pam.

The three women were now looking straight ahead, each performing their minor repair jobs.

"Are you fucking my husband?"

Judy's lipstick slid from her lower lip to a point halfway down her chin, leaving a bright streak of red. Pam blinked, but that was the only indication that her composure had slipped for even a millisecond. It was regained instantly. A silence siphoned all of the air from the room.

"I think that's something you should talk to Bryden about," said Pam coolly.

"I'll take that as a 'yes'," said Grace, and with that, her right fist flew across her body and caught Pam flush on the right cheekbone.

The force of the blow sent Pam to her left and down slightly, where her head made a solid connection with the paper towel dispenser. She was out cold before her rear end hit the tile floor.

"Oh, my God!" cried Judy.

Grace bent down and carefully removed the diamond earrings from Pam's ears.

"Oh, my God!" cried Judy. "Is this a hold up?!"

Grace rose and turned for the door. Judy stood over Pam for a moment. She wanted to bend down and feel the woman's pulse but because of her tight dress, that was out of the question. Instead, she poked at Pam's arm with the toe of her high-heeled shoe. Nothing. She poked a little harder. Pam groaned and her head turned to the left. There was a patch of spittle in the corner of her mouth and a small cut on her left temple.

"Oh, my God," said Judy, and then she turned and quick-stepped out of the washroom.

Grace approached the table where Bryden and Ron had been joined by a graying man whom Grace recognized as Donald Heinz, the District Attorney for Maine's York County. Bryden and Donald Heinz stood as Grace approached. Ron was a little slower on the uptake but seeing the other two men rise, he too stood, bottle of Budweiser in hand.

"Grace, you remember Donald Heinz, don't you?" Bryden said as Grace reached the table.

"Yes, of course. Hello, Donald."

Donald took Grace's hand and cupped it with both of his. "Grace, you look beautiful tonight."

"Oh, thank you."

"I was just telling your husband here about the pitfalls of being a District Attorney, but he seems hell bent on it anyway. Maybe you can talk some sense into him." Donald smiled at Bryden good-naturedly.

"Oh, I doubt that," said Grace, and she opened her hand to show Bryden the diamond earrings set in cloverleaves. "We're leaving."

Bryden looked at the earrings. He then looked around the room in an attempt to locate Pam Carpenter.

"She's out cold in the ladies room," said Grace. "Now, let's go."

"Grace, not now. Not tonight," said Bryden in a hushed tone that made Donald Heinz lean in a little closer so as to hear better.

"Oh, yes, tonight, Bryden. Now, are we leaving, or shall we discuss this here?"

"Grace, I can't walk out on the Governor."

"All right, then, we'll discuss it here. How long have you been humping Pam Carpenter?"

Donald Heinz now sensed that this conversation was not meant for his ears and he turned, desperately looking for someone else to move to. "Richard?" Donald waved to a group of six people off to his left. "How are you?" Donald moved away from Grace and Bryden, and right on past the group of six and disappeared into the crowd.

Ron Winkley took a sip of his Budweiser, sat down, and watched Grace and Bryden. To him, this stuffy affair was finally getting interesting.

"Oh, my God," Judy said as she approached the table. She put her hand on Ron's shoulder and bent down as close to his ear as her dress would permit. "Ron, you won't believe what just happened."

"Not now, Judy," Ron said. He was waiting for Bryden's reply to the 'humping' question.

"I'm telling you, Grace, do this here, right now, and you'll be sorry."

"Is she a good fuck?"

Judy gasped and Ron took another quick sip, spilling some beer down his chin onto his shirt. Bryden turned and walked across the dance floor towards the entrance hall of the Governor's mansion and its large front doors. Grace followed.

"Good-bye, Grace," Judy said. "Good luck."

Bryden reached the front door five steps ahead of Grace. A doorman dressed in black tie and tails pulled the door open for them.

"Bryden?"

Bryden and Grace turned towards the sound of the voice. It was Thomas Antonetti, the soon-to-be-retired District Attorney of Penobscot County. Bryden's boss.

"You're not leaving already, are you?"

"Uh..yes, I'm afraid so, Thomas," said Bryden.

"But, the night is young. There are a lot of people who want to meet you yet."

"I know, Thomas, but . . . ."

"Important people, if you know what I mean."

"Well, Grace isn't feeling well and she'd like to go home and lie down."

"Oh, I'm sorry to hear that. What is it, Grace, that flu bug that's going around?"

"No," said Grace, "I think it might be crabs."

Bryden grabbed Grace by the wrist, as a father might grab his insolent child.

"Give my apologies to the Governor, Thomas," Bryden said, and he led Grace out the door to the parking lot.

*

"Are you waiting for somebody?"

"What?" Grace looked up to find the waitress standing there.

"Well, three hours and four cups of coffee. I figure you must be waiting for somebody."

"Oh." Grace looked at her watch. Had she been there that long? "No, I'm just . . . well, yes, I am waiting for someone actually."

"Thought so. Well, can I get you something to eat?"

"No, thank you."

"You sure? Bill's a helluva cook."

"Who?"

"Bill Shiner. The man who owns the place. He makes a wicked club sandwich."

"Oh, well..uh..no thank you. Maybe later."

"Okay. I'll check back with you in another hour or two."

Grace smiled. The waitress patted her twice on the shoulder. Grace felt sympathy in the touch as if this waitress knew that Grace's life was in upheaval. The waitress moved to a man three tables down and stood writing out a check. The man was in his early forties and wearing a jean jacket over a cream-colored cotton shirt. Grace saw him come into the restaurant about a half an hour earlier. She crossed him off her list of potential rides because he had a toothpick in his mouth.

When the waitress handed the man his check, she patted him on the shoulder twice and then moved back towards the counter. Grace held up a hand timidly, and when she did, she realized that this wasn't like her. Where did this timidity come from? She had always been assertive. Confident. Had Bryden turned her into a simpering milksop in less than twenty-four hours?

"Change your mind?" asked the waitress.

"Pardon me?"

"About the club sandwich."

"Oh, no, no. I uh . . . ." Grace hesitated. Was this really what she wanted to do? Really? Maybe she just ran out on Bryden to teach him a lesson. Maybe he's learned that lesson now and maybe she should forget about running away. After all, she had ten years invested in this marriage and in Bryden's climb to power. She had given up a career for this man. Couldn't she just forget about what he did to her in the parking lot of the Governor's mansion last night? Couldn't she?

"I need a ride."

"A ride?"

"I need a ride out of town. Out of the state. Tonight. Now."

As the waitress looked at Grace now she noticed a slight puffiness around her right cheekbone, and under the thick layer of makeup, a darkened area on the cheek itself. A birthmark maybe. Or a bruise.

"You in some kind of trouble?"

"Not really. I just want to get away for awhile."

"Uh-huh. From a man?"

"Yes."

The waitress nodded as if she had seen women in this situation before. Maybe she had been in the situation herself.

"You sure this is what you want to do, Hon? Maybe you'll feel different about things tomorrow."

Grace looked up at the woman with steel in her eyes. The simpering milksop had disappeared without a trace.

"This is what I want to do, *Hon*."

The waitress took Grace at her word now. "A ride, huh? Okay. From one of these guys?" Without looking behind her she pointed over her shoulder with her pen, in the general direction of the diner's clientele.

"Yes, but I want someone I can trust. A nice guy. Are there any nice guys here?"

"They're all nice guys. Doesn't mean you can trust them."

"Well, can you recommend one to me? I mean, you must know them, right? Are there any that a woman could feel safe with?"

"Well, personally, I like the ones you can't feel safe with. But, different strokes, right?"

"Please. There's got to be one here."

The waitress turned around now and took a good look at the customers. She turned back to Grace and looked down at her clothing. Grace felt uneasy for a moment. Was there a stain somewhere? Were her buttons done up unevenly?

"What's wrong?"

"You got any casual clothes in that suitcase?"

Grace looked down at herself and then back to the waitress. "These are casual clothes."

"Not in here they aren't. You got any jeans? A sweatshirt?"

"I've got jeans, yes. Why?"

"Well, look, why don't you go into the ladies room there and change into something more appropriate for the road? When you come out, I'll have your man for you."

"Oh. All right. Thank you." Grace slid out of the booth and pulled her suitcase out behind her.

"Don't mention it."

"Thank you."

"I said don't mention it."

"No, that thank you was for the 'don't mention it.'"

"Oh . . . . Well . . . . Don't mention it."

"Thank you."

Grace headed for the ladies room. The waitress turned and looked towards a booth to her right.

*

"Bryden, you're hurting my wrist."

They were walking through the side parking lot of the Governor's mansion. Bryden had waved off the kid from valet parking when they exited the mansion.

"Where's the black BMW?" he said to the kid brusquely.

"Which one?" replied the kid. "There must be about twenty of those here."

Bryden didn't wait. He would find the car himself. The last thing he was going to do was stand on the goddamned steps of the Governor's mansion waiting for some squeaky-voiced kid to locate his car while his wife assaulted him with her obscenity-laced questions.

"Bryden, let go!"

Bryden looked down the row of cars. Lincolns, Cadillacs, BMWs, Pam Carpenter's Lexus–she had performed oral sex on him in that car in a parking lot behind the Justice Building – Ron and Judy Winkley's Ford Taurus, several of those gas-guzzling four-wheel drive vehicles, and finally Bryden's black BMW. He pressed a button on his key case and the BMW's doors unlocked from about thirty feet.

He let Grace go when they reached the car and he walked around to the driver's side and climbed behind the wheel. Grace got in the passenger side of the vehicle and began rubbing her wrist.

"So, you didn't answer me. Was she a good fu . . . ."

Before Grace could finish her question, Bryden's left hand swung around and caught her flush on the right cheek. Grace felt the slap before she saw it. She wasn't expecting it, and it turned her head so hard to her left that she banged her chin on her left shoulder. Before she realized what had caused the loud 'thwack!' and the stinging pain on her face, he hit her again. Same cheek. Only this time, instead of bringing his hand around in a reflex motion from the steering wheel, as was the case with the first slap, he brought this one down from the top of the front windshield, as far up as he could reach in the confined space. The second slap caused Grace to let out an involuntary 'grunt' as her head was forced back into the headrest. In the instant of the second slap, she knew what was happening. She knew that her husband had hit her, not once, but twice. In that same instant, even as the left side of her face was rebounding off the leather of the passenger seat headrest–in that very instant – she knew that this marriage was over.

"How dare you?!" growled Bryden. "How fucking dare you??!"

Grace didn't answer. She put a hand up to her cheek, and looked at her husband in disbelief. Inside her mouth she could taste her warm blood. One of the blows had forced her cheek to scrape against her teeth, causing a small cut inside.

"Don't you ever humiliate me in public like that again. Ever!!"

Bryden's shoulders were heaving and his breathing was rapid. His adrenalin was pumping uncontrollably. He seemed to realize this and he put both hands on the steering wheel and gripped it tightly in an attempt to get control of himself. He took a few more deep breaths and then he turned to Grace again. The look on her face hadn't changed. Her right hand still comforted her cheek.

"I'm warning you Grace. There is no one . . . not you . . . not Pam Carpenter . . . no one, who is going to get in the way of what I have to do. Do you understand? I was put on this earth to do some good for people who can't do it for themselves. That's why I'm here. And the higher up I go the more I can do for them. And I'm not just talking about being the goddamned District Attorney for fucking Penobscot County! That's just the start. I'm talking about being Governor, and maybe even beyond Governor. So, if you think that I'm going to let your being upset because I had a few nights in the sack with Pam Carpenter ruin all that, you are sadly fucking mistaken. My mission is more important than you or me or our marriage."

"We don't have a marriage anymore," Grace said as she reached into her purse and pulled out a tissue. She wiped tears from the corners of her eyes. They were not tears of sadness. They were tears brought on by two slaps to the face.

"What did you say?"

"I said we don't have a marriage anymore, you bastard. I don't stay married to a man who hits me."

"Oh, I'm afraid that's where you're wrong, Grace. We will stay married for as long as I need you."

"What do you mean, need me?" said Grace. "You just said I wasn't important."

"I said you weren't as important as the cause. You are important though. You see, voters can tolerate their leaders having a sexual indiscretion now and then. Christ, they're used to that. But, when a wife doesn't stand beside her man in times of discord, then that tells the voters that the man cannot be trusted. I mean, if his own wife won't stand by him, why should they? So, you will stay Grace . . . ."

"The hell I will."

"Oh, you will. Because if you don't, then I'll have to find an acceptable excuse for your departure. An excuse that will put the voters on my side. And there are only two excuses that qualify. You went crazy, or you died."

Grace didn't recognize this man in the car next to her. She had never seen this side of Bryden before. Mission? He was on a mission? She just thought he wanted to be district attorney, not Mother Teresa for Christ's sake. "You went crazy or you died." What did he mean by that? Was that a threat? Would he kill her just to keep his public image intact? No, of course he wouldn't kill her. This was the man she loved. This was the man she adored . . . . This was the man who had just slapped her hard twice.

Bryden started the car and backed out of the parking space.

"Let's go home," he said calmly.

*

Grace came out of the diner's washroom wearing a pair of jeans and the Gap t-shirt. She carried her suit jacket over her arm now. She would have brought more clothing with her but she didn't want to take the time in case Bryden came home unexpectedly.

The night before she didn't sleep at all. She lay in their bed, on her side, as far away from Bryden as she could get. "You went crazy or you died." She grew more paranoid by the minute. After all, Bryden was a lawyer. If he wanted to prove that his wife was crazy and have her locked away in an institution somewhere, he probably could. And where would he get the evidence? Well, just look at the night at the Governor's mansion. Grace punched a woman in the washroom, stole the woman's earrings, and then she told the District Attorney for Penobscot County that she thought she had crabs.

That morning, after Bryden left, Grace poured herself a cup of coffee and pondered her options. Maybe she could call somebody. The police? Right. And accuse someone high up in the District Attorney's office of hitting her in the face? Her husband no less. The authorities would just chalk that up to a domestic dispute and in the process she would make Bryden even angrier. That option was ruled out by the time she had had her first sip of coffee. Maybe she could go to her parents' place in Chicago. No. That would be one of the first places Bryden would look for her.

For the next few hours, she vacillated back and forth between leaving and telling herself that she was over-reacting. The phone rang twice that morning, but she didn't answer it. The morning turned into afternoon, and finally at two o'clock, she made her decision. She had to get away. Just for a while so she could think without Bryden being around. She had to work this problem out. Decide what to do. She ran upstairs and hurriedly threw a few things into her suitcase, and then ran downstairs to the kitchen and called a cab. She waited at the front door for ten agonizing minutes before the red and white taxi arrived, and then she rushed out and climbed into the back seat, throwing the brown leather suitcase in ahead of her.

"Where you going?" asked the cabby.

"Take me to a place where the truck driver's eat," she said.

This was another idea that had come to her in her paranoid state the night before. If she took a bus or a train or a plane out of town, Bryden would be able to trace her movements, but by finding a truck driver to drive her away from Bangor, she would eliminate that eventuality.

"Truck drivers?" asked the cabby.

"Yes," said Grace curtly. "You do know a place where the truck drivers eat, don't you?"

The cabby turned his head and looked into the back seat at the well-groomed woman wearing the wool blend pant suit, the Gap t-shirt and the diamond earrings.

"Okay, but I hope you have a reservation," he said. "The maitre de doesn't like it when people just show up there unannounced." Fifteen minutes later, the cabby dropped his fare off at Shiner's Truck Stop. And now here Grace stood, dressed down in a pair of jeans and waiting to meet her trucker.

"Well, that's a little better," said the waitress from behind the counter. "Now you're ready for the road."

"So . . . did you find somebody?"

"Oh, yeah. You bet. I think I've got just the fella for you." The waitress turned toward the row of booths near the window. "Dan?"

The man in the jean jacket looked up. The toothpick was still in his mouth. The waitress waived him over to where she and Grace stood.

"Him?" said Grace.

"That's right. He's the nicest guy in the place."

Grace looked around quickly at the rest of the patrons. Did the waitress mean that this was a nice guy, or was he just the lesser of the other evils in the establishment?

"Dan, this is the lady I was telling you about. This is..I'm sorry I didn't get your name, hon."

"Grace." The name was out of her mouth before she thought to give a false answer. Being Bryden's wife and being introduced to strangers at hundreds of functions had downloaded that habit into her hard drive.

"Grace. Dan, this is Grace."

The man took the toothpick out of his mouth the way other men would doff their caps when they met a lady. He held his free hand out to Grace.

"How do you do, Grace?"

"Hello."

"I understand you're looking for a ride."

"Uh . . . yes. Yes, I am."

"'Scuse' me folks," the waitress said. "I've got customers waiting." She moved to a group of three men seated at a table in the middle of the diner. She patted one of the men twice on the shoulder.

"Well, I'm heading north into Canada. You're welcome to ride along if you like."

"Thank you. That's very kind of . . ."

"No problem," said Dan, cutting Grace off and moving towards the front door of the diner. "Let's hit the highway then."

"But . . ."

"But, what?" Dan stopped.

"Well, I don't know anything about you."

"Of course you don't. We just met."

"Well, I think I should find out a few things about you first."

"Things? What things?"

"Well, I'd just like to ask you a few questions before I climb into the truck with you."

"Fine. You can ask me as many questions as you can fire off between here and the truck." And having laid down his conditions, Dan was out the door.

Grace hesitated long enough to take one more quick look at the diner patrons, all of whom had their eyes fixed on her again. She quickly moved out the door after Dan.

"Have you ever been arrested?" she said, hurrying to catch up to him.

"Nope."

"Never been in any trouble with the law?"

"Nope."

"Do you have a substance abuse problem?"

"No."

"Are you short-tempered?"

Dan stopped and turned to face Grace. "Well, now you're starting to piss me off."

"That was a joke, right?"

"That was a joke."

"Good."

Dan turned and began walking again. Grace continued the chase across the dusty parking lot.

"Are you married?"

"No."

"Why is that?"

"Haven't found a woman tall enough."

"Well, that's a pretty ridiculous reason for not getting married."

"Well, that short-tempered question was kind of stupid too."

Dan reached the truck, pulled open the driver-side door and climbed in. Grace stood there for a moment and looked around at the other trucks that inhabited Shiner's parking lot. Maybe she should wait. Maybe this wasn't the guy. She looked back towards the diner. The waitress stood in the doorway. Grace shrugged her shoulders to her as if to say, "What do I do?" The waitress gave a couple of backhanded flicks of her wrist, the kind of urging a mother would give to a child who was shy about asking for a hockey player's autograph. Grace gave a sigh and walked quickly around to the passenger door. Unable to reach the door handle, she rapped on the door with her fist. Dan leaned over, opened the door from the inside and looked down at her.

"Can you give me a hand, please?" Grace held up her hand to the truck driver.

"Well, hold on now," said Dan. "I think I should ask you some questions first."

"What?" said Grace, staring up.

"Well, a fella can't be too careful about who he's driving with. I'd like to find out a few things about you first."

"Like what things?"

"How far did you go in school?"

"I've got a degree from the University of Maine."

"What's your favorite vegetable?"

"Green beans."

"Do you sleep in pajamas or a man's football jersey?"

"I sleep in the nude."

"Climb on up," Dan said, and he reached down and held out his hand to Grace.

Grace grabbed hold of Dan's hand and took a big step up in an attempt to reach the running board of the huge cab, but Dan's pull was so strong that she missed the running board completely and was unceremoniously hauled head first into the cab, suitcase and all. Upon landing in the cab, Grace righted herself, pushed the hair away from her eyes, and nonchalantly crossed her legs in a futile attempt to appear unfazed.

"Thanks."

"Don't mention it."

Grace looked back towards the diner where the waitress now stood in the doorway with one hand on her hip. She smiled and gave Grace a wave. Grace started to give a small wave back, but at that same moment, the big truck lunged forward throwing Grace back against the seat. The Kenworth pulled out of the parking lot and turned north onto Interstate Ninety-Five. It was five-oh-seven p.m.. In two hours they would be passing by a small town just over the Canadian border. Rainbow, New Brunswick.

-5-

You hope and pray you'll find
A love to last all time
Not until you know
The art of letting go.

Dan's cassette player expelled the sounds of Kenny Loggins.

You're dying to believe
In love eternally
Not until you know
The art of letting go.

They drove on in silence. Both just listening. Song after song.

You get one chance at a life
To give it all and get it right
And after all this time in mine
Everything I thought I knew
Was tellin' me to give it up
And leave it all behind.

Grace twirled a lock of her hair around her index finger over and over again, a habit she had acquired in her childhood, and something she didn't even realize she was doing most of the time. She finally spoke.

"You don't talk much," she said.

"I didn't think you wanted to talk."

"Why?"

"Well, you're troubled. I figured you wanted some quiet time."

"Oh . . . . Thank you."

"You want to talk now?"

"Maybe."

"What do you want to talk about?"

Grace hesitated. She looked out the window as the big rig passed over the Penobscot River. She looked back at Dan. "Men like women who sleep in football jerseys, don't they?" she said.

"Oh, yeah. Definitely."

"Why?"

"Because it's sex and sports in one package. It's a dream come true for us."

"And they like it even more than say, something from Victoria's Secret?"

"I'll tell you something, Grace. If Victoria's Secret ever put their name on the back of a football jersey, they'd clean up."

Grace smiled. It was her first smile in almost twenty-four hours. "Do you ever take that toothpick out of your mouth?"

"Can't."

"What do you mean, you can't?"

"I quit smoking. This is my replacement. It's my oral gratification."

"Oral gratification? How do you know about oral gratification?"

"How do I know? Well, there's these things out there in these stores, Grace, and they're called books. And these stores are called book stores, ya' see, and every once in a while I wander into one by mistake because I'm kinda stupid and I can't read and I think the sign out front says 'Beer Store' . . . ."

"All right, all right. I'm sorry. That's not how I meant it."

"Sure it is. That's *exactly* how you meant it. You see a truck driver chewing on a toothpick and you assume that all I know about is Clint Eastwood movies and country music."

"You don't like country music?"

"I love country music. Doesn't mean I can't like classical music too."

"You like classical music?"

"I hate classical music. I was just using that as an example."

"Oh. Well, I'm sorry. You're right. I did assume that because you're a truck driver and you chew on a toothpick that maybe you were . . . . under-schooled."

"Under-schooled. I like that. You're a bit of a snob, aren't you, Grace?" Dan said with a grin.

"No, I'm not, no." This was an affront to Grace who had always prided herself on her liberal ways, and of course a liberal-thinking person would never sell a man short simply because of his class standing.

"Oh, I think you are," said Dan, his grin widening. "You're a rich bitch snob."

"I am not a bitch."

"But, you're rich."

"No, don't be ridiculous. Rich."

"Well-to-do then."

"What makes you say that?"

"The earrings. Look like diamonds. Are they diamonds?"

"I didn't buy these earrings. They were a . . . . a gift."

"Oh. I see."

After a brief pause Grace changed the subject. "So, how long have you been a truck driver?" she asked.

"Going on four years now."

"Four years? That's not very long. What did you do before that?"

"I was a baseball player."

"A what? A baseball player?"

"Yeah."

"You mean a professional baseball player?"

"Uh-huh."

"Who did you play with?"

"Well, I bounced a round quite a bit. I played with The Red Sox organization for two years and I spent a few years in the Houston Astros farm system and the Dodgers farm system and the Tigers farm system. I didn't see much time in the majors really."

"So, why did you quit?"

"Wasn't good enough."

"Well, you were good enough to make it farther than most."

"Yeah, but I wasn't good enough to make it over that last hill. There are only a very few who are that good. Anyway, that frustrated me, so I quit."

"Just like that, huh? You didn't find it hard, walking away from it like that?"

"It would've been a lot harder to stay and watch all the young players coming through on their way up."

"Oh."

Two more miles passed under the truck's wheels before the next words were spoken.

"So, what are you running from?" Dan asked.

Grace was surprised at the suddenness of his question and it caused her to hesitate.

" . . . . A man."

"Figures."

Walkin' on my own
Absolutely free
Solitary life
Only life for me.

"So, this man, he your husband?"

"Hmm-hmm," Grace nodded.

"Must be pretty bad to make you hitch a ride with a strange truck driver."

"Yeah, it's pretty bad."

"He give you that bruise?"

Grace reached up involuntarily and touched her right cheek. "I didn't think it was noticeable."

"Only close up. Once you're outside of twenty feet you can hardly see it at all."

Grace smiled again. She was relieved that she could smile after what had transpired since the Governor's Ball. And that someone could make her smile twice, well, that was almost a comfort to her.

"So, what do you think you'll accomplish by running away?"

"Getting away I guess."

"It doesn't sound like you gave it much thought."

"I gave it as much thought as I needed to, believe me."

"Uh-huh. So, what if things don't get any better where you're going?"

"Then I'll go somewhere else."

"And what if it isn't any better when you get to somewhere else?"

"Well . . ." Grace paused and looked into the distance beyond Interstate Ninety-Five. "I'll just keep looking. There's got to be a rainbow somewhere."

"What?"

"It's something my grandfather told me when I got married. We were dancing at the reception and he said if ever things got me down, you know, if I'm having a bad day, I should remember that there's always a rainbow somewhere."

She turned and looked out the window again and twirled a lock of her hair around her index finger. They passed a sign that read 'Houlton 21 miles.' There they would find the Canadian border, and customs.

*

"Grace?? . . . . Grace!!"

Grace woke up to hear a woman calling her name. She had fallen asleep about ten miles away from the border and now she awoke to find a man in a uniform handing some papers to Dan the truck driver through the driver side window. Her first thought was "How did that man get up so high? He's got to be ten feet tall." Then she realized that the man was standing on a platform. Where were they?

"Grace!?"

That voice again. She was awakening from the worst kind of sleep. The ten minute sleep that seems to tire you out more than it rests you. "Customs," she thought. "We're going through customs."

They were. They were in the 'Trucks Only' lane at the Houlton border crossing.

"Thank you," Dan said to the customs inspector.

"Have a safe run," the inspector said, and he backed away from the window.

"Grace?! Yoo-hoo!"

"Somebody out here seems to know you," said Dan.

Grace craned to look out Dan's window. Standing three lanes over was a woman in a customs inspector's uniform. She was waving. Judy Winkley, from the Governor's Ball the night before. Judy was waving, but there was no friendly 'Nice to see you' smile on her face. It was more of a 'What the hell are you doing in an eighteen wheeler with your Gap t-shirt on' kind of look. Grace held up her hand. She gave Judy a tentative wave. A 'I just woke up and I can't believe you're the first person I see' kind of wave.

"Do you want to talk to her?" asked Dan.

"No."

Dan didn't ask why. He put the truck into gear and pulled away. Grace took one last look at Judy. Judy's wave had slowed so that it was barely noticeable. Her dumbstruck expression hadn't changed. She watched the truck cross into Canada.

-6-

"How far is Halifax from here?" Grace asked as they turned onto the Trans-Canada Highway.

"Bout' six hours. Is that far enough away for you?"

"Hmm?"

"Halifax. Is that gonna put enough distance between you and your husband?"

Grace shrugged. She didn't know the answer. She didn't know how far she wanted to go. She didn't know what she was going to do when she got there. She started to get angry at herself again. How could she have put herself in this spot? How does an intelligent woman do this?

"Looks like they've had some rain here," said Dan. The highway in his headlights was damp now and he could hear the sound of his tires rolling through the wetness.

Out of the horizon of darkness that lay before them, a highway sign came into view in the eighteen wheeler's headlights. The sign said 'Watch for Moose.'

"They put those signs every seven kilometers," said Dan.

"Hmm? What signs?"

"The 'Watch For Moose' signs. We just passed one. They're every seven kilometers. You know why?"

Grace didn't know why and she didn't really care.

"You see they did a study and they found that if they put the signs every six kilometers, then people saw too many of them, and after a while they didn't pay any attention to them. But if they put them every eight kilometers, then people didn't see enough of them and they forgot to watch for the moose. That's why they're every seven kilometers. It's the perfect distance."

Grace waited for the next sign. And in those seven kilometers she tried to put a bit of her past behind her. Her husband. The Governor's ball. The next sign came and she told herself that in the next seven kilometers she would put more behind her. The punch up in the ladies room. The slap in the face in the car. And the next sign came. And the next. And with every sign, Grace jettisoned more of her past. Then Grace noticed a different sign. Not the smaller 'Watch For Moose' sign, but a bigger green highway sign. It read 'Rainbow Business District, 1 Kilometer'.

"Slow down!" Grace shouted.

"What?!!"

"The next exit! Get off at the next exit!"

"What, Rainbow??"

"Yes."

"You want to go into Rainbow?"

"Yes."

Dan took a bewildered pause and then one final time he said, "Rainbow?"

"Yes. Right here. Please?"

They were at the exit now and Dan took the 50 kilometer per hour exit ramp at about 80 kilometers per hour. The brakes puffed and wheezed as he geared down and held the truck in as wide a turn as he could so as not to allow it to flip. Dan finally brought the Kenworth to a stop just off the ramp on Nylander Street. Across the road was a small park with a large gazebo in the center of it. Grace saw a sign that said 'Moran Park'.

"Well, what now?"

"Uh . . . I don't know," said Grace. "But, I think this is as far as I want to go for now."

"Here."

"Yeah."

"And what are you going to do here?"

"I . . . uh . . . I'm going to think. I'm going to take some time, gather my wits and think. Thanks very much for the ride, and . . . uh . . . . well, thanks."

Grace grabbed her suitcase and reached for the door handle. As she did, she felt a hand on her left arm. She jumped and let out a high-pitched yelp.

"Whoa," said Dan, pulling back his hand. He held up both his hands to show Grace that he meant her no harm.

"I'm sorry," said Grace, her back against the truck's door now. "I'm sorry."

"No, I'm sorry. I shouldn't have grabbed you like that. But, you were about to jump out here in the middle of nowhere. I can't let you do that."

"Well, there's a town here somewhere isn't there? I mean, there's a gazebo."

"The town's about half a mile down the road. I'll drive you in."

"No, that's okay."

"No, I'm not dropping you off until I know you're gonna be all right."

"Well . . . ."

"It'll take two minutes. Now sit back and relax."

"Funny," said Grace, "That's what my husband used to say."

"What?"

"It'll take two minutes. Now sit back and relax."

Dan looked at Grace for about a two count, and then the joke suddenly struck him. He threw back his head and roared. He had a great laugh. A robust man laugh. Grace chuckled, both at Dan's laugh and at her joke. She was relieved that she could joke about Bryden, even if what was implied in her joke was a complete falsehood. Bryden was a very good lover, but in the tradition of divorced women–which she felt she would soon be–she found herself, almost by reflex, bad-mouthing the ex-husband with a crack about his poor sexual performance.

Dan moved the big truck ahead to the next stop sign where he turned left onto Main Street. About five hundred yards down the road, Grace saw what she assumed must be the lights of the town of Rainbow.

"There isn't much here," Dan said.

"You've been here before?"

"Yeah, a couple of times. Pulled in to get some food was all."

They passed Proctor's Electric, a Sobey's grocery store, and a medical center housing the offices of an optometrist, two general practitioners, and a dentist, Doctor Duffy Higgenson. But, there was nobody on the street. No signs of life.

"Where is everybody?" Grace said as she looked out at the deserted sidewalk.

"Beats the hell out of me. Looks like one of those science fiction movies, doesn't it? Where everybody's disappeared for some mysterious reason."

"Here."

"What?"

"You can let me off here, at this restaurant."

Dan pulled the truck over and stopped behind a police car. Through the front window of the restaurant Grace could see a policeman seated on a stool, and a man standing behind the counter. They appeared to be looking up at a television set. The man behind the counter turned and looked out at the truck. He said something to the policeman and the policeman looked out the window as well.

"Are you sure about this?" Dan asked.

"Yes."

"But, what about a place to stay? Did you think about that?"

"I'll find a place. I'll be fine."

"Do you have any money?"

"I have credit cards."

"Uh-huh, well I wouldn't go using those if you don't want your husband tracing your whereabouts."

"I have a little cash too. I'll be fine." Grace put her hand on the truck's door handle. "Thanks for the ride . . . and . . . well, for everything. You've been good company. I could've done a lot worse when I was looking for a ride back at that truck stop."

"Oh, hell, half the guys in there would've been good company for you."

"Yeah. Well . . . thanks just the same."

Grace opened the door and climbed down from the cab slowly. She had to jump the last two feet to the pavement. Once on the sidewalk, she turned around and Dan handed her suitcase down to her. Grace took the suitcase and reached up to close the truck's door. She could see Dan leaning over to look down at her.

"Good-bye," she said.

"Listen," Dan called down to her. "I'm coming back this way tomorrow. Probably at about the same time. If you're still here, and if things aren't working out for you and you want a ride back to Bangor . . . well, you could meet me here."

"No, you don't have to do that."

"Do what? It's no big deal. I pull off the road, takes me two minutes to get here. It's not even out of my way. Okay?"

"Okay. Thanks."

"Tomorrow. Same time."

"Right."

"Right here."

"Right."

"Okay."

"Can I close the door now?"

"Be my guest," said Dan.

"Good-bye."

"Take care of yourself."

"I'll do my best."

Grace gave a hard push and the truck door slammed shut. She could feel the heat coming off the engine as it revved. The truck pulled out from behind the police car and turned into a parking lot across the street. Then it backed out, turned around, and headed back the way they had come. As he drove by, Dan held a hand up and gave Grace a smile. Grace waved back. She smiled too. Both smiles lacked confidence. The truck disappeared down Main Street, past Moran Park and the gazebo, and back onto the Trans-Canada Highway. Grace pushed open the door of The Frying Dutchman.

-7-

"What's that truck stopping out there for?" said Henry.

"Hmm?" said Pete turning to look out the front window of 'The Dutchman'. "Don't know. You expecting a delivery?"

"Not tonight."

"Well, maybe he just pulled off the highway to try some of your fine cooking."

"Yeah, be just my luck. Right when Jeopardy's starting."

Now entering our studio are today's contestants," came the Jeopardy voice-over announcer from the Magnavox. *"A real estate agent from Tempe, Florida, Gail Standish."*

The audience applauded as a middle-aged brunette took her place behind her podium.

"A furniture salesman from Rainbow, New Brunswick . . . ."

"There he is!!" shouted Henry as Mickey Welton walked to the podium that, through some electronic wizardry, had his name hand-written on the front of it.

"Mickey Welton."

"Well, I'll be damned," said Pete. "I'll be goddamned. Mickey Welton on national television."

"He looks good, doesn't he? That's a nice suit. Real nice. Oh, he's gonna do good. I can feel it. Look at him. He's got his game face on."

"And our returning champion, a computer programmer from Dayton, Ohio. David Chong."

"Well, that's it," said Henry, slapping his tea towel against the counter. "Mickey's fucked. A goddamned computer nerd. And a Chinese computer nerd at that. He's double fucked."

"Oh, come on, Henry," said Pete. "They haven't even started yet."

"It's over, Pete. Forget about it. How the hell is he gonna beat a goddamned Chinese computer nerd? Fix!!" Henry shouted at the television.

"And now, here is the host of Jeopardy, Alex Trebek."

The front door of The Frying Dutchman swung open and Grace Downey walked inside. Pete and Henry turned to look at her. She was carrying a leather purse and a medium-sized brown leather suitcase. Pete noticed that the suitcase looked like your high-end piece of luggage. If this was New York City, they would call it 'chic'.

As Pete looked at the attractive woman who was now avoiding his gaze, his first thought was of the Sesame Street song, 'One Of These Things Is Not Like The Others.' This woman looked very much out of place here in 'The Dutchman.'

"Good evening," said Henry, and without waiting for a response, he turned and looked back at the television.

"Hello," said Grace, and she moved to a booth against the side wall at the back of the restaurant.

"Good luck, contestants as we test your knowledge in these categories; Ancient History, Body Parts, Musical Instruments, Famous Firsts, Poets and Television. Gail, you won the toss backstage and you'll begin."

"I'll take Body Parts for one hundred, please."

"If you are clumsy, your fingers may be all these . . . . Gail?"

"What are thumbs?"

"Correct. Gail, select again."

"Body parts for two hundred."

"Act bluntly and you shoot from this . . . . Gail?"

"What is the hip?"

"Shoot from the hip. Correct."

"Henry," said Pete, "I think the lady would like some service." Pete cocked his head towards Grace who had settled into the booth and now sat with hands folded on the table.

"Yeah, all right," replied Henry, and he turned up the volume on the television set so he wouldn't miss anything while he was at the back of the room.

"What is a trigger finger?"

"Correct."

"Come on, Mickey," said Henry as he backed towards Grace. "Get in the game!"

"Body parts for four hundred."

"Hard workers always put this to the wheel."

"The shoulder, Mickey! The shoulder!", Henry cried as he continued his backward route towards Grace.

"Gail?"

"What is the shoulder?"

"Oh, for Godssake. He's gettin' killed, Pete. By a real estate saleswoman."

"It's still early yet, Henry. Give him a chance. He's probably nervous."

In his excitement, Henry backed right into Grace's table, rattling the salt and pepper shakers.

"Oh, sorry ma'am. We're watching Jeopardy."

"Yes, so I see."

"What can I get you?" Henry said, looking away from Grace to watch the television again.

"Just a coffee please."

"That's it?" Henry asked without taking his eyes off the television. "How about a piece of our raspberry pie? Best raspberry pie in the world. And if you don't think so, it's on the house."

"The best in the world?"

"Uh-huh."

"Really? Well, if it's the best in the world then maybe I'd better try it."

Henry didn't respond. He stood watching the Magnavox.

"Hello?" said Grace.

"I'm sorry. What did you say?" Henry's eyes were still riveted to the television set.

"I said I'll have the pie as well."

"As well as what?"

"As well as a coffee."

"Raspberry pie and coffee. It's on the way."

"Famous firsts for one hundred."

"The answer. With Vince Lombardi as it's coach, this team won the first Super Bowl in nineteen sixty-seven . . . . Mickey?"

The Packers, Mickey!!"

"Who are the Green Bay Packers?"

"Correct."

"Yeah!" said Henry, pumping his fist into the air. "Yeah!!"

"There you go," said Pete. "He's on the board."

Grace watched the two men as they played along with the contestants on Jeopardy. The voice of Alex Trebek was saying something about Kitty Hawk.

"Who was Orville Wright?"

"Correct. Mickey, select again."

"Oh, yeah! Look at that. Mickey's got three hundred and the computer guy's got zip! He's gonna bury him!"

"I think it's the real estate woman we've got to worry about," said Pete.

"Yeah. She looks focused. Very focused."

"Who was Roberta Flack?"

"Correct."

"Yes!"

Henry held up a hand to Pete expecting a high five in return.

"Yeah, yeah," said Pete waving him off.

"What? Come on! Give me a high-five for Mickey."

"I don't give high-fives."

"What do you mean?"

"Who was Craig Breedlove?"

"Correct. David, your turn to select."

"Oh-oh. China just checked in," Henry observed. Then he turned his attention back to Pete. "What do you mean you don't give high-fives?"

"I just don't. I feel stupid doing a high-five. Only athletes should do high-fives. The rest of us always get it wrong and we look ridiculous. You know, we catch half a hand or we miss completely and someone gets whacked in the nose. We haven't had enough practice at it, so we shouldn't do it."

"What was the Mercury Program?"

"Correct. The Mercury Space program. Select again."

"Television for one hundred, Alex."

"He was on the run from Lieutenant Phillip Gerard .... Mickey?"

"Who was The Fugitive?"

"Correct. Doctor Richard Kimble."

"Way to go, Mickey!! He's holding his own, Pete. He's staying close," enthused Henry, as he removed a raspberry pie from the display case near the cash register and quickly cut a piece for his customer.

" .... take a short break, and we'll be right back to talk to our contestants."

"All right. Perfect timing," said Henry. He grabbed the plate with the piece of raspberry pie on it, and a pot of coffee and headed to Grace's table.

Pete turned to watch as Henry served the lady.

"Here, we go. Raspberry pie and a coffee."

"Thank you."

"You going somewhere?" asked Henry.

"I beg your pardon?"

"The suitcase."

"Oh..Uh..no, no. I just arrived in town."

"Oh. You didn't come in on the SMT did you?"

"The what?"

"The SMT. The bus line here. Because that's not supposed to come through for another hour yet. I always have a couple of pots of coffee ready for them. They stop just up the street and sometimes the passengers wander down here for a pick-me-up."

"No, I didn't come on the SMT."

"Oh. So, where you coming in from?"

"Well, I'm from out west actually."

"Oh. Say, you didn't just get out of that truck that was out front, did you?"

"As a matter of fact, yes." Grace was wishing this line of questioning and the proprietor would both go away.

"Henry, can I get a refill, please?" Pete held up his empty cup from across the room.

"Sure. Scuse' me, ma'am."

Henry moved away from Grace and went back behind the counter to freshen Pete's coffee. Grace looked at the policeman who had just rescued her from the Spanish Inquisition. He gave her a quick, almost shy smile, and looked away.

-8-

"Mickey, maybe you should give Miss Hoyt a call."

"No, Mom, it's okay."

"But, the show's started. She said she was going to be here to watch it with you."

"Well, maybe something came up. Maybe she got busy."

"Or maybe she fell asleep," said a worried Myrna. "Maybe she's lying on her couch right now, not even knowing that she's missing the show that you two worked so hard to prepare for. I think you should call her."

"Mom, please . . . ."

"Mickey it says here that you are a furniture salesman back home."

"That's right, Alex."

"Give the store a plug," said Jack.

"I've been there for two years now."

"Give the store a plug!"

"You must enjoy it then, do you?"

"Well, I've met some interesting people there, yes."

"What are you doing?"

"What?" said Mickey, not trying to mask his annoyed state.

"What the hell are you doing?"

"What?!"

"You didn't give the store a goddamned plug."

"What do you care if he gives the store a plug?" said Peggy. "It's not your store."

"I know it's not my store, Miss 'Talk-to-your-parents-as-if-they-were-idiots', but don't you think the man who *does* own the store would be grateful if his store got mentioned on national television? Grateful enough to perhaps supply us with some free furniture? Possibly the new living room set that your mother's been wanting so badly for the past nine years?"

"Jack, shhhh!" said Myrna. "I can't hear what Mickey's saying."

"Well, do you want a new living room set or don't you?"

"The one we have will do."

"No, it won't. Damn it, you deserve better and I think your son should've taken it upon himself to try and get it for you when he had the chance."

"Goddamn it, Jackie, shut the Christ up!" said Gran, and she picked up a cushion she was using for back support and threw it across the room at her son, hitting him on the side of the head.

"*. . . . an actor.*"

"What?" Myrna looked at Mickey. "What did you just tell Alex?"

"He's Canadian you know?" said Gran.

"I know he's Canadian, Gran. We're all very proud. Now, what did you just say to Alex, Mickey?"

"Nothing. It was just small talk."

"What? What did he say?" said Jack.

"Did you tell Mr. Trebek that you wanted to be an actor?"

"An actor?" said Jack.

"I couldn't think of anything to say so I just said that. I thought it might be more interesting than the furniture store stuff."

"You want to be an actor?" asked Myrna, still baffled by this news. "Why haven't you told us this before?"

"I've just been thinking about it. Just thinking. It doesn't mean I'm going to be one."

"Actor? Where the hell would you act?" said Jack. "There's no acting going on here in Rainbow for Christ's sake."

"Well, now, Jack, there is that group of folks from St. Paul's Church. They put on two or three shows a year in the church basement. They did 'Cat On A Hot Tin Roof' last spring and I heard it was wonderful."

"No, Mom," said Peggy, "They did 'Fiddler On The Roof'. Not 'Cat On A Hot Tin Roof'.

"Well, I knew it was one of the roof plays," said Myrna.

In the den just off the living room, Buster, the Welton family patriarch, still in a deep sleep, began to mumble.

"Can't have that for Godssake. Get your hands off that woman."

"It's all right, Dad," Myrna called from the living room. "Go back to sleep,"

"Mickey, you had the last correct response, so you'll select."

"I'll take Poets for one hundred, Alex."

"Poets?? What the hell do you know about poets?" said Jack.

"Shhhh!", said Peggy waving her hand at her father in an effort to get some quiet.

"Don't you shush me, Miss 'I-Think-I-Own-The-House-And-Can-Talk-To-My-Parents-Anyway-I-Want.' What you need is a damn good . . . ."

Before he could finish, Jack was hit on the side of the head by the second cushion that Gran had been using for back support.

"One of these days, old woman," said Jack, pointing his finger at his mother, "you're going to throw one pillow too many and it'll be the last goddamned thing you ever throw."

"In 1827 he enlisted in the army under the pseudonym Edgar A Perry . . . . Mickey?"

"Who was Edgar Allan Poe?"

"Correct."

"Poets for two hundred."

"He wrote the line, 'Then he climbed the tower of the old north church.' . . . . Mickey.

"Who was Longfellow?"

"Is correct."

"Poets for three hundred."

"This poet and his wife Elinor were co-valedictorians at Lawrence High School in Massachusetts . . . . Mickey?"

"Who is Robert Frost?"

"Correct."

"Poets for four hundred."

"In 1809 he took his seat in the House of Lords . . . . Mickey."

"Who is Lord Byron?"

"Right again."

"Poets for five hundred."

"This Percey Shelley work begins with the title character bound to a precipice . . . . Mickey."

"What is 'Prometheus Unbound."

"That is correct."

"Whoo!!!" Peggy cried. "Way to go, Mick!" And with that, she threw her arms around her brother who was seated on the floor in front of her.

Myrna leaned back in the couch and let out her first breath in almost a minute.

"We really should call Miss Hoyt," she said. "If she misses this she'll die."

-9-

Wood Lynch turned his police cruiser onto Lilac Road and took notice of how this street, like Fairlawn before it and Yarbro before it, was devoid of any pedestrian or vehicular traffic. He knew why of course. Mickey Welton was appearing on Jeopardy tonight. He looked at his watch. Seven thirty-nine. He would be back at the police station in about four minutes, just in time to see Double Jeopardy and the final Jeopardy answer. Wood wasn't a regular Jeopardy viewer but he, like many others in Rainbow, had taken to watching it when they found out that one of their own was going to be on the program.

Lilac was a pretty street, lined with trees, as most streets in Rainbow were, and as he turned onto Lilac from Fairlawn he passed the imposing structure of St. Paul's Church on the corner. As children, he and his brother Donnie had attended this church with their mother Deborah, and after church, his mother would visit with Reverend Warren Figures in the rectory at the rear of the one hundred year-old structure, for counseling. She would be there for what seemed like hours, in the boys' minds, but what were certainly only a few minutes of real time. Deborah, of course, had recently been deserted by her husband and the Reverend Figures was diligently seeing to the healing of one of his flock.

During these sessions, Wood and Donnie would wander out behind the church to where the cemetery was located and they would look at old tombstones. The oldest one they found was that of a woman named Caroline Thornton. She had been born in the year eighteen thirty-seven and died at the age of sixty-four in nineteen oh-one. The boys would run their hands over her gray, worn marker and make educated guesses about what was left of her down there in the ground. Was there anything left? What did they bury people in way back then? Was it wooden boxes like the ones they had seen the victims of the O.K. Corral laid out in in photographs from that day? Donnie suggested to his younger brother, Bobby, that people back then were too poor to purchase coffins, wooden or otherwise, so most folks were just rolled up in bubble wrap and tossed into the grave by cemetery workers after the deceased's loved ones had left the grave site following the funeral service. Wood believed that story for a while, but he eventually caught on that this was just a case of his older brother acting like an older brother and having a laugh at his expense.

For Wood, Sunday was his favorite day as a child. Mainly because when his mother emerged from her sessions with Reverend Figures, she seemed relaxed. At peace with herself. It was as if the weight of the world had been lifted from her shoulders, and now she had the strength to begin another week of raising her boys alone.

Years later, Wood better understood his mother's Sunday rejuvenation when it came to light that Deborah and the Reverend Figures had fallen in love during her healing process, and had carried on a torrid affair in the rectory during the after-service sessions. This startling piece of news was revealed in a 'death-bed' confession by church organist Eloise Landers.

It seems that one Sunday, Wood's mom and the Reverend Figures had been discovered in the throes of passion by Mrs. Landers, when the organist had innocently entered the rectory to drop off her hymn suggestions for next Sunday's service. When Eloise opened the carelessly unlocked rectory door, she was greeted by the sight of Deborah Lynch sitting astride the good Reverend as he lay flat on his back on the rectory floor.

"Oh my God!" Eloise had cried. "Reverend, are you all right??"

Eloise suspected that the Reverend had suffered a collapse of some sort and that Deborah Lynch had leaped into action and was giving him cardiopulmonary resuscitation from her position atop his pelvis. Upon closer examination though, Eloise noticed that the Reverend's robes were hiked up above that pelvis, and his hands were up inside Deborah's rose-colored blouse.

"Sweet Jesus!!" Eloise cried, placing her hands over her eyes. "Sweet merciful Jesus!!"

The organist turned and made an attempt to bolt from the room. Unfortunately for Eloise, with her hands covering her eyes to block out the evil vision which lay before her, she misjudged where the doorway was and caught the flat edge of the big wooden rectory door straight on. The force of the collision stunned her momentarily, and then, giving her head a shake in the same way a cartoon character might after an anvil has fallen on his head, she lunged for the door again. She lasted exactly four steps before the bang on the forehead took effect and brought her to her knees in the hallway outside.

"Eloise," Reverend Figures called out. "Are you all right?"

Still sitting atop the good Reverend, Deborah Lynch stared out into the hallway in stunned silence. There she could see Eloise on her knees, hands covering her face, ready to pass out from the collision. And after three or four seconds, she did pass out, falling face first into the hall carpet.

"Deborah, you'll have to get off now," Reverend Figures said calmly.

"Hmm?"

"You'll have to get off."

"Oh! Yes!" said Deborah, and she did just that, sliding her right leg over and releasing the Reverend from her love grip.

Deborah then gathered up her white silk underwear which had been tossed behind the Reverend's desk early on in the counseling session, and she made a hasty exit into the hallway, being careful not to step on the organist's hands as she did so. Once outside, she called to Bobby and Donnie out in the cemetery, telling them to hurry up, they had to leave now. The boys joined their mother in the car and the threesome sped away into the heat of a Sunday afternoon.

After the Reverend revived Eloise and calmed her down, the two of them discussed what had transpired for close to an hour. During that talk, Reverend Figures somehow managed to convince Eloise that if news of his tryst with Mrs. Lynch leaked out, it could be very bad for the church's standing in the community. And even though neither Reverend Figures nor Deborah Lynch were married at the time of the involvement, he was probably right. He knew that parishioners liked their church leaders to be free from the bonds of lust. He knew that falling in love with and having relations with a woman he was counseling would be considered improper and unprofessional behavior, and he knew that the news of the positioning of Deborah on top and astride his lower half would raise more than a few eyebrows at the next choir practice. Having convinced his church organist of the perils of having this clandestine relationship made public, Reverend Figures then persuaded Eloise to swear on his rectory Bible that she would never talk about what she saw that day. And he swore too, that he would break off the relationship with the lovely divorcee, Deborah Lynch, immediately.

Seventeen years passed. The Reverend and Deborah did break off their relationship after being discovered by Eloise, and the Reverend eventually moved on to another parish hundreds of miles away. Deborah dated several other men, none of whom did for her what Reverend Figures did, and Eloise Landers kept her promise and never talked about what she saw on the floor of the rectory that day. That is, until she was stricken with pneumonia.

At the time of her battle with pneumonia, Eloise was seventy-one years old. The pneumonia had rendered her immobile and for three days she lay in a hospital bed, barely able to raise her head, while a steady stream of friends and family filed through to wish her well and pray with her for a speedy recovery. But, by the evening of that third day, Eloise felt herself losing the battle. She would be in a sweat one moment and was chilled to the bone the next. She drifted in and out of consciousness, and at one point, awoke to find a priest standing over her. Standing next to the priest and hanging another bag of clear fluid on a metal pole beside her bed was nurse Marilyn Mott. As it turned out, the priest, a new man in town, had been directed to the wrong room by the hospital receptionist and was supposed to be attending another patient down the hall, but seeing his robed figure standing there, Eloise surmised that this must surely be her last moment on earth, and she mustered all the strength she could and grabbed the holy man by the sleeve.

"Father," she gasped weakly. "There's something . . . I must . . . . tell you."

"What is it, Sandra?" the priest asked, leaning closer.

"What?" said Eloise.

"Your God is listening, Sandra? Speak, my child."

"Eloise."

"What?

"El..oise."

Eloise? Who's that?"

Eloise coughed and almost let go of the priest's sleeve, but her will was strong and she hung on.

"That's her, Father," said Nurse Mott.

"Her father? Her father is named Eloise?"

"No, Father. *Her* name is Eloise. Eloise Landers."

"It is?"

"Yes," said Nurse Mott, now straightening the sheets at the end of Eloise's bed.

"But, I'm here to see Sandra Hackett."

"Room two-thirteen," said Nurse Mott.

"Two-thirteen?"

"Two-thirteen."

"Oh my. Well, this is awkward, isn't it? I'm sorry, dear," he said to Eloise. "I'm afraid I've bungled into the wrong room."

The priest straightened up from Eloise's bedside and turned to leave, but Eloise had a death grip on his sleeve now and as he moved, he dragged the poor woman with him and she slid halfway out of the bed.

"Oh, goodness gracious!" said the priest, and he grabbed Eloise by the shoulders and set her back in her original position. Being in the wrong room, he of course wanted to leave everything exactly the way he had found it.

"Father . . . . I have been . . . . keeping . . . a secret," said Eloise desperately. "A dark . . . secret . . . . for many years . . . and I'm afraid that if I don't confess it now . . . . I will not be allowed into the Kingdom of . . ."

Eloise was out of breath. She could scarcely get the words out now.

"The Kingdom of . . . ." Eloise coughed. The pneumonia had filled her lungs with phlegm and she was coughing it up now every few minutes.

"The Kingdom of what, my child?" asked the priest.

"I think it's the Kingdom of Heaven, Father," offered Nurse Mott.

"Oh, yes. The Kingdom of Heaven! Of course," said the priest. "All right then, what is this secret? I will hear it now."

"Should I leave, Father?" asked Nurse Mott.

"Why?"

"Well, if you're hearing her confession, isn't that supposed to be private?"

"Well, I don't think she's giving a confession. She just has a secret to tell us. Isn't that right, dear?" He raised his voice when he spoke to Eloise.

Eloise nodded her head slowly once.

"There you see?" the priest said. "Now, what's the secret, dear?"

"I saw . . . . Reverend Figures..and . . . and . . . Mrs. Lynch . . . ."

"You saw what?" The priest turned to Nurse Mott. "What did she say?"

"Reverend Figures and Mrs. Lynch. Reverend Figures was a minister here a few years ago and Mrs. Lynch must be Debbie Lynch. She works over at the Allemane Inn."

"The Allemane. Oh, they have a wonderful steak and kidney pie over there," said the priest. "I had it last night."

Eloise grunted and gave a tug on the priest's sleeve in an attempt to regain his undivided attention.

"Yes, my child, yes. Go on."

"They were . . . . They were . . . ."

"Yes? They were what?"

"Having . . . relay . . . . shuns."

"Relay . . . shuns? Oh! Relations?"

Eloise nodded her head.

"Good, good. Relations. Good. What kind of relations?

"Se . . . . Se . . . .

"Se?

"Sexual," said Nurse Mott.

"What? Sexual relations? Oh my." The priest looked at the nurse incredulously, then back to Eloise. "Is that what they were having, Sandra?"

"Eloise", Nurse Mott corrected him calmly.

"Eloise. Right. Is that what they were having, Eloise? Sexual relations?"

Eloise nodded again, and with that burden off of her chest, her hand finally let go of the priest's sleeve.

"Well, how about that?" said Nurse Mott.

"Oh, dear," said the priest. "Maybe you should leave after all, Nurse."

"Too late now, Padre," said Nurse Mott. "In for a penny, in for a pound." And with that, she pulled a visitor's chair up close to the other side of the bed, sat down and leaned in to Eloise. "Where, Eloise? Where was Reverend Figures doing it to her?"

Eloise closed her eyes tightly as if trying to block out the sinful image in her mind.

"Come on, sweetheart," Nurse Mott urged. "The father has to know all the details."

"No, I don't," said the priest.

"Shhh!" said Nurse Mott. "Now, come on, Eloise. Where was he doing it to her?"

Eloise turned her head away from the nurse. Her eyes closed tighter still.

"In the . . .", she began.

"Yes," urged Nurse Mott. "In the what?"

"In the . . . in the rect . . . ."

Nurse Mott sat upright and the priest took a step back from the bed, covering his mouth to stifle a gasp.

"Rectory," said Eloise.

Nurse Mott and the priest let out one simultaneous breath in relief.

"All right," said the priest. "That's enough, dear. You rest now." He patted Eloise on the forearm. "The Kingdom of Heaven will welcome you now. Bless you, my child."

"Wow, that was somethin' huh?" said Nurse Mott. "I'll bet you didn't expect to hear that when you popped by tonight, Father."

Turning to look at the priest, the nurse saw only the hem of his robe disappearing out the door of the room as he sprinted down the hall to give the last rites to Sandra Hackett in room two-thirteen.

The pneumonia didn't take Eloise Landers that night. Nor the next night. In fact, Eloise made a full recovery and now, at eighty-four years of age, was residing at Birchmount Manor, the senior's home on Koonary Road. And to this day, she had never again uttered a word about what she saw that Sunday in the rectory of St. Paul's Church. Nurse Mott, however, did. To any and all who would listen.

Wood looked at the church as he drove by. He had been there in the spring to see a production of Fiddler On The Roof. When he approached the next block – the corner of Lilac and Winston Road–something caught his attention out of the corner of his eye. Movement. A person running. Now, had this been a normal evening when there were folks out walking, or children playing, he might not have noticed the figure off to his right. But, on this night, with pretty much the entire population of Rainbow indoors watching Mickey Welton, he more than noticed it. The running figure broke into the still evening so abruptly, it almost startled him. He slowed down and looked up Winston Road. The figure, a woman, was running across the lawn of the second house on the right. She tripped and fell, but then pulled herself up quickly and continued out onto the road. Wood knew instantly that something was wrong and that this wasn't just another Rainbow citizen rushing home to catch Mickey Welton on Jeopardy. He knew, because when the woman fell, she got to her feet and continued running without stopping to clean herself off. She was either being chased by someone, or had to get to somewhere in a life or death hurry. She bolted straight across the road and up onto the sidewalk on the other side. Wood was just past the intersection now and he stopped his cruiser. He saw that the woman was Opal Peacock's girl, Gabrielle Lasalle. Opal and Fraser Peacock were the owners of the Rainbow Golf and Country Club and Gabrielle had married Tom Lasalle, the golf pro at the club, three years ago. Now, as Wood watched from his cruiser at the end of the street, Gabrielle ran toward her house at eighteen Winston Road and Wood was close enough to see a look of distress on her face. He opened the cruiser door and stepped out, setting one foot on the pavement, and the other up on the cruiser's rocker panel. He looked over the top of his vehicle to where Gabrielle was.

"Gabby?!" he called.

Gabrielle Lasalle stopped just as she was about the climb the front steps to her home. She turned towards the sound of Wood's voice.

"Gabby, are you all right?"

"Wood!" Gabrielle started running toward Wood and his cruiser. Her tan-colored slacks had grass and mud stains on both knees from her fall on the wet lawn – one of the knees had a hole torn in it – and the front of her cardigan sweater was muddied as well.

Wood closed the cruiser door and moved around to meet Gabrielle on the sidewalk. When she reached him, Gabrielle grabbed onto Wood's arms to steady herself. She was shaking.

"Gabby, what's wrong?"

"Bonnie," said Gabrielle, her shoulders heaving as she gasped for breath. "Bonnie Hoyt. I think she's dead."

"What?!"

Wood looked across the street to Bonnie Hoyt's house. It was the house that he had seen Gabrielle running from. She had fallen on Bonnie's front lawn.

"She's dead, Wood. I know she is."

"What do you mean? Where is she? Is she in her house?"

"Yes," Gabrielle nodded.

"You saw her?"

"Through the window."

"You saw her through the window?"

"Uh-huh. She's on the floor in there. There's blood."

"All right, stay here," said Wood calmly. "I'll have a look."

Wood started toward Bonnie's house. Behind him, Gabrielle moved, almost involuntarily in the same direction, only at half the speed of the police officer. When Wood reached Bonnie's lawn, and was about twenty feet from the front door of the house, he turned back to Gabrielle.

"Okay, where, Gabby? Where did you see her?"

"Right through there," Gabrielle said, and she pointed with a shaking hand to a big picture window to the left of the front door.

"All right. Now you stay there. Don't come any closer," Wood said.

Bonnie Hoyt's house had a veranda that ran the length of the structure, and Wood moved across the lawn, stepped up onto the veranda and moved to the front door. He knocked.

"Bonnie?!" Wood called out. He didn't know exactly why he was calling to Bonnie but he knew it was the proper thing to do before you went looking in somebody's window. "Bonnie, it's Wood Lynch. You in there?"

There was no answer. Wood looked back at Gabrielle who had now moved up to the edge of the lawn. She was biting her lower lip now and it made both lips seem as if they had been sucked into her face. Wood moved left to the big window that looked out onto Winston Road. The curtains covering the window were closed, but not all the way, and there remained a small space between them about two inches wide. Wood cupped his hands on the glass and peered in. There were no lights on inside, but even in the slim natural light provided by dusk, Wood could still see what Gabrielle saw – what made her run from the veranda and across Bonnie Hoyt's lawn in terror. A body. On the floor of the living room. It was Bonnie Hoyt, on her back, a bathrobe closed, but not tied around her. Under her head, Wood could see a red patch on the carpet. Blood. He backed away from the window slowly, until his butt bumped against the white wooden railing which bordered the veranda.

"Did you see her, Wood?" Gabrielle asked.

For a split second, Wood couldn't answer.

"Wood?"

"Yeah. Yeah, I saw her."

"Oh, God." Gabrielle hung her head. "Oh, God."

Wood suddenly snapped out of his momentary shock, moved quickly to the front door and tried the knob. The door opened and Officer Lynch entered the house.

"Bonnie?!" he called quietly as he moved into the living room. He was momentarily frozen as he looked down at Bonnie Hoyt. Then he took a couple of steps forward and knelt down beside the woman on the floor and felt her neck for a pulse. He found nothing. "Shit. Bonnie?!"

He put his ear to her nose hoping to feel a breath, but again there was nothing. He felt her neck again. It was cool. He stood up and looked down at the body of the high school English teacher.

"Is she dead?"

Wood jumped back with a start. Gabrielle stood in the archway between the hall and the living room.

"Jesus, Gabby, you scared the hell out of me."

"I'm sorry."

"I told you to stay where you were."

"Well, I got scared out there by myself. So . . . is she?"

Wood looked down at Bonnie. "She's dead."

"Oh, Wood," said Gabrielle sadly. Having Wood Lynch confirm her fear put a finality to it for Gabrielle, and she began to weep.

"Come on, Gabby," Wood said, moving to her. "You shouldn't be in here. This is a crime scene now."

"Crime scene? You think somebody killed her?"

"I think so."

"But, maybe she fell. Maybe she hit her head. Maybe that's where the blood came from."

"Hit her head on what? The carpet? She's lying in the middle of the floor."

Gabrielle looked down at Bonnie. "Oh, God."

Wood put his arm around Gabrielle again, and escorted her from the house. "Let's get you over to your place."

As they moved across the street again, Gabrielle told Wood about how she had happened to see Bonnie's body.

"I was bringing a magazine over for her. I saw her car there and figured she was home, so I took the magazine over but she didn't answer her door. Then I just decided to leave the magazine on the table on the veranda where she would find it. That was when I walked by the window and happened to look in and . . . Jesus Christ, Wood, who would do that?"

"I don't know, Gabby."

They arrived at Gabrielle's front door. The police officer looked back toward Bonnie Hoyt's house, and then to Gabrielle. In twelve years on the force, this was his first murder.

"I'm going to have to leave you now, Gabby. I've got to call this in to Pete. Will you be all right for a few minutes? Is Tom home?"

"No, he hasn't come home yet. He had a late lesson."

"Well, maybe you can go next door to Mrs. Kenny's for a while."

"No, I'll be all right, Wood. You go ahead."

"You sure?"

"I'm fine. You go do what you have to do."

"Okay then. I'll come back soon and check on you."

"That's Okay, Wood. Tom should be home anytime now."

"Yeah. Well, I'll come back anyway."

"Thanks," said Gabrielle.

Wood turned and jogged back to the corner to his awaiting police cruiser. Gabrielle pulled her mud-stained sweater around her to keep out what she thought was the evening chill, but what in fact, was a side effect of the mild shock she had just experienced. She looked across the street to Bonnie Hoyt's house, then down at the watch on her wrist, and then up the street towards Lilac Road. Far beyond Lilac, across town on the outskirts of Rainbow, was the Rainbow Golf and Country Club, and, Gabrielle hoped, her husband Tom.

-10-

"And now, contestants, it's time to play Double Jeopardy. And here are your Double Jeopardy categories. Astrology, Places in Canada, The Beatles, For The Birds, The Outlaws, and American Presidents. David, you'll select first this round."

"I'll take American Presidents for two hundred, Alex."

"Nother' coffee, Pete?"

"No thanks, Henry. I want to get some sleep tonight."

"Who was Ulysses S. Grant?"

"Correct."

"So, what do you make of her?" Henry cocked his head towards Grace who was watching her spoon make slow circles in her coffee cup.

"What about her?"

"Well, a woman all by herself, wandering into town in the middle of the night with one suitcase."

"It's ten to eight, Henry. I'd hardly call that the middle of the night."

"All right then, what about that bruise on her cheek?"

"What bruise?" Pete started to turn towards the woman but stopped himself for fear of being too obvious.

"She's got a bruise on her cheek. I noticed it when I gave her the pie. She's tried to cover it with make-up but the trained eye can still see it."

"You've got a trained eye?"

"Sure, I do."

"And how'd you get that?"

"Watching out for counterfeit bills is how. I check every bill bigger than a ten."

"Oh. And have you ever found any?"

"Not one in twenty-two years. Nobody passes bad money in a town this size. You only find that in the big city."

Pete thought about asking Henry why he was watching for the counterfeit money if it's never passed here, but he decided that he didn't want to go around that horse track again.

"Who was Woodrow Wilson?"

"Correct."

"Shit, this computer guy is cleaning up on the presidents," Henry said, turning his attention to the t.v. again. "Come on, Mickey. Buzz in!"

Pete pushed his coffee cup off to his left, enabling him to cast a nonchalant look in Grace's direction. She was still stirring the coffee, her pie sat untouched. Pete couldn't see a bruise but then, he thought, maybe his policeman's eye wasn't as well-trained as a restaurateur's. Pete had done his police training at Holland College, the same as Wood, but Pete's training was done with the financial assistance of the town of Rainbow. Chief Walt Steeves liked this vagabond Torontonian for some reason, and he thought that Pete would make a good police officer, so he got the town to foot the bill for Pete's training, and when it was finished, he gave Pete a job on the force.

"Who was Richard Nixon?"

"That's correct."

"There you go! He's back in it, Pete."

"The Beatles for two hundred."

"And the answer is, the youngest of the Fab Four."

"Who is George?" said Pete calmly.

"Mickey?"

"Who is George?"

"George Harrison. Correct."

"Beatles for four hundred."

"Paul McCartney's brother had a brief solo career using this pseudonym."

"Mike McGear," said Pete.

"What is Mike McGear?"

"Is correct."

"Six hundred."

"She picks up the rice in the church where her wedding has been . . . Mickey?"

"Eleanor Rigby," said Pete.

"Who is Eleanor Rigby."

"Correct. Select again."

"Beatles, eight hundred."

"The album entitled, 'The Beatles", is more commonly known as this."

"What is The White Album," said Pete.

"Mickey?"

"What is The White Album?"

"Correct."

"The Beatles for one thousand."

"Finishing off the category, in the song Ob-La-Di Ob-La-Da, this was Molly's occupation."

"A singer in a band," said Pete.

Pete and Henry stared up at the Magnavox. There was silence. None of the contestants were buzzing in.

"Come on," Pete urged quietly. "A singer in a band."

Henry was less reserved. He yelled up at the television. "A singer in a band, damn it!!"

"Mickey?"

"What is, 'A singer?"

"Correct!"

"Yeah, baby!!" Henry shouted, and almost by reflex he held up his hand to Pete expecting a high-five.

Pete looked at the hand and then at Henry, and then feeling that perhaps he was taking some of the enjoyment out of the evening for Henry, Pete held his hand up reluctantly. "All right, go ahead," said the officer.

"Yes!" said Henry, and he gave Pete's hand a firm smack. Unfortunately, on the recoil, Henry's elbow hit a sugar dispenser on the counter and knocked it to the floor where it shattered, leaving a small pile of sugar and glass at Henry's feet..

"Aw shit," the Dutchman said, and he then proceeded to clean up his mess.

Pete shook his head and smiled, and then cast another glance in the direction of the woman at the back of the restaurant. His policeman's eyes still could not detect any bruising around that cheek, but this time they did detect something else. Tears.

✱

"What is, 'A singer'?"

"Correct!"

Grace could feel the tears welling up. The orchestra had been playing Ob-La-Di Ob-La-Da when Grace saw the earrings at the Governor's Ball, and now suddenly, everything that had happened to her in the last twenty-four hours had caught up with her right there in a greasy spoon in some Godforsaken place called Rainbow, New Brunswick. She should have known it would hit her sooner or later. You don't up and leave a life you've lived for ten years and not break down at some point.

"*Places in Canada for two hundred.*"

"*And the answer is, 'Renamed in the eighteen thirties, this city and it's river were both originally called Little Thames.'* . . . *Mickey?*"

"*What is Stratford?*"

"*Home of the Shakespearian Festival. Correct.*"

Grace pulled her pie plate closer to her. Maybe if she had a mouthful of raspberry pie it would stop her from crying. She sliced a small section off with her fork and put it into her mouth. Then she heard herself sob. A sob! She was mortified. She was sobbing in a public place in front of two strange men whose lives seemed to revolve around the game show Jeopardy. When she heard herself sob a second time, it made her moan in despair. Now she was sobbing and moaning and chewing her pie. She wiped a tear from her cheek with the back of her fork hand and inadvertently replaced the tear with a small dab of raspberry.

"I take it you don't care too much for the pie."

Grace looked up to see the police officer standing there.

"Hmm? Oh, no. No, the pie's *(sniff)* fine *(sniff)*," she said.

"Well, I like it myself, but I must admit, it's the first time I've ever seen it reduce a person to tears."

"No..no, it's not the pie..it's.. *(sniff)* ..something else."

"Uh-huh." The policeman pointed to Grace's face. "You've got a..uh.."

"A what?"

"On your cheek there," he continued. "You've got some..uh.."

"Oh, I fell," Grace said.

"What?"

"I was running and I fell. That's how I got the bruise."

"No, I didn't mean the bruise. You've got some raspberry there."

"Oh!" Grace picked her napkin off the table and wiped away the raspberry. "Did I get it?"

"Yeah."

"Thank you."

"*This city hosted the nineteen seventy-six Olympic games* . . . . *Gail?*"

"*What is Montreal?*"

"Correct."

"I'm Pete Golliger." The policeman held out his hand to Grace.

"Grace," she said, shaking his hand. She cursed in her head for once again giving her real name.

"Can I sit for a minute?"

"Uh . . . well . . .

"Just for a minute."

" . . . Sure. Go ahead." Grace pointed to the seat opposite her.

"Thank you."

"What is Vancouver?"

"Correct. Gail select again."

"You folks are big Jeopardy fans I see," said Grace, finally getting her sobbing under control.

"Hmm? Oh, no, not really. But the fella in the middle there, that's Mickey Welton. He lives here."

"Oh," Grace said, looking up at the television. "How's he doing?"

"Not bad."

Grace took another bite of her pie and then pushed the plate aside. She had eaten only half of it but she didn't want to continue while the police officer sat there watching her. As she wiped her mouth with her napkin, the officer spoke.

"And how are you doing?"

Grace looked at the policeman sitting across from her. He was a good-looking man with warm eyes set deeply into his rugged face. "Me? Oh, I've been better."

"Is there anything I can do?" the officer asked.

"No. Thank you."

"Are you sure? I mean, it's a slow night and I really don't feel like I'm earning my pay, so if I could be of some service to you it would make me feel a little better."

"Really?" Grace asked with just a hint of a smile.

"Definitely."

"Well . . . I need a place to stay. Could you point me towards a hotel?"

"Oh, I can do better than that. I'll drive you over to The Allemane and introduce you to Kate Leger. Kate owns the place. She'll look after you just fine."

"Well, thank you, but you don't have to drive me. Just tell me where it is and . . ."

"No, I'll drive you. It's no problem.

"You're sure?"

"Positive. Yeah, I stayed at The Allemane myself for about a month when I first moved here."

"Oh, so you're not from here then?"

"No, I'm from Ontario. Toronto."

"Oh."

"And the Final Jeopardy category is, Ancient History. We'll be back to test your knowledge in that area after this."

"And where are you from?"

Grace hesitated before answering. How trustworthy were those warm eyes of his? When she introduced herself to him she was careful only to give her first name, but now he wanted to know where she was from. Would this get back to Bryden somehow through channels? Through a police station network? You never know. Bryden sends word to a police station in Houlton asking them to keep an eye out for her. The Houlton force passes the word north into Canada, to Rainbow maybe, maybe to this very officer. Who knows? "Chicago."

"Chicago? Well, you're a long way from home. Did you travel all the way from Chicago in that truck?"

"No. No, I came by bus most of the way."

"Oh. And where did the truck driver pick you up?"

"Boston."

"Boston?"

"Yes."

"Well, you have been doing some traveling, haven't you? So, you took the bus from Chicago to Boston?"

"Yes. You know, if you don't mind, I think I'd like to get to that hotel now."

"Sure. It's not a hotel though. It's just an inn. They have about eight rooms over there. It's nice though. Very nice."

"Good," said Grace, sliding out of the booth with her suitcase. "Can we go now?"

"Sure thing," said the officer, and as he stood, he reached out for Grace's suitcase. "Here let me take that for you."

"Oh, thank you," said Grace.

Grace turned and headed for the counter where the cash register sat. As she moved, she reached into her purse and took out some money.

"Oh, don't worry about that," said the policeman. "This one's on the Rainbow Police Force."

"No, you don't have to do that. I can pay."

"I'm sure you can, ma'am. I wasn't implying that you couldn't. I was just trying to show you what a friendly town we have here, that's all. I mean, maybe it'll get back to your friends in Chicago and it'll boost our tourist trade."

"Oh," said Grace with yet another small smile. "Well, all right. Thank you."

"Henry, put the lady's coffee and pie on my tab, will ya?"

"You're not goin', are ya'?" asked the proprietor.

"Well . . ."

"It's Final Jeopardy. Mickey's only eight hundred bucks behind the real estate chick. You can't leave now."

Pete looked at Grace. "Do you mind?" he asked.

"No, not at all. I'm kind of curious now myself."

"Thanks.

Pete set the suitcase on the floor in front of the counter and sat down at one of the stools. Grace sat down on the stool beside him and the three inhabitants of 'The Dutchman' stared up at the Magnavox.

"And the Final Jeopardy clue is . . . 'This Babylonian King took over Judah's kingdom in six-oh-two B.C..'"

"Oh-oh," said Henry. "That's a tough son-of-a-bitch." He looked at Grace, apologetically. "Pardon my French, ma'am."

"No, you're right," replied Grace. "It is a tough son-of-a-bitch."

Pete and Henry looked at Grace and then at each other. Grace continued to watch the television. The camera panned down the line of contestants. David, the returning champion wasn't writing. He was thinking.

"He's stumped!" said Henry, his hopes rising. "Sayonara, buddy."

"That's Japanese," Pete said.

"Close enough."

The camera panned to Mickey. Mickey had finished writing his answer and was setting down his pen.

"Mickey's got it!" cried Henry. "Look at him. He's got the damned answer!"

"Well, let's hope it's the right one," said Pete cautiously.

The camera panned to Gail, the 'real estate chick'. Gail was writing her answer out.

"Oh-oh. This one worries me," said Henry. "She's worried me from the very beginning."

"I thought the computer nerd worried you from the beginning," Pete said with a wry smile.

"They both worried me. Now shhhhh!"

"All right, contestants, your time is up. And we'll begin with David, our champion, who has five thousand six hundred dollars. David, what is your response?"

The electronic podium in front of David lit up his answer.

"Who is Hammurabi?" I'm sorry, that's not the Babylonian king we were looking for. And what was your wager?"

Again the electronic podium did it's job and David's wager was displayed.

"Five thousand five-hundred and ninety-nine dollars. That leaves you with one dollar."

"Hit the road, Dave!" said Henry enthusiastically.

"And now Mickey, with seven thousand, four hundred dollars, what did you put down? . . . . 'Who was Nebuchadnezzar?' He came to power after Hammurabi, and that is the correct response."

"Yes!" Henry did a three hundred and sixty-degree turn where he stood, barely managing to keep his balance by grabbing the counter top when the rotation was completed. "Yes! Yes!"

"Good for you, Mickey," said Pete. "Good for you."

"And congratulations, you even spelled it correctly."

"You hear that?" asked Henry. "He even spelled the name right. Damn he's good!"

"And how much did you wager? . . . . All of it. Which leaves you in first place right now with fourteen thousand, eight hundred dollars."

"Whoo!!" shouted Henry. "Fourteen thousand!

"Easy, Henry," cautioned Pete. "We've still got one more contestant to go."

"And now Gail, with ten thousand, five hundred dollars, did you have the correct response? 'Who was Nebuchadnezzar?' Yes. And how much did you wager?"

The electronic podium in the television studio in Los Angeles, California, illuminated Gail's wager and broke the heart of a small town thousands of miles away.

"Four thousand, three hundred and one, which brings your total to fourteen thousand, eight hundred and one dollars, and you are today's winner by one dollar. Congratulations."

"What?!" said Henry incredulously. "No!"

"Too bad," said Pete.

"No!" cried Henry again.

"He came close," said Pete. "It was a real nice try."

"One dollar? He lost by one stinkin' dollar?"

"That's a shame," added Grace. "But, he did well. You should be proud of him."

"Oh, we are that," said Pete. "We're very proud of Mickey. Aren't we, Henry?"

"One stinking dollar," said Henry. "Shit." He slumped onto a stool that he kept behind the counter. "And he doesn't even get to keep the cash. He has to settle for some lousy consolation prize."

"Runners-up on today's show will receive a handsome selection of earthenware from Huntley's of Beverly Hills. Huntley's, the home of good taste for your home."

"You see that," said Henry. "Earthenware."

"We've gotta go, Henry." Pete, slid off the stool and reached down to pick up Grace's suitcase. "You all set, ma'am?"

"Yes." Grace stood and followed the police officer to the front door of the restaurant.

"See ya later, Henry," said Pete, as he pulled the door open for Grace.

Henry didn't answer. He merely held up his hand without looking in their direction, and then muttered to himself. "One stinking dollar."

Outside, a brisk wind blew down the rain-soaked street. The air was pure September. It was fresh and had a crispness to it that was a harbinger of October.

"So, how long are you going to be in Rainbow?" asked Pete.

"Well, I'm not sure," replied Grace. "A day or two maybe. Depends."

"On what?"

"A lot of things."

"I'm sorry," said Pete. "I didn't mean to sound like I was prying."

"But, you are, aren't you?"

"Oh yeah. Absolutely. I just didn't mean for it to sound like I was."

"Well, you're a police officer. It's your job to pry, I suppose."

"Yes, it is," said Pete, opening the cruiser door for Grace. "I'm only doing my duty."

Grace slid onto the front seat. Pete opened the back door and gently placed Grace's suitcase on the back seat. That was when he heard his two way radio crackle.

"Pete? Are you out there? Pete, this is Wood. Answer me, will ya?"

Pete walked around to the driver's side of the cruiser and climbed in the front seat. Wood's voice had an urgency to it. Pete hoped he wasn't calling to say he would be late for his shift.

"Pete? Come in, Pete."

"Yeah, Wood, I'm here. What is it?"

"Pete, we've got a situation over on Winston Road. A real situation."

"What kind of situation?" With his free hand, Pete put his keys in the ignition and turned on the engine.

"We've got a . . . . ete."

When Pete turned the engine on, the radio cut out momentarily and Pete missed the middle of Wood's communication.

"Say that again, Wood. I didn't catch it."

"We've got a dead body, Pete. A dead body."

"Where are you?"

"I'm in my cruiser at the corner of Lilac and Winston."

"I'll be there in two minutes." Pete put the microphone back in the cradle, and then shifted the cruiser into drive.

"Pete," came Wood's voice again. " . . . . It's Bonnie Hoyt."

Pete didn't lift his foot off the brake. He stared down at the radio for a moment, then looked up at the deserted street in front of him. "Oh, God."

"Pete? Did you hear me?"

Pete lifted the microphone out of the cradle again. "I heard you. I'm on my way." And with that, Pete wheeled the cruiser out onto Main Street.

"We have to make a stop on the way to The Allemane," he said to Grace.

"I'm in no hurry," she replied.

-11-

"Earthenware? You won a bunch of goddamned earthenware?"

"I like earthenware," said Myrna. "That'll get put to good use around here, Mickey. Don't you worry."

"I'm proud of you, Mick," said Peggy as she gave her brother a hug. "You did real good."

"Thanks, Peg."

"I'll tell you where you went wrong," said Jack on his way to the kitchen. "You let that woman get all those 'Places in Canada' answers. And she's not even from Canada. You're from Canada. Christ." Jack reached into the refrigerator, pulled out a can of beer, and returned to the living room.

"He got the Stratford question," countered Peggy.

"Big freakin' deal. Stratford. Bunch of 'Nancy boys' in tights is all that place is. I'd rather he *didn't* get that one. I mean, 'Home to hockey's Canucks?' How the Christ could you miss that?"

"I knew the answer but she buzzed in ahead of me."

"Earthenware. Jesus." Jack sat down and took a pull on his beer.

"Well, I think he did just fine," said Myrna. "You did just fine, Mickey. Now, why don't you call Miss Hoyt and see if she watched the show?"

"Aw, I don't know . . . ."

Before Mickey could finish, the phone sitting on the end table next to the couch rang.

"Oh, I'll bet that's her now."

Peggy was the first one to the telephone. "Hello? . . . . Oh, hi, Mr. Petty."

It was Doug Petty, Mickey's employer from the La-Z-Boy store.

"Yeah, we watched. Of course we watched . . . . Yeah, one dollar. What a piss-off."

"Oh, Peggy," said Myrna. "Language on a public utility."

"But, he did good though, don't you think?" Peggy continued.

"He's probably calling to tear a strip off of you for not mentioning his store," said Jack.

"Oh, Jackie, shut up, ya' Goddamned potato head." Gran Welton wasn't really leaping to the defense of her grandson as much as she was taking another free shot at her son. "The boy's got more brains in his little finger than you've got in that entire fat ass of yours."

"Yeah, he's right here," said Peggy. "Hang on. Mickey. For you." She held out the receiver to her brother.

"Hello? . . . . Oh, hi Mr. Petty . . . . Thanks . . . . Well, it was exciting to be there, that's for sure . . . . Uh-huh . . . . Uh-huh . . . . No, I knew it was Vancouver but she buzzed in ahead of me . . . . Yeah . . . . Yeah, well, I've been thinking about acting, but . . . . Yeah . . . . Well, I was just trying to say something interesting. They like you to make it interesting during the interview part . . . . No, I wouldn't leave the store without giving you some notice, no . . . . No, you don't have to worry about that . . . . A month? Sure, I'll give you a month. But, I'm not planning on leaving anytime soon . . . . Yeah . . . . Okay . . . . Okay, thanks a lot. Bye." Mickey hung up the phone.

"Well, was I right?" asked Jack.

"No, Dad, you weren't," replied Mickey. "He didn't mention my not talking about his store at all."

"Well, then he's a goddamned idiot. The man had some free nationwide advertising go right down the toilet and he doesn't even know it."

"Maybe he doesn't care," said Mickey. "Maybe he was just glad for me because I did okay."

"And that's all you did was okay."

"That's all I wanted to do."

"That's all you ever do."

Mickey hesitated. Did he really want to get into it with his father now? Was it really worth it? One day he would tell his father exactly what he thought of him. One day. But, this was not the day. Fortunately, at that moment, the telephone rang again, and Mickey turned away to answer it.

"Hello? . . . . Oh, hi coach." It was coach Tudder Halliwell from the high school. Mickey had gone out for the football team in his final year and wound up playing first clarinet in the school band. "Well, thanks coach. Thanks a lot . . . . No, I don't get to keep the money . . . . No, only the first place finisher gets to keep their cash . . . . Uh-huh . . . . Earthenware . . . . Earthenware. It's like, you know, dishes. Plates and goblets and stuff. . . . Yeah . . . . Uh-huh . . . . No, I knew it was Vancouver, but she buzzed in first."

-12-

Bonnie Hoyt was born and raised in Rainbow and until the day she died, she lived in the house that she grew up in on Winston Road. Her mother had died of cancer four years ago and shortly after that, her father moved to Calgary to live with Bonnie's sister, Lynn. He wanted to watch his grandchildren grow, and Bonnie, being single and childless, could not offer him that luxury.

Bonnie had only been away from Rainbow for four of her thirty-four years. That was when she went off to teacher's college in Halifax to pursue her dream of becoming a high school teacher. Upon completion of her studies there, Bonnie returned to her home town and took a job at the same school she had graduated from four years earlier. There, she became a very popular English teacher and coach of the Rainbow High girl's volleyball team.

Socially, Bonnie dated often, but she never found a man that she was completely sold on settling down with. The longest relationship she had had was with Tom Lasalle, the golf pro at the Rainbow Golf and Country Club. They dated for close to two years, but Bonnie broke it off when she found out that Tom had begun sleeping with Gabrielle Peacock. Gabrielle and Tom would later marry and much to Bonnie's surprise, they bought the house right across the street from her house three years ago.

The day they moved in, Gabrielle marched right across the street to Bonnie's house for a woman to woman talk. Bonnie, who was watching the Lasalles move in from her front window, saw Gabrielle coming, and met her at the door before her new neighbour could even ring the bell.

"Hello, Gabby," said Bonnie.

"Hi, Bonnie."

"How are you?"

"Fine."

"Long time no see."

"Yes. Look, I wasn't crazy about the idea of living across the street from my husband's ex-girlfriend. In fact, I'm still not crazy about the idea, but Tom convinced me that this house was too good a deal to pass up, and he's right. I mean, it's just what we're looking for and well within our price range, and it's got three bedrooms to accommodate the family that we're planning on starting soon. Well, not right away but two or three years down the road because after all I am twenty-seven now and I don't want to wait too long. Well, you know what I'm talking about. Anyway, I hope that we can get along as neighbours because I don't have any bad feelings towards you and maybe you do towards me, I don't know, but if you do, I hope we can bury the hatchet and get along, all right? That's all I wanted to say."

"Gabby," said Bonnie, "Tom and I broke up years ago and I'm pretty much over it now, so don't worry about any hard feelings on my part."

"Well, I know it was a long time ago, but I was the reason you broke up, remember?"

"I remember."

"And you know what they say about a woman scorned."

"I'm familiar with the saying."

"And you've stayed single so I thought maybe you've been carrying a torch for Tom all this time."

"No. There's no torch."

"There isn't?"

"No."

"Well, good. Well, that's all I wanted to know. I'm glad we cleared the air."

"Oh, yes. Clear air is good."

"Good. Well, maybe we can be friends then. Maybe we can have coffee together once in a while. I mean, I'm right across the street."

"Well, let's just see how the neighbour thing goes first, okay? We'll work up to friends."

"Oh. Okay. That's fair dinkum."

"What?"

"That's fair dinkum. It's an Australian expression. It means . . . . well, fair."

"Oh. Well, fair dinkum it is then."

Bonnie and Gabby did not become friends. There was no coffee together. They just kept to themselves, Gabby on the south side of Winston Road, and Bonnie on the north.

One of the other men Bonnie had dated over the years was police officer Pete Golliger. That relationship was very short-lived. Six or seven dates about five years ago was all it amounted to. Pete liked Bonnie but she was running him ragged with her health-conscious lifestyle. She was after him to go jogging with her, and bike riding, and hiking, and as much as Pete admired Bonnie's conditioning regimen, he had no intention of adopting it. For her part, Bonnie liked Pete a lot but she wanted a man who she could share her activities with. She didn't feel that she could completely respect someone who didn't share her passion for a healthy lifestyle. Pete and Bonnie parted as good friends though and had remained so until this evening, when Pete pulled his cruiser up in front of Bonnie's house at twenty-one Winston Road.

*

"She's on the floor in the living room." Wood Lynch was waiting for Pete out on the sidewalk in front of Bonnie Hoyt's house. He pointed across the street to a figure standing alone on a set of concrete steps. "Gabby Lasalle found her."

Pete turned and looked in the direction that Wood was pointing. There he saw Gabrielle Lasalle standing on her front steps, still holding her sweater closed tightly around her.

"She said she was bringing a magazine over and she happened to look in the window and saw Bonnie lying there." As he spoke, Wood glanced into the front seat of Pete's cruiser and saw a woman there looking towards Bonnie's house. "Who's that?"

"Hmm?" Pete looked at Wood, and then back to his cruiser. "Oh, that's a woman who's looking for a place to stay. I was taking her over to The Allemane. So, what happened? How did she die?"

"Well, it looks like she was hit on the back of the head."

"Oh, Jesus. You mean it's a murder?"

"That's what it looks like."

"Shit."

"So, what do we do?" asked Wood. "I've never worked a murder before."

"Neither have I."

"So, what do we do?"

"Well, the first thing we do, I guess, is secure the area. Keep everybody away from the scene."

Pete and Wood looked around the street. The north side of the street was empty. They looked across to the south side. Gabby Lasalle was still on her front steps. Off to their left in a driveway two doors down from Gabby's next to Mrs. Kenny's house, they saw a man with a dog. It was Louis Little, a widower who lived at twenty-two Winston Road. Louis was the artistic director of the Rainbow Theatre Guild, a group based out of St. Paul's church, and he had directed their production of Fiddler On The Roof earlier that year. On this night, he was walking his Scotch terrier, Zero, whom he had named after the late Broadway great, Zero Mostel. Every evening at about this time, Louis would take Zero for a walk up to The Allemane Inn where 'Kate's Place', a local pub, was located. Louis would tie Zero to a fence outside the pub and then proceed inside for a pint or two of his favourite dark ale. Louis wore an overcoat and a royal blue Kangol hat and carried a very dapper walking stick in his right hand as he and Zero moved down the driveway and onto the sidewalk.

"Louis?" Wood called across the street.

"Oh, good evening, Wood," replied Louis, noticing the two officers. "Good evening, Officer Golliger."

"You stay back now, you hear, Louis?" warned Wood.

Louis had no idea what was going on. He gave Wood a quick, oblivious acknowledgment with his walking stick, and kept right on walking at the same pace.

Wood looked at Pete. "Well, that's done. Now what?"

"Well, I guess we'd better have a look inside."

Pete and Wood moved up the shrub-lined walk to Bonnie's veranda. Officer Golliger observed that there were two patio chairs at the end of the veranda and also a small wicker footstool. When he arrived at the closed front door, Pete, by reflex, held up his hand to knock. He caught himself before he completed the act. "I guess I don't need to knock, do I?"

Pete turned around to see Wood staring at the patio table on the veranda. Wood then turned around and looked across Bonnie's front lawn. Then out onto the street.

"Wood? What's the matter?"

"Nothing," replied Wood bringing his gaze back to the lawn, then to Bonnie's walk. "I'm just wondering where the magazine is."

"What?"

"The magazine. Gabby said she was bringing a magazine to Bonnie. She said she was going to set it down on the table there and she happened to glance in and saw Bonnie through the window. But, it's not on the table. It's not on the lawn. Gabby didn't have it when I saw her on the sidewalk there. I'm just wonderin' where it is."

"Maybe she set it on the table and it blew off. Maybe it's in the yard next door."

"Maybe."

"We'll find it later."

Pete turned the door knob and pushed the door open.

"Was the door unlocked before?" asked Pete.

"Yeah."

Pete stepped inside and Wood came in behind him and pointed to the living room on the left.

"She's in there."

"Yeah," replied Pete.

Pete knew the layout of the place having been here a couple of times when he and Bonnie had dated. He moved into the living room and upon seeing the body, stopped in his tracks so abruptly that Wood almost walked up his heels.

"Christ," Pete muttered.

"It's something, isn't it?" said Wood. "It's just bloody awful."

Pete moved closer and knelt down beside Bonnie's body. He put the back of his hand against Bonnie's cheek, the way a mother would when checking her child for a fever. "And you say she was hit on the head?"

"Well, that's what it looks like, doesn't it?"

"Well, did you take a look at her head?"

"Well . . . not really."

"You mean you didn't look at the wound?"

"Well, why would I do that?"

"Well, maybe she was shot."

"Shot?"

"Maybe."

"Well, wouldn't there be an exit wound in the front of her head if she was shot?"

"Not if the bullet lodged in her brain," replied Pete.

"Oh Jesus, Pete, do we have to talk about this?"

"Wood, we're the police. This is what the police talk about."

"Well, you look. I don't want to look."

Pete lifted Bonnie's head gently towards his chest with his right hand. As he pulled her head up, two of his fingers inadvertently slipped into a two inch long slice in the back of Bonnie's head.

"Oh, shit!" he said.

"What's the matter," asked Wood.

"Oh, shit!" Pete straightened his fingers across Bonnie's blood-matted hair so that his hand now cradled her head below the gash.

Wood could now see the gash as well. "Oh, man."

"She was hit all right," Pete said, laying her down again.

"Damn. Jesus. How long do you figure she's been here?"

"I don't know. Two or three hours maybe. Her hair is damp."

"From the blood?" asked Wood.

"No, it's damp all over. Like she's been in the shower. So, if her hair hasn't had time to dry yet, I figure two or three hours tops." Pete stood up and looked down at Bonnie. "Is this the way you found her?"

"Yeah."

"With her robe closed like that?"

"Yeah," replied Wood. "Just like that."

Pete bent down again and opened Bonnie's thick white bathrobe. She was naked beneath it.

"Well, that's weird."

"What is?" asked Wood.

"Her robe, closed like that and not tied."

"What's wrong with that?"

Pete stood again. "Well, what are the chances a woman gets hit over the head with some object and then falls to the floor, and her bathrobe winds up closed nice and neat like that?"

"You think whoever killed her was concerned for her modesty?"

"I don't know."

"All right, here's something else. If she was hit on the back of the head, wouldn't she fall on her stomach instead of her back. The blow would knock her forward, wouldn't it?"

"Yeah, you'd think so."

"So, how do you explain her lying on her back like that?"

Peter looked around the living room. It was small. About twelve feet by sixteen feet. There was a sofa, an easy chair, a footstool with gold-coloured wheels, and covering one entire wall, a large bookshelf filled with hundreds of books of almost every description. Novels, plays, history books, books on gardening, golf, volleyball, travel, animals. Almost every topic imaginable. Pete's gaze moved to the beige carpeting in the room.

"I don't see any blood anywhere else. This must've been where she fell."

"What if she was killed in the shower and then carried out here?" Wood asked.

"But, why?"

"I don't know."

"Hi, Pete," came a voice from behind Wood.

"Oh, Jesus!" Wood jumped and turned to see Gabby standing there. "Jesus, Gabby, will you cut that out?!"

"I'm sorry," said Gabby.

"I told you to stay out of here. This is a crime scene."

"Well, I got scared over there all by myself. I mean, what if whoever did this is still around somewhere?"

"I told you to go over to Mrs. Kenny's, didn't I?"

"Oh, yeah, like I'll feel safer with a seventy year-old grandmother by my side."

"Where's Tom?" asked Pete.

"He's not home yet. He had a late lesson."

Pete looked at Wood. Wood turned his back to Gabby and raised his eyebrows slightly so that only Pete could see it. Both men knew that Tom Lasalle had a penchant for the ladies and both figured the 'late lesson' line had been used on Gabby many times during her marriage.

"Have you got any clues yet?" Gabby continued.

"Uh..not yet," said Wood. "Listen, Gabby, what did you do with that magazine?"

"What magazine?"

"The one you were bringing over when you saw Bonnie."

"Oh, I..uh..I put it on the table out on the veranda."

"Well, it's not there now."

"Well, I don't know. It must've blown off I guess."

"Well, let's you and I go out and have a look for it."

"What for?" asked Gabby. "What do you need the magazine for?"

"Because it's a part of the puzzle, that's all. We need to put all these pieces together during an investigation."

"Well, I don't see why that's so important," said Gabby, closing her sweater as tightly as it would go around her torso. "It's only a stupid magazine. It's got nothing to do with Bonnie lying there dead."

"I know, but . . . ."

"What magazine was it?" Pete interjected.

"What?" asked Gabby.

"What magazine? Was it People, Maclean's, National Geographic?"

"It was Good Housekeeping."

"Good Housekeeping?" asked Pete.

"Yes, there was a recipe in it that I thought Bonnie might like to try."

"Oh. Did you and Bonnie exchange recipes often?" asked Pete.

"Once in a while. What's that got to do with anything? Jesus, Pete, Bonnie's lying there dead and you're asking me about a fucking magazine? Christ!"

"All right, Gabby, come on," said Wood, taking Gabrielle by the arm. "We're all a little shaken by this mess. Let's just go outside and find the magazine, okay?"

Wood led Bonnie out of the living room and onto the veranda. Pete moved to the big bookshelf and looked more closely at Bonnie's collection of reading material. Charles Dickens, Dave Barry, Ernest Hemingway, Carl Sagan, Elmore Leonard. The variety was endless. Pete then moved into the dining room which was just off the living room. The dining table was not set for dinner, but as he moved on into the kitchen, Pete noticed a styrofoam container and some leftover Chinese food on the counter. Bonnie had obviously gotten take-out after school, come home and eaten, and then went to the bathroom to shower. Pete made a rough estimate of the time it would have taken to do all of these things, and concluded that the death would have occurred sometime after five o'clock or five-thirty. Then in one corner of the kitchen counter, beside the toaster, Pete saw a bottle of champagne. "For what?" he wondered. "Some sort of celebration? A birthday? Anniversary?"

He moved to the counter and tore off two sheets of paper towel from a rack that was fastened beneath one of the cupboards. He then used the paper towel to open each cupboard door so he could look inside without leaving his fingerprints or smudging any which might be there already. Inside the cupboards he found the usual kitchen fare. Glasses, dishes, cereal, canned goods, one cupboard filled with seven or eight travel mugs, another filled with crystal wine glasses and two or three scented candles.

Having finished his examination of the kitchen cupboards, Pete moved out of that room and down the hall to the bathroom. Here he found two damp towels hanging over the shower's curtain rod, and a damp bath mat as well. This confirmed his suspicion about Bonnie having had a shower fairly recently. Pete then opened the medicine chest. Tylenol, cold medicine, eye drops, an assortment of prescription drugs which seemed to be for the treatment of migrane headaches, a box of band-aids, two disposable shavers for women, Q-Tips, and there on the bottom shelf . . . a box of condoms. Pete closed the medicine chest. He felt like an intruder, as if he shouldn't be looking into this woman's private possessions. He turned to leave the room, and as he did, his gaze fell on a wastebasket next to the sink. Inside were a few make-up stained tissues, another disposable shaver, and . . . . he reached into the container and flicked one of the tissues aside with his finger . . . . a condom wrapper.

"Pete?" came Wood's voice from another part of the house.

"Yeah?" Pete left the bathroom and moved out to the front hallway.

"We found it," said Wood, showing Pete a Good Housekeeping magazine that he held in his hand. The magazine was wet and wrinkled from having fallen onto the damp grass at the side of the house.

"Are you satisfied now?" asked Gabby in an irritated tone.

"Oh, Gabby, cut it out," said Wood. "We're only doing our jobs here."

"Is that Tom?" asked Pete, looking past Gabrielle and out the opened front door into the street.

Gabrielle turned and looked across towards her house. The lights of a car in the driveway were just being turned out.

"Oh, thank God," she said. "Can I go now?"

"Gabby, I told you I didn't want you here in the first place," said Wood. "Now, go on home."

"We'll have to talk to you again though, Gabby," Pete added.

"Fine. Whatever," answered Gabrielle, and she burst out the front door, across the lawn and straight to her husband Tom, who was now waiting on the other side of the street, looking at the two police cruisers parked in front of his ex-girlfriend's house.

"A late lesson, huh?" said Wood.

"Yeah. We'll have to find out who that late lesson was with," said Pete.

"What do you mean? You don't think Tom has anything to do with this?"

"Well, he and Bonnie went out together at one time."

"So did you and Bonnie."

"Bonnie and I went out for three months. Tom damn near married her." said Pete, and then he motioned Wood over towards the big bookshelf. "Come ere."

"What? You find something?"

"Just come ere' for a sec."

Wood followed Pete to the bookcase. The two men stood looking at the collection of reading material.

"Take a look at all these books," said Pete.

"Yeah, she was quite a reader, wasn't she?"

"No, that's not what I mean. Take a look at the types of books up there. What do you see?

"Well, let's have a look now." Wood took a step closer to the shelf and started from the top left and worked right. "The War of 1812. Famous Civil War Battles. The Complete Book of Modern Art. The Impressionists." Wood's eyes skipped over the books more rapidly. "The Love You Make, The Godfather, The Grapes Of Wrath, Neil Simon Rewrites, The Complete Bartender, Unabridged Super Trivia, Barnes and Noble Book of Quotations. I don't know, Pete. I see all kinds of books. What am I looking for?"

"How about a cookbook?" replied Pete.

"Cookbook? Hmmm." Wood scanned the shelves again. "No, I don't see any."

"That's right."

"But, usually, you know, you keep cookbooks in the kitchen. That's where Jeannie keeps them. In a cupboard in the kitchen."

"No," said Pete. "I checked. There are no cookbooks in the kitchen. None. And you know why?"

"Why?"

"Because Bonnie hated to cook. I remember that about her from when we were dating. She hated to cook. She didn't even like eating that much. To her, eating was an annoyance. A distraction. Something you had to do."

"Okay. So what?"

"So, Gabby says she and Bonnie exchanged recipes once in a while? Well, I don't think so."

"Aw, come on, Pete, you and Bonnie dated years ago. Who says she didn't change her mind about cooking in that time?"

"Well, she could've I suppose, but, there's a big container of Chinese take-out in the kitchen that tells me she hadn't. And here's something else. Look at those curtains." Pete pointed to the pale yellow curtains covering the living room window.

"What about em'?"

"They're closed. There's only a little slit there where a person could see in from outside."

"Yeah, I had to cup my hands over the window to get a good look myself."

"Exactly. And you said that Gabby just happened to look in and saw Bonnie lying there."

"That's what she said. But, she would have to get right up close and look in like I did, wouldn't she?"

"That's right. So, what was she doin' that for?"

"Maybe she was just checking to see if Bonnie was home. Maybe she figured Bonnie didn't hear her knock."

"Yeah. Maybe."

"So, what do we do now?"

"Well, I've got to get that woman over to the Allemane. You'd better call the RCMP boys and tell them we need a forensics team over here right away." Pete took a couple of steps in the direction of the front door.

"Right. Maybe they can pull some prints," said Wood.

Pete stopped at the front door and turned back to Wood. "Maybe they can what?"

"Pull some prints. Fingerprints."

"Yea, I know what prints you're talkin' about, but 'pull some prints?' Where'd you get that?"

"I saw it on t.v.. Some cop show."

"Oh," Pete said. "I have got to start watching more television," he thought.

Pete looked out towards his cruiser. Grace sat in the front seat, slowly twirling a lock of her hair around her right index finger and staring straight ahead. Pete spoke without turning to Wood.

"Wood, do you know if Bonnie was seeing anybody these days?"

"You mean did she have a boyfriend?"

"Yeah."

"Not that I know of. Why?"

"Well, there's a bottle of champagne on the kitchen counter in there and I found a condom wrapper in the bathroom."

"Well, if she did have a boyfriend, it shouldn't be too hard to find out who it was in a town this size."

"Yeah." Pete looked across the street to where Tom and Gabby Lasalle stood in their driveway. "Shouldn't be too hard at all."

-13-

The Allemane Inn was located at the corner of Yarbro and Nelson Streets, about a half a mile from Bonnie Hoyt's house. The inn was one of only two places to stay in Rainbow, the other one being The Howard Johnson's on Nylander Street on the opposite side of town just off the Trans-Canada Highway. Pete thought that Grace would be a little more at home at The Allemane because it didn't feel like a motel. It was more like a large bed and breakfast. They had eight comfortable rooms in the two storey building, a dining room located at the front of the inn on the first floor, and the small pub, 'Kate's Place', around the side. Tenants parking, what little there was of it, was around back and that was where Pete parked his cruiser when he and Grace arrived at about eight-forty-five.

"This looks nice," said Grace, as Pete pulled her suitcase out of the back seat.

"Oh, yeah, I think you'll like it here just fine."

"Hi, Pete!" came a voice from above.

Pete and Grace looked up, and there, sitting on a second floor balcony that overlooked the parking area sat Leo Terrio. Leo was an ex-heavyweight boxer whose most famous moment came back in nineteen sixty-six. Leo, nicknamed 'The Lion', was about to sign a contract to fight Canadian Heavyweight Champion George Chuvalo in March of that year. Leo and his wife Marie had flown to Montreal where the deal was going to be signed, but while he was there, and just twenty-four hours before he and Chuvalo were to put their signatures on the dotted line, Chuvalo got an offer to fight then World Heavyweight Champion Muhammad Ali instead. Chuvalo accepted the lucrative offer and went on to fame as one of the few boxers to extend Ali to the full fifteen rounds without being knocked down, while Leo 'The Lion' fought for another ten years without ever getting that title shot. He retired the same year that his wife Marie died, and he moved to Saint John where he attempted to live off of the earnings from his eighty-four professional bouts. Unfortunately for Leo, his manager was not being as frugal as Leo would have hoped, spending a lot of his pugilist's money on women and nightclubs. Six months later the boxer's funds dried up and Leo had to take a job on the docks loading cargo. He worked at that job until he tore something in his back during a friendly wrestling match with one of the other dock workers after his shift one day. Unable to claim any workman's compensation for the off duty injury, Leo decided to return to Rainbow, the town he had lived in until he went off to seek his boxing fortune at the age of twenty-one. A man of fifty when he arrived back in Rainbow, Leo had no skills to speak of and no education past grade eight, which in most instances, would translate into a problem procuring gainful employment. Fortunately, Leo had a lot of fans in Rainbow, one of them being high school football coach/music teacher Tudder Halliwell, who talked the Reverend Erskine Biggs into hiring Leo to be the caretaker of St. Paul's Church. Reverend Biggs had taken over for the Reverend Warren Figures after Reverend Figures left town following his scandalous tryst with Debbie Lynch.

So, Leo had the caretaking job, plus, three times a week – up until the current school year at least–Coach Halliwell brought Leo in to meet with the Rainbow High School boxing club where he would instruct the boys on the finer points of the 'gentleman's sport'. This year though, Leo had been informed that his services would no longer be required by the school boxing club. The school had received some complaints over the summer from concerned parents who said they didn't want their children being instructed by a man whose faculties appeared to be dwindling daily. Bonnie Hoyt was the one who gave Leo the bad news back in August. The task fell on Bonnie's shoulders because Tudder Halliwell was vacationing in Spain at the time the decision came down, and Bonnie being the volleyball coach, was considered the second in command in the athletic department.

And so now, Leo had no connection to the boxing world at all. He did have the caretaking job at the church though. The pay wasn't great, but it kept him active and off the dole, and as a result, kept the man's enormous pride intact. Leo's other 'job' in town was as the official greeter at Kate's Place in the Allemane. Kate Leger, the owner of the inn, offered the position to Leo with one stipulation. She could not afford to pay him a wage, so in return for sitting in her pub and interacting with her clientele night after night, Leo would have to accept room and board at The Allemane as payment. This offer came at a most opportune time for Leo, shortly after he returned to Rainbow and found that most of the lodging in town was beyond his budget. What luck that Kate would discover a need for a greeter around that very same time.

"Did you see Mickey?" Leo called from his balcony.

"Sure did," replied Pete.

"Missed it by one dollar, huh? One dollar. He got the earthenware though. Can't complain about that. No sir. Can't complain about that."

"How you doin' tonight, Leo?"

"Good. Good. Just finished watching Mickey on the t.v.. Did you see him?"

"Yeah," replied Pete. "And what are you doing outside? A little cool, isn't it?"

"No, I'm fine," the big man replied. "Some rain we had tonight, huh? Clear now though. Cleared right up. I'm watching the stars. I love to watch the stars. I mean, just look at them all. Do you know how many stars there are up there, Pete?"

"No idea," replied the police officer. "Must be millions."

"Seventy-eight."

"Seventy-eight?" asked Pete.

"Seventy-eight stars. That's a lot, isn't it? But, that's how many there are. I counted them once."

Leo's eighty-four fights had taken quite a toll on his brain cells. Some statistician once sat down and figured out that the average boxer gets hit two hundred and fifty times during a ten round bout, and if that was true–and Leo was fighting when many of the bouts were scheduled for twelve or even fifteen rounds – then Leo had received approximately twenty-one thousand blows during his career, and if only one half of those were blows to the head, then that meant that Leo had been hit over ten thousand times in the cranial area. Ten thousand punches to the head. At age sixty now, Leo was clearly exhibiting the aftereffects of his chosen profession.

"Who's your lady?" asked Leo, looking at Grace.

"This is Grace," replied Pete. "Grace, I'd like you to meet Leo Terrio. Rainbow's most famous citizen. Back in the sixties Leo was that close to becoming the Canadian Heavyweight Champion."

"Really?" said Grace, genuinely impressed.

"That close," echoed Leo from above. "Chuvalo chickened out though. Chickened right out."

"Well, it's nice to meet you, Leo," said Grace.

"You too, Grace." Leo's puffy face stared down at the woman. He scratched his cheek with one of his meaty hands and then he looked at Pete. "She's pretty."

"Thank you," said Grace.

"You remind me of my Marie. She was pretty too. Prettiest girl I've ever seen. I've got her picture inside. You wanna see?"

"We haven't got time right now, Leo," said Pete. "But, I'm sure Grace would love to see it some other time."

"Yes, I would," Grace agreed.

"Okay."

Pete and Grace took another couple of steps toward the southwest corner of the building.

"She your girlfriend, Pete?"

They stopped and looked up at Leo again. "No, Leo. Grace is just visiting for a while."

"Gonna be staying here?" asked Leo.

"That's right," replied Pete. "And I want you to take good care of her, you hear?"

"Oh, I will. I will. That's what I'm here for. Make the customers happy and see to their every need. That's me."

"Good. Well, we'll see you later, Leo."

Bye, Pete. Bye, Grace!" The ex-boxer raised his voice when he said Grace's name, as if it was more important that she hear his goodbye than Pete.

"Goodbye, Leo," said Grace. She watched as the man on the balcony above her leaned back in his chair and stared up at the night sky.

"Leo's harmless," said Pete, as they rounded the corner of the building. "He's just been hit too many times."

"Was Marie his wife?" asked Grace.

"Yeah. She was killed about twenty-five years ago. Her and Leo were swimming in Grand Lake, diving off a houseboat they'd rented. I guess Marie slipped as she was about to dive and she banged her head on the side of the boat. Went into the water unconscious they say. Leo went in after her but he couldn't find her. Her body washed up on shore the next day."

"Oh, how awful."

"Yeah. I think that had a bigger effect on his mental condition than all those punches he took."

The two approached a sign that jutted out from the red brick wall of the inn. The sign read 'Kate's Place' and beneath it was the entrance to the pub. Beyond the entrance was a wrought iron fence surrounding a patio which was quite a popular spot with the locals in the summer months. Tied to the fence was Zero, Louis Little's Scotch Terrier. The dog got to his feet as Pete and Grace approached, blinked a couple of times and then sat back down again. Pete pulled open the door to the pub and motioned for Grace to go inside.

"Kate's probably in here," he said.

Kate's Place was a very small bar, but it had a wonderful atmosphere. There was a bar at which maybe seven or eight people could sit, and there were four small tables for two over by the wall. The walls were adorned with everything from a movie poster from the Paul Newman film 'Nobody's Fool', to a Ken Danby painting of Bobby Orr sitting in a chair in the middle of a hockey rink, to a framed Bruno Bobak print. There was also the Leger family coat of arms, a large blown up black and white photograph which showed the Rainbow downtown area circa nineteen twenty, and an autographed framed photograph of Leo 'The Lion' Terrio in his boxing heyday. The room was dimly lit by four small lamps which were fixed to the walls, and by two slightly larger lamps behind the bar. Seated at the bar were Louis Little, still wearing his Kangol hat and holding his fancy walking stick, and on the stool next to Louis, a woman in her mid-forties. She had jet black hair down to her shoulders, bright red lipstick, and a Spanish-looking dress, the kind that sported puffy sleeves which sat off the shoulders. This was Kate Leger, the proprietor. She and her husband Maurice were the owners of the inn, but Kate ran the place while Maurice tended to his full-time job as a lawyer. As Grace and Pete entered the pub, Kate and Louis were steeped in conversation.

"Hi, Louis," Pete said.

"Why Officer Golliger. We meet again," said Louis.

"Hello, Kate."

"Pete," Kate replied, while looking Grace up and down.

"I hope we're not interrupting anything." said Pete.

"No, no, no," replied Louis. "Kate and I were just discussing the possibility of her appearing in our Christmas production this year. We're doing Who's Afraid Of Virginia Woolf? Don't you think she would make a splendid Martha?"

"Virginia Woolf? For your Christmas production? Do you think Rainbow is ready for that?" asked Pete.

"I don't care whether they're ready or not. Theatre is about challenging the audience, Peter. You cannot let them just sit back and have trite material wash over them like a tepid shower. You must scald them! You must prick their senses!"

"Uh-huh," said Pete. "Well, I'm not sure the basement of St. Paul's Church is the place for scalding and pricking at Christmastime."

"On the contrary," countered Louis. "The church basement is precisely the location for enlightenment."

"Well, could be," said Pete.

"Oh, and I hope you weren't arresting Miss Hoyt tonight."

"What do you mean arresting?" said Kate.

"Because she's our Honey," continued Louis.

"She's your what?" asked Pete.

"What do you mean arresting?" Kate repeated.

"Our Honey. The young wife of the biology professor in Virginia Woolf. Sandy Dennis played her in the film and was absolutely brilliant. I only hope Miss Hoyt is one tenth as captivating."

"Louis, what the hell do you mean arresting? Pete, what does he mean?"

"Well.." Pete began, but Louis didn't allow him to finish.

"There were two police cruisers parked in front of Miss Hoyt's house this evening. Zero and I saw them on our way here."

"Two police cruisers?" said Kate. "Wow. That would be the entire Rainbow force wouldn't it, Pete?"

"Every man we had available was there."

"So, what's going on?" Kate asked.

"Oh, I'll tell you all about it when I have more time. Right now I'd like to get a room for the lady here."

"Oh, sure," said Kate, climbing down off the bar stool.

"This is Grace. Grace this is Kate Leger, and Louis Little."

"Pleasure," said Louis touching the front of his Kangol hat with his thumb and index finger.

"Hi there," said Kate. She took notice of Grace's bruised cheek and then moved behind the bar.

"Hi," said Grace.

"How long will you be wanting the room for?" asked Kate.

"Oh, I don't know," replied Grace. "A couple of days I guess."

"All right." Kate plucked a key from a group of keys on hooks behind the bar. "We'll put you up on the second floor if that's all right."

"That'll be fine," said Grace. "Thank you."

"Right this way then."

"Pleasure meeting you," said Louis.

Kate led Grace and Pete through a doorway at the end of the bar. The doorway led into a small hall and then out into the Allemane's main dining room. Just off the dining room was a staircase to the second floor.

"So, did you see Mickey tonight?" asked Kate as they climbed the stairs.

"Sure did."

"Not bad, huh? He only lost by one dollar. I think he did us really proud."

"Yeah, Mickey's pretty smart all right."

"Okay, here we are."

Kate stopped in front of a door on which there was a bronze plaque that read, 'The A.R. Wetmore Room'. The eight rooms in the inn were not numbered, but instead, were named after famous New Brunswickers. A.R. Wetmore was the province's first premier after Confederation. Other rooms at the inn were named after, Sir Charles G.D. Roberts, a New Brunswicker who was dubbed 'the father of Canadian Poetry', Willie O'Ree, the first black hockey player in the National Hockey League, actress Mary Pickford, artist Bruno Bobak, Charles La Tour, an early settler, Louis Robichaud, another premier, and finally, Marianne Limpert, a swimmer who had won a silver medal at the Atlanta Olympics a few years ago.

Kate opened the door to reveal a very pleasant room which featured a sunken living area with a love seat, a chest of drawers, a television set and one chair, and then up two steps was the bed which was covered with one of the most beautiful quilts Grace had ever seen, and beyond the bed, a small bathroom with a shower.

"I hope this will be all right," said Kate.

"Oh, yes, this is very nice," said Grace stepping down into the living area.

"It's forty dollars for one night, but if you want it for a week or more, I can give you a rate."

"Good," said Grace. "Thank you."

Pete stepped inside and set the suitcase down next to the love seat. "I'll just leave this here for you, Grace," he said. "I've got to get back."

"Oh, certainly. Thank you. I appreciate all your help."

"No problem. If there's anything else you need, you just tell Kate here, or you can give me a call at the station."

"Thank you."

"Have a nice night," Pete said, and then he stepped outside into the hallway.

"The dining room is open from seven a.m. to nine p.m.," said Kate. "Would you like something before I close it up for tonight?"

"No, no, I'm fine, thanks."

"Good. Well, enjoy."

Kate closed the door and she and Pete moved down the hallway towards the stairs.

"So, what's her story?" asked Kate.

"I don't know. I just met her."

"Did you see the bruise?"

"Yep."

"I wonder how she got that. A jerk husband I'll bet."

"She said she was running and she fell."

"And you believe that?"

"Well, she could have."

"Yeah, well, thank you, Sherlock. I'll give you a call the next time I need to find the nose on my face."

"Hey, I'm just repeating what she said."

"Uh-huh. Well, in the first place, a woman who carries herself the way she does and wears diamond earrings like that, that kind of woman doesn't run anywhere. She's gets chauffeured. And in the second and most important place, I've got a sixth sense about things like this."

They reached the bottom of the stairs and made their way through the empty dining room. Kate looked around the room and made a clucking sound with her tongue.

"I didn't have one customer in here tonight," she said. "I had to let Debbie Lynch off early. I guess everybody stayed home to watch Mickey."

"Yeah, I guess so."

As Pete and Kate entered the bar again, Louis exhaled the smoke from a freshly-lit tiparillo and waved a match in a slow rythmic motion to extinguish it's flame.

"Did I hear someone mention young Mickey?" he asked, his eyes squinting through the white smoke.

"Yeah, he's the reason my business is off tonight," said Kate.

"He's my Nick you know," Louis said to Pete.

"Your what?" asked Pete.

"My Nick. The young biology professor in Virginia Woolf. Mickey got the part. He's quite good actually. He's a little young for Miss Hoyt's Honey but it's barely noticeable."

"Listen," Pete began. "I think I should tell you two something. The reason Wood and I were over at Bonnie's tonight, is..uh . . ."

"What?" asked Kate, setting herself down on a stool at the end of the bar.

"Well, the fact is, we found Bonnie dead."

There was a short gasp from Kate and she put her hand to her mouth as if the gesture would keep her heart from jumping out of her throat and onto the floor.

"Oh, dear God," said Louis.

"She's what?" whispered Kate in disbelief.

"Someone hit her over the head."

Kate gasped again.

"We don't know who yet or why or anything."

"Oh, dear God," said Louis. "That poor sweet woman."

"Louis, you live right across the street from Bonnie. You didn't see anything, did you? Someone going into or leaving Bonnie's house between five and seven today?"

"No. No, I was, uh..let me see now..I would have been downstairs for most of that time. That's where my work area is and I was making some notes concerning the set for Virginia Woolf."

"Uh-huh. Well, if you do remember seeing anything, let me know, would you?"

"Most definitely," said Louis.

"And do me a favour and don't go running out and telling everybody about this, all right? You too Kate. I don't want a crowd gathering over there tonight."

Kate, still holding her hand to her mouth, stared down at the bar. Her eyes were glistening with newly-formed tears. Louis tapped his tiparillo into an ashtray on the bar and took another drag.

"I'll see you later," said Pete, and he left the bar.

Kate took her hand from her mouth. "Bonnie Hoyt," she said. "I don't believe it."

"Yes," said Louis. "So much for my Honey."

Upstairs in the A.R. Wetmore Room, Grace lay back on the quilt and stared up at the ceiling. She let out a breath that told her this day was finally ending. Before long, a tear rolled down her cheek and came to rest on the crisp, white pillowcase that cradled her head.

Down the hall and out on the balcony of the Charles La Tour room, sat Leo Terrio, staring up at the stars, but seeing only the face of a beautiful blond twenty-something woman he knew long ago. She smiled down at Leo the way she had always smiled at him as he lay in their bed after one of his fights. Her hand reached down and brushed his hair back off his forehead. A caring finger gently traced a scar over his left eye. Her lips kissed the puffiness of a swollen cheek in an effort to make it better. "Marie," he whispered, and a tear rolled slowly to the corner of his mouth.

-14-

Bryden Downey arrive home from work at about eight-thirty on the evening of September the twenty-first to find his house dark and his wife gone. He had called four times from his office that day and didn't get an answer. He suspected that Grace was still pissed off about last night and was teaching him a lesson by not answering the phone. He called her name as he entered the house and received no reply. He checked the house thoroughly and found no one. Then he noticed that Grace's brown leather suitcase was gone from her walk-in closet upstairs. He looked in the closet to see if there were any clothes missing, but he paid so little attention to what his wife wore in the first place that he couldn't tell if anything was missing or not.

"Son of a bitch," he whispered angrily.

Bryden tore off his tie and threw it on the bed. He marched downstairs to the kitchen thinking he might find a note there explaining his wife's absence and her whereabouts, but there was nothing. He checked the living room. Again, no note. Bryden then went to the den, a room which he and Grace had transformed into a home office for himself, containing a big oak desk, a computer, fax machine and a separate phone line. Maybe Grace would leave a note for him here, where he spent much of his time, but there was nothing. He opened a liquor cabinet next to the desk, poured himself a small glass of Brandy and downed most of it in one gulp.

He set his Brandy glass down on the desk beside the telephone and took two steps towards the hallway. Then he stopped and looked back. The telephone. If she was going to her parents' house in Chicago or to her friend's in North Carolina she would have called them first to let them know. He moved back to the phone, picked up the receiver and hit the redial button. The phone on the other end rang four times and then Bryden heard a woman's voice.

"Hello. You've reached the offices of Landry, Grossman and Bennett. Our offices are closed right now, but if you would like to leave a message . . . ."

Bryden hung up. He had called Charlie Bennett yesterday afternoon from this phone to see if the lawyer wanted to plea bargain a client to a lesser charge in an armed robbery case. Bennett took the offer. Bryden returned to the kitchen and picked up the receiver of the phone which sat on a desk built into a small nook in the corner next the pantry. He pressed the redial button. The phone on the other end rang twice before Bryden heard a man's voice.

"Young's Taxi."

Bryden hesitated. Whatever the man had said, he said it so fast that Bryden didn't catch it.

"Pardon me?"

"Young's Taxi. Can I help you?"

"Oh, yes," said Bryden. "Is this Young's Taxi?"

"That's what I said. What can I do for you?"

"Uh..this is the Bangor Police calling. We're uh..we're trying to locate a woman who we believe may have taken one of your cabs earlier today, and we were wondering if you could help us out."

There was a pause at the other end of the phone.

"Help you out how?"

"Well, we'd like to know where she was dropped off. You keep those kinds of records, don't you?"

"Sure we do."

"Good. She was picked up at . . ."

"What do you want to get hold of her for?"

"What was that?"

"I said why do you want to get hold of her?"

"Oh, well, it's an urgent family matter. Her husband has to get in touch with her."

There was a second pause on the other end of the phone. Then the voice said, "Doesn't he know where she went?"

"Well, no, you see, they're separated, and their daughter's been in an accident and her husband wants to let her know."

"So, how do you know she took one of our cabs?"

"How do we know?"

"Yeah."

Bryden paused and then coughed.

"Sorry. Didn't mean to cough in your ear. The whole station house has caught this cold that's going around." He cleared his throat. "A neighbour saw her leave the house and get into one of your cabs. That's how we know."

There was a third, longer pause at the other end.

"So, could you help us out?" said Bryden.

"Why didn't you just send one of your officers over here to get the information?"

"Why would I do that?"

"Well, it would be nice if I could see a badge."

"Well, I could do that if you want . . ."

"I mean, how do I know you're not a stalker? How do I know you're not going to hurt this woman?"

"You're right. That's a good point, and I'm glad to see there are still a few conscientious citizens out there. I'll send a car over then. I just thought it might be faster over the phone, that's all. I mean, the daughter's condition is pretty serious. So, we'll get someone over there as soon as we can free up a car. Thanks for your trouble."

Bryden waited for the man to say good-bye, but heard nothing.

"Hello?" said Bryden.

"What's the address?"

"I beg your pardon?"

"The address where the woman was picked up. What is it?"

"One-fourteen Garrison Court."

"Hang on."

Bryden picked up a pen from the desk and shuffled a few papers around until he found a blank sheet.

"We picked a woman up at that address a little after two this afternoon," came the voice at the other end.

"And where did she go?"

"Shiner's Truck Stop."

"Shiner's?"

"Shiner's Truck Stop, on the interstate just past exit twenty-eight."

"Okay, thank you very much." Bryden scribbled the name down on the sheet of paper. "Appreciate your help."

"No problem."

"Good-bye."

Bryden hung up the phone feeling quite pleased with himself. "Nice try, Grace," he whispered.

He left the kitchen and climbed the stairs to the bedroom he shared with his wife. He wouldn't go to the truck stop tonight, nor tomorrow either. A smart man, Bryden calculated the reasoning for Grace's cab ride to the truck stop. No trains. No planes. No buses. No way to track her movements. He would give Grace a day or two to get over that snit of hers. Did she think he wasn't serious when he said if she didn't stay with him, he would find an 'acceptable excuse' for her departure? An excuse the voters would understand and perhaps even sympathize with?

He moved to the bedroom and closed the door. He would give Grace a couple of days to come to her senses. If she wasn't back by his side in two days, she would find out how serious he was.

-15-

"How much does Daddy love you, Ev?" asked Wood.

"Bigger than a . . . elephant?" replied the voice on the other end of the phone.

"Way bigger," said Wood. "Now you get to bed, you hear? It's past your bedtime."

"Okay."

"Put Mummy back on."

"Mummy!?" The young boy's voice sounded distant to Wood as the child turned away from the phone to summon his mother. Then the phone clunked as if dropped.

"Hello." said Jeannie.

"Hi."

"Sorry. He dropped the phone."

"Yeah. So anyway, I just thought I should call you to let you know so you'll lock your door tonight."

"Well, thanks, Bobby," said Jeannie. "but I always lock my door anyway."

"Well, I just wanted to be sure," said Wood. "I mean, I doubt if whoever did it is going to be like on a rampage or anything, but better safe than sorry."

"Fine, Bobby, I'll lock my door," said Jeannie. "Jesus."

"I'm only . . ." Wood caught himself before he finished. " . . . you know."

"Only what?" asked Jeannie. "Only trying to look out for me?"

"Well, is there something wrong with that?"

"Never mind," said Jeannie.

"I know. You don't want me being protective of you. Fine. Fine then. Leave your door unlocked. Leave it wide open in fact. And while you're at it, why not walk around the house naked with the curtains open just in case if the killer happens to be driving by your house, you'll get his attention."

Jeannie smiled on the other end of the phone. "Bobby, I'm sorry. I know you mean well."

"Oh Christ," moaned Wood.

"What?"

"Jeannie, that is the worst thing you can say about a man."

"What is?"

"He means well," said Wood.

"What's wrong with 'he means well'?"

"Well, it implies that the person means well, but he's kind of a dope. Kind of a loser."

Wood was speaking on the phone in Bonnie Hoyt's living room. He sat on the couch with his feet across the coffee table so that his boots were hanging over the other side so as not to leave a mark on that particular piece of Bonnie's furniture.

"Oh, don't be stupid, Bobby. You know what I mean. Just . . . will you stop worrying about me so much?"

Wood looked between the toes of his boots to where Bonnie lay dead on the floor. "Jeannie, if you could see Bonnie lying here with her head cracked open, you'd be worried too."

"Someone's going to have to call her father out west," said Jeannie.

"Yeah. Pete's gonna do that right away. Listen, you don't know if Bonnie was involved with anybody, do you?"

"A boyfriend you mean?"

"Yeah."

"Well, I haven't seen her with anybody. Why?"

"Well, Pete found a condom wrapper in the house here, so we think she may have had sex recently."

"Lucky her," said Jeannie.

"What?"

"You heard me."

"Yes, I did hear you. So, am I to assume from that comment that you're not getting any?"

"Well, what do you think?" replied Jeannie.

"Well, I don't know. We've never talked about whether or not either of us have been having sex since we've been separated."

"What about you?"

"What about me?"

"Well, have you?"

"Have I what? Had sex? No."

"Oh, come on."

"I haven't," said Wood.

"I don't believe you."

"I'm telling you, I haven't had sex the whole time we've been separated. Two years."

"You've had no sex."

"No sex," replied Wood. "Nothing. Zip. Not even a meaningful strip search."

Wood heard someone nearby clear his throat and looked up to find a tall man in a blue nylon windbreaker standing in the archway between the living room and the hall.

"I've gotta go," he said into the phone.

"What?"

"I've gotta go."

"Right now? Just like that?"

"I'll call you tomorrow."

"But, Bobby . . ."

"And lock your door. Good-bye."

Wood hung up the phone and pulled his feet off of the coffee table. As he did, his left foot accidentally kicked a Zeller's 'Club Z' Catalogue that was lying there and it slid off the table and onto the floor where it landed on Bonnie's ever-stiffening right hand.

"Oh, Christ!" said Wood, and he reached down, picked up the catalogue and set it back on the table. "I'm sorry, sir," he said to the stranger in front of him. "This is a crime scene. You can't come in here."

"I'm McCaffrey," said the man, reaching into his pocket. "RCMP." He pulled his identification out of the pocket and held it out so that Wood could see it.

"Oh. Uh . . . I'm Wood Lynch. Hi." He moved to the man and shook his hand.

"Hi."

"Boy, you fellas work fast, don't you? I just called a few minutes ago."

"Well, we're in the process of setting up an office in the area, you know, to facilitate the changeover, so I was in the neighbourhood."

"Uh-huh. Right. The changeover. September twenty-eighth."

"Right. So, this is the body, huh?"

"Yep. Boy, you can't put anything over on you RCMP boys, can you?" Wood said with a smile. "You recognize a dead body right off." Wood continued to grin his friendly grin, but he could see that this McCaffrey fellow wasn't in the mood for a laugh.

McCaffrey bent down and felt Bonnie's hand. Then he took her chin between his thumb and forefinger and moved her head from one side to the other, at one point, holding the head as far right as it would go so that he could look at the back of it.

"She was hit on the head," offered Wood.

"Uh-huh."

"Is the forensics team on the way too?" asked Wood.

"Yeah, they'll be here in a while."

"Good. Maybe they can tell us more about what happened here. Pull some prints."

"Maybe."

Wood felt a sense of vindication that this RCMP fellow seemed to know what the phrase 'pull some prints' meant.

"So, was it domestic do you think?" McCaffrey asked.

"Domestic? No, Bonnie wasn't married or anything."

"Forced entry?" asked McCaffrey.

"No. No sign of that."

"Any suspects?"

"Not yet, no."

"Weapon?"

"Didn't find one. No."

McCaffrey reached down from his kneeling position and took one side of Bonnie's robe in his hand.

"She's naked underneath," said Wood. "You don't have to look."

McCaffrey didn't respond. Instead he flipped open the left side of Bonnie's white robe. Then he flipped open the other side so that Bonnie's body lay completely exposed.

"You see, you didn't have to do that," said Wood. "She's naked. See?"

McCaffrey continued to stare down at the body.

"So, why don't you just close it back up again and we'll wait for the forensics people?"

McCaffrey put his hand on Bonnie's hip and rolled her up on her side slightly, so that he could see her buttocks.

"Hey, come on," said Wood uneasily. "What are you doin' that for? You don't have to do that."

"I'm looking for evidence," McCaffrey said calmly.

"Yeah, but Bonnie was a friend and I don't think she'd like you and me standing here looking at her all naked and spread-eagled like that. So close it up, will you?"

"Believe me, officer, your friend is far from feeling anything at this point."

"What the hell's going on here?" came a voice from the archway.

Wood and McCaffrey turned to find Pete Golliger standing there.

"What are you doing?" asked Pete as he moved towards the body.

"This guy's with the RCMP, Pete," said Wood.

Pete bent down, closed Bonnie's bathrobe, and then stood again to find himself facing McCaffrey.

"Sergeant Dale McCaffrey," the man said.

"Pete Golliger. Are you with forensics?"

"No, but I . . . ."

"Well, then let's leave the examination of the body to the forensics experts, okay?"

"Sure," said McCaffrey. "Whatever you say. You the guy in charge?"

"No, we're both in charge," replied Pete.

"Really?" said McCaffrey curiously.

"That's right," said Wood.

"Well, you know," McCaffrey began," When two men ride the same horse, one's gotta ride behind."

Pete and Wood looked at the Sergeant for a moment, and then to each other.

"Mind if I look around a bit?" the Sergeant asked.

"Help yourself," answered Pete.

McCaffrey moved casually into the kitchen and Wood took two steps closer to Pete.

"I tried to tell him to leave her alone, but he wouldn't," Wood said quietly.

"What's he doing here?"

"He just showed up," replied Wood. "Said he was in the neighbourhood. He says they're setting up an office nearby for when the takeover happens."

Sergeant McCaffrey called to the men from the kitchen. "What's out here?"

"What?" asked Pete, moving to the kitchen.

McCaffrey was looking out the window which was located over the sink.

"What's out back here?"

"Just the back yard," replied Pete.

"Anybody had a look yet?" McCaffrey asked as he moved towards the back door.

"I was out there for a couple of minutes," said Wood, entering the kitchen. "But I didn't see much. Too dark."

McCaffrey flipped a light switch next to the door and three quarters of the yard was immediately illuminated.

"Ah, that's better," said Wood.

In the back yard there was a small aluminum shed off to the left near the fence and next to the shed was a gas lawn mower. The six-foot high fence ringed the entire yard, and at the end of the yard there was a gate leading into the darkness beyond.

"What's beyond the fence?" asked McCaffrey.

"Not much," replied Pete. "A bicycle path, and on the other side of that, a church and a cemetery."

McCaffrey turned the knob on the back door.

"It's unlocked," he said. "Was it like this when you found her?"

"Yep," said Wood.

"Hmm." McCaffrey moved back into the living room.

"Nothing unusual about that though," said Pete as he and Wood followed McCaffrey. "I mean, it was the middle of the afternoon. No reason for Bonnie to have her door locked in the middle of the afternoon."

"No?" replied McCaffrey. "Well, the woman's lying dead in her living room with the back of her head bashed in. I'd say that's a reason." McCaffrey ripped a paper towel off of a rack fastened beneath one of the kitchen cupboards. He folded it twice and shoved in down into the drain of the sink.

"My guess is she knew whoever did this," countered Pete. "I mean, there's no sign of a struggle anywhere."

"Yeah, her being a school teacher," added Wood, "and a lifelong resident here, there's probably not a whole lot of people Bonnie didn't know."

McCaffrey pulled the paper towel out of the drain. It was now coloured with pinkish stains.

"What's that? Is that blood?" Wood asked as he bent closer to the paper towel in the Sergeant's hand.

"Yeah. Whoever did this must have rinsed the murder weapon off in here. You'd better rip the sink out of here and let the forensics team have a look at it."

"If it's Bonnie's blood, it's not gonna tell us anything," said Pete. "Bonnie could have cut herself some other time and that's why the blood would be in there."

"Did you see any cuts on her hands?" McCaffrey asked.

"No."

"Uh-huh. So, you're the only two cops left in town, is that right?" McCaffrey moved back into the living room.

"That's right," said Pete following the big man. "We've sort of been deserted by everyone else."

"Yeah, I heard," said McCaffrey. "Well, we'll be glad to take this case off your hands for you." He turned and looked at the big bookcase against the wall.

"What, the RCMP?" asked Pete.

"Yeah."

Pete looked at Wood. Wood gave a quick shake of his head to indicate his disapproval of the sergeant's offer.

"Actually," Pete began, "I think we'd rather handle this one ourselves."

"Why would you want to do that?" asked McCaffrey still looking at the bookshelf.

"Well, she's one of ours. She was a friend, and I think we should be the ones to look into it."

McCaffrey turned to face the two Rainbow police officers and slipped his hands into his windbreaker pockets. "I take it you don't get too many murders here."

"No, we don't," replied Pete. "In fact, this one is pretty much it."

"Yeah, well I just got transferred here from Ontario a couple of months ago," said McCaffrey. "We get our fair share back there and believe me, it's better if you don't know the victim. That way your emotions don't get in the way."

"So, you don't care about the victims?" asked Wood.

"I didn't say that," replied McCaffrey. "I said I don't get emotionally involved."

"Well, all the same," said Pete, "I think we'd like to handle this case ourselves."

"Okay, but don't forget, you're done here in seven days. If you don't close it by then it's gonna land in our laps anyway."

"Well," said Wood, "We'll take it as far as we can, okay?"

"Suits me." McCaffrey started for the front door. As he did, he pulled his identification wallet out of his jacket pocket. "Here," he said, and he held out a business card an equal distance between Pete and Wood. "This is my card. If there's anything I can do, anyway at all we can assist you, you let me know."

"Thanks," said Pete, taking the card.

The sergeant looked at the card in Pete's hand, and then at Wood. He smiled. "I guess that means you're riding behind," he said to Wood.

The RCMP officer left the house and made his way to an unmarked police car in Bonnie's driveway. Pete and Wood stood in the doorway and watched the burly officer strut down the sidewalk.

"Oh, by the way," McCaffrey called out as he opened the driver's side door. "The weapon? Judging by the gash on the woman's head, I'd say you were looking for something with an edge, like a piece of lumber or a dull axe. But, then you probably knew that already, huh?"

Pete and Wood both nodded. "Uh-huh," they said in unison.

"And you might want to throw a sheet over your friend's body," McCaffrey added. "Just as a courtesy." The sergeant climbed into his car and backed it down the driveway and onto Winston Road.

"Am I riding behind?" asked Wood.

"What?"

"The card. You took his card. Does that mean I'm riding behind?"

"No," replied Pete. "It doesn't mean anything. I just took his card, that's all. He held it out and I took it."

"Well, I could've taken it."

"Well, why didn't you?"

"You didn't give me a chance."

"Well, do you want it?" Pete held the card out to Wood.

"No, I don't want it."

"Go ahead. Take it."

"No," said Wood, "You took it. You keep it. I'm just wondering if you took it because you thought you were riding in front, that's all."

"No. Not at all. In fact, if anybody's riding in front, you are. You've been on the force longer than I have."

"Yeah, but you're older. I thought maybe you thought because you're older that you were riding in front."

"No. Absolutely not."

"Fine."

"Not at all."

"Good."

"Good."

The two men stood side by side on the front veranda and looked up and down Winston Road. There was silence between them for about ten very long seconds.

"So, what now?" asked Wood.

"Well, what do you think we should do?" asked Pete. "We'll probably have a bit of a wait for the forensics team."

"Well, one of us should throw a sheet over Bonnie I guess."

"Good idea," said Pete. "And one of us should probably talk to the neighbours. Find out if anyone saw anything."

"You want me to do that?"

"If you want," said Pete.

"Because you can do it if you want to," said Wood.

"No, you go ahead. I'll throw the sheet over Bonnie and check out the back yard."

"Okay," said Wood.

"Okay."

They stood silent for another ten seconds, neither one of them moving to perform their newly-assigned tasks.

"Well, we'd better get to it," said Wood, and he started across the street towards Mrs. Kenny's house.

"Yep," agreed Pete and he stepped inside and closed the door.

After he had covered Bonnie's body, Pete went to the back door and stepped outside onto a small deck which ran along the back of the house for about ten feet, ending directly beneath the kitchen window. On the deck to the left of the door were two deck chairs and a gas barbecue. To the right of the door, leaning up against the house, was a set of golf clubs. Pete walked to the end of the deck where the barbecue was and looked down into a flower garden which had obviously seen better days, and then he straightened up to find himself staring directly into the kitchen window. Through the kitchen, Pete could see into the front hall and to the front door. On the wall inside the front door was a full length mirror in a mahogany frame, probably for one last check before Bonnie headed out of the house on her way to work every morning. He pictured her there, looking at herself, brushing lint off of her coat and then tying a scarf around her neck so that it lay in a fashionably correct manner over her collar. As he looked at the mirror, and Bonnie's imagined image disappeared, Pete could see that Bonnie's living room was reflected in the mirror, and there on the living room floor, he could see the sheet which now covered the slain high school teacher.

Pete moved to the stairs of the deck and stepped off onto the lawn. He walked to the shed and in the decreasing light, he could see that the lawnmower was covered in raindrops. Wet from the brief storm that had blown through town earlier. He opened the unlocked shed. Inside was an electric 'weed eater', some gardening tools, a wheelbarrow, and Bonnie's multi-speed bicycle. This brought to mind another activity which Bonnie had tried to encourage Pete to become involved in during their brief relationship. She wanted him to go riding with her, but Pete didn't own a bike, so he borrowed one from Wood who got it from his wife, Jeannie. Unfortunately, it was a woman's bike and a bit on the smallish side as well, and as a result, Pete's manhood took a severe beating as he and Bonnie – her on her noticeably larger bike – road through town that Saturday afternoon.

Pete closed the shed door and walked another forty feet to the very end of the yard where the gate led out through the fence to the bicycle path. The light was at a premium back here but there was still enough illumination for Pete to notice that the gate was not locked. Then, looking down at a patch of mud left by the rain just inside the gate, he saw what appeared to be two shoe prints. The lawn had been worn down to dirt back here and the shoe prints were quite visible leading away from the grass. Pete bent down for a closer examination and saw that there was one more print inside the gate. This one belonged to someone traveling towards the house. Pete determined that someone going out of the yard would have had to stop here to open the gate, thus the two prints leading away, whereas someone coming into the yard would have pushed open the gate from the outside and their stride had left only the one print in the short patch of mud between the gate and the lawn.

"Were these the killer's prints?" Pete wondered. "Could we be that lucky?"

He turned and walked back to the house. When he stepped onto the deck he could see that it too was still wet from the rain, the drops having beaded on the treated wood. He looked at Bonnie's golf bag, leaning against the house. Bonnie had taken up golf when she was dating Tom Lasalle, and it was not unusual for her to head out to the Rainbow Golf and Country Club early in the morning so she could squeeze in nine holes before school began. The heads of the golf clubs were wet, leading Pete to conclude that Bonnie had been murdered before the rain blew through town. If she had still been alive she would have brought the clubs inside or put them in the shed when the rain began. She wouldn't leave them out to get wet like this. Same with the lawnmower. This confirmed Pete's guess about the time of Bonnie's death. Somewhere between five and six. The storm had come through at around six-fifteen or six-thirty as he recalled. He would call the weather office tomorrow to get the exact time. Then Pete turned and looked back towards the end of the yard and the gate.

"But, if the murder occurred before the rain," he wondered, "then how did the footprints get in that mud? Someone had to have come in and then gone out after the rain." This didn't make sense to the officer. Maybe he was wrong. Maybe Bonnie just forgot about the clubs. Maybe she . . . . "Shit! I don't know what to make of this," he thought.

Pete reached for the back door, but stopped suddenly and looked back down at the golf clubs. The clubs were all wet. All but one. The eight iron. There was no moisture on this club. It was completely dry. And it was clean. The other club heads had signs of play on them. Dirt which the rain had failed to wash away completely.

"I'd say you were looking for something with an edge, like a piece of lumber or a dull axe," Dale McCaffrey's word's echoed in Pete's mind.

"Or a golf club," Pete whispered.

-16-

News travels at the speed of light in a town of only nine thousand citizens, and by the time the morning of September the twenty-second arrived in Rainbow, the report of a local high school teacher's sudden and felonious demise was on the lips of just about everyone, and every storyteller had a different tale to tell. "She was hit over the head with a lead pipe," said one. "They found her naked on her bed like Marilyn Monroe", said another. And still another said, "She was stabbed in her shower like the woman in that Psycho movie." And everyone had an opinion as to who could have done it. Some thought it must be a transient because surely no one from Rainbow could commit such a heinous crime. Others said it was a student who was out to avenge a failing grade. And some thought it must be a jilted lover. Those with a flair for the sensational speculated that it could be a lesbian lover, and when queried as to their assessment of Bonnie's sexuality, they claimed not to know for certain, but after all, Bonnie was very athletic, and she did coach the high school girl's volleyball team, and she did golf, and she was still single at the ripe old age of thirty-four. How could she not be a lesbian?

On this morning, in The Allemane's dining room, Grace was overhearing a silo full of such speculation from two sixty-something ladies seated at a table across the room from her. Grace had come down for breakfast at eight o'clock and shortly after that, the two ladies arrived, said a cordial good morning to her, and then sat down at their table and immediately began discussing Rainbow's first murder in eighteen years.

"Well, I'll be sleeping with one eye open tonight, I can tell you that," said the first lady. "I won't be his next victim."

"You think he'll strike again?" asked the second.

"Well, Helen Fry's girl Roberta said the killer left a note."

"Go on!"

"That's what Roberta said. Said the note warned the police that they'll never catch him and that he can kill whenever he pleases."

"The note said that?" asked the second lady in surprise.

"That's what Roberta said, and she should know. I mean, her fabric shop is right next door to the police station. She sees those officers coming and going all day long."

"The two of them you mean."

"Pete Golliger and Debbie Lynch's boy, Bobby, right."

"Well, what do you know about that?"

There was a brief pause in the rumor-filled conversation during which the first lady looked down at herself and in a proper, business-like fashion, smoothed the grey skirt that covered her to her knees. "So, did you see Mickey last night?" she asked in an lighter tone of voice.

"Hmm?" said lady number two, lost in thought.

"Mickey Welton, on Jeopardy. Did you see him?"

"Oh, Mickey, yes. Wasn't that exciting?"

"Lost by one dollar."

"One dollar."

"His mother must be proud."

"Oh, she must be. She must be. Although, she's a bit of an odd bird."

"Mickey's mother?"

"Yes."

"Don't know her."

"Well, she's an odd one. He is too. The father. I don't care for him much."

There was a pause. Lady number two pulled a lost thread from her sweater, held her arm out away from the table and let the thread glide to the floor. "The earthenware was nice," she said.

"Oh, yes," said lady number one. "Very nice."

Just then, Pete Golliger entered the dining room. He was wearing the uniform that he had worn last night when he drove Grace to The Allemane. This morning though, it was in a slightly disheveled state. In fact, as Grace looked up and saw Pete standing there, she wondered if he had slept in the uniform.

"Good morning," Pete said, approaching Grace's table.

"Hello," said Grace.

"Everything okay for you here last night?"

"Yes, yes. It was just fine, thank you."

"Good." Pete looked to the two women seated nearby. "Good morning, ladies," he said.

"Good morning," said lady number two.

Lady number one didn't waste her breath on pleasantries. She got right to the question of the day. "Did you find Miss Hoyt's murderer yet?"

"Uh..no, not yet," replied Pete. "But, we're working on it."

"Do you think he meant what he said in that note?" asked lady number two.

"Note?" asked Pete. "What note?"

"The note the killer left."

"I'm sorry, but we didn't find any note," said Pete.

"Oh. We heard there was a note."

"No."

"That's all right, Officer," said lady number one. "We know you can't discuss the specific details of the case." She looked at her companion. "They have to hold some of the details back from the public so that if they get a confession from somebody, they can use those details to verify the suspect's story."

"Actually ma'am, I'm not holding back any details. The fact is, there was no note."

"Oh. Well, that's too bad," the lady said. "I mean, it would have been a break if the killer had left some piece of evidence like that for you to examine. Something you could pull his prints from."

"Yes, yes, it would have been," replied Pete. "Excuse me." He turned his attention to Grace. "Mind if I join you?"

"Uh . . . No, go right ahead," said Grace.

"Thank you." Pete pulled out a chair and sat opposite Grace.

"Did you get any sleep last night?"

A little smirk crossed Pete's mouth. "Why? Do I look that bad."

"No, I just meant . . ."

"No, that's all right," Pete said, removing his hat and setting it on an empty chair to his left. "The fact is, I didn't get any sleep at all. The forensics people showed up at about ten and I stayed with them most of the night, and then I went back to the office to call the woman's father and give him the news. And then I had to get a start on the paper work. I'm just heading home to catch a couple of hours now, but I thought I'd stop in here for some breakfast first."

"Oh," said Grace. "Do you eat breakfast here a lot?"

"Oh, yeah. All the time," replied Pete.

"Oh. So, did they find anything? The forensics people?"

"Well, we've got one or two things to work with so far, but we won't get their full report until later today or tomorrow."

Deborah Lynch entered the dining room through a swinging door that led to the kitchen. She wore a white blouse and dark slacks as she did every day at The Allemane, and she was carrying a fresh pot of coffee. Deborah was fifty-eight years old but looked ten years younger. The years of raising Wood and his brother Donnie by herself, driving them back and forth to their hockey games and football games and soccer games, picking up after them, cooking meals for them, doing endless loads of laundry and in general, trying keep two active boys on the straight and narrow, had not run her into a ragged state as one would expect. In fact, all of the activity of those years appeared to have kept her in the best of shape.

"Oh, good morning, Pete."

"Morning, Debbie," the officer replied.

"What are you doing here?"

"What do you mean what am I doing here?" said Pete trying to veil his embarrassment at the untimely question.

"Well, I thought you always had breakfast over at The Dutchman."

"The Dutchman? No. Well, sometimes yeah. But a lot of the time I have breakfast here too."

"Really? I've never seen you in here," said Debbie. "Coffee?"

"Please," said Pete.

"I've never seen you here either," said lady number one from across the room. "And we're here every morning?"

"Really?" said Pete.

"Every morning for the last nine years. Since my husband passed," said lady number two

"Well, I'm usually here a little earlier," countered Pete. "I guess we've just missed each other."

"So, what would you like?" asked Debbie.

"Uh . . . . I think I'll have my usual. The French toast." He looked at Grace. "I love the French toast here."

"We don't have French toast here," said Debbie.

"What?" said Pete trying to force a laugh. "Since when?"

"Since never. We've never had it."

"That's right," said lady number one. "We've been coming here for nine years now and I've never seen French toast on the breakfast menu."

"Never. In nine years," added lady number two.

"Two eggs over hard with bacon and toast then," said Pete. "Is that on the menu?"

"Sure is. That's the Sunshine Breakfast Special," said Debbie.

"Is it really?" asked Pete.

"Has been for five years now," said Lady number one. "Since my Merle passed away."

"Has it been five years?" asked Lady number two.

"Five years next month."

"I thought he'd been dead longer."

"Nope. Five years next month. The seventeenth."

"Uh-huh," interrupted Pete. "Well that's what I'll have. The Sunshine Breakfast Special."

"Coming up," said Debbie, and she moved to the two ladies across the room and took their orders as well.

Grace was now wearing the smile of a Cheshire cat. "So, you come here all the time do you?"

"Well, not all the time."

"You're checking up on me."

"Oh, I wouldn't call it checking up."

"What would you call it then?"

"I just want to make sure you're enjoying your stay, that's all."

"Oh, I see."

"So, are you?"

"Yes."

"Good." Pete looked at ladies number one and two and noticed that they had halted their conversation about dead husbands and were now listening intently to what he and Grace had to say. He smiled at them and nodded his head.

"So," he said to Grace, "What part of Chicago are you from?"

"Do you know Chicago?" she asked.

"No," he replied. "Well, I know that the southside of Chicago is the baddest part of town."

"Oh?"

"Yeah. And if you go down there you'd better just beware of a man named Leroy Brown."

"Right. Jim Croce."

"Right."

"Well, I'm from Lincoln Park." Grace wasn't lying. She was indeed from the Lincoln Park area of Chicago. Her parents still lived there, but Grace had moved to Maine to attend university years ago and upon completion of her studies she got a job with a Bangor public relations firm and she had lived there ever since.

"And uh..what brings you to Rainbow?" asked Pete.

"Oh, just sightseeing. I've never been to this part of your country before."

Pete looked at the gold wedding band on Grace's left hand. "Your husband doesn't mind you traveling all this way by yourself?"

"No," Grace replied.

"Because I'd be worried about letting my wife go off on her own like that," said Pete. "Especially if she was an attractive woman like yourself. And especially if she's going to be hitching rides with truck drivers along the way."

Grace didn't answer. The conversation was beginning to make her uncomfortable. Pete noticed this but he didn't back off. There was something about this woman that intrigued and worried him, and it began with that bruise on her cheek. He suspected, as did Kate Leger the night before, that it was given to her by a 'jerk husband'. He leaned into Grace, closing the space between them, set his elbows on the table and crossed his forearms. "Your bruise is looking better today." Pete spoke quietly so the two other patrons couldn't overhear.

"Thank you," Grace replied.

"You want to talk about it yet?"

"There's nothing to talk about," Grace replied, and she leaned back, gaining the personal space that had been stolen from her seconds before. "I just fell, that's all."

"Uh-huh. So, do you have any kids?"

"No," replied Grace. "You?"

"No. Not married."

"Oh. You were once though, right?" Grace was now trying to divert the line of questioning away from her story.

"What makes you say that?" asked Pete.

"Well, what are you, forty? Forty-five? Half the population has been married and divorced by that age. Some more than once."

"Yeah, I was married. Back in Toronto."

"So, what happened?" asked Grace.

"It didn't work out."

"Why?"

"Well . . ." Pete began to formulate an answer that would avoid his appearing like a loser in Grace's eyes, but she didn't give him a chance to get it out.

"Did you cheat on her?"

"No."

"Did she cheat on you?"

Pete poured some cream into his coffee cup and thought for a moment. "All right," he said. "You've made your point. I won't ask you any more questions. Not right now at least."

Debbie Lynch entered from the kitchen carrying Grace's breakfast order. "Here you go," she said, setting a small plate on the table in front of Grace. The plate held an English muffin and a slice of orange.

"Thank you," said Grace.

"I can't believe what happened to Bonnie," Debbie said to Pete. "It's terrible."

"You been talking to Wood?" asked Pete.

"He called me last night and told me to make sure my doors were locked."

"Well, Debbie, I don't think there's any danger of the killer doing this to someone else. I think this was a one time thing."

"That's not what he said in the note," interjected lady number one from across the room.

"There was no note," replied Pete.

"I mean, who's to say he won't strike again?" continued lady number one, ignoring Pete's statement of fact. "I've heard that sometimes, after someone kills for the first time, they get a thirst for it, and they want to do it again. Bloodlust they call it."

"Well, I really don't think . . ." Pete began, but was cut off by lady number one.

"Maybe he went in to burglarize Bonnie's house and she walked in on him and he killed her and maybe it excited him and now he's got the bloodlust."

"Oh, my!" gasped lady number two.

"Look," said Pete. "I don't want everybody getting in a panic over this. There was no burglary. I don't think it was a random killing. We think Bonnie knew whoever did it. Okay?"

"Should you be talking about the case in such detail?" asked lady number two.

"No, I shouldn't be," replied Pete. "I just want to try and put your minds at ease, that's all. I mean, Debbie here is worried about locking her doors, and your friend is talking about bloodlust. There's really nothing to worry about. This town is just as safe now as it's always been."

"So, are you saying we shouldn't lock our doors?" asked lady number one.

"No, you should. You should lock your doors anyway. Regardless of what happened to Bonnie."

"Oh," said lady number one. "Because I always lock my doors and I'm not about to start leaving them unlocked at this stage. Not just because a policeman tells me to."

"I didn't tell you to," replied Pete nearing frustration. "Lock your doors. By all means. Lock your doors and your windows. Lock everything up as tight as a goddamned drum!"

There was a pause as the four women in the room looked at Officer Golliger. Then lady number one looked across her table at lady number two. "Well, that didn't put my mind at ease," she said.

It was at this juncture in the conversation that Leo Terrio entered the Allemane dining room. It was a part of Leo's daily routine to stop in here for a breakfast of four eggs, toast and grapefruit juice before heading off to his caretaking job at St. Paul's Church. As he entered the room, the robust ex-boxer noticed the two sixty-something ladies and approached their table. The ladies were usually here when Leo came down each morning, and the three of them would often pass the breakfast hour steeped in conversation about recent goings on in Rainbow. Some of the talk was small town gossip and conjecture, and some was of a more important nature, such as why did the Legion want the town to build them a bigger hall when their membership was dwindling due to death by natural causes?

"Good morning, dear ladies," said Leo.

"Good morning, Mr. Terrio," said lady number one with a coy smile. She held her hand out to Leo and he took it, raised it to his lips and kissed it in a gentlemanly fashion. Lady number two held out her hand, and Leo repeated the debonair act with her. It was obvious that this exchange occurred each and every time the three crossed paths at the Allemane.

"And how are we this morning?" Leo asked.

"Well, quite frankly, sir, we are shaken, as is most of Rainbow," said lady number two.

"Shaken? Over what?" Leo had not heard the news about Bonnie.

"Well . . ." began lady number two, but before she could finish, Leo noticed Grace and Pete sitting at a table across the room.

"Pete!" said Leo, moving to Grace's table. "What are you doing here?"

"Well, Leo," said Pete with just a hint of irritation in his voice, "I'm here for breakfast."

"Wow. Since when did you start coming here?"

"Today, Leo. Today. This is my first day. This is it."

"Well, welcome," Leo reached out and shook Pete's hand. "Welcome to the Allemane. And I see you brought your girlfriend with you too? Good morning, Grace," he said and he took her hand in his and kissed the back of it."

"Good morning, Leo," said Grace.

Leo's voice suddenly went up an octave. "Hey did you see Mickey last night?" He then turned to the ladies across the room. "Did everybody see Mickey?"

The ladies nodded enthusiastically.

"Yeah, I think everybody in town probably saw him," said Pete. "Leo, why don't you sit down? Have breakfast with us."

"Oh, I wouldn't want to interrupt you love birds," said Leo.

"No, really," insisted Pete, reaching over and pulling out the chair to his right. "Join us."

"Well . . . . all right then. Sure," said the big ex-boxer shyly. "Thanks." Leo sat down with a pleased look on his face, happy that Pete wanted to have breakfast with him.

"Leo," Pete began after Leo was seated, "I don't know if you've heard yet or not, but, something's happened to Bonnie Hoyt."

"Oh yeah? What?" asked Leo, the smile still lingering from the breakfast invitation.

"Well . . . . she's been killed."

Leo's happy expression did not change instantly. He looked at his friend Pete for a moment, still smiling, and then to Grace who he was sure would wink at him as if to say that Pete was having a little fun at his expense. But, there was no wink from Grace, and Leo knew that Pete was not the kind of man who would play a cruel joke like this on someone. His smile slowly faded and he looked back at the police officer seated to his left. "Killed?" he asked. "Miss Hoyt?"

"I'm afraid so," said Pete.

"How?"

"She was murdered last night," replied Pete.

Leo's face registered the shock of someone who had just been punched hard in the stomach. He was not a close friend of Bonnie Hoyt's, but he had known her through his work at the high school. He had often seen Bonnie running laps around the gym with her girl's volleyball team. Sometimes while working at St. Paul's Church, he would glance out a window and see Bonnie coming through her back gate with her bicycle, heading out for a ride on the bicycle path. And now, the idea that this vibrant woman's life could be ended at such a young age seemed to affect him deeply.

Pete leaned in closer to Leo so as to shield his conversation from the two ladies at the other table. "Did you work at the church yesterday, Leo?"

"What?" Leo was lost in thought.

"Did you work yesterday? At the church?"

"Yeah. Worked there all day," Leo replied.

"Til' when?"

"How was she murdered?" asked Leo.

"She was..uh..she was hit."

"Beaten up?"

"Well . . . ."

"She wasn't beaten up, was she? A man didn't beat her up, did he?"

"She was hit once. Just once."

"It makes me mad to think that some guys beat up on the women they say they love. That makes me real mad. Don't these men know how lucky they are to have someone to love? And then to . . . to treat them like that . . . ."

"What time did you work until, Leo?" asked Pete.

Leo paused. When Pete's question finally registered, he answered. "Six. Knocked off at six like I usually do."

"Uh-huh." Pete began to push a spoon around on the table in front of him. "Did you see anything unusual say between and five and six? I mean, maybe you happened to glance across towards Bonnie's house and maybe you saw someone or something."

"Would you like me to leave?" Grace asked.

"Leave? Why?" asked Pete.

"Well, it seems like you're conducting an interrogation here, and maybe it's something I shouldn't hear."

"No, this isn't an interrogation," said Pete. "I'm just talking to my old friend Leo here. Right, Leo?"

"Right," replied Leo.

"There, you see?" Pete said to Grace. "Unless we're putting you off your breakfast with all this murder talk. Is that it? Is that why you want to leave?"

"No. No, I don't care about that," replied Grace, and she pushed her small plate aside and pulled her cup of coffee in front of her.

"Oh, I have put you off your breakfast. I'm sorry," said Pete.

"No, no not at all. I'm just not very hungry this morning."

"I saw Tom Lasalle," said Leo. His words cut through the conversation like a razor.

Pete looked at the big man to his right, who was now staring down at the table. He was playing with his spoon the same way that Pete had been. "What did you say?"

"I saw Tom Lasalle."

"You saw Tom Lasalle when?"

"Last night when I was leaving work. I came out the back door and I saw him coming out of the graveyard towards his car."

"Tom Lasalle?"

"Yeah."

"Well, did he say anything to you?"

"No. I don't think he saw me."

"And what time was this, Leo?"

"Oh . . . five after six maybe. Ten after."

"And you're sure it was Tom Lasalle."

"Sure I'm sure. I know Tom when I see him. His dad and me grew up together."

Pete's mind was suddenly filled with a thousand thoughts. What was Tom Lasalle doing in the graveyard at six o'clock? The graveyard is a stone's throw from Bonnie Hoyt's house. Was Tom involved? Maybe Tom saw somebody leaving Bonnie's house through the back gate. Five after six, said Leo. Maybe ten after. The rain. The boot prints. The weather office. What time did it rain? Pete suddenly found himself standing.

"Are you leaving?" asked Grace.

"Hmm?" Pete looked down at Grace and Leo. "Uh . . . yes. Yes, I have to go now. It was nice seeing you again."

"But, you just ordered breakfast."

"I know, but, uh . . ." Pete fumbled in his pocket for some cash. He finally pulled out a five dollar bill and set it on the table. "Leo, you can have my breakfast, okay? It's on me. I've gotta run."

Without giving Leo a chance to accept his offer, Pete turned and was gone. Lady number one watched the officer leave the dining room and then turned to lady number two.

"I don't care what he says. I'm locking my doors tonight."

-17-

Wood Lynch had arrived home at around midnight the night before. He and Pete had decided that one of them should get some sleep in order to have a rested officer on duty the next day, so Wood called it a night while Pete stayed on with the forensics team at Bonnie's.

Wood lived in an apartment on Hickson Road out near the Rainbow Arena. He had taken the apartment when he and Jeannie split up, but it had never really felt like home to him. The sparsely-furnished apartment had a temporary feel to it, as if Wood was telling himself that he wouldn't be here for long. That pretty soon, he and Jeannie would work out their problems and return to being a family again. It was a hope that Wood was clinging to like a drowning man to a life ring.

On the morning of September the twenty-second, Wood left his apartment at seven-thirty and drove to Bonnie Hoyt's house to find out how the evening had gone with Pete and the forensics team. Pete had already returned to the police station by then to get started on the paper work that a case such as this required, and so Wood touched base with the head of the forensics unit, a woman named Carrie Jardine. Ms. Jardine gave the officer the facts as she knew them so far, and a little speculation as to what might show up in her final report. She put the time of death somewhere between five-thirty and six-thirty p.m.. This estimate was based on the rate at which the blood had clotted and the coagulation. It appeared that Bonnie died as a result of a single blow to the head, probably from the golf club that Officer Golliger had found in the golf bag on the deck. The forensics team found traces of blood in the grooves on the club head even though it appeared that someone had made an effort to wipe the entire club clean. There were no fingerprints found anywhere on the eight iron in question. As for fingerprints elsewhere, they found three different sets in Bonnie's house.

One of the shoe prints left in the mud near the back yard gate was perfectly preserved and Ms. Jardine felt that if they could find the shoe that made the impression, they could match it up with no problem at all. She said it appeared to be a boot print. Probably a hiking boot like those Doc Martens.

"Wouldn't all Doc Marten style hiking boots have the same tread print?" asked Wood.

"Only when they're brand new," replied the expert. "When there is wear on the boot, nicks and gouges occur and the boot takes on an impression that is uniquely it's own."

Ms. Jardine's team found some hair at the scene as well. Hair which appeared to be from someone other than the victim. These hairs were found in the carpet near the victim's feet.

But, the most interesting detail that Ms. Jardine shared was her speculation as to how the death blow was struck. She said it appeared to have come in a sideways motion from above, the kind of swing one might take if they were chopping down a tree with an axe. Wood asked if this would mean the killer was taller than Bonnie and Ms. Jardine replied only if the killer was about seven feet tall. She said she felt that the angle of the blow was such that Bonnie might have been on her knees when she was struck.

"Maybe she was sitting in a chair," offered Wood.

"No," replied Ms. Jardine. "I thought about that but we didn't find any blood on or near any of the chairs in the house. The only other blood we found was around the hot water tap on the kitchen sink, but that could've come from the victim while she washing dishes one day. Maybe she cut herself. Who knows?"

"Any signs of her being assaulted sexually?" Wood didn't want to ask this question but he knew he had to.

"Well, there's no vaginal bruising," replied Ms. Jardine. "There were fluids found but until we conduct a more detailed examination of the victim, we won't know."

"Okay," Wood said with a finality which told Ms. Jardine that he didn't want to know any more about the process involved in her 'detailed examination'.

As he was leaving Bonnie's house, Wood saw Tom Lasalle's car pulling out of the driveway across the street. Tom was heading off to the golf course as he did every morning about this time. On this particular morning he had a group lesson scheduled for nine. The group was made up of three women who took lessons from Tom once a week. This would be their final lesson of the season.

As Tom's car pulled away and headed east towards the Rainbow Golf and Country Club, Wood saw Gabby Lasalle standing at her front door. Wood waved to Gabby and Gabby waved back, and then Wood started across the street towards her. "You got a minute, Gabby?" Wood asked as he reached the sidewalk in front of Bonnie's house.

"I suppose," replied Gabby halfheartedly.

Wood crossed the street and made his way up Gabby's walk to her front door. "How you doin' this morning?"

"Okay," she replied.

"I just want to ask you a couple more questions about last night."

"Well, I already told you everything that happened."

"Uh-huh." Wood looked down the street in the direction that Tom's car had gone. "Tom off to work, is he?"

"Yeah."

"Boy, must be nice to have a job like that. Spend your whole day on a golf course. I wouldn't mind doin' that myself."

"I didn't know you golfed."

"I don't, but if I'd known I could have a job like Tom's one day, I might've taken it up when I was younger."

"So, what do you want to know?" Gabby asked. "I was just about to do the laundry."

"Oh, sure. Uh..can I come in for a sec?"

Gabby hesitated and then without answering, went inside, leaving the door open for Wood. Wood wiped his feet on the door mat outside and followed Gabby into the living room. The room was bright and big. Tom and Gabby had done some renovations after moving in, knocking down a wall between the kitchen and the living room so that the space was an open concept now. There was a fireplace against one wall and on the mantle over the fireplace was Gabby and Tom's wedding picture which was sandwiched in amongst Tom's many golfing trophies. Tom had won the provincial championship twice and the club championship five years in a row. In a corner on the other side of the room was a fish tank containing five or six colorful tropical fish.

"Have a seat," said Gabby.

"Thanks," replied Wood and he sat himself down in a wooden rocking chair near the front window.

"You want a coffee?" Gabby asked.

"Uh..sure, if you've got some made. Thanks."

Gabby moved into the kitchen area and took a coffee mug from a cupboard to the right of the sink.

"This is the first time I've ever been inside your house," said Wood.

"Well, sorry about the mess," Gabby said.

Wood looked around the room. It was spic and span. There wasn't a book, a newspaper, or even a piece of junk mail out of place. The hearth of the fireplace was spotless as if it had been vacuumed within the last ten minutes. The firewood in the wood box next to the fireplace was stacked neatly and there were no errant bark chips on the carpet around the box. The water in the fish tank was crystal clear. So clear, in fact, that even the fish looked as though they had been polished recently. Wood leaned over and looked directly down at a small end table beside the rocking chair. He could see his reflection in the tabletop. And in the kitchen, there were no dishes in plain view, which seemed to indicate that no humans had eaten breakfast there this morning. "Yeah, you've really let the place go," said Wood. Gabby didn't catch the sarcasm in Wood's voice. In fact, her lack of reaction made him think that she didn't hear him at all. "So," he continued, "About last night."

"Do you know who did it yet?" asked Gabby.

"Well, no, not yet, but we've found some evidence that might help. You know, fingerprints and stuff." Wood paused for a second and then went into investigator mode. "So, tell me about how you came to see Bonnie through the window, Gabby."

"I already told you. I was setting the magazine down on the table on her veranda and I saw her through the window."

"Did you just happen to glance in and see her? Is that what happened, because you know, the curtains were pulled closed and there wasn't much of a space to see in."

"Well," Gabby began, "I turned and I just..well, something caught my eye inside and so I looked a little closer and that's when I saw her."

"Something caught your eye?"

"Yeah. A foot maybe, or just something that didn't seem right. How do you take your coffee?"

"Just a little cream please. So you didn't just happen to glance in then. You looked in with some intent, right?"

"Well, I guess I looked in, yeah. What do you mean intent?" Gabby opened the refrigerator and took out a container of half and half cream. She poured a small amount into the coffee mug.

"Well, you wanted to see inside."

"I wanted to see what I saw a little better, yeah," said Gabby returning the container of cream to its place inside the refrigerator.

"But, you weren't, you know, snooping or anything?"

Gabby began to bristle at the officer's suggestion. "Snooping? No, I wasn't snooping. I was bringing her a recipe. Why would I be snooping?"

"Well, it was hard to see in, that's all. I'm just asking how you saw in."

"And I told you." Gabby moved to Wood, took a coaster from a stack of coasters on the end table beside him and set it and then the coffee mug down on the table.

"Thanks. All right let me ask you something else. Did you happen to see anybody going into or coming out of Bonnie's house yesterday afternoon? Say between five and six-thirty."

"No. Well, I saw Bonnie come home." Gabby returned to the kitchen, picked up a dishcloth from out of the sink and began wiping the counter in the area of the coffee maker.

"You saw Bonnie?'

"Yeah, I was sitting where you are and I saw her car pull into the driveway. She got out with her briefcase and a couple of bags."

"What time was that?"

"Oh, about quarter to five." Gabby turned to face Wood and leaned against the kitchen counter. "You see, that's why I thought she was home when I took the magazine over. Because I saw her come home earlier." She turned back and began wiping again.

Wood paused and looked at the fish tank. The fish shone back at him. "I should put my sunglasses on," he muttered.

"What?"

"Nothing." Wood took a sip of his coffee and looked out the front window to Bonnie's house across the street. "Do you know if Bonnie was seeing anybody these days?" he asked.

"No idea," Gabby answered.

"She didn't talk to you about having a boyfriend or anything? I mean women friends talk about their boyfriends, don't they?"

"Bonnie and I weren't friends. I mean, not that kind of friends."

"Oh. I thought you talked a lot. I mean, you exchanged recipes and everything."

"Well, we exchanged recipes, sure, but we didn't get together and talk on a regular basis." Gabby placed the dish cloth on the sink next to the hot water tap and turned to face Wood, leaning back against the counter again. This time she folded her arms and crossed her feet. A body language expert would have told Wood that he should probably leave now. When Wood didn't ask another question, Gabby filled in the silence. "So, I mean, I wouldn't know whether she had a boyfriend or not."

"What about Tom?" Wood asked.

"What about Tom? What are you saying?"

"Well, would he know if Bonnie had a boyfriend?"

"Oh..uh..no, he wouldn't know. He and Bonnie didn't talk."

"Yeah, but you know, sometimes men talk to other men and maybe he heard something."

"No, he didn't."

"Oh." Wood took a final sip of his coffee and stood. "Well, I guess that's all then." Wood moved to the front door. Inside the door, off to the left out of the way of traffic, and placed as neatly as everything else in the Lasalle household, were two pairs of shoes on a rubber mat. One a woman's pair, and the other a man's. "Does Tom own a pair of hiking boots?" Wood asked.

"Tom doesn't hike," Gabby replied.

"Well, most of the people who own hiking boots don't hike," said Wood. "It's like those folks who own four wheel drive vehicles. I'm sure ninety-eight percent of those people don't drive through the bush on their way to the office every day. I just wondered if Tom owned a pair."

"No." Gabby's answer was curt.

"Okay." Wood moved out onto the front steps while Gabby stayed inside with her hand on the frame of the front door. "So, what do you do with yourself all day, Gabby?"

"What do you mean?"

"Well, do you just stay inside all day? Do you jog, do you bike, what do you do?"

"What, because I don't have a job you think I don't do anything all day?"

"No, that's not what I meant. I'm just curious as to how you fill your time, that's all."

"I've got a lot to do, Wood. A lot. In fact, I should be getting to it right now."

"Sure, okay," said Wood. He wasn't asking her the question in relation to the Bonnie Hoyt case. He was just curious. He liked Gabby. He had liked her since he first met her in high school when she was a cheerleader and he was dropping passes for the Rainbow High football team. Gabby was a freshman then and Wood was a senior, and he was taken by her vivacious, outgoing personality. Sadly, that personality had flat-lined since she married Tom, and Wood suspected that her husband's dalliances had taken a toll on Gabby's happiness. And now, he just wanted to know how her life was going. "Well, I'll see you later then. Have a nice day."

Gabby said good-bye and closed the front door. Inside she would begin another day. Laundry. Watching television. Cleaning the house, even though it did not appear to need cleaning. Paying bills. Sitting in the rocking chair by the window, watching her neighbours walk by occasionally. Louis Little with his dog, Zero. And Mrs. Kenny next door on her daily outing to play bridge with her friends at Charlotte Gormley's house two streets over. Gabby was insecure about her importance in this life. In her husband's life. She had no job. She had no children to care for. She didn't play any sports. She didn't have a hobby. She wondered if her husband Tom, who was seven years her senior, found her interesting enough. Challenging enough. She knew of Tom's reputation with women. She knew it when she married him, but, he had assured her that she was the only woman for him, that he would never need anyone else, and she took him at his word. Her insecurity would not ease up though. It ate away at her on a daily basis. It was this insecurity which made her cross the road to Bonnie Hoyt's house last night at seven thirty. It was the same insecurity that made her peer with intent into Bonnie's front window, through closed curtains which she had to strain to see through by cupping her hands over her eyes and then leaning up against the glass.

The Rainbow police station looked more like the office of a small business than a law enforcement headquarters. In the main area of the station there was the receptionist's desk and behind that, three other desks, each one set up with its own computer and telephone system. A room off to the left of the receptionist's desk housed the office of the Chief of Police, but due to Walt Steeves' departure from that position three months earlier, that office, at present, stood unoccupied. Wood Lynch and Officer Pete Golliger each had a desk in the main area of the station, but since becoming the sum total of the Rainbow Police Force, the two men rarely had time to make use of them.

Beyond the main area of the station, through a door at the back of the room, were three holding cells. The last time any of the cells were used was two months ago after Huntzy Hunt fired a shotgun into the air to scare his neighbor's dog out of his wife's vegetable garden. Unfortunately, he fired the weapon into an overhead hydro wire and sheered the wire in half, plunging his entire street into darkness for two hours. Huntzy was charged with the unlawful discharge of a weapon, creating a disturbance, and public mischief, but after due deliberation, Pete and Wood decided just to hold Huntzy overnight to make him sweat, then they sent him home and made the paper work disappear.

Wood arrived at the police station at nine o'clock on the morning of the twenty-second. He missed Pete by about an hour according to station 'Information Coordinator', Lori Higgenson. Lori, the twenty-seven year old niece of local dentist, Duffy Higgenson, dreamed up the 'information coordinator' title for herself because she didn't want to be called a receptionist. She felt that the term 'receptionist' did not fully describe her duties at the police station, duties which included answering the telephone, accepting payment of traffic fines, dispatching calls to officers in the field, and miscellaneous filing and sorting.

Lori arrived at work at eight that morning just as Pete was leaving. She and Pete didn't talk for long. She asked him if he had seen Mickey on Jeopardy the night before and Pete said yes and Lori bragged about how she went to school with Mickey. "Well, we weren't in the same class. He was two years behind me, but I saw him in the halls quite a bit." Pete then told Lori about Bonnie Hoyt and warned her that she might be fielding a lot of calls about the murder this morning.

"And if somebody calls with any information about the case," Pete said, "try and get their name, but if they don't want to give it, then at least get the information down correctly." Pete had learned that sometimes people preferred phoning in any tips they might have, rather than face the police in person. "Will you do that?" Pete said to Lori.

"Pete, what's my title?" Lori asked, putting her hands on her hips in a challenging manner.

"Your title?"

"My title. What's my title?"

"Information coordinator," Pete replied.

"That's right. So, if somebody was to call with any INFORMATION, don't you think I would be sure to get the INFORMATION down correctly?"

"Yeah, I guess you would," said Pete, too tired to argue.

"Yes, mister, I guess I would. And you should get yourself a cell phone."

"A cell phone? What for?"

"Well, with this murder I might need to get hold of you when you're off duty."

"Lori, when I'm not on duty, I'm at home and you have my home phone number. When I'm on duty I'm here or in the squad car which has a two-way. Why in the hell would I need a cell phone?"

"It's the twentieth century, Pete. Get with it."

"I am as with it as I care to be, thank you very much."

Approximately forty-five minutes later, Lori's information coordinating prowess would be tested when Pete's voice crackled over the two-way radio. Pete had just left The Allemane and was on his way to the Rainbow Golf and Country Club. He wanted Lori to call the weather office and find out what time that rainstorm had blown through town the night before. She did, and five minutes later she was on the two-way informing Pete that the storm had drenched Rainbow at six-twenty. Another task performed to perfection, and it wasn't even nine a.m. yet.

When Wood arrived at the station, Lori wasted no time in filling him in on how hard she had been working for the past hour. "I've been answering this phone ever since I sat my sweet little butt down in this chair," she said.

"Did anybody have anything for us about last night?"

"No," Lori replied. "Everybody wanted to know if what they heard was true."

"I hope you didn't give them any details," cautioned Wood.

"I couldn't. I don't know any details."

"Good."

"So?"

"So what?"

"So, what are the details?"

"I'll let you know as soon as I know more, Lori," said Wood, sidestepping Lori's question. Wood knew that Lori often had coffee with Roberta Fry who managed the fabric shop next door. Sometimes it seemed that Roberta had more information about the comings and goings of the Rainbow Police Force than either Wood or Pete did, and Wood suspected that Lori's loose lips may have been the source of Roberta's vast knowledge.

"I heard the killer left a note," said Lori, trying to prime the information pump.

"Who told you that?"

"One of the people who called."

"No, there was no note," replied Wood.

"Okay, no note. Was she found naked on her bed like Marilyn Monroe?"

The phone on Lori's desk buzzed. Lori stared at Wood, waiting for an answer to her Marilyn Monroe question. The phone line buzzed again.

"Lori," said Wood, "shouldn't you be answering the phone?"

"Oh, it'll just be someone else asking about Bonnie. So, naked or not?"

"Lori, would you answer the phone please? It might be someone with a lead for us."

"Oh, all right," said Lori.

"Thank you."

Lori picked up the receiver. "Cop shop," she said.

Wood's eyes opened like saucers and his jaw dropped. Lori grinned at Wood and pushed down a button which connected her to line one. "Good morning. Rainbow Police," she said, still smiling at Wood. " . . . . Just a minute please." Lori set the receiver causally on her shoulder. "It's your wife. I mean, your ex-wife. No wait, she's not your ex-wife yet, is she? How's that going anyway? Are you two getting back together or is it splitsville for good?"

"Lori," Wood said pointing to the receiver on Lori's shoulder. "Did you put her on hold?"

Lori looked at the receiver and then down to the phone on her desk. "Oops." She put the receiver to her ear. "Sorry, Mrs. Lynch. Here's Wood."

Wood moved to his desk and answered the phone. "Hi, Jeannie."

"Hi, Bobby."

"Sorry about that," he said.

"Bobby, I've got some news," Jeannie began, getting right to her reason for calling.

"What news? Oh, shit, is this what you wanted to talk to me about yesterday?"

"Yes."

"Oh, I'm sorry. With this whole Bonnie Hoyt mess I forgot to get back to you about that."

"That's okay, Bobby. Listen. I've got a chance to manage a new Howard Johnson's that they're opening next month, and I..uh..I think I'm going to take it."

Wood didn't answer. His mind was racing.

"Did you hear what I said?" asked Jeannie.

"Yeah," replied Wood, feigning composure. "Manager, huh?"

"It's a really good opportunity for me, Bobby. You know, more money, a move up. But, even more than that, it shows that they have faith in me. I mean, they're going to let me run a brand new hotel. Me!" In her attempt to emphasize the positive side of her news, Jeannie sounded almost giddy on the other end of the phone. She paused briefly expecting Wood to ask where the new hotel was. He didn't. "So, uh . . . anyway," Jeannie continued, "they want me there next week. I know it's not a lot of time, but, uh..I have to get there to get everything organized before the hotel opens because I'm going to be in complete charge, you know, and I want everything to be right. Now, I was thinking that you could move into the house when we leave if you wanted to. Or should we sell it? I don't know. We could sell it I guess and divide up the..uh..you know, whatever we make on it." Jeannie paused again and then answered Wood's unasked question. "Bobby, the hotel's in Kingston . . . . Ontario."

Wood's mind stopped racing, halted by the name of city nine hundred miles away. The driving time to this city was about twelve hours, give or take. Nine hundred miles. Twelve hours. How often could he make that trip to see Jeannie and Ev? Nine hundred miles. Twelve . . . .

"So, what do you think?" Jeannie asked.

Her voice penetrated Wood's world and he struggled to muster an opinion for her. He wanted to tell her he didn't want her to go, that it would break his heart for her and Evan to be so far away from him. He wanted to tell her that they should have never split up, that they should be together right now and if they were, he would go wherever she wanted to go. He formed the words on his lips as he sat in the chair behind his desk. He would tell her right now and end this silly separation.

"Sounds like a big step," he said finally.

"It is. But, I think it's going to be so good for me," Jeannie replied. "It's a chance to prove myself. I mean, you never know what you can do until you try, right? Well, I want to find out. I want to find out just how much I can do."

"Well, I'm happy for you," said Wood.

There was a pause. Wood had given all the encouragement he could. He dared not say another word for fear that his voice would crack and expose the emotion that was being pent up inside him at this moment.

"I'm sorry, Bobby," Jeannie said, the exuberance leaving her voice. "I know it's far away, but . . . ."

"But what?" Wood asked after a slight hesitation.

" . . . . But, I've got to do it."

"Yeah. Look, Jeannie, I have to go. It's nuts around here right now with this Bonnie Hoyt thing going on, so . . . .

"Oh. Okay. But what about the house? What do you want to do?"

"Sell it," said Wood abruptly.

"You sure?"

"Yeah. Sell it."

"Because you could move in if you . . ."

"Sell it."

Jeannie paused for a second after Wood cut her off. "Okay. I'll call the realtor today then."

"Anything else?" Wood asked.

"No."

"Good. I'll talk to you later then."

"Yeah."

"Bye." Wood waited for Jeannie's goodbye from the other end of the phone line, but there was only silence. "Jeannie?" He wanted to get off the phone right now. He felt that if they spoke any longer she might deliver more bad news. "Oh, by the way, I've found another man and we're getting married," she would say. "He's rich, handsome and Evan calls him Daddy." After what seemed like forever, Wood finally got his wish.

"Yeah. Bye," came Jeannie's voice, and she hung up.

"Wood, I'm going to take my break now. Can you watch the phones?"

Lori's voice seemed to come from a faraway place. It reached into Wood's rapidly crumbling world and pulled him back to his desk at the Rainbow Police Station.

"What?" Wood asked quietly.

"I'm taking my break. Will you watch the phones for me?" Lori was gathering up her purse from the floor beneath her desk.

"Yeah, sure."

"Thanks. Can I bring you back a coffee?"

"Uh . . . yeah. Please."

"Okay. See you in a bit."

Lori breezed out of the front door of the police station. Wood watched the pretty young woman as her feet met the sidewalk outside and a gust of wind caught her shoulder length hair and pushed it across her face. Lori gave her head a gentle toss and like magic, the hair fell into place again and she disappeared from view. Wood continued to stare blankly at the street outside and within seconds of Lori's departure, a car pulled up to a parking meter directly across from the station and directly into Wood's view. Wood recognized the blue Toyota four-door as the one belonging to the Welton family. Behind the wheel sat Myrna Welton. She brought the car to a stop and Wood watched as she carefully put the vehicle into park. Then, she just sat there, staring straight ahead. After about thirty seconds, Wood decided that she must be waiting for someone. It couldn't be her mother-in-law because that woman never left the house, and it probably wasn't her daughter Peggy because she would be in school by now. Another thirty seconds passed and Myrna reached down and shut the car's engine off. Then she turned her head slowly towards the police station and looked in through the front door. Wood couldn't tell whether or not Myrna could see him in there. His desk was set back against the wall and the glass in a door can hamper a person's view if the sun is reflecting off of it a certain way, but just in case, Wood raised his hand slowly and gave Myrna a quick wave. She didn't respond. Instead, she opened the driver's side door and climbed out of the car. She clutched her purse in front of her with both hands, and without looking left or right, she started towards the police station. Wood heard the blast of a car horn off to his right and saw Myrna jump back against her car as another vehicle passed by, narrowly missing her. This brought Wood to his feet and he moved quickly to the front door. He stepped outside and looked at Myrna Welton who was now frozen in terror against the blue Toyota's driver side door.

"Myrna?" Wood called, "Are you all right?"

The woman didn't answer. Instead she looked left, then right, and then crossed the street to where Wood was standing. She looked up at the police officer and Wood could see, instantly, that she was troubled.

"Wood," she said, "we have to talk."

-18-

The Rainbow Golf and Country Club was on the eastern edge of town, built on what used to be Fraser Peacock's dairy farm. Fraser had long ago realized that farming was not going to provide adequately for his retirement and so, with some help from the bank and the provincial government's Business Initiative Support Program, Fraser and his wife Opal built an eighteen hole golf course on the property. That was fifteen years ago, and now, Fraser and Opal were the proud owners and operators of what had last year been rated as the third finest golf course in all of the Maritimes. Fraser, a man of only fifty-six, could now retire if he chose to, but he was enjoying this life too much to do that. Most of his days were now spent in the club's 'Duffer's Lounge', swapping stories over a flagon of beer with the many friends he had made since opening the golf course. Fraser didn't play the game himself, having never been bitten by the infamous golf bug, but he enjoyed the company of those who did play. He found them to be a grand group of storytellers who had no doubt mastered the art of the tall tale while filling out their scorecards.

Opal enjoyed the life as well, and found it far more to her liking than farming, which had never become her. She was more of a city girl at heart. She had grown up in Halifax and had met Fraser when the two attended university there. They were married a short time after graduating and were living in an apartment in Halifax when Fraser's parents were killed in a car accident. The elder Peacocks had just spent a week visiting their son and daughter-in-law and were on their way back to the family farm in Rainbow when they drove into a snow storm in an area known as the Tantramar Marsh. The Tantramar Marsh is a stretch of flat marshland just inside the Nova Scotia border, and it is famous for it's white-outs, a blowing snow which lowers visibility to the proverbial 'hand in front of your face', and makes driving an extremely treacherous undertaking. On this day, Mr. And

Mrs. Peacock's westbound automobile wandered over the center white line into the path of a large eastbound moving van. The impact crushed the car like a beer can and killed it's occupants instantly.

This tragedy left Fraser with a decision to make. He had grown up on the farm in Rainbow, and he knew that it would have been his father's wish that his son move back and work the place as it had been worked by three previous generations of Peacocks. Fraser, at twenty-five, now had to decide whether he and Opal should move to preserve the farming tradition, or stay in Halifax and begin carving out a new direction for the family name. He knew what the answer would be before the question was asked, and so, even though his heart wasn't in it, and even though Opal took some sizeable convincing, the two packed up and moved to the farm. Sixteen years later, Fraser wondered what his father would think of his son turning the cherished family property into, of all things, a golf course. He placated his conscience by telling himself that the old man wouldn't mind, so long as a Peacock still owned it.

Opal had only one stipulation about moving to the farm; she would not be expected to be a farmer. Moving there was gesture enough on her part, she thought, and so she took a job in Rainbow as a legal secretary, working for Maurice Leger, who had just hung out his shingle. The job was as much for Opal's sanity as it was for her salary, and she stayed with Maurice for the next sixteen years, taking only one leave of absence during that time period. That leave was to give birth to her daughter, Gabrielle. When they opened the golf course though, Opal knew that it would require an abundance of hard work to make a go of it, and so she left Maurice's employ, and settled in to help Fraser run the fledgling operation.

As much as Opal enjoyed the new life, she enjoyed even more, the way it changed her husband. As a farmer, he was in a sour mood at the beginning of the day and dead tired by the end of it. But, as a golf course owner, Fraser couldn't wait to get started each morning. He was a new man, or rather, he was the man he was when he and Opal first met, and this translated into an almost instantaneous improvement in their relationship as husband and wife.

The change in Fraser crystallized in Opal's mind the evening before they opened the Rainbow Golf and Country Club. Fraser wanted to take one last ride around the course to make sure that all was in readiness for opening day, and he invited Opal to join him. They drove the course in a motorized golf cart and talked about how their lives had twisted and turned over the past eleven years. They were both nervous and excited at the same time as they rode the dew-covered fairways in the May twilight, and at one point, Fraser reached over and laid his hand on Opal's hand and told her he was glad that they were going through this experience together. He would have been too scared to go it alone, he said.

As they approached the number fourteen green, and with the sun disappearing behind a wall of trees in the distance, Fraser brought the cart to a halt just off the edge of the green, and spoke of how he was excited about their future here and about how he felt that everything that had happened in the past sixteen years, good and bad, beginning with the deaths of his parents, had led he and Opal to this moment.

As he spoke, Fraser's hand slid gently off of Opal's hand and touched down on her slacks, on her inner thigh, a good distance above the knee. He seemed almost unaware of what he had done, for he continued to talk and gaze around at the panoramic view that lay before them in the dim light of dusk. But, Opal was acutely aware, and she parted her legs slightly to allow her husband's hand to nestle in more comfortably. After a moment, she reached down and slowly pulled his hand in tightly to her. His eyes left the countryside and turned to meet hers. In the next second, he leaned in and kissed his wife with a passion neither of them had felt in years. Then, without saying a word, Opal lifted Fraser's hand from between her legs and, still holding his hand, she stepped out of the cart, drawing Fraser with her. She backed up the slight incline towards the raised green, and when she reached the manicured grass where the fringe meets the smooth putting surface, she released Fraser's hand, stepped out of her shoes, and reached down and undid her slacks. Then, in one fluid, sensual motion, she took hold of her slacks at the hips and slid both the slacks and her powder blue underwear to the grass at her feet. Standing up straight now, and looking into her husband's eyes, she lifted her left foot out, and then her right, and the garments were off. Opal then laid herself down on the green, and Fraser came to her and made love to her as if it was the last time he ever would.

*

"Morning, Tom," said Pete, climbing out of his cruiser.

Tom had turned away when he saw Officer Golliger's cruiser pulling into the parking lot, and when the blue and white police car came to a stop beside his Cherokee, Tom kept his head down and pretended to be looking for something in the rear of his vehicle.

"Oh, morning, Pete," replied Tom, forging a look of surprise. "I didn't see you there."

"You didn't?" asked Pete.

"No, I was looking for my golf glove."

"Oh," continued Pete. "I thought I saw you looking my way when I pulled in through the gates back there.

"No," said Tom. And then he said it again as if once wasn't convincing enough. "No."

"I thought our eyes met."

"What?"

"I thought our eyes met. I thought we made eye contact."

"No," said Tom, "I didn't see you until just now."

"Oh."

"If I had of seen you I would have acknowledged you."

"Yeah, I guess you would have."

"I would have waved."

"And I would've waved back."

"I just didn't see you, that's all."

"I guess you didn't."

"Not until you said hi just now."

Pete was reminded of a line from a Shakespeare play. 'Methinks thou dost protest too much.' "So, did you find it?" asked Pete.

"Find what?"

"The golf glove."

"Oh!" replied Tom. "Yeah, it's in my golf bag."

"Gee, that would've been the first place I would've looked," said Pete.

"It *was* the first place I looked," replied Tom.

"Well, that would explain why you found it so quick."

Tom didn't answer this time. He sensed that Pete was having fun with him, in a cat and mouse kind of way, and he wanted no part of it. He reached inside the Cherokee, pulled out his golf bag and leaned the clubs against the back bumper.

"Don't they have lockers here?" asked Pete.

"What?"

"Lockers. Don't they have a place where you can store your clubs? I mean, geez, you're the pro here. You'd think they have a place where . . ."

"I've got a locker here," Tom interrupted. "I took my clubs home to clean them."

"Oh. I see."

"Was there something you wanted to talk to me about, Pete?"

"You cleaned them last night?" Pete said, ignoring Tom's question. He ran his hand over the head of Tom's shiny metal driver.

"Yeah. Why?"

"Well, it's just that with what happened to Bonnie last night, and knowing that you used to be her boyfriend, well, it's hard to picture a man in that situation sitting down to polish up his golf clubs the night of the murder. I would've thought you would've been . . . I don't know . . . not in the mood."

"On the contrary. I found it very therapeutic." Tom reached in and grabbed his golf shoes and then closed the rear gate of the Cherokee.

"You clean your shoes too?"

Tom looked down at the white and tan golf shoes in his hands. "As a matter of fact, I did."

"More therapy?" Pete asked.

"What do you want to know, Pete?"

"What?"

"Well, you've obviously come here to talk to me about Bonnie, so talk. I've got to give a lesson in ten minutes." Tom picked up his golf bag and began walking towards the club house.

"Oh, all right," Pete said, walking with Tom. "What were you doing in the graveyard last night?"

Tom stopped and gave Pete one of those furrowed eyebrow looks, the kind that says "How did you know that?"

"You said you had a lesson in ten minutes," Pete began, "so I thought I'd jump right to the important questions."

"I was visiting my father's grave." Tom began walking again.

"You do that every night?"

"Every night?" Tom chuckled. "No. We weren't that close. I do it once a year, on September twenty-first, the anniversary of his death, just to reassure myself that the old fuck is still dead."

Tom's father, Marty 'Sally' Lasalle, was a womanizer and a bully, who had driven Tom's mother, Virginia, to suicide when Tom was fifteen years old. Marty died two years later, the result of a hit and run accident on Rainbow's main drag, Main Street. The hit and run driver was never found, and up until Bonnie Hoyt's murder the night before, Marty's was the last suspicious death on the Rainbow police blotter.

"You're a good son, Tom," said Pete sarcastically.

"I try," replied Tom, his tone matching Pete's stride for stride.

"Well, did you happen to see anybody coming out of or going into Bonnie's backyard about the time you were there?"

"No, but, then I wasn't looking."

"I mean, the graveyard's only about what, fifty yards or so from Bonnie's place, right?"

"I said I wasn't looking."

"Oh." Pete sensed that Tom was annoyed by the questioning. It was a reaction that was encouraging to Pete. "Do you know if Bonnie was seeing anybody these days? Was she dating?"

"Couldn't tell you."

"You didn't talk to her?"

"No."

"You lived right across the street and you never talked to her?"

"No."

"What about Gabby? Did she talk to Bonnie much?"

"I doubt it," Tom snorted.

"Well, you knew that Gabby was the one who found her, huh? When she was taking that magazine over to her?"

Tom hesitated. "Yeah," he said finally. "Gab told me." Tom never called his wife 'Gabby' or Gabrielle. 'Gab' was more to his liking. Short and to the point.

"So, they must have talked some, if they were exchanging recipes."

"You'd have to ask Gab about that." The two men reached the clubhouse area and Tom placed his golf clubs on the back of one of a line of golf carts, and began strapping them in. It was a relatively easy process, pulling the strap around the outside of the bag and through a securing loop on the other side of the cart, something which Tom had done a thousand times before, but this time, he was fumbling with it.

"So, you don't know of anybody who had something against Bonnie, huh? A student maybe? A lover?"

"No."

"Oh."

"Hi, Tom." The cheerful voice chirped down from the steps leading to the front door of the clubhouse. It was Cindy Keller, one of the three women that Tom would be instructing on this morning. She smiled at Tom as she pulled on her red golf glove and fastened the velcro snap tightly at the wrist. Cindy wore a white tank top and yellow shorts out of which flowed a pair of long, creamy legs that reminded Pete of his ex-wife, Heather.

"Hi, Cindy," said Tom. "You all set?"

"All set," replied Cindy. "Francine and Kathy are already on the practice tee."

"Good. I'll be over in a couple of minutes."

"Okay." Cindy glided down the stairs as if Fred Astaire himself was waiting to greet her at the bottom, and then she grabbed the handle of a pull cart waiting for her there just off the cart path. "Hi, Pete," she said.

"How you doin', Cindy?"

"I heard about Bonnie." Cindy's tone of voice had suddenly shifted from cheerleader to sympathetic mother. "That's awful."

"Yeah, it was something," said Pete.

"Did you see Mickey last night?" The sympathetic mother had disappeared as quickly as she had appeared, and now the cheerleader was back. "Pretty good, huh?"

"Yeah, that was something too," said Pete.

"See you later,' said Cindy, and she and her pull cart moved off towards the practice tee.

Pete watched Cindy's legs and the ripple effect they had on the flesh encased by her yellow shorts as she walked. He was struck by how easily a person could express pity over a dead woman and then delight over a Jeopardy contestant in the space of two seconds. And then he thought, "What am I talking about? I'm investigating a friend's murder and being held spellbound by a woman's ass simultaneously."

"So, is that it?" Tom's voice broke into Pete's philosophical musings. Tom was sitting in the driver's seat of the golf cart now, and was taking off his shoes. He threw them into a wire basket behind the seat and began putting on his golf shoes.

"Uh . . . just one more question," Pete said. "You had a lesson last night?"

"Yeah."

"And what time was that?"

"Six-thirty."

"Who with?"

"Shelly Burtt." Tom had his legs crossed and was now putting on the second golf shoe.

"They don't have spikes," said Pete.

"What?"

"Your shoes. They don't have any spikes."

Tom looked down at the shoe in his hand. They were a new brand of golf shoe that featured raised treads instead of spikes. "No, the course doesn't allow metal spikes anymore. Just soft spikes or treads. Most golf courses are like that now."

"Oh."

"So, is that it? I've got people waiting."

"Yeah, that's it," Pete said, still looking at Tom's shoe.

Tom put the golf cart in reverse, causing the small vehicle's high-pitched beeping back-up signal to kick in. He backed the cart up onto the gravel path, put the gear into forward, and drove off towards the practice green without any hint of a goodbye. Pete didn't notice the absence of courtesy in Tom's exit. He was thinking about the golf shoe and how closely its tread resembled that of a hiking boot.

"Hi, Pete."

Pete's thoughts were interrupted yet again, this time by the pleasant voice of Opal Peacock. Pete looked towards the entrance to the clubhouse where Opal stood, hands on hips, like one of those sassy women that Barbara Stanwyk used to play in the movies. "Hi, Opal. How's the prettiest woman in Rainbow this morning?"

"You looking for a free round of golf, Copper, because you're going about it the right way."

"No," Pete smiled. "I'm just out here asking around about Bonnie Hoyt."

"Oh, God, Pete that is such a sin. Gabby called me last night after it happened and I felt as though I was going to be sick."

"I know," said Pete. He hung his head and kicked at the gravel with his boot.

"I mean, we loved Bonnie out here. She always had a smile and a friendly word. I just can't imagine."

"You don't know if Bonnie was seeing anybody, do you, Opal? Maybe somebody from the club here."

"Not that I know of. She used to come out here and play nine all by herself most mornings. Some mornings she'd hook up with Tom, but that was just . . . well, you know Tom's married to Gabby now and all."

"She played with Tom Lasalle?"

"Once in a while."

"Uh-huh." Pete looked off in the direction of the practice tee where Tom was now surrounded by his three students. "Listen, Opal, yesterday, do you remember Tom taking off between five and six?"

"Yes. He played a round with a couple of our members in the afternoon and then he went for supper at about five or quarter after."

"And he was back at six-thirty?"

"Yes, to give a lesson to Shelly Burtt."

"Uh-huh. How did he seem when he came back from supper?"

"What do you mean?" asked Opal.

"Well, did he seem normal? Was he acting, you know, different in any way?"

"No. Not that I noticed. The only thing different about him was that he had changed his shirt."

"His shirt?"

"Yes, he had a different shirt on when he came back. But, that's not unusual. Tom usually changes his shirt after a round. You know, it gets kind of sweaty when you're walking around out there."

"In September?"

"Well . . . I don't know about that, but, Tom always likes to look his best. In fact, he carries an extra shirt in his golf bag. Sometimes he changes right in the middle of a round."

"He carries an extra shirt in his bag?"

"Yeah. He's a bit of a narcissist, isn't he?" Opal laughed. "But, I'm not complaining. I mean, I could've wound up with a worse son-in-law."

"Uh-huh. All right, I want to get this straight, Opal, okay? I'm a little slow this morning. I haven't had much sleep. Now, when Tom came back from supper, you saw him wearing a different shirt, is that right?"

"Well, when he came back he had his jacket on. But, then he went to his locker to get his clubs and when he came back out, that's when I noticed the different shirt."

"So, he could've changed it at his locker."

"Well, he could have I suppose, but why would he go for supper wearing a dirty shirt and then change into a clean one when he came back? That doesn't make much sense."

It made sense to Pete, if Tom had gotten blood on the shirt during the time away from the golf course. "No, you're right, it doesn't," said Pete. "Like I said, I'm a little slow this morning."

"Why are you asking about Tom? You don't think he had anything to do with it, do you?"

"No, I'm just asking," said Pete. "Right now I'm like a drunk stumbling around in the dark trying to find a light switch. I'm reaching for anything. I'll see you later, Opal. Thanks." Pete turned away from Opal, but before he could take one step towards the parking lot, her voice turned him back to her.

"He's not messing around on my Gabby, is he?" Opal asked.

"What?" Pete heard the question clearly, but he was stalling until he could think of a diplomatic reply.

"I mean, I've heard the stories about Tom and I know what his father was like and . . . well, they say the acorn doesn't fall too far from the tree, so . . ."

"Opal, I don't know if he is or not," Pete said. "I honestly don't know."

"Maybe with one of them?" Opal nodded towards the three women standing on the practice tee with Tom. One of them, Cindy Keller, threw her head back and laughed and then gave Tom a playful slap on the arm. "I mean, I see him out here with these women all the time, giving them lessons, flirting with them, but I tell myself that nothing ever comes of it. Meanwhile, my little girl is . . . well, she's not the girl she used to be, Pete. He's changed her. She's . . ." Opal swallowed her next word and looked off to a spot on the horizon. Pete could see that she was on the verge of tears and it hurt him. He reached up and touched Opal soothingly on the forearm.

"I don't know if he's cheating or not, Opal. I honest to God don't."

"Well, if you find out that he is . . . would you shoot him for me?"

"Oh, absolutely. You can count it."

"Thank you."

"Now, I've got to go. Okay?"

Opal nodded and forced a smile across her lips. "You come back for that free golf game sometime, huh?"

"I will."

Pete turned and started back towards the parking lot and his awaiting police cruiser. He ran over the facts, as he knew them, in his head. Tom was seen in the graveyard, only fifty yards from Bonnie Hoyt's house around the time that Bonnie was killed. When he came back to the golf course, Tom was wearing a different shirt. His golf shoes could have left the tread marks in the mud. "No," thought Pete. "No. Shit. The rain didn't happen until twenty after six. Tom was seen in the graveyard at about five after. Well, maybe he went back. Maybe he forgot some . . . . No. Shit. He made his golf lesson at six-thirty. He wouldn't have had time to go back to Bonnie's and still be at the lesson by six-thirty. Shit!"

Pete was angry at himself for not being better trained for a case like this. Whatever he did learn about murder investigations at Holland College all those years ago had atrophied due to a lack of practical application. Then, before he even realized he had walked this far, his hand was opening the police cruiser door.

"Pete?"

Pete turned around to see Tom Lasalle sitting in his golf cart at the rear of the cruiser. The officer was so lost in thought, he hadn't heard the golf cart whirring across the gravel in the parking lot.

"Leo Terrio."

"What? What about him?" asked Pete.

"Well, you were wondering if Bonnie had any enemies and I was thinking Leo might have something against her because Bonnie was the one who had to tell him that the parents didn't want him instructing the high school boxing club this year."

"Oh," Pete laid his arm across the top of the squad car and looked at Tom. "Did Bonnie tell you this during one of your golf games with her?"

" . . . . I see my mother-in-law has been sticking her nose in where it doesn't belong, huh?"

Pete ignored Tom's dig at Opal. "I thought you and Bonnie didn't talk," he said.

"I was being discreet, all right? I didn't want you to think that Bonnie and I had a thing going. News like that travels fast in Rainbow."

"Did you have a thing going?" asked Pete.

"Forget it," said Tom. "I told you about Leo because I was trying to help. You don't want to look into it, fine with me. Go fuck yourself."

Tom stepped on the pedal and the golf cart lurched forward.

"Tom?!" Pete yelled. Tom stopped the cart and looked back at the police officer. The two men appeared as though they were preparing for a mini show down right there in the parking lot of the Rainbow Golf and Country Club, some three thousand miles northeast of the historic O.K. Corral. "You changed into a different shirt after supper last night. Any reason?"

"Yeah, I spilled food on myself."

"Uh-huh. And where's that shirt now? The one with the food on it."

"At home. Probably washed by now. Gab was going to do a laundry this morning."

"Okay, then," Pete began, "Why don't I just cut the bullshit and ask you the big question, all right? Where were you between the time you left here at about five yesterday and the time you were seen leaving the graveyard?"

"Gee, Pete, you sound like a real policeman when you put it that way," Tom said with a smile that made Pete want to give him a sand wedge enema.

"Well?"

"I went to Burger King and got a cheeseburger and some fries. I used the drive-thru where I was waited on by some blotchy-faced sixteen year-old. I don't know who it was and I doubt if he knew me in case you're looking to corroborate my story. I ate the burger and fries in my car in the church parking lot, where I spilled some ketchup on my shirt, then I went to the graveyard and I was there until a little after six."

"You were visiting your father's grave for that long? I thought you didn't care for the man."

"My mother's buried there too. She's worth the time." Tom stepped on the pedal on the floor at his feet and he and the golf cart moved off towards the practice tee and his eagerly awaiting students.

Pete watched the Shriner-like vehicle trundle off with its passenger, and then he climbed into the front seat of his cruiser. "Fucking jerk."

-19-

Bryden Downey awoke on the morning of September the twenty-second to find himself alone in the queen size four-poster bed that he and his wife Grace had shared for the past ten years. Groggy at first, it took him a couple of minutes to recall the events of the night before when he had come home to an empty house. He remembered the conversation with the dispatcher at the cab company, remembered how cleverly he had gotten the information he wanted from the dispatcher, remembered there was a truck stop. Shiner's Truck Stop. Tomorrow he would go to Shiner's and, using his position of power in the District Attorney's office, he would get some answers from someone there. Today, however, would be business as usual. A meeting at ten o'clock with the outgoing District Attorney of Penobscot County, Thomas Antonetti. Following that, an important eleven o'clock briefing with the team handling the state's case against an accused child killer. Bryden would inform the team at this meeting that he would be stepping in to handle the case personally. It was a very high profile case, the kind that would help Bryden in his upcoming run for the District Attorney's job.

Following the eleven o'clock briefing, Bryden would meet with Pam Carpenter in the law offices of Huddleston and Greenblat on the other side of town. Pam was recovering nicely from her assault at the hands of Grace at the Governor's Ball two nights ago, and the only remaining sign of the one-sided tussle was a slight cut on Pam's left temple where her head had slammed into the paper towel dispenser.

In Pam's office, Pam and Bryden would split a Chef's Salad which Bryden would pick up on his way over, they would discuss a plea bargain offer that Bryden had made to Pam yesterday and which Pam had planned to talk over with her client last night, and then, with business out of the way, they would almost certainly make love on Pam's maroon-colored leather couch. They had done this so many times before that it had developed into a routine. Pam would go to the couch, reach up under her skirt and pull off her pantyhose and panties. While Pam was doing this, Bryden would remove his pants and lay them over the back of the chair in front of Pam's desk. That would be followed by the removal of his suit jacket which he would drape over the back of the same chair. He would then go to Pam who would now be sitting on the couch with her skirt or dress hiked up to her waist and her lower body exposed. Bryden would kneel down on the floor between Pam's open legs, and they would kiss for a moment. If there was time, Bryden would put his face between Pam's legs and bestow some oral foreplay on his mistress. If time did not allow them the luxury of said foreplay, Bryden would simply enter her and complete the act in somewhere between two, and two and one half minutes. Bryden was nothing if not consistent.

After the lunch/meeting/conjugal visit, Bryden would head back to his office for a one-thirty meeting with a man who Bryden had recently hired as his campaign manager for his run at the DA's job. The two men would discuss campaign strategy for an hour or so, and then Bryden would spend the remainder of the afternoon tying up loose ends on a couple of other cases, and clearing his calendar for the following day. He wanted tomorrow to be free and clear.

At approximately the same time that her husband was arriving at his office in downtown Bangor, Grace Downey was approaching the corner of Main and Grandy Streets in downtown Rainbow, one hundred and twenty miles to the north. Grace had spent a pleasant few minutes chatting with ex-boxer Leo Terrio over breakfast at The Allemane Inn, and then she excused herself to go for a walk and take in whatever sights the town had to offer. As it turned out, the sights were few and far between, and by the time Grace reached her present location, her interest had been piqued only once, about a block ago, by a little antique shop called 'Teeks' next door to the Frying Dutchman. She hadn't noticed the shop last night when she climbed down from Dan's eighteen wheeler, or when she sat in Pete Golliger's police car listening to Wood Lynch break the news to Pete about Bonnie Hoyt. She decided that on her way back to the Allemane, she would stop into the antique shop and have a look around. She wouldn't buy anything though, for what would be the point? What sense did it make for a woman on the run to be toting an antique lamp or a small statue of Stalin with a clock in his stomach.

Standing now on that corner in Rainbow, Grace was suddenly startled by the blaring sound of a car horn off to her right. She looked up the street in the direction of the sound and saw a woman backed against a blue Toyota four-door. The woman clutched her purse to her chest and appeared frozen there in fear. Then, from a doorway across the street, under a sign which read, 'Rainbow Police', a uniformed officer appeared. It was the same officer that Grace had seen at the crime scene last night.

"Myrna?" the officer called out, "Are you all right?"

The woman didn't answer. Instead she moved across the street to where the officer stood, said something to him, and then the two disappeared into the police station. The next thing Grace felt was something bumping into her legs just above the knees. The bump caused her to stumble forward and, feeling she was about to tumble face first to the sidewalk, she reached out to stop herself, only to look down and find her outstretched hand heading straight for a blue baby's bonnet. The bonnet was secured to the head of an infant who lay there in his stroller, innocently chewing on a baby's rattle, while his mother stood staring into the window of Doug Petty's La-Z-Boy Furniture Store. Grace quickly altered her hand's course to a higher flight path and managed to avoid contact with the tyke's noggin, but her forward momentum carried her crashing into the mother who, having felt the bump against her baby's stroller, was now staring at Grace with ever-widening eyes. Grace's right hand glided over the woman's shoulder and clothes-lined the window-shopping mommy just as the woman began a startled scream. The scream was instantly transformed into a muffled 'Arggg' when the crook of Grace's arm met the woman's larynx.

"Shit!" said Grace. "I'm sorry." The out-of-towner righted herself and removed her arm from around the mother's neck.

"That's . . ." the woman choked as if trying to dislodge a wad of hair from the recesses of her throat. "That's all right," she said finally.

"No, it's not," said Grace apologetically. "I wasn't watching where I was going. I heard a car horn up there and . . . ."

"No, it's fine," said the woman. "I didn't even see you. I was looking in the store window."

"Are you all right?" Grace asked.

"Yes, fine. Thank you."

As the two women stood gathering themselves, a baby's rattle catapulted out of the stroller and came to rest on the sidewalk near the curb. Grace picked up the rattle from the pavement and placed it back in the infant's hands. "There you go, sweetie," she said. Grace watched the baby put the rattle up to his mouth and begin licking and drooling over it.

"Oh, honey, let me clean that off before you put it back in your mouth," the mother said. Then she took the rattle from her child and rubbed it back and forth on her Chino-clad hip for a few seconds. "There you go. That's better." And she handed the rattle back to her baby.

"He's a cute little guy."

"Thank you."

There was an awkward pause as the mother and her sidewalk assailant looked down at the baby.

"Well . . . goodbye," said the mother, and she pushed the stroller forward and continued on her way.

"Goodbye," said Grace. "Sorry." Grace watched as the young woman pushed the stroller along the sidewalk. She looked at her watch. Nine twenty. Bryden would be in his car on the way to the office right now. Or would he go into work today? Would the sudden disappearance of his wife cause him so much anxiety that he wouldn't be able to function properly? Would he be worried about her? Would he be looking for her? She didn't care about the answers to the first two questions, but the third one was disquieting. Should she keep moving, get out of this town, or should she stay put. 'Lie low', as they say in those old detective movies. Yes. She would wait here for a day or two and then head to her parent's home in Chicago after Bryden's search, if there was one, had de-intensified.

Grace watched the woman with the stroller cross to the other side of the street at a crosswalk, and then, without realizing it, she sighed, and turned, and walked smack into a young man who was headed towards the front door of Doug Petty's La-Z-Boy. Both she and the young man said "Excuse me" simultaneously. Grace, feeling much like a human pinball at this point, backed up a step and looked at the victim of her most recent assault. He was about twenty-four or twenty-five she surmised, and under his tan windbreaker he was wearing a white shirt and a tie which featured a pattern of small yellow diamonds. "I'm so sorry," she said.

"That's okay," replied the young man, and then he took a set of keys out of his windbreaker pocket. Looking down, he selected one of the keys on the Montreal Canadiens key chain, and eased it into the lock on the front door of the La-Z-Boy store.

Grace stood there and watched. She knew this young man. She had seen that face recently, but where? The young man attempted to turn the key in the lock but it resisted. He turned it back to the left until it was straight up at twelve o'clock again, and then he turned it to the right once more. Grace heard a click and the young man pushed the door open and went inside. Turning to close the door, he was surprised to find the woman he had just collided with, staring at him. He gave her a slight, awkward smile and began to close the door. He closed it slowly, for the woman looked as if she was going to say something to him . . . but she didn't. Instead, her eyes narrowed in a manner reminiscent of Clint Eastwood, and she continued to stare. The young man was closing the door in an excruciatingly slow fashion now, and staring back at the woman through the ever-shrinking door opening. He raised his eyebrows, inviting that comment which he knew was lurking on the end of her tongue, a hairbreadth from her lips, but the comment was not forthcoming and the door was barely open a sliver now.

"Oh-h-h-h," Grace finally said. "Oh, that's it."

The young man pulled open the door and looked at Grace.

"You were on Jeopardy last night, "she said. "Yes, I watched you at that restaurant up the street here."

Mickey Welton looked up the street to where this stranger was pointing. "The Frying Dutchman?" he said.

"Right. That's the place. Yes. You were good. I thought you did well."

"Thank you."

"Yeah, that Babylonian King question was a tough one."

"Who was Nebuchadnezzar?"

"Yeah, Nebuchadnezzar, wow. Good for you."

"Thank you," said Mickey.

"You work here, do you?" Grace said after a cumbersome pause.

"Yeah," said Mickey. "We open at ten if you're looking for something."

"No. No, I'm not in the market for any..uh.." Grace looked through the showroom window to see what was for sale inside. "Furniture! I'm not in the market for any furniture right now. So..uh..anyway, I'll let you go,"

"Okay," said Mickey.

"Nice talking to you."

Grace had never been star struck in her life, not even when she was introduced to James Taylor after a concert in Bangor a few years ago. She conducted herself in a very composed way during that backstage meeting. She didn't even tell the singer how much she enjoyed his music, even though he was an idol of hers and even though she had called in all of the outstanding favours she was owed in order to secure the backstage pass. But now, here she was making a fool out of herself over a Jeopardy contestant. She shook her head and started back for her room at The Allemane.

-20-

"Have a seat, Myrna," said Wood, pulling out a chair for the obviously troubled woman who stood before him.

"Thank you," Myrna replied, and she sat down, holding her purse in her lap and her gaze to the floor.

Myrna Welton had grown up in the small mining town of Minto, New Brunswick, about forty miles to the north of the capital city of Fredericton. Her parents, Jewel and Peter Daneko were strict Baptists who raised Myrna and her sister Jillian to be mindful of their elders, and to be faithful to the word of God. Jillian took those teachings to heart and became a missionary, and she was now working, selflessly, to help the poor in Guatemala. Myrna, on the other hand, had a great affection for children, and she decided that motherhood was to be her calling. She dreamed of the day when she would fall in love, get married and have toddlers of her own that she could hug, and laugh with and sing to sleep at night. So anxious was she for her dream to come true, that many felt she had neglected to wait for the right man to come into her life. Instead she married a slightly bent over young fellow named Jack Welton whom she met on a bus trip from Minto to Moncton.

Myrna was traveling to Moncton on a buying trip for her mother. The family car was in the shop with a blown transmission and Myrna's mother Jewel was badly in need of her favourite brand of denture adhesive. They sold denture adhesive at Kelly's Konvenience in Minto, but it was the Fasteeth powdered brand adhesive and Jewel much preferred the holding power of Fixodent which came in a tube. She had run out of her Fixodent two days before, and when the garage called to say that their car wouldn't be ready for another week yet because their mechanic was down with the flu, Jewel decided that she simply could not go on that long with her upper teeth unfastened and bouncing around inside of her mouth like a plastic hockey puck, so she gave Myrna bus fare, and instructed her to go to the Shopper's Drug Mart in Moncton and buy up as much Fixodent as she could carry.

When Myrna boarded the green and white SMT bus that morning, she found there were only two seats available. One was next to an older gentleman who had drifted off to sleep and had a rivulet of drool running from the corner of his mouth, down his chin, onto his neck and into his shirt collar where it finally disappeared. Myrna found herself glancing at the man's pant cuffs to see if perhaps a little drool delta was forming at his feet. It wasn't, and Myrna moved on to the next available seat beside a young fellow with round shoulders.

Myrna would later claim that she was attracted to Jack by his handsome tweed sports jacket with the suede elbow patches. She thought a jacket like that spoke volumes about a man. He must be an English professor, she assumed, or perhaps something even more exciting, such as a poet on his way to perform a reading of his works at a university.

As it turned out, the tweed jacket was on loan from a neighbour and Jack explained that he was headed to a meeting with the manager of a Moncton grocery store where he was sure he was going to land the assistant manager's job. His father, Buster had set up the meeting with the manager, an old friend of his, much in the same way that Willy Loman had set up a job interview for his son Biff in Death Of A Salesman. Sadly, in Jack's case, the results were much the same as Biff's. Jack wound up getting into an argument with his father's old friend over the price of apples, and the meeting careened madly downhill from there.

"How come," Jack began, "when you pick apples at a u-pick, you can get them for about ten cents a pound, but when you buy them in your store, they're marked up to forty cents a pound? How come?"

"Well, Jack," the manager replied, "when you buy them in the store, someone else has already done the picking and the shipping for you."

"And that gives you the right to jack the price up four hundred percent?" asked Jack.

"Well, I wouldn't call it jacking the price up," the manager said patiently, "It's a price that we've found to be reasonable and competitive in today's market."

"Reasonable my sorry ass," Jack continued. "It's a goddamned ripoff."

"I beg your pardon?"

"It's a fucking ripoff."

"A fucking ripoff?" said the manager calmly. "Oh, good. I thought you said it was a goddamned ripoff."

"It's both! I mean, the ordinary Joe hasn't got the money to buy half of the shit you're selling here."

"Shit?"

"Yeah," said Jack, "I'll tell you something. When I get to be the assistant manager here, I'm going to start marking these prices down so people like me can afford to buy this stuff."

"*When* you get to be the assistant manager? Don't you mean, 'if'?"

"What do you mean, 'if'?" Jack replied. "Dad said you were an old friend of his and that you were going to give me a job."

"I told your father I would give you an interview," the manager replied.

"An interview?"

"Yes."

"A job interview?"

"Yes."

"You mean like where we sit down and you ask me about my qualifications and stuff and I try and make a good impression on you?"

"Yes, one of those."

"Oh. And is this it now?"

"Now? No. No, I'm afraid that was it that just ended. Now – this moment right here? – is you and I parting ways. Have a nice day, Jack."

Jack spent that night at the Thriftylodge Motel next door to the Moncton bus station. He passed the evening lying on his bed, hands behind his head, staring up at the water-stained ceiling, wondering what he did wrong in the interview. Maybe the manager didn't like Jack's tweed jacket. As he lay there in room one fourteen, his mind drifted to the young lady he had met on the bus today. She said her name was Myrna Daneko, and she talked to Jack as if he was somebody that mattered. As if he was a valuable human being. Jack didn't get that kind of treatment very often, and he liked the way it felt, so on his way back to Rainbow the following day, he got off the bus in Minto and found the nearest pay phone.

"Hello?" Myrna said.

"Hello, could I speak to Myrna please?"

"Speaking."

"Oh. Myrna, this is Jack Welton."

"Yes?"

"We met on the bus yesterday, remember?"

"Oh, yes! Of course, I remember," said Myrna with a smile. "Well, isn't this a surprise? Are you calling from Moncton?

"No, I'm in Minto."

"Oh. Well, how did you find my number?"

"Well," explained Jack, "when I got off the bus here, I went to a phone booth and looked up Daneko in the phone book, and there was only one Daneko there, so I figured it must be the number."

"Oh. Well, it is," Myrna giggled.

"So, uh, did you get your mother's Fixodent all right?"

"Yes. Yes, I did, thank you for asking," replied Myrna. "They had a case of it in the back and I purchased the whole thing. Mother thinks it should last her a good two years if she doesn't eat too much corn on the cob."

"Great," said Jack. "That's great. So, listen, I was wondering if you'd like to do something tonight."

"Do something?"

"Yeah. I mean, I'm in town and I thought we could . . . you know, go out."

"Tonight? Uh . . . . well, what about your new job? Don't you have to work?"

"I didn't take the job," replied Jack. "Inferior benefits."

"Oh, I see. That's too bad. Well, um . . . . well, sure, we could do something I suppose. What would you like to do?"

"I don't know," said Jack. "What do people do here for fun?" There was a pause at the other end of the telephone. An unusually lengthy pause. "Hello?" said Jack.

"Yes, I'm still here," said Myrna. "Let me see now. For fun. Uh . . . ."

"Never mind," said Jack. "How about if I just come over to your place and we can figure out something when I get there?"

"Oh, all right. I live at thirty-seven Kellogg Street."

"Kellogg. Okay, and how do I get there from where I am?" asked Jack.

"Well, where are you now?"

Jack looked around at the area surrounding his phone booth. There was a small convenience store to his left, a couple of houses across the street, and to his right, an Esso full service gas station. He looked at the sign above the convenience store. "I'm in a phone booth right next to a place called 'Kelly's Konvenience.'"

"Kelly's Konvenience?" asked Myrna. "Is Konvenience spelled with a K?"

"Uh . . . ." Jack looked over at the convenience store again and checked the sign. "Yeah."

"And you're in a phone booth next door to it?"

"Uh-huh."

"Okay, do you see the house across the street? The white one with the green trim?"

Jack looked at the two bungalows across the street. The house on the left was white with red trim. Next door was the white with green trim. "Yeah, I see it."

"Well, I live in the house next to it. The one with the red trim."

Jack looked to the right of the front door of the red-trimmed house and into a large picture window where he saw Myrna standing with a telephone in her hand.

"Hi Jack!" Myrna said waving. "Come on over."

Jack did go over and eight months later the couple was married and planning a family together. They would have four children, they decided, one right after the other so that the children could be playmates. Jack was without siblings growing up and he had always felt alone in the world. The fact that he was a completely unlikable person and tended to repel anyone who might think to befriend him never entered his mind as being a reason for his loneliness.

And so, having drawn up the blueprints for the brood they were going to assemble, Myrna and Jack set about laying the foundation. For the first three years of their marriage they tried desperately to have children. Their efforts were yeoman-like. They had more sexual intercourse than Myrna thought was permissible under the Baptist guidelines, but try as they did, she was not getting pregnant. She went to her doctor to see if perhaps she was what her mother would term 'barren', but the tests proved that Myrna's would be a fertile garden for any seeds that might be planted there, and this prompted the doctor to suggest that perhaps the problem rested with the gardener, Myrna's husband Jack.

"There's nothing wrong with me," Jack insisted when Myrna suggested he get himself checked. "I could knock up any woman off the street tomorrow if I wanted to." Myrna proposed that they should save the 'street test' as a last resort, and that Jack should go to the doctor now to see if there was anything amiss with his plumbing. After weeks of protest and several more sessions of non fruit-bearing intercourse, Jack finally acquiesced and paid a reluctant visit to the doctor. When the test results showed that Jack lacked the necessary sperm count to impregnate so much as a field mouse, it was as if someone had lopped off his testicles and sent them wheeling across the tile floor. He felt inadequate. He felt incomplete. He felt betrayed.

Eventually, Jack and Myrna would adopt young Mickey, and after that, their daughter Peggy, but Jack was never the same man. The sexual liaisons between he and his wife dropped off to what Myrna now felt was far below the minimum required under Baptist law. Nevertheless, she didn't harp at Jack, for that was not Myrna's way. Instead, she tried as best she could to create a pleasant home environment for her family. But now, here she sat opposite officer Wood Lynch in the Rainbow Police Station, and her heart felt as though it would break into pieces at any moment.

"What is it, Myrna?" Wood asked. "What's the problem?"

"Well, I don't quite know how to approach this," she said, as she fidgeted idly with the clasp on her black purse.

"Approach what?"

"Well . . . . it's . . . it's my Mickey."

"What about Mickey?"

Myrna took her eyes off of her purse for a moment and glanced at the police officer across from her. She was too ashamed to hold his gaze though, and she quickly looked back down at her purse. "I think he killed Miss Hoyt."

"What?!" Wood leaned forward over the desk.

"I . . .," Myrna began. "I think my Mickey killed Miss Hoyt."

"You think . . . ." Wood took a moment to reflect on what this woman had just said. Mickey Welton? Mickey was a good kid. A real good kid. Why would he kill anybody? And why would his mother, a loving woman who always seemed to have her children's best interests at heart, be saying this? "I don't understand, Myrna. You think Mickey killed Bonnie Hoyt?"

"Yes."

"Why? Why do you think this?"

"Well . . . a number of reasons."

Myrna paused and continued to fuss with the clasp on her purse. Wood leaned back in his chair and opened his arms wide. "I'm listening," he said.

"Well," Myrna began slowly, "it has something to do with Jeopardy."

"Jeopardy?"

"Yes. You see, when Mickey came home from Los Angeles, he told us that he wasn't allowed to tell anyone how he did on the show before it aired on television. He said if he told someone, they would take away his prizes."

"The earthenware," said Wood.

"Yes, the earthenware."

"All right, go on."

"Well, I think that maybe Miss Hoyt got it out of Mickey somehow – You see, Mickey was very fond of Miss Hoyt and they had become quite close during the time that she was helping him prepare for the show–so anyway, I think that Miss

Hoyt got the information out of Mickey somehow, and then after realizing what he had done, and realizing that he might be in danger of losing his winnings . . . . well, after realizing this, he felt that he had to . . . ."

"Okay, wait a minute, Myrna. Wait a minute. Are you going to tell me that Mickey killed Bonnie Hoyt because he didn't want to lose his earthenware?"

"Well, he was very insistent that he couldn't tell anyone. He wouldn't even tell his own family how he did on the show."

"Well, sure, but, Myrna, come on."

"Well, let me finish, now, Wood, please. I mean, I have other reasons for thinking this. I wouldn't just come in here and accuse my own son of such an act if I didn't have cause."

Wood let out a sigh. "All right," he said impatiently. "What else?"

"Well, Miss Hoyt was supposed to come over to our house last night and watch the show with us, but she didn't."

"That's because she was dead."

"Yes, but when she didn't show up in time for the beginning of the broadcast, I suggested to Mickey that he should call her, but he declined."

"Yeah. And?"

"Well, I think that maybe he knew that she was dead and that's why he didn't call her. That's why he didn't seem surprised that she hadn't arrived yet."

"All right, look Myrna," Wood said, getting to his feet. "I know you mean well, but . . ."

"But, she had called earlier to say she would be there. She said she was bringing a bottle of champagne to celebrate Mickey's appearance on the show."

Finally, Myrna had Wood's attention. This would explain the bottle of champagne that was found on Bonnie's kitchen counter. "Bonnie called Mickey earlier?"

"Yes."

"Gee, Myrna, I wish you'd told me this sooner. This information could be important in solving this thing."

"What do you mean sooner?"

"Well, before now."

"But, it's only nine-thirty. How much sooner could I have told you? I mean, the murder only happened last night, and this morning I had to get Jack off to work and Peggy off to school, and . . ."

"All right, Myrna, all right. Never mind."

"Maybe if I could see the note."

"The what?"

"The note that the killer left. If I could see that then I could tell if it's Mickey's handwriting."

"There was no note."

"There wasn't?"

"No."

"I heard there was a note."

"No, there was no note. Could we get back to Bonnie's phone call? What time was that?"

"Around five o'clock. Mickey wasn't home from work yet and I took the call."

"What time did Mickey get home?"

"About five-thirty I think."

"You think or you're sure?"

"No, it was five-thirty. I'm almost positive."

"Well, the time of death was put at sometime after five-thirty, Myrna, so if that's accurate then Mickey couldn't have done it."

"What?" asked Myrna.

"That's right, so Mickey's off the hook."

Myrna let out a big breath and her body relaxed for the first time since she had heard about Bonnie's death. "Oh, my. Oh, Wood, that is such a relief. You're sure now, are you?"

"Well, like I say, if the expert is accurate, then you've got nothing to worry about."

Myrna smiled and Wood could see moisture forming in her eyes. "Oh, I'm so glad. Thank God. Because Mickey was home at five-thirty and he didn't go out again until six-thirty. Oh, thank God."

"He went out at six-thirty?" Wood asked.

"Yes, just after that rain we had. He went out to get some potato chips so we could have something to snack on while we watched Jeopardy. Well, that is a load off of my mind, I can tell you." Myrna stood and held her hand out to the police officer seated across the desk from her. Her hand was shaking. "Thank you, Wood. Thank you very much. Praise Jesus." Myrna turned and headed for the door, the weight of the world no longer on her shoulders.

"Myrna?" Wood said.

"Hmm?" Myrna stopped at the door and turned to face the officer.

"Does Mickey own a pair of hiking boots?"

"Hiking boots? Yes, he does. He bought a pair when he was in Los Angeles. They were cheap, he said. Of course with the exchange, I'm not so sure how much of a bargain they were." Myrna smiled. "Why do you ask?"

"Well, I might need to see those boots, just so we can clear Mickey for once and for all. I mean, we found some boot prints at the scene so, uh . . ." Wood spoke casually, not wanting to send Myrna into a relapse of concern, but he felt that if Mickey was out after the rain last night and if Mickey owned a pair of hiking boots, then it was his duty to check into it.

"But, you said, he couldn't have done it," Myrna said, her smile quickly disintegrating.

"Absolutely," Wood reassured her, "Absolutely. It's just that I have to check everybody who owns a pair of hiking boots. Everybody. It's nothing."

"Oh . . . all right," Myrna said haltingly. "Uh . . . I could bring them by later if you like."

"Whenever you can."

"I've got a few errands to run first. Maybe after lunch?"

"Whenever."

"Or around eleven maybe. I have to go over to the church to prepare the meals for the shut-ins, but I could be done by eleven I think."

"Eleven would be fine."

Myrna paused and then pushed on the door, opening it slightly and letting in the street noise from outside. She took a step and then stopped halfway through the door and turned back to Wood. "I'll get them for you now," she said.

"No, Myrna, listen . . ."

"No, I'll get them for you now. I want to put my mind at ease. I'll drive home and get them for you right now." And with that, the woman was out the door and heading across the street to her blue Toyota.

"Hi, Mrs. Welton!" Lori's voice called out.

Wood could see Myrna turn in the direction of the disembodied voice. She stood in the middle of the street now. Just then Lori came into Wood's view and she leaned her back against the front door, opening it slightly as she spoke to Myrna.

"I saw Mickey last night," Lori said. "He was great."

"Thank you," Myrna replied, still standing in the street.

"You're going to love that earthenware."

Myrna put her hand to her mouth and began to sob right there in the middle of Grandy Street. She turned and moved quickly towards her car.

"No, really," shouted Lori. "It's good stuff!"

Myrna sobbed a little louder and climbed into the Toyota.

"Really," said Lori trying to reassure the woman.

Wood watched as Myrna pulled her car away from the curb and disappeared from his view. Lori pushed open the police station door with her rear end and turned to face Wood. "What the fuck did I say?"

-21-

The sound of an eighteen wheeler gearing down to a stop always reminded Dan of an angry bull. It huffed and it snorted and, if it could, Dan was sure it would paw at the pavement to show its displeasure. This image jumped into his mind as he pulled his rig up in front of the Frying Dutchman in downtown Rainbow on the evening of September the twenty-second. He checked his watch and saw that it was seven-thirty. He had made good time from Halifax on this run. A little under six hours. He would stop here for a short while to check on the woman he had given a ride to the night before, then he would head on to Bangor, stopping at Shiner's Truck Stop for a meal, maybe catching some sack time in his truck in Shiner's parking lot, and then he would complete the trip to Boston tomorrow morning.

He had promised the woman – Grace, she was introduced as by Luanne, the waitress at Shiner's – he had promised her that he would be here tonight at about this time just in case she had changed her mind and wanted a ride back to Bangor to face whatever it was she was running from. She had told him it was her husband, and that he had given her the bruise which perched like an intrusive flaw on her otherwise immaculate face. The woman was very attractive and Dan was taken by her sense of humor, especially considering the situation she was in. Had the conditions been right, he would have flirted with her. Maybe he would have made an outright pass at her. But, under the circumstances, that would have been entirely inappropriate. And so, he dropped her off at The Frying Dutchman, wished her luck, and drove off into the night.

Parked out front now for the second time in as many nights, Dan chewed on his toothpick as he leaned down to look out of the passenger side window and into the restaurant. He could see the man behind the counter, the same man who had been talking to the policeman the night before when Grace climbed down from the big rig. The man appeared to be watching something on television now, as he and the policeman had been last night. Dan looked at the stools which lined the restaurant's counter. They were empty. In fact, the whole restaurant was empty except for a mother, a father and their two boys seated in a booth along the wall to the left. The two boys appeared to be about ten and seven years old. The three males of the family wore ball caps. The woman wore a smile as if this was a wonderful night out for her, and it probably was. Probably glad she didn't have to cook supper and wash up after these three tonight.

Dan began to sit up straight again when something caught his eye beyond the father's ball cap. There, in the very last booth, by herself, sat a woman twirling her hair around her index finger, and staring off into someplace located far behind her eyes. It was the woman he knew only as Grace. Dan felt his heart begin to beat a little faster as he climbed out of his truck, threw his toothpick to the pavement, and entered the diner.

"Evening," said the man behind the counter. He gave Dan a quick look and a nod and then turned his attention back to the television set.

"Hi," Dan replied. Dan looked up at the t.v. and saw Tom Brokaw's face. The NBC Nightly News was on. The truck driver walked towards the back of the restaurant past the family in the booth. As Dan passed, the father's gaze followed him. Dan noticed that all three males were wearing Boston Red Sox ball caps.

"Hello there," Dan said to the woman in the last booth.

Grace seemed startled, as if she had been shaken from a dream. "Oh, hi," she said, and she smiled up at the driver. "I'm sorry. I didn't see you come in."

"Can I join you?" Dan asked.

"Yes. Yes, of course," Grace replied, pointing to the seat across from her.

Dan sat himself down in the booth, and as he did, he noticed that the father in the booth behind him was still looking at him.

"So, you came," said Grace.

"I said I would," Dan replied.

"Well, that's very nice of you."

"No, like I told you last night. It's right on my way, so . . ."

"Well, it's very nice of you anyway."

"So, I don't see a suitcase anywhere. Does that mean you're staying?"

"Well, for another day or two I think," Grace replied.

"But, you came to meet me here anyway. Why?" Dan was hoping that the woman would say that she wanted to see him again. That she enjoyed his company yesterday and she thought it might be nice to spend a few minutes with him tonight. Maybe she would invite him to go out for a drink with her. There must be a bar somewhere in this town. They would go for a drink, maybe a couple of drinks, and then Grace would invite him back to her room. They would sit side by side on the small couch provided by the motel she was staying in, and every once in a while, Grace would laugh at something Dan said and she would reach out and touch his forearm innocently or slap him on the shoulder playfully, and if this warm discourse continued for a respectable length of time, Dan would take a chance and lean in to give her a kiss, and to his delight she would kiss him back, not hard, but gently as he suspected was her way, and then they would part and look into each other's eyes and they would both know that a far more passionate kiss was to follow, and it would, and Dan would hold Grace in his arms as they kissed and she would put her hand on the back of his neck and softly run her fingers up into his hair, and . . . .

"Well, I didn't want you to be waiting around here wondering whether I was or wasn't coming for that ride you offered," Grace said.

Dan's wishful daydream exploded into a million pieces. "Oh, I wouldn't have waited," he said.

"You wouldn't?" Grace asked with a hint of surprise.

"Yeah, I probably would have." Dan's stab at nonchalance had been thwarted almost immediately. "So, uh . . . you like it here, do you?" he asked.

"Well, it's an interesting place," Grace said. "It's quite interesting actually."

"How so?"

"Well, there was a murder here yesterday."

"A what?"

"Yeah," Grace said. "A murder."

"Go on."

"I was at the scene in fact."

"You what?"

"Yeah. Well, this police officer was giving me a ride to where I'm staying and we had to stop at the crime scene, so . . ."

"Wow."

"And I met an ex-boxer who lives in the place where I'm staying. And this morning I met a guy who was on Jeopardy last night."

"What?"

"Yeah. This young guy. Mickey something. He was on Jeopardy last night and he lives right here in this town."

"Well, you have had an interesting twenty-four hours," Dan said with a smile.

"Get you something?" asked Henry Van Etten as he approached the table.

"Uh . . . no thanks," said Dan. "I'm not staying."

The proprietor nodded and made a one hundred and eighty degree turn without even breaking his stride. He returned to his position behind the counter.

"So," Dan continued, "You're okay then, are you?"

"I'm okay," Grace replied, somewhere between self-assurance and not-so-sure.

"Good. Well . . . I, uh..I guess I'll get going then."

"Thanks for coming," said Grace.

"No problem," Dan said as he slid out of the booth. "You know, like I say, it was on my way. I hope everything works out for you. I'll see you."

"Take care," Grace replied. "Have a good trip."

"Thanks." Dan turned and headed for the front door of the Dutchman.

"Excuse me?"

Dan stopped. The father with the Red Sox cap was looking up at him.

"You're Dan Miller, right?"

"Yes, I am," Dan replied.

"I knew it!" the Dad replied, giving his wife a little nudge with his elbow. "I saw you play once at Fenway. It was about..oh..must have been . . . ."

"Fourteen years ago," said Dan.

"Right, fourteen years. Good memory."

"Well, I only played there for half a season so it's not easy to forget."

"Third base, right?"

"Third base," said Dan.

"You hear that, kids?" the father said to his boys. "This fella played third base for the Boston Red Sox."

"Well, not for long," Dan reminded them.

"Yeah, tough break. I mean, we had Boggs, right? There was no place for you."

"Yeah."

"Yeah, I'm a huge Red Sox fan. Have been all my life."

"Well, you'd have to be to remember me," Dan said humbly. He looked at Grace and saw that she was watching the encounter with a lingering smile. Dan had seen that smile before. When he was a boy just starting out in baseball, if he had played a good game, he would see that smile on his mother's face as they walked back to the car together. It was pride mixed with contentment. "Anyway," Dan continued. "It was nice meeting you. I'll see you all later." He moved to the front door, turned to give Grace a small wave, which Grace and the Red Sox fan returned, and then he stepped outside, fully prepared to climb back into his truck and continue his journey. He got as far as the driver's side door of the truck, and he stopped. "Aw, what the hell," he said out loud, and he marched back into The Frying Dutchman.

"Evening," said Henry Van Etten from behind the counter. He gave Dan a quick look and a nod and then turned his attention back to the television set as he had done when Dan entered for the first time three minutes ago. Henry was so transfixed by the newscast that he hadn't even noticed that it was Dan returning and not a new customer.

"Hi," Dan replied, and he marched to the booth at the back of the restaurant where Grace sat twirling her hair around her index finger. "Would you like to go for a drink?" Dan asked.

"A drink?" Grace was caught by surprise. "Uh . . . well . . ."

"Just one though because I'm driving."

" . . . . All right. Sure."

"Good. Where would you like to go?"

"Well, there's a little bar at the place where I'm staying," Grace offered. "We could go there."

"Sounds great," said Dan. His wishful daydream was quickly being pieced back together.

"Good. Well, let's go then."

"Get you something?" asked Henry, approaching the table.

"Uh, no," replied Dan. "We're just leaving. Here, this is for the lady's coffee." Dan reached into his pocket and handed the man two dollars.

"She didn't have a coffee," Henry replied.

"Oh, well, then this is for whatever she had."

"She didn't have nothin', did ya, ma'am?"

"No, I didn't."

"You see?" said Henry. "And the fella who came in before you didn't have nothin' either. I guess nobody's in the mood for refreshments tonight."

"Well, here," Dan said, putting the two dollars into Henry hand. "This is for your trouble then."

"Well, thank you," said Henry, staring at the two dollars.

"All set?" Dan said to Grace who was standing beside him now.

"Yep."

"Good. We're off then."

Dan and Grace headed for the front door.

"Wasn't no trouble though," Henry said as the couple walked away. "I mean, I gotta be here anyway. The fact is, I kinda appreciate the company."

Without looking back, Dan waved at Henry over his shoulder.

"Come again," said Henry, and he moved back to his place behind the counter and turned up the volume on his Magnavox.

*

Dan and Grace sat at one of four small tables against the wall of Kate's Place. The dimly lit bar entertained three other customers this night. One was ex-boxer Leo Terrio, who wasn't actually a customer, but the official greeter of the establishment, and indeed he had greeted Dan and Grace with a hearty "welcome" when they arrived. Leo now stood at the end of the bar with a glass of scotch in his hand. Grace recognized one of the paying customers as Louis Little, the man she was introduced to last night when Officer Golliger brought her over to check into the Allemane. Louis wore the same Kangol hat he had worn the night before and he sat on the same stool. Three stools down from Louis sat a young woman who looked to be barely of legal drinking age, if that. She wore tight jeans and a loose-fitting red blouse which highlighted her mane of bright red hair. Behind the bar was Kate Leger, the proprietor.

In the forty-five minutes or so that they had been in the bar, the conversation between Dan and Grace ran the gamut of topics from Dan's baseball career to Grace's home town of Chicago, to American politics. It had yet to touch on Grace's flight from her marriage.

"So, what do you think?" asked Dan.

"About what?"

"About what you're going to do?" he said. "Have you made up your mind yet?"

"You mean about my husband?"

"Yeah."

"Well, I think I'll just stay here for a day or two and then I'll make my way to my parent's place."

"Uh-huh. Make your way how?"

"I don't know. Find the nearest airport and fly down I guess."

"Nearest airport's Fredericton," Dan said. "About an hour east."

"Well, that's where I'll go then."

"Uh-huh." Dan paused and took a sip of his beer. "You know, I'll be back through here in three days. If you want to wait that long, I could give you a ride into Fredericton."

"No, I couldn't ask you to . . . ."

"Hey, it's no problem. It's right on the way."

"Again?"

"What?"

"Everything seems to be on your way," Grace said with a grin.

"Well, it is on my way. It's right on the way to Halifax."

"Hmm-hmm."

"Aw hell, even if it wasn't on my way," he said, "I'd still come and get you."

Grace seemed slightly embarrassed. She looked down into her glass of dark Canadian beer. "So, why aren't you married?" she asked.

"I told you back at the truck stop," Dan replied. "I haven't found a woman tall enough."

"Besides that," Grace said with a good-natured smile.

"Oh, I don't know," Dan said. "I guess I spent so much time trying to make my baseball career fly that I didn't have any time left over for a relationship."

"A lasting relationship you mean," Grace corrected.

"Any relationship," Dan said.

"Well, you must have had short-term relationships along the way. Months, weeks, days . . . . hours."

"Well, yeah, I mean, I didn't take a vow of celibacy. They don't make you do that as part of spring training."

"And what about after you quit baseball? Were there no relationships then?"

"I'm on the road too much," Dan replied.

"Oh."

There was another pause as Dan sipped his beer and Grace cast her eyes to the other patrons at the bar.

"I would, you know," Dan said finally.

"Would what?"

"Come and get you."

Grace looked into Dan's hopeful eyes and tried to find the words that would tell him that she liked him, but at the same time would let him know that she was not about to encourage him. "Look," she began, "you don't even know my last name."

"So, what is it?"

"Dan," Grace said, avoiding the question, "this..uh . . . this is a really bad time for me."

"I know it is. I just want to help you out."

"No, I think you want to do more than help me out."

"And if I do, what's wrong with that?"

"Well, what's wrong is, if I were to let something get started between you and I—and believe me, under better conditions, I would be quite open to that. Quite open.–but, if I did it now, then I wouldn't be any better than my husband, would I?"

"Oh. He cheated on you, did he?"

"Yes, and I found out about it and we had a fight and . . . well, here I am, bruised cheek and all."

"Uh-huh. Okay," said Dan. "I understand completely. I'm not happy about it, but I understand. And the offer still stands, by the way. I mean, if you want that ride, it's yours. No problem. I mean, it's . . ."

"Right on the way," Grace finished Dan's sentence for him.

"Right. Can I ask you one question though."

"Sure," replied Grace.

"That room of yours upstairs, does it have a small couch in it?"

"You mean a love seat?"

"Yeah, a love seat."

"Yes it does. Why?"

"No reason," Dan replied, and he downed the remaining contents of his glass of beer. "Well, I'd better get going."

"I'll walk you to your truck."

Dan and Grace rose from their table and moved to the bar where Dan reached into his pocket for some money.

"No, this one's on me," said Grace. "Kate, will you put these drinks on my room bill please?"

"Sure thing, Grace," said Kate.

"Thanks."

"You know," Louis Little piped up. "You would make a divine Honey."

"A what?" asked Grace.

"Honey. In my production of Virginia Woolf. You possess that look. You're a little mature for the part perhaps, but I think we could make it work."

"No, I won't be around long enough to be in your show. Sorry."

"Oh, so am I. Miss Hoyt was going to be Honey. You know, the poor woman who was murdered?"

"Yes."

"But, now I'm forced to recast. I thought of young Miss Welton here," Louis pointed to the redhead at the end of the bar. "But, her brother Mickey is playing Nick and somehow a brother and sister as husband and wife . . . well, there's something about it that compels one to shower, isn't there? So, now I'm up Shirley Booth Creek without a girdle."

"Well, sorry but I can't help you out," said Grace.

"What about your swarthy friend there?" Louis said, looking at Dan. "There's never a shortage of roles for strapping men in their thirties. We're doing Picnic in the spring. You'd be perfect. Take off your shirt."

"Pardon me?" said Dan.

"Your shirt. Take it off a la Bill Holden."

"Sorry, I don't live here. I won't be able to do your play."

"Well, take it off anyway." Louis burst into laughter.

"All right, Louis. Stop pestering my customers," said Kate, but she was laughing too.

"Goodnight," Grace said through her smile.

"Night, Grace," said Kate.

"Night, Grace!" Leo chimed in, and he moved to the front door and held it open for the departing couple.

Dan's truck was parked in front of the Allemane on Yarboro Street. When they reached the section of sidewalk nearest the passenger side door of the truck, Grace stopped and held out her hand to Dan.

"Well, I guess this is it," she said.

"Yeah," said Dan, shaking Grace's hand. "Listen, I hope everything works out for you."

"Thanks. I'm sure everything will be fine. And thank you for all your help."

"My pleasure."

Dan still held Grace's hand. He liked the way it felt and he didn't want to let go. If he dragged out this goodbye, maybe he could hold it for a few more seconds. But, before he could think of something else to say, Grace removed her hand from his and put both her arms around his neck, pulling herself in close to him and hugging him. "I don't know what I would've done if I hadn't run into you," she whispered into his shoulder. Dan put his arms around Grace's waist and softly returned her embrace. He ached for what was not going to happen between them.

No more words were spoken by the pair. The goodbye was complete now and they both knew it. Dan climbed into his truck and eased the impatient bull away from the curb and into the night. Grace stood and watched as the eighteen wheeler moved down Yarboro Street to the corner of Mary Street where it's taillights brightened as it slowed to a stop, preparing to turn right onto Mary, after which it would travel on to Main Street and then out of town to the highway. Grace raised her hand, even though Dan couldn't see it in the darkness of his rearview mirror. Inside his truck, Dan raised his hand, even though Grace couldn't see it from her place on the dimly lit sidewalk.

-22-

Wood Lynch rolled down the cruiser window and looked at the lone figure sitting on the bus stop bench across the street.

"Hi, Peggy."

"Oh, hi, Wood."

"Whatcha doin'?"

"What does it look like? I'm waiting for a bus."

"The buses stopped running a half an hour ago, Peggy."

"Oh. Well, I guess I've got a long goddamned wait ahead of me then, don't I?"

It had been a long day for Wood. After Myrna Welton had dropped off Mickey's hiking boots, Wood ran them over to Bonnie Hoyt's house and left them with Carrie Jardine, the head of the forensics team. Ms. Jardine said she would take the boots and the imprint from Bonnie's yard back to Saint John with her that afternoon, and she would probably have a full report for Wood and Pete the next morning. That errand completed, Wood returned to the police station where he met up with Pete who had just had a rather acerbic question and answer period with Tom Lasalle at the golf course. Pete expressed the opinion that Tom should be placed on the top of their list of suspects in Bonnie's murder. Wood agreed, but he also pointed out how the scenario of Tom being the murderer was just too neat a package. A woman is murdered with a golf club, her ex-boyfriend is a golf pro, and he lives right across the street from the victim. Federal Express could not have packaged this any better.

When his shift ended at four o'clock, Wood drove over to Jeannie's house to pick up Evan, and he and the boy went to Moran Park to play catch with Evan's mini football. After an hour or so of this, Wood treated his son to a supper of fast food at the MacDonald's in the Hawthorne Mall, and then it was back home to Jeannie's where Wood dropped the boy off at exactly five-thirty.

"How much does Daddy love you, Ev?"

"Bigger than a . . . . dinosaur?"

"Way bigger."

Evan ran up the walk to his mother's waiting arms as Wood watched. Jeannie invited Wood to come inside for a minute, but the officer declined saying he had to get an hour or two of sleep before his next shift. As he drove away from the small house he once shared with his wife and child, Wood thrust his arm out of the cruiser window and gave a big wave. The woman and child stood at the foot of the home's front steps, Evan smiled widely and waved his arm in broad strokes from side to side. Jeannie held up a hand. There was no smile. That image was still with Wood when he laid himself down on his bed fifteen minutes later, and it kept him from sleep for the next several hours, eventually forcing him to surrender any notion of rest before his next shift. His quest for slumber defeated, he rose, showered, and headed back out onto the quiet streets, hoping that work would eradicate the thoughts of his wife and child's impending departure to another province.

"Have you been drinking, Peggy?" Wood asked the attractive young redhead.

"I'm legal," she replied.

"That's not what I asked you, Peggy. I asked you if you'd been drinking."

"As a matter of fact I have."

"How much?"

"Four double scotches if it's any of your business, Wood Lynch."

"All right, come on," Wood said, climbing out of his cruiser. "I'll give you a ride home." He closed the cruiser door and walked across the deserted street to where Peggy Welton sat at the bus stop in front of the Allemane Inn. As he approached the young woman, the neon sign outside of Kate's Place went dark. "You must have closed the place, did you?" remarked Wood.

"Sure did," replied Peggy. "Me and that theatre dweeb."

"What theatre dweeb?"

"Louis Little."

"Oh, Louis. Stayed a little late tonight, did he?" Wood reached down and took Peggy by the arm. "Okay, let's go, Peggy."

"Okay," said Peggy wistfully and she rose and walked beside the officer towards his car. "Where are we going?"

"I'm taking you home," replied Wood.

"Oh, that's no fun. Let's do something."

"Peggy, it's one o'clock in the morning. You should be at home in bed."

"I don't want to go home."

"Don't you have school tomorrow?"

"I'm not going."

"Why not?"

"I don't know. I don't fit in there. They're all so immature. All they ever talk about is who's going out with who and who's having a party this weekend and which band is the best band. I mean, who gives a shit?! It's all kid stuff. Who needs it?"

"Oh, and you're all grown up I suppose."

"More than most."

"Uh-huh. Well, I don't care what you do tomorrow, but right now you're going home." Wood opened the passenger door of the cruiser and ushered Peggy inside. Then he walked around to the driver's side door and climbed behind the wheel. "Put your seat belt on," he said.

"You do it for me."

"What?"

"Please. I'm not feeling too well. Things are starting to spin." Peggy leaned her head back on the headrest and closed her eyes.

"You were feeling all right ten seconds ago."

"Yeah, well, I feel like dog shit now," Peggy replied, running her left hand across her stomach.

"You shouldn't close your eyes. If you close your eyes, things will start to spin even more and you'll throw up."

Peggy didn't answer. She continued to rub her stomach with eyes closed. Wood reached across Peggy with his left hand and grabbed hold of the passenger side seat belt. As he started to pull it across the front of the young woman to fasten it, she reached up with her right hand and pulled his head in tight to her face. "Surprise," she whispered, and then she put her parted lips on his and kissed him. Before he could react, Wood felt Peggy's soft tongue push its way into his mouth, and her left hand came up from her stomach and wrapped itself around his shoulders. In the next instant, Wood pulled himself away and let go of the seat belt, which recoiled and snapped Peggy flush on the nose.

"Fuck!" She mumbled through her left hand which now covered her face.

"What are you doing?" The startled officer asked.

"I'm showing you how grown up I am," She replied. "Fuck." Peggy rubbed her nose one last time and then she lunged at Wood, forcing him to back flat up against the driver side door. She was so close now that her breasts pinned his left hand against his chest, and feeling reluctant to move it for fear of unintentionally fondling the young woman, he instead used his right hand to push Peggy away by her shoulder.

"Jesus, Peggy, cut it out! What's the matter with you?"

"Oh, come on, Wood. I know you want me."

"What?! Want you? Whatever gave you that idea?"

"All the men want me. I know that."

"What the hell are you talking about? I'm almost twice your age!"

"So? I've been with older men. In fact, I prefer older men. Now, come over here." Peggy reached out and grabbed Wood's uniform tie and attempted to pull him to her, but Wood snatched the tie out of her hand and clung stubbornly to his safe haven against the door.

"Cut that out!" Wood demanded.

"Come on, Wood." Peggy moved closer to the officer, who now had both hands covering his tie.

"All right, that's it. You're gettin' in the back seat."

"What?"

Peggy's 'What' fell on deaf ears. Wood was already outside of the cruiser and was walking around to the passenger side door.

"Wood?"

Wood opened Peggy's door and stood there with a father's stern look on his face.

"Out," he said.

"What?

"Get out."

"No way." Peggy folded her arms stubbornly.

"Okay, fine." Wood reached in and took the girl by the right arm and pulled her firmly out of her seat. He then closed the door, still gripping Peggy's arm and opened the rear door of the vehicle.

"This is police brutality," Peggy cried.

"Aw, shut up, Peggy. Watch your head." With that, Wood put his hand on Peggy's head and bent her over so she wouldn't bump herself on her way into the cruiser. Wood then walked around to his side of the car, mumbling to himself. "Shit. Like I need this right now. Jesus Christ." Wood climbed into the driver's side of the cruiser and put the car in gear.

"I want your badge number," came the voice from the back seat.

"Peggy, there's only two of us cops in town and you know my name. You don't need my badge number. God."

"I'm going to report you."

"To who?"

"To the authorities."

"I am the authorities. Now, sit there and shut up."

Wood pulled away from the bus stop and headed back up Yarbro Street. Yarbro Street wound around the perimeter of Rainbow and would take Officer Lynch and his passenger straight to Bagnall Street, where Peggy lived.

"I'm fucked up, Wood," came the sorrowful and drunken voice from the back of the cruiser.

"I know you're fucked up, Peggy. That's why I'm drivin' you home."

"No, I don't mean fucked up drunk. I mean fucked up. Just plain fucked up."

"Naw, you're just having a bad . . . few years, that's all."

"Is that your idea of consoling someone? Because if it is, you suck at it."

There was a break in the conversation during which time, Wood figured maybe Peggy had fallen asleep. If Peggy wasn't asleep, she was usually talking.

"I feel sick."

"What?"

"I feel sick. I think I'm gonna throw up."

"I'm not pulling the cruiser over Peggy, to let you out so you can run off on me, so forget it. Nice try."

"Fine."

Exactly three minutes later the police cruiser pulled into the Welton's driveway on Bagnell Street. The car had barely come to a stop when Myrna Welton emerged from the front door of the house and stood on the dimly-lit porch. Wood climbed out of the vehicle and spoke to Myrna as he moved to the rear door of the vehicle.

"It's okay, Myrna. It's just me."

"Wood? Wood Lynch?"

"Yep. I'm just bringing Peggy home."

"Peggy? You were out with my Peggy tonight?"

"No, Myrna, I . . ." His voice lowered. "God."

Wood opened the rear door of the vehicle and motioned to the young woman inside. "Come on, Peggy. Let's go."

"I threw up."

"What?" Wood looked into the back seat and saw the thick puddle of vomit on the floor at Peggy's feet. "Aw shit, Peggy."

"Well, I told you I was going to be sick."

"Come on then." Wood took Peggy by the arm and helped her out of the cruiser. "Are you okay now?"

"Well, now that I've thrown up I am. I must have eaten something that didn't agree with me."

"Right. I don't suppose it was the four double scotches."

Peggy smacked Wood across his chest before moving towards the house. "Fuck you," she muttered.

"You're welcome," replied the officer, and he closed the cruiser door.

"I don't understand. What's going on?" asked Myrna, moving off the porch and onto the front walk.

"It's nothing, Myrna. Peggy just needed a ride home, that's all."

"Oh." Myrna looked at Peggy who was now walking in a serpentine manner up the front walk. "Did you thank the officer, Peggy?"

"I tried to but he made me sit in the back seat."

"Oh." Myrna would not attempt to make sense of that reply a right now. She would save that for later, when she was lying in bed trying to make sense of everything else that was going on in her life at the present time.

"Goodnight," Wood said from the driveway. He opened the driver's side door of the cruiser and had one foot inside when the smell of the vomit hit him. "Oh, Jesus," he muttered.

"Wood?"

"Yes, Myrna." He was trying to hide his impatience and his revulsion at the smell of his car all at once but it was a futile attempt at best.

Myrna moved down the walk to where Wood was standing by his vehicle. He hadn't moved. His right foot was still inside the cruiser, as if leaving it there would hasten the impending conversation.

"Wood," Myrna said in a lowered voice, so Peggy wouldn't hear. "Did you get the report back on Mickey's boots yet?"

"Not yet, Myrna. I expect it first thing in the morning." Wood eased his body into the cruiser, making sure his head was the last part to enter the vehicle so as to avoid the full force of the vomit smell for as long as he could.

"It's just that I'm concerned that's all."

"I understand." Wood pulled the car door closed and immediately rolled the window down. He looked up at Myrna who was now standing beside the squad car. "Is that it?"

"Oh yes, yes. That's it."

"Good." Wood put the vehicle into gear.

"You'll call me when you hear, won't you?"

"You'll be the first one."

"Good."

Wood looked at Myrna, who again, looked back at the officer silently. He could see the concern on the woman's face – this woman, who had such a burden on her, living with a husband like Jack, and trying to keep a family together that was coming apart at the seams. – "I'll call you in the morning, Myrna. Even if I don't hear. Okay?"

"Thank you."

Wood backed out of the driveway. Myrna stood and watched from her position on the walk as the police cruiser disappeared down the street. It was as if she was hoping he would stop and come back and tell her that it was all right. Mickey's boots didn't match. Everything was going to be okay. From behind her, a voice broke the crisp September air.

"What about Mickey's boots?" asked Peggy.

-23-

Dan hadn't planned on sleeping this long. He had pulled his rig into the Shiner's Truck Stop parking lot at about eleven-fifteen the night before and then had gone inside for a club sandwich and a short chat with proprietor, Bill Shiner. He thought it would be a short chat, but business was slow that night and Bill had nothing but time and bacon fat on his hands. And so, the two men chatted for a little over an hour. Bill told Dan about the Massachusetts trucker who had pulled in earlier, running on too little sleep, and who had taken out the phone booth that stood just to the left of the entranceway to the gravel parking lot. The young hitchhiker who was using the phone at the time got a bit of a scare, but managed to leap clear of the booth before it was demolished. It worked out for him in the end though because the trucker felt so sick about the near miss, that he gave the hitcher a ride. They disappeared into the night about two hours ago, the hitchhiker still a little shaken, and the trucker still running on too little sleep.

"Well, I'm gonna get some sleep myself," said Dan, pushing himself away from the counter.

"You want some pie for dessert?" asked Bill.

"No thanks."

"You don't want my raspberry pie? It's the best raspberry pie in the whole state."

"Really?"

"I guarantee it," said Bill, leaning both hands on the counter and smiling proudly.

"Well, I hate to tell you this, Bill," Dan began. He was halfway to the front door now and he turned around and spoke to Bill while walking backwards. "But there's a fella up in Rainbow who says he's got the best raspberry pie in the whole world."

"What?"

"That's what he says?"

"In the world?

"That's right."

"How can somebody make that claim? A person can't say that."

"Well, this fella does." Dan's hand reached for the front door.

"What were you doin' up in Rainbow?"

"Oh, I just stopped in for a bit. You know, cup of coffee."

"The best pie in the world, huh?" Bill looked over at his display of raspberry pie, and then turned back to the front door. He was about to argue his point further, but it was too late. The door was closing behind Dan. Bill shook his head and looked back to his pie display. "How can a person say that?"

It was nine-fifteen the next morning now, September the twenty-third, and Dan's hand was once again reaching for the front door of Shiner's Truck Stop. He looked back at the black BMW he had just strolled passed in the parking lot. It wasn't very often he saw a high end automobile like that parked outside of Shiner's. Someone was either lost, or that raspberry pie really did have some drawing power. Stepping inside he noticed about seven or eight other customers spread throughout the diner, and then his eyes fell on the day shift waitress, Luanne, standing at the counter talking to a man in a tan overcoat. When Luanne noticed Dan, she pointed in his direction and the overcoat man turned to look at him. Dan walked the few steps to the end of the counter closest to the door, where the cash register was located. He stood and waited for Luanne to approach him.

"Dan?" said Luanne, moving in his direction. "This gentleman here is looking for that woman who hitched a ride with you the other day."

"Uh-huh. Could I get a large coffee to go, please?" Dan reached into his pocket for some change. He didn't look at the overcoat man. He pulled the change out of his pocket and began counting it.

"He's trying to get hold of her because of some urgent family business."

"Luanne? Large coffee to go please?"

"Right." Luanne turned to the overcoat man. "This is Dan. He can help you." Luanne moved away and went about fixing Dan's coffee to go.

"Hi," came the voice from atop the overcoat.

"What can I do for you?" replied Dan. He didn't look up. He counted his change for a second time.

"Is this the woman you gave a ride to?" Bryden Downey held a photograph of his wife, Grace, out for the trucker to see. The trucker didn't look at the photograph. Instead, he continued to count his change. Bryden moved the photograph into the trucker's line of vision. In the photo, a woman with a broad, infectious smile was posing in front of a fountain. Dan recognized it as the Trevi Fountain in Rome.

"Who wants to know?" asked Dan

"I'm with the Penobscot County District Attorney's office."

"Uh-huh."

"We're trying to find this woman."

"On some urgent family business?"

"That's correct."

"Do they often send someone from the District Attorney's Office on errands like this? This would be more of police matter, wouldn't it?"

"Well . . ."

"Wouldn't they just send a patrol car out here to ask these questions? Seems like kind of a trivial matter to have someone important like Bryden Downey on the case."

"You know who I am then."

"Every once in a while a newspaper falls into my line of vision too."

Bryden almost presented a smile, partly because of the trucker's wry sense of humour, and partly because he took a measure of satisfaction from being recognized. "So, is this the woman?"

"What'd she do? She kill someone?"

"No."

"Because she doesn't look like a killer. She looks like a nice person."

"Like I said, it's a family matter."

"Well, I don't know if that's her or not. It's not a very good picture. You got any other pictures? A wanted poster maybe?"

"The waitress says it's her. She said the woman said her name was Grace."

"Well, sir, it sounds like the waitress knows a lot more about this than I do. Maybe you should talk to her."

Bryden heaved an audible sigh and looked away from Dan and towards the other patrons. By now, everyone in the establishment was watching the encounter at the cash register.

"All right, then, just tell me this. Where did you take the woman you gave the ride to?"

Dan was not about to tell this man anything about Grace's whereabouts. Grace had told him that her husband gave her that bruise on the cheek. That, coupled with Dan's infatuation with Grace, was enough to make him want to keep her location a secret no matter what. "Sorry, Mister Downey. I can't help you."

"Here you go, Dan." Luanne set Dan's coffee to go on the counter.

"Thanks, Luanne." Dan set the exact change down and picked up the Styrofoam cup.

"Boy, you sure upset Bill last night," Luanne said as she swept the change into her hand.

"What's that?" asked Dan.

Bryden hadn't moved. He was putting the photo of Grace into the breast pocket of his overcoat.

"With all that talk about the raspberry pie up in Rainbow," Luanne continued. "That's his grandmother's recipe and, by God, he thinks there's nothin' finer," Luanne laughed. She punched a button on the cash register and it sprung open to the sound of a bell.

"Uh-huh," replied Dan. He turned towards the door.

"What are you doin' eatin' at a restaurant in Rainbow? Our food isn't good enough for you?" Luanne winked at Dan and pushed the cash register closed.

"Rainbow? That's just across the Canadian border, isn't it?" Bryden looked at Dan, but he was expecting the answer to come from the verbose waitress.

"Yes sir. About two hours from here," Luanne chimed in on cue.

"Thank you, Luanne." Bryden put a five dollar bill on the counter. "Thank you very much." He brushed past Dan and exited the diner.

Dan watched Bryden Downney walk at a stern pace across the parking lot and climb into the black BMW. He turned back to Luanne.

"Jesus, Luanne. What the hell's the matter with you?"

"What?"

"You don't know when to keep your mouth shut, do ya'?"

"What? The raspberry pie?"

"No, not the raspberry pie. Him!' He pointed out to the parking lot. "What'd ya tell him about the woman for?"

"He said it was an urgent family matter. I thought I was being helpful."

Dan pushed open the truck stop door and ran out of the diner.

"What did I do?" Luanne called after him.

As Dan quick stepped across the parking lot he fumbled in his pocket for some coins and pulled out two quarters. He would call The Allemane Inn, where Grace was staying, and warn Grace that Bryden Downey was headed her way. He could drive to Rainbow himself to warn her but with him in his eighteen wheeler and Bryden in his BMW, the overcoat man would get there at least a half an hour in advance of him. Looking at the change in his hand, Dan heard the sound of tires spinning on the gravel parking lot. He looked up and saw the black BMW pull out onto Interstate Ninety-five, heading north. As he watched Bryden Downey's car, Dan stopped at where he thought the phone booth should be and reached up to pull open the phone booth door. At his feet sat a telephone receiver and what resembled a pile of phone booth kindling.

"Shit!"

Dan turned quickly and ran back towards the diner.

-24-

At eight-fifteen on the morning of September 23'rd, Gabby Lasalle stood at the kitchen sink, finishing up the breakfast dishes. Even though the Lasalles had a dishwasher in their kitchen, Gabby preferred to hand wash every dish after every meal. She washed the pots and pans as she cooked, and then scrubbed the plates, glasses, and cutlery the instant the meal was consumed. Gabby would not trust her dishes to a machine. She had tried the dishwasher when they first moved into the house, but too often she would find a speck of food between the prongs of a fork, or water spots on her glasses. Besides, washing the dishes by hand was one more way to pass a little more time in each of her elongated days.

It had been approximately thirty-seven hours since Gabby had peered into Bonnie Hoyt's window and made the gruesome discovery which now had every tongue in Rainbow wagging. Across the street from the Lasalle home, Bonnie's house was now ringed with yellow police tape. The investigation was ongoing. A forensics team had packed up their gear and left the house at about six o'clock the previous morning. Gabby had heard them pull away as she lay in bed beside her husband Tom. Tom went to work that morning even though Gabby had urged him not to. She was still shaken by her experience of the night before and she did not want to be alone. Tom said she was being silly, and at the front door he gave her a less-than-comforting peck on the cheek, barely grazing her skin, before heading down the walk to his car. Gabby stood at the front door and watched Tom's Cherokee pull out and drive off. Then, out of the corner of her eye, she noticed someone approaching from across the street. She turned to see police officer Wood Lynch. The officer waved to Gabby and she waved back.

"Got a minute, Gabby?"

"I suppose," replied Gabby halfheartedly.

Gabby invited Wood inside and Officer Lynch questioned her on the previous evening's events. How did she happen to be looking into Bonnie's window that evening? Was she snooping? Did she know if Bonnie had any boyfriends? What about Tom? It was at this point that Gabby became rattled, thinking that the officer was suggesting that Tom might be one of Bonnie's boyfriends, when in fact he was asking whether Tom might know if Bonnie had any boyfriends. Gabby recovered from the misstep and the questioning continued without incident. The fact was, Gabby *was* snooping last evening. She did not walk over to Bonnie Hoyt's house to pass along a recipe. The magazine was merely an excuse in case Gabby's worst fears were not realized and Bonnie turned out to be alone in the house. She would ring the doorbell and if Bonnie answered, Gabby would offer her the magazine, saying she thought Bonnie might like to try the recipe inside. If there was no answer, Gabby would peer into the windows to see what was going on inside. She would start with the front window and work her way around the house to see if she could catch a glimpse of her husband Tom, somewhere inside.

Gabby had no proof, but she had long suspected that Tom and Bonnie were carrying on an affair, and she fully-expected to see the couple inside Bonnie's house on this day. The day when Tom had told her he had yet *another* late lesson at the golf course. She would see them embracing, kissing, or worse. Instead, she saw Bonnie, robe closed, lying dead on the floor.

On this, the second morning after the murder, Tom Lasalle was leaving for work a little later than usual. He had trouble sleeping last night and at about three a.m., Tom got out of bed and poured himself a glass of Jim Beam, hoping it would assist in his quest for some much-needed slumber. He felt uneasy about the question period he had gone through at the hands of Pete Golliger that afternoon. He did, after all, tell the police officer to go fuck himself. Pointing a finger at Leo Terrio was a smart move though. A punch drunk ex-boxer? It would be natural for someone to assume that Leo could fly off the handle and kill a person. He surmised that Pete should have thought of that possibility himself. Tom, glass of whiskey in hand, wandered into the living room and looked out the window, across Winston Street, towards Bonnie's house. The yellow police tape was whipping in the wind. The end of the tape that was attached to the left side of Bonnie's veranda had come loose and was now flapping freely, and every so often it would slap against the veranda's wooden railing.

"Tom?"

The voice behind him startled Tom and cut like a knife into his vision of Bonnie lying dead on that living room floor across the street, robe open and life departed.

He turned to see his wife standing in the archway between the stairs and the living room.

"Jesus, Gab. You scared the hell out of me."

"What are you doing?"

"I couldn't sleep. And what are doing? Come down to do some dishes, did you?"

"I woke up and you weren't there." Gabby was softened by the way Tom alluded to her housecleaning habits. Softened in the same way a sirloin steak is softened by the constant beating of a chef's tenderizing hammer. "I wondered where you went."

"Well, now you know."

'Is something wrong?"

"Wrong? Gee, no Gab, unless you count our neighbour being murdered." Tom's gaze shifted from Bonnie's house to his glass of Jim Beam. He judged that he had maybe three sips left. He used up one of the sips and then looked back across the street.

"Come back to bed, Tom."

"In a few minutes."

" .... We can make love." Gabby proposed this to Tom as she would propose an outing to her parent's house for Sunday dinner, an activity she suspected Tom would not be enamored by. They had not made love in over two weeks, and before that last encounter for another three. Gabby suspected that Tom must be finding sexual comfort elsewhere. Maybe in the arms of Bonnie Hoyt. Or maybe Cindy Keller, one of the women that Tom gave golf lessons to on a regular basis.

"I said I'll be up in a few minutes."

"Promise?"

"I'll be up in a few minutes," Tom repeated, slowly and with more emphasis as if to crystallize his point for Gabby.

Gabby left Tom's presence as silently as she had entered.

Tom continued to gaze across the empty street. His mind flashed on two other dead bodies from his past. His mother, Virginia's, as it lay on her bed the afternoon that Tom returned home from school and found her there. A bottle, which once contained sleeping pills, lay next to her. The same sleeping pills which Virginia regularly ingested to escape the hell inflicted by her brutish husband Marty. Marty's body was the other that flashed through Tom's mind, lying broken, bloodied and lifeless on Rainbow's main street, two years after Virginia's death. Young Tom had reasoned that if he waited two years, then no one would suspect him of exacting the revenge that he so desperately craved. And so he waited, marking time until he could finally repay the man who had made life no longer an option for his mother. Tom stopped the car for only a few seconds that night, checking in the rearview mirror to make sure the body didn't move. To make sure that the man was dead. If it did move, he would back up and drive over it again. It didn't, and seventeen year-old Tom Lasalle drove off at a casual speed, disappearing down Main Street, and attracting no attention.

Tom finally went to bed one hour and one more glass of whiskey later. Finding his wife asleep was a relief, and the whiskey soon surrendered him as well. Instead of waking up at his usual six-fifteen on this day, he slept in until seven forty-five. He had no lessons scheduled this morning though so there was no urgency in getting to the golf course. Still, he hurried to shower and dress and eat breakfast. After brushing his teeth, he returned downstairs to find his wife at the sink, as usual, cleaning the breakfast dishes while they were still warm from the heat of his two fried eggs.

"I'm doing a laundry today," Gabby announced. "Are your shirts in the hamper?"

"What?"

"Your golf shirts from the last two days. Are they in the clothes hamper? Because I only saw one there. Shouldn't there be two?"

"You count the clothes in the dirty clothes hamper?"

"No, I don't count them. I was just checking to see what was there."

"Oh, well that makes much more sense. You weren't counting them. You were just checking up on them." Tom said this as he slipped into his windbreaker.

"So, where's the other shirt?"

"I threw it out."

"What?" Gabby turned away from the sink and looked at Tom. She dried her hands, using the neatly folded tea towel on the counter to her left. "Why did you do that?"

"Because it was old and I didn't like it anymore."

"So you just throw it out?"

"Yes."

"Well, that's a little wasteful, isn't it?

"Gab, I'm a golfer. I've got fifty golf shirts hanging in my closet. Believe me, I won't miss one shirt. God."

Gabby folded the tea towel, set it back in its place on the counter to her left, and returned to washing the dishes. There was a brief pause as Tom sat down on the bench just inside the front door to put his shoes on.

"I'll be late again tonight," Tom said as he picked up one of his shoes.

"Do you have another late lesson?"

"Uh-huh."

"Who with?"

"What?"

"Who's the lesson with?" Gabby didn't look at Tom. She faced the sink, scrubbing a plate which was already beyond clean at least thirty seconds ago.

"Why?"

"Because I'm interested. Can't a wife be interested in her husband's work?"

"Cindy Keller I think."

"You think? Don't you know? Don't you have it written down?"

"It's Cindy Keller. I'm pretty sure." Tom was now tying up his left shoe. He was only a few feet from the front door and the sweet relief of escaping his wife's line of questioning.

"She's been taking lessons for about four months now, hasn't she?"

"I don't know for sure how long it's been." His left shoe was now tied. One more to go.

"No I think it's been at least four months."

"Fine. It's been four months. So what?" His right shoe was now on Tom's foot. It only needed to be tied and he would be gone.

"Well, isn't she getting any better? How many lessons does a person need?"

"That depends on the person." He fumbled with the lace. "Come on," he whispered urgently, as if coaxing the lace to tie itself.

"Well, doesn't there come a time when she would say, 'I've had enough goddamned lessons. Shouldn't I be able to play this goddamned game by now?!' Doesn't there come a time when she would say that??!!"

The sound of the plate breaking in the sink was followed closely by the sound of the front door closing behind Tom.

*

At eight-fifteen on the morning of September twenty-third, Information Coordinator Lori Higgenson entered the Rainbow police station. Officers Pete Golliger and Wood Lynch sat silently at their desks. Wood had come off his shift fifteen minutes ago. It had been a relatively quiet night, with only the over-imbibed Peggy Welton to deal with. Wood was tired after his eight hour shift but instead of heading home, he was waiting around for the forensics report. It had been approximately thirty-seven hours since Officer Lynch had seen Gabby Lasalle running frantically across Winston Street towards her home. Approximately thirty-seven hours since he had entered Bonnie Hoyt's house and found the murdered woman's body. The leader of the forensics team, Carrie Jardine, had promised to call sometime this morning with her findings.

"Sorry I'm late," Lori said, throwing her bag onto her desk, setting her large Tim Horton's double double coffee down, and taking off her coat. "Traffic was awful."

"Traffic?" asked Pete, without concealing his skepticism.

"Yeah. The four way stop at the end of my street was nuts this morning." Lori hung her coat on the freestanding oak coat rack in the corner.

"You had time to stop at Tim Horton's though, huh?" Wood said.

"I need my Tim's, Wood. You don't expect me to start my day without a coffee, do you?"

Wood smiled at Pete and Pete responded with light-hearted shake of his head.

"So, get me up to speed, boys. What's new on the Bonnie Hoyt case?" Lori didn't look at the officers. She was busy brushing away the lint left by her coat on her short black skirt. She stood, legs slightly parted, and brushed the front of the skirt with both hands. She heard no reply from the two officers, and looking up, she noticed both of them staring at her in her rather provocative stance. "Boys? Hello?"

Shaken from his trance, Wood responded clumsily. "Uh . . . nothing new. We're waiting for the forensics report."

"Yeah, they should be calling any minute," Pete added. He looked to the top of his desk and moved a file from one side of the desk to the other.

"Yeah, any minute," echoed Wood. He looked for something to shuffle on his desk but there was nothing, so he just blew away some dust.

"You fellas need to get laid," Lori said. She moved to the chair behind her desk, sat down, removed the lid from her coffee-to-go and took a sip while peering over the top of the cup at the two officers.

"Well, Miss Information Coordinator," Pete began. "In the past twenty four hours, that's about the first piece of information you've gotten right."

Pete looked over at Wood and the two officers broke into broad, victorious smiles. Wood sat back and hoisted one foot onto his desk.

"Speaking of getting laid, did you have a good time with Peggy Welton last night, Wood?" Lori placed the lid back on her coffee-to-go.

"What?" The victorious smile disappeared from Officer Lynch's face and the foot slipped off of the desk and hit the floor.

"What?" Pete looked at Wood. The smile was absent from his face now as well.

"Well, I hear you two were having quite the session in your squad car last night. Yes, quite the session indeed."

"Where'd you hear that?" asked Wood.

"Roberta Fry called me this morning. She lives across the street from The Allemane Inn. The bus stop is right at the end of her walk."

"What kind of session is she talking about, Wood?" Pete swiveled in his chair and faced his fellow officer.

"Peggy was drunk last night. I gave her a ride."

"What kind of ride?"

"Home! A ride home!"

"Well, according to Roberta, you two were going at it pretty good before you pulled away from the bus stop." Lori removed the lid again and took another sip of coffee.

"Well, Roberta's got it all wrong," replied Wood.

"She said she saw you and Peggy kissing."

"You were kissing Peggy Welton?" Pete's disbelief was growing by the second.

"No, Peggy was kissing me."

"What?!"

"Yep," said Lori. "Roberta saw the whole thing."

"Well, did she also see me get out and put Peggy in the back seat?"

Pete sat straight up now. "You did *what* to her in the back seat?"

"She came on to me, Pete. So I pulled her out of the front seat and put her in the back seat and then I drove her straight home. God." Wood looked back to Lori. "Did Roberta Fry tell you that?"

"No, she didn't mention that." Lori replaced the lid on her coffee-to-go one more time. "She just told me about the kiss."

Pete swiveled his chair around to face Lori. "What time did Roberta call you, Lori?"

"Oh, about a half an hour ago."

"A half an hour, huh?"

"Yep."

"So, you probably talked for what, five or ten minutes?"

"I don't know. Maybe."

"Well, she didn't just call and say, 'Lori! I saw Wood Lynch and Peggy Welton kissing last night' and then hang up, right? She probably said 'How are you?' and you said 'I'm fine' and she said 'Guess what I saw last night' and you said 'What' and she told you all about Wood and Peggy and you asked her some questions and she told you some more and you said something like 'Well, what do you know about that' and then you gossiped about it for a few minutes longer, because Roberta does like to gossip and you do too, and then you looked at the clock and said 'Damn, I'm going to be late for work and then you went to Tim Horton's and showed up here fifteen minutes late."

"That's good police work, Pete. Real good." Lori removed the lid from her coffee-to-go yet again and took another sip.

"Lori, why do you keep taking the lid off and putting it back on every time you take a sip?" There was more than just a trace of irritation in Wood's voice. "Why don't you just take the lid off and finish the damn thing?"

"It lasts longer this way," replied Lori. "It doesn't get cold as fast." She casually replaced the lid.

The minor confrontation was interrupted by a tapping on the front window of the police station. Pete, Wood and Lori looked up to see a woman standing outside the glass waving to them. It was Roberta Fry, on her way to work at the fabric shop next door. She stood, smiling and waving. Pete waved back to Roberta and gave her a friendly smile. Wood just stared at the woman. Lori looked at Roberta, pointed to Wood, nodded her head and then gave a thumbs up as if to signal Roberta that everything Roberta had told her this morning was true. Lori smiled as Roberta moved past the window and into her work day.

"Lori, what'd you do that for?" asked Pete, in the same the way a father would ask his teenage daughter why she intentionally cut a hole in one knee of her new jeans.

"Kicks," came Lori's reply. And she removed the lid from her coffee-to-go.

"Morning, gentleman. Ma'am."

The voice came from the front door of the police station. Pete, Wood and Lori looked up to see a big man in a blue nylon windbreaker standing in the doorway.

"Shit!" muttered Lori, and she reached for a tissue from the Kleenex box on her desk. She wiped up a few drops of coffee that had spilled when she was startled in mid-sip by the tall stranger.

"Sergeant McCaffrey," offered Pete. "What brings you here?" Pete didn't rise to greet the RCMP officer. He remained seated at his desk.

"Oh, I just thought I'd stop by and see what kind of facility we're going to be moving into." McCaffrey looked at Wood. "Officer Lynch."

"Morning," replied Wood.

"You look tired."

"Yeah, I just came off an eight hour shift."

"Yes, I hear you had quite the night with a Miss Welton."

"What?" Wood looked at Pete and then at Lori. "How'd you hear that?"

"Population nine thousand. That's how." McCaffrey moved to Lori and held out his hand to her. "Hi. Dale McCaffrey. Sergeant. RCMP."

Lori took the man's hand and squeezed it lightly, which was her way of shaking hands. "Lori Higgenson. Information Coordinator. RPD."

"Beg pardon?"

"Rainbow Police Department."

"Oh, right. Well, pleased to meet you." McCaffrey looked around the small office. "So this is it, huh?"

"This is it," replied Pete.

"Hmm. Pretty close quarters. That an office in there?" McCaffrey pointed in the direction of Police Chief Walt Steeves old office to the left of Lori's desk.

"Yeah."

"Holding cells?"

"Three. Out back."

"Uh-huh. Well, I suppose this will do for a while. We'll have to find something a little bigger before long."

"How many officers are you gonna have here?" asked Wood.

"Five to start. But we'll be covering the outlying areas as well so I figure we'll have to bump that up to nine or ten eventually." As he spoke, Sergeant McCaffrey moved towards two filing cabinets next to Wood's desk.

"Are those your case files?"

"Yep." Wood replied. "Well, the cabinet on the right is the case files. The one on the left is where I keep my golashes."

"Golashes?"

"Yeah. You know, in case it rains."

"Right." McCaffrey rested his hand on the top of the filing cabinet to the right. "Mind if I take a look?"

"Why? They're just golashes."

"No, I meant take a look at the case files."

Pete didn't wait for Wood to answer the Sergeant's question. "You can have a look on the twenty-eighth," he said. "When you take over officially. We'll leave everything here for you."

"That's fine. Probably not much in there anyway, right?" McCaffrey moved to the front window of the station, shoved his hands into his back pockets and looked out onto the street. "Pretty quiet town, huh?"

"Oh yeah," replied Wood. "She's sleepy all right."

"How's your murder investigation going?"

Wood looked to Pete and Pete held up his hand to stop Wood from replying.

"It's going." Pete replied finally.

"Got the forensics report back yet?"

"Soon."

"Find the murder weapon?"

"Think so."

"Was it something with an edge like I thought?"

"Yep."

McCaffrey turned to Pete. "So, what is this? Monosyllabic day at the office? Christ. We're on the same side here, Officer. What's the harm in giving me information that I'm going to get when I take over the investigation anyway? Huh?"

"Who says you're gonna take over the investigation?" Pete was still seated and appeared unrattled by McCaffrey's sudden swing. "I expect we'll have this all wrapped up by the time you fellas move in."

"I expect so too," Wood chimed in.

McCaffrey didn't acknowledge Wood's addition to the conversation. He assumed Pete was the lead dog in this office. "Well, you didn't do so well with the other murder in this town so what makes you think this one is gonna be any different? Now, I'm not trying to insult you. Not at all. It's just that you haven't got the experience in these areas. You should be asking for my help. I've got a lot of resources at my disposal. Resources you could use."

"What other murder?" Pete asked.

"The hit and run back in nineteen-eighty."

"Nineteen-eighty?" Pete scoffed. "I wasn't even working here then."

"Neither was I," Wood added. "And besides, it was a hit and run. It wasn't a murder."

"Oh, yeah? Well, let's review it for just a second, Officer. Man leaves a bar after having only two drinks, so he's not considered drunk. It's one o'clock in the morning so there's not a whole lot of traffic on the street, and yet this relatively sober man walks right out in front of a car. Probably the *only* car around. No. It doesn't wash. What probably happened was this car was waiting by the curb when the fella came out of the bar. The man looks both ways to cross the street, sees nothing, begins to cross, and the car pulls out and runs him down before he knows what hit him. Seems awfully straightforward to me. And yet it's still on the books. It was never solved. I mean, if this town is so damned 'sleepy' as you put it, you'd think you'd have time to dig up an old case like that and look into it. Hell, it'd be good practice for you."

"How do you know so much about the case?" Pete was starting to feel slightly inferior to the Sergeant about now, and feeling a little defensive about it.

"Well, sir, this is what I do. It's all I've done for the last thirty years. And it's not something I just dabble in. It's not a hobby. It's something I do passionately. It's cost me two wives – two wonderful women – because I couldn't leave it at the office. Wife number one called it a sickness. Wife number two called it a mistress. I'm not sure what I call it. Maybe it's both. I just know that I'm damn good at it."

"So, you like to put the bad guys away, huh?" said Wood.

"No, that's not the attraction. That's just the end result. It's a perk. The attraction is the process. Putting the pieces of the puzzle together. It's my crack cocaine."

The phone on Lori's desk buzzed. Lori picked up the receiver and pressed the button which indicated line one.

"Rainbow police station . . . . Just a moment please." Lori looked at Pete. "It's the forensics woman."

"Well, it's about time," said Pete and he picked up the receiver of the phone on his desk. He was about to press the button for line one, when Wood spoke up.

"Are you gonna to take it?"

"What?" Pete's finger stopped about an inch from the button.

"Are you going to take this call or do you want me to take it?"

"Uh . . . . Well, you can take it if you want. Or I can take it. It doesn't matter to me." Pete knew what this was. Wood didn't want to appear to be 'riding behind' with Sergeant McCaffrey standing there.

"Well, it doesn't matter to me either," Wood offered. "I mean, either one of us could take it and it wouldn't mean anything. I mean, if I took it, it wouldn't mean that I'm any more official than you are."

"No, of course not," Pete replied.

"Of course not."

"So, do you want to take it?" Pete's finger retreated from the area of the button.

"I could. Sure. Or you could."

"It doesn't matter to me."

"Me neither."

"Well, shit, would one of you take it please?" Lori interjected with her usual aplomb. "Good God."

"Put it on the speaker phone," said Pete.

Lori pressed the hold button, replaced the receiver into its cradle and pushed the speaker button. Sergeant McCaffrey reached for the front door of the police station and pulled it open.

"Sergeant McCaffrey?"

McCaffrey stopped in the doorway and turned back to Pete.

'Stick around. You might want to hear this," said Pete.

McCaffrey hesitated only for a moment, then he stepped back inside the police station and let the door swing closed. Peter turned to Wood.

"Go ahead."

"What?"

"Talk to her."

"No, you can do it," Wood said.

"Are you sure?"

"Yeah, it's fine."

"You're sure? Because if you're not sure . . ."

"I'm positive. Really."

"Hello?" Carrie Jardine's disembodied voice called out from the speaker phone.

"Hi there," Pete responded loudly so that his voice would travel the distance to the speaker phone. "This is Officer Golliger, Miss Jardine. We've got you on the speaker phone if that's okay."

"That's fine," came the woman's voice. "And you can call me Carrie."

"Ooh that movie creeped me out," said Lori, giving her shoulders a shake.

"Pardon me?" The voice on the speakerphone sounded bewildered.

"I said that movie creeped me out!"

"Who is this?"

"Lori Higgenson. Information coordinator." Lori removed the lid from here coffee and took a sip, making a loud slurping noise as she did.

"Carrie, we're anxious to hear what you found out." Pete leaned forward and crossed his arms on his desk. He wanted to hear every word. "Can you fill us in please?"

"Well, first of all, the golf club is the murder weapon. You were right on that one."

No one in the office said a word at that news. The three men were awfully sure of that fact anyway so that wasn't a surprise.

"And it was your victim's blood in the drainpipe of the sink."

Again, no surprise.

"And your victim had sex very near her time of death."

Wood leaned forward on his desk. "So was it a rape then?"

"She said she had sex, Wood," Lori piped up. "Rape isn't having sex. God."

"Well, that's splitting hairs, isn't it, Lori?" replied Wood.

"No, it's not splitting hairs. What the hell is wrong with you men? Shit. Rape is an affront. It's a violent act. It's theft of the worst kind. Sex is what you had with Peggy Welton last night."

"I did not have sex with Peggy Welton last night!"

"Excuse me?" came the disembodied voice from the phone. "Can I continue? I've got other cases I have to get to this morning."

"Sorry, Carrie," Pete offered. "Continue, please." Pete looked at Wood as if to admonish him for his untimely argument with Lori.

"I did not have sex with Peggy Welton!" Wood spoke in a hushed, angry and yet defensive tone.

Pete looked at Lori with that same look of admonishment. Lori removed the lid from her coffee cup and took a loud sip.

"All right, time of death we had right," Carrie continued. "Sometime between five-thirty and six. The contents of her stomach indicated she had eaten not long before she died. The hairs that we got from the carpet were male hairs. All right, listen, you want to know what I think? Lemme just skip right to it, and this is just me making an educated guess, but I think she was having sex WHEN she was killed."

Nobody in the Rainbow police station said a word. Lori stared at the phone. Sergeant McCaffrey turned around and looked to the street outside. The two Rainbow police officers looked at each other. Pete leaned back in his chair.

"Hello? Did you hear me?"

"We heard you, Carrie."

Lori set her coffee down and leaned into the phone in front of her. "So, was she killed by the person she was having sex with?"

"Lori?" Pete interrupted. "Do you mind?"

"Well, it's the next logical question, isn't it?"

"She's right," Offered McCaffrey, without turning around.

"Yeah, it probably is the next question." Wood chimed in.

"Even so," Pete was firm as he spoke this time. "I don't think Lori is the one to be asking the questions at this point."

"He's right, Lori," Wood said. "Why don't you just finish your coffee and leave the questions to the experts."

"And who would that be?" snapped Lori.

From his place near the window, Sergeant McCaffrey smiled without turning around.

The disembodied voice chirped up again in an attempt to move this conversation along. "No, I don't think she was killed by the person she was engaging in sex with, Lori. I think she was sitting on top of her lover. That's why we got his hairs from the carpet. And while she was sitting on top of him, I think that's when she was struck with the golf club."

"Sweet Jesus." Wood gasped.

"Maybe this was part of a sex game," Lori said.

"What?" Pete asked incredulously.

"Well, you know how some people like to be choked while they're having sex?"

" . . . . What?" Pete's 'incredulous' level had not dropped one iota.

"Some people, women mainly, like to be choked when they're having sex because the lower supply of oxygen to the brain enhances the sexual sensation and gives you a heightened orgasm. They say it makes it easier to come too."

" . . . . So, are you suggesting that Bonnie wanted to be whacked on the head with a golf club because it heightened her sexual pleasure?" Pete asked.

The three men stared at Lori, waiting on tenterhooks for whatever wisdom would flow from her lips next.

"Well, when you put it that way," Lori began, "It does sound kind of far-fetched."

Wood leaned towards the phone from his place at his desk. "Carrie, can we assume that the person she was having sex with would know who killed her?"

"Well, I can't say that for sure but I think he probably might, yes."

"Well, that's it then. All we have to do is get hold of who she was sittin' on and he can tell us who the killer is."

"Well, Wood," Pete's voice had a tinge of impatient sarcasm in it as he began his response. "We would have heard from this fella already, don't ya' think, if he wanted us to know who he was. But obviously he doesn't. Obviously he doesn't want us to know he was having sex with Bonnie."

"Or he's dead too." Sergeant McCaffrey finally put his two cents worth in. "Maybe the killer killed him too, and then took his body away to dispose of it somewhere else."

"Why do that?" asked Pete. "If you've already got one dead body, why not just leave the second one there too?"

"I don't know. Just thinking out loud."

"One more thing, folks," Carrie continued over the speakerphone. "Those boots you brought me yesterday? They match the footprints we took from the back gate."

"Say that again, please?" Pete wanted to be sure that he heard what he heard.

"The boots that your deputy gave me yesterday, they're the boots that made the prints in the mud in your victim's yard."

"He's not my deputy," Pete corrected her.

"Well, whatever he is."

"I'm the co-investigator on the case", said Wood, raising the volume of his voice slightly while at the same time lowering it an octave.

"Good. Terrific. I'm happy for you. So, that's it. That's all I've got for you at this point."

"Okay, thanks, Carrie. Thanks for everything," said Pete.

"Thanks, Carrie," Lori added.

"Bye, Lori."

"Bye now." Lori pressed the button on the phone and Ms. Jardine was gone. The Information Coordinator then picked up the receiver and dialed a number.

"Shit." Wood looked at Pete.

"Yeah, shit."

"So Mickey was in the yard right after Bonnie was killed," Wood stared at his desk now, trying to get this right in his mind.

"It looks like." Pete suddenly looked at Lori and gave her a stern look of warning. "Lori, not a word about this to anybody, ya' hear?"

"Oh, who am I going to tell?" Lori then spoke into the phone. "Hi Roberta."

Pete jumped up, moved quickly to Lori's desk, grabbed the receiver out of her hand and hung up.

"Pete!"

"I said, not a word."

"Oh, fine. God, you're no fun at all."

"So, I guess we'd better have a talk with Mickey huh?" Wood offered. He was surprised that Mickey's boots turned out to be the right boots. And surprised that Myrna Welton might actually be right about her son being involved in this mess somehow.

"Yeah, I guess we'd better," replied Pete.

"That would be my call anyway," offered Wood, without trying to force his point. "I don't know how you would feel about it. I mean we are co-investigators here so maybe we should come to a consensus on what to do next."

"No, I think talking to Mickey is the next step," Pete agreed.

"Good."

"Good."

"Jesus Christ," Sergeant McCaffrey grunted, and he pushed open the door.

"Sergeant?" Lori's voice stopped the RCMP officer at the door. He looked back to the pretty young woman at the desk. "When you RCMP boys take over here, will I still have a job?"

"Well, we'll need someone who has their finger on the pulse of what's going on in this town. We'll need someone like that to funnel information, that's for sure."

"Well, I'm your girl then," Lori smiled. "No one knows more about what goes on in this town than me. And no one can get the information out there faster."

"That's good to know." Sergeant McCaffrey exited onto the sidewalk outside and moved off. Just before he disappeared from sight past the police station window, Pete noticed him shake his head in disbelief.

Pete stood up from his desk. There was reluctance in his movement now, as if interrogating Mickey Welton was something he did not look forward to. He liked Mickey. Mickey was a good kid. Pete didn't want to find out that Mickey was involved in this terrible crime somehow. He didn't want his worst fears to be realized. He would rather be a thousand miles away right now.

"All right," Pete said, standing but not really making a move to go anywhere. "Let's go talk to Mickey."

"Right. Let's hit it," said Lori and she grabbed her coat from the oak coat rack.

"Where do you think you're going?" asked Pete, challenging the information coordinator with a stern look.

"We're gonna talk to Mickey."

"No, you're not going to talk to Mickey. We are." Pete's hand moved back and forth between himself and Wood Lynch so that Lori wouldn't miss the point.

"Aw come on, Pete. This is just getting good."

"No. You stay here and do your job."

"Pete?" Lori whined once more as if this tactic might just convince Officer Golliger.

"No." It didn't convince him.

"Hang on, Pete," said Wood, still sitting at his desk.

"What?"

"Well, Doug Petty's La-Z-Boy doesn't open until ten."

"So?"

"So, it's only eight forty-five. Mickey won't be at work for another hour and fifteen minutes yet."

"Well, you know what, Wood?" Pete was being as patient as he could with his co-investigator. "We're police officers. We can actually go right to Mickey's house and question him there."

"I'd rather not do that, Pete," said Wood. "I mean poor Myrna is jumpy enough already about this thing. If we go over there and question Mickey in front of her, it just might send her tumblin' over the edge of normal."

Pete thought about this but didn't answer.

"I'm just thinkin' about poor Myrna, Pete. I'm just tryin' to look at it from a mother's point of view. And Mickey's not going anywhere. He'll be at Doug Petty's this morning like he always is."

"And how do you know that?" Pete asked.

"Because Mickey's dependable."

Pete smiled at this notion for a couple of reasons. First of all, Mickey *was* dependable. And even if he was involved in Bonnie's death somehow, this dependable young man would still feel obligated to show up for his shift at work the next day so as not to let anyone down. Pete liked that about the boy. Secondly, here were Pete and Wood investigating a murder, and they were willing to let a suspect finish his breakfast and show up for work on time, rather than go to his house and upset his mother by interrogating him there. Pete liked that about the small town of Rainbow.

"All right. We'll wait til' Doug Petty's opens."

"Good," Wood nodded his approval. "Thanks Pete."

"Why don't you hit the cot for an hour, Wood?" asked Pete. You've had a long shift.'

"No, I think I'm gonna head over to The Allemane and grab some breakfast. See my mom." Wood stood and moved towards the front door of the office.

"The Allemane?" Pete asked.

"Yeah." Wood was at the door now and was just about to push it open.

"You know what? Maybe I'll head over there with you."

Wood stopped in his tracks. He looked back at Pete who was moving towards the door. "You"

"Yeah."

"What do you want to go there for?"

"Breakfast. What do you think?"

"You've never eaten breakfast at the Allemane."

"I have too. I was there yesterday."

"You were?"

"I sure was."

" . . . . Why?" Wood hesitated because he couldn't quite fathom this new fact.

222 | NORM FOSTER

"Because I was hungry."

"And because he's sweet on that new woman in town," Lori added. "Grace? Right? And she eats breakfast over there because that's where she's staying until her bruise goes away and she can move on without being noticed in the next town she runs to."

Officers Golliger and Lynch stood in the doorway of the Rainbow Police station and looked back at Lori. Lori removed the lid from her Tim Horton's double double coffee and took a long loud sip. She punctuated the sip and her last statement with a refreshed, "Ahhhhh."

-25-

Bryden pulled up to the Houlton border crossing at about eleven-thirty on the morning of the twenty-third of September. His wife, Grace, had been gone for two days now and he was in warm pursuit of her. He would have been in hot pursuit but Bryden had a sterling reputation to protect and he didn't want that reputation sullied by a speeding ticket. The press these days would jump on the tiniest misstep of a politician, and Bryden was careful not to open any doors that the fifth estate could slink through. The town of Rainbow, New Brunswick – a town he had barely heard of, let alone ever visited – was only a half an hour away now. The truck driver back at Shiner's had been secretive about where he had dropped his passenger off a day and a half ago, but the waitress with the big mouth at Shiner's had pretty much put the pieces together for him.

"Where you headed today?"

The voice came from just outside of Bryden's car window and stopped Bryden's musing in its tracks.. He turned to look at the custom's officer in the booth. "Uh . . . Rainbow."

"Where do you live?"

"Bangor."

"Citizenship?"

"American."

"And what's the purpose of your . . . . Hey? It's you."

"Pardon me?" Bryden looked at the uniformed man in the booth. The man was sporting a large grin.

"It's you. How ya' doin', Mr. Downey?"

"Oh. Fine, thank you," Bryden felt a little bubble of pride over having been recognized yet again.

"My wife Judy and I are still talkin' about that Governor's Ball. Boy that was something."

"I beg your pardon?"

"The Governor's Ball the other night. Quite the do."

Bryden finally realized who the grinning man was. The contest winner who was seated at his table at the Governor's Ball three nights ago. His wife was wearing that dress that made her walk like a geisha girl. He forgot both their names, but he wouldn't be here long enough to make that an uncomfortable situation anyway. "Right. That was a night all right," said Bryden.

"Yeah, I'll bet it's not often you get a good old fashioned donnybrook at the Governor's mansion. No sir."

"No, sir indeed. So am I okay to go through?"

"Hmm? Oh, sure. Yeah, you go right on through. Meetin' up with your wife, are you?"

"Pardon me?" The custom's officer now had Bryden's undivided attention.

"Mrs. Downey. She came through here a couple of days ago in a big rig. Judy saw her."

"Right, right. Yes, I'm meeting up with her, yes."

"Where?"

"Excuse me?"

"Where ya' meetin' up with her?" It never occurred to Ron Winkley that Bryden Downey meeting up with his wife somewhere might be a private matter and not fodder for the public rumour mill.

"Well, we want to keep that a secret. We don't get away very often and when we do, we don't like to be disturbed."

"Gotcha," Ron said with a wink. "Yeah, nothin' like make-up sex."

Bryden ignored the last inappropriate comment. He moved on to more important matters. "I don't suppose my wife told Judy where we were meeting, huh?"

"No sir. She was tight lipped. Don't you worry about that."

"Good." Bryden flashed one of the many insincere smiles that he had in his politician's repertoire.

"So, why was your wife ridin' with that trucker? He a friend of yours?"

"A friend?" Bryden searched his calculating mind for a suitable response. He always had the right answer for every question. This talent would stand him in good stead further on down the political road. "No. Not a friend. A relative."

"A relative, huh?"

"My wife's cousin. A loose cannon. Never quite got his life together, so we help him out whenever we can. My wife is keeping an eye on him."

The customs officer looked at Bryden with a blank stare. Apparently this answer needed more elaboration.

"Drugs," added Bryden.

"Ohhhh. Well, you can't choose your relatives, right? Okay, off you go then."

Bryden flashed one final politician's smile at customs officer Ron Winkley, stepped on the accelerator and moved off into Canada.

-26-

Grace Downey's first stop on her second morning in Rainbow was the Allemane's dining room. She would have breakfast and then take another walk around the town. She did the same yesterday and discovered there wasn't very much to see, but she allowed that maybe she hadn't seen everything the town had to offer, and today she was going to give it a second chance. That fact was, she *had* seen everything the town had to offer. Her explorer's coffers were not going to get any richer on this day.

"Good morning, Grace."

Grace turned to see Leo Terrio sitting with the two sixty-something women who had been in the dining room the morning before. Yesterday morning Leo had offered Grace a big ear to ear smile. This morning there was no smile. Leo was obviously still affected greatly by the news of Bonnie Hoyt's death.

"Oh, good morning, Leo. Good morning, ladies."

"Good morning," the ladies replied as one.

"Good morning," a new voice came from behind Grace.

Grace turned again and saw waitress Debbie Lynch coming out of the dining room kitchen. She was bringing a pot of tea to the two ladies.

"Oh, hi," Grace responded. She smiled a quick, friendly smile at Debbie. The volley of good mornings was completed now, and Grace moved to an empty table near the window.

"Good morning," came a voice from the front door.

Grace looked up to see Pete Golliger and Wood Lynch entering the dining room through the door that led to the street.

"Good morning," Grace said for the third time.

"Morning," said Officer Lynch.

"Grace, I don't think you've met Wood," said Pete as the two officers moved toward her table. "Wood, this is Grace."

"Hi," said Wood, removing his hat and offering a noticeable bow in Grace's direction.

"Hello," responded Grace.

"I saw you in the squad car the other night."

"Hmm? Oh, right. At the uh . . . at the house."

"The murder scene," Wood said.

"Right."

"Bobby. Pete." Debbie Lynch joined the trio at Grace's table.

"Hi, Mom," said Wood. He gave Debbie a peck on the cheek.

"Hi Debbie," said Pete. He removed his hat as well and fiddled with it at his belt buckle.

"Pete, you're here again?" Debbie looked gobsmacked by Pete's second appearance in as many mornings.

"Yep."

"Two days in a row. Wow," Debbie turned in the direction of Leo Terrio. "Leo, Pete's here again."

"Good morning, Pete," Leo shouted from across the room.

"Leo," replied Pete.

"Good morning, officers," the two ladies said in unison.

"Good morning," replied Pete, wondering if the two ladies practiced speaking together like that or if it was just years of being with each other that made it come naturally.

"Good morning," yelled Wood, taking his volume cue from Leo. Wood thought he had to yell, not because of the size of the room, but because of the age of the two women he was speaking to.

Grace made this the tenth 'good morning' that had been offered up so far.

"Do you mind if we join you?" Pete asked Grace.

"Not at all. Be my guest."

"I think I'll just sit over here, Pete," said Wood. "I'm gonna talk to my mom for a while."

"Oh, okay. Sure Wood," Pete actually welcomed the idea of sitting alone with Grace. He wasn't looking to make any romantic overtures here, but being a man, the thought of sitting alone with an attractive woman was always appealing.

Wood moved to a table in the furthest corner of the room and sat by himself. Debbie gave him a sign as if to say she would be right there, and then she moved to Grace and Pete.

'What it'll be this morning, folks?"

"I'll just have a coffee and grapefruit please," replied Grace.

"Coffee and grapefruit," echoed Debbie. She didn't write the order down. She could handle coffee and grapefruit all right. "Pete? The breakfast special again?"

"Sounds good to me."

"You gonna eat it this time?"

"What?"

"Well, you ordered it yesterday and then you bolted out of here before you ate it."

"Oh, right," Pete thought back to yesterday morning. Leo Terrio had told Pete that he saw Tom Lasalle in the graveyard on the evening of Bonnie's murder. This prompted Pete to rush out of the dining room to drive to the golf course to have a little talk with Tom. This was the memorable 'go fuck yourself' conversation. "No, I think I'll finish it this morning, Debbie."

Debbie left the dining room and headed to the kitchen to place the orders.

"How's the investigation going?" asked Grace. "Or is that confidential?"

"Well, there isn't a whole lot that's confidential in a town this size," Pete replied. He assumed, correctly, that Information Coordinator Lori Higgenson had kept the Rainbow citizenry well-informed about the on going investigation. "We've got a couple of leads that we're going to follow up on here shortly."

"Good."

"And you?"

"What about me?"

"Well, how was your day yesterday," asked Pete.

"Oh, quiet."

"And that's good, right?"

Grace smiled. "Yes, that's very good."

"Well, I hope you'll have another quiet day today. Any plans?"

Debbie Lynch entered from the kitchen with a pot of coffee. "Here's your coffee." Debbie stood beside the table and poured coffee in the two cups in front of her customers. Their conversation came to a grinding halt as she performed this task. This break in the proceedings did not go unnoticed by the waitress. "Did I interrupt?"

"Nope," Pete replied quickly.

"Are you sure?" continued Debbie. "Because I heard you ask her if she had any plans today and then as soon as I arrived the chatter seemed to stop, meaning either she has no plans, or she has plans that she didn't want me to overhear. So, which is it, Dear?"

"Debbie? Please?" Pete turned his palms up indicating that he wanted Debbie to stop her line of questioning.

"Just being friendly, Pete. Just being friendly." Debbie gave Pete a playful wink and moved off to talk to her son at a table in the furthest corner of the dining room.

"So, was she right?" Pete smiled at Grace. "Do you have plans that you didn't want her to overhear?"

"No," Grace relied with a smile of her own. "I'm just . . . In my current situation I'd rather not make my plans public knowledge."

"I understand."

"I really have no plans today. I was just going to take a walk around town."

"Didn't you do that yesterday?" asked Pete.

"How did you know that?"

Pete looked at Grace and raised his eyebrows slightly as if to say 'How do you think I knew?'

"Oh, right. Small town."

"That's it."

"Well, yes I did, but I don't have anything else to do so what the hell?"

Pete noticed a sign of resignation in Grace's voice. And then, out of the blue, he was suddenly struck with a brilliant idea. "Hey, why don't you let Leo show you around?"

"Leo?"

"Sure. No one knows this town better than Leo. He could give you a walking tour. Show you all the high points," Pete turned to Leo, still seated two tables over with his two lady friends. "Leo? Come ere' for a second."

Without hesitation, Leo excused himself and move to Pete and Grace.

"Leo, I've got a job for you."

"Sure. What job?"

"I want you to show Grace around town today. Give her the grand tour. Tell her all you know about the place?"

"Really?" replied Leo.

"Sure. Grace? Would you like that?"

"I think that would be lovely. If it's all right with you, Leo." Grace looked up at the big man standing beside her.

"It's all right with me. I know a lot about this town."

"You're being modest, Leo," Pete interjected. "You know *everything* about this town."

"Yeah, I guess I do", replied Leo, with a noticeable puffing of his chest. "More than most anyway."

"Then it's a date," said Pete.

Leo looked at Pete with a big question mark in his eyes.

"Well, not a date. Not a date date," Pete backpedaled feverishly. "It's a get together. A stroll through town." Pete saw a release of pressure in Leo's eyes as if they were heaving a sigh of relief. "So, Leo, as soon as Grace and I are finished breakfast, you two can head off. How's that sound?"

"Good," replied Leo.

"It's a date," added Grace, and she smiled at both men.

Without realizing it, Pete had killed two birds with one stone. He had a tour guide for Grace, and he had given his boxer friend Leo something to take his mind off of Bonnie Hoyt's untimely end.

*

"You look tired, Bobby," Debbie Lynch observed as she poured coffee into her son's cup.

"Well, I just came off shift," replied Wood. "I'm a little groggy."

"Are you sure that's all it is?" She sat in the chair opposite Wood and set the coffee pot down.

"Yeah, I'm just tired," said Wood, putting a spoonful of sugar into his cup of coffee. "Just tired."

Debbie reached her hand out and laid it on top of her son's. Wood didn't look up from his coffee cup. He just stirred the sugar round and round. If he looked up, his mother might see a hint of moisture appear from behind his eyes, for the mere touch of her hand had caused his sadness to the break the surface.

"Jeannie's moving. To Kingston. Next week. She got a job." Wood broke one sentence into four, fearful that he might choke on the words if he tried to string too many of them together at once.

"Oh, Bobby," Debbie whispered as her hand now grabbed Wood's hand. She watched as her son swallowed hard.

"It'll be okay though," Wood continued, in attempt to allay his mother's fears more than his own. "I can visit. You know, I can visit a lot." Wood looked at Debbie ever so briefly and flashed a reassuring smile that vanished as quickly as it had appeared.

"What kind of job?" asked Debbie.

"Hotel. Managing a hotel," Wood replied, still keeping his sentences short. "Yeah, it's a good job. A good move for her. A move up. She'll be happy."

Debbie searched for the right words but Wood changed the subject before those words could be spoken.

"Boy, this Bonnie Hoyt murder has taken a strange turn," he blurted.

"How so?"

"Well, we're going to be interviewing a person of interest here right after breakfast. I can't tell you who it is just yet, but it will set this town on its heels if it turns out he had anything to do with it." Wood shook his head and lifted his coffee cup to his lips.

"Oh, you mean Mickey Welton."

"What?" The coffee cup stopped just short of Wood's mouth and hung there in limbo.

"Mickey Welton. Your person of interest. That's who it is, isn't it?"

"Who told you that?" Wood set the coffee cup back in its place on the saucer.

"Kate told me," Debbie said matter-of-factly, as if this inside police information was common knowledge.

"Kate? Kate Leger?"

"Yeah."

"Well, who told Kate?"

"Helen Fry's girl Roberta."

"Roberta Fry?"

"Yeah."

The pieces immediately fell into place for Wood. Roberta Fry was Information Coordinator Lori Higgenson's friend and confidante. Lori had struck again.

"Jesus, we only found out about this twenty minutes ago," Wood said with astonishment. "The news made it over here quicker than we did."

"Well, Roberta called Kate on another matter this morning," Debbie explained. "She was wondering if she left her scarf here last night when she was here for dinner. And in the course of their conversation, Mickey's name came up because of the Jeopardy show and then it naturally segued to Bonnie's murder. She hadn't though."

"Hadn't what?"

"Left her scarf here."

"Oh Jesus. Pete?" Wood called across the room to his co-investigator Pete Golliger who appeared to be enjoying his conversation with the new woman in town, Grace, and retired boxer Leo Terrio.

"Yeah?" Pete turned to look at Wood.

"My mother knows about Mickey."

"What?!" Pete was no less surprised than Wood was at hearing this news and his tone indicated as much.

"You mean Mickey Welton being a suspect in Miss Hoyt's murder?" lady number one chimed in from her table. "We were shocked to hear that as well, weren't we?" She looked across the table to lady number two.

"I nearly choked on my Shredded Wheat," replied lady number two.

"Oh, shit," muttered Pete. He looked at Wood. "How the hell did this happen?"

"Roberta Fry," Wood answered.

"Oh, shit."

"Did she find her scarf?" asked lady number one.

"What?" Pete looked at the woman in bewilderment.

"I was talking to Mrs. Lynch," said lady number one.

"No, she didn't," replied Debbie.

"Oh, that's too bad. She bought that in Halifax you know. Last Valentine's Day."

"That's the one with the hearts, right?" said lady numbered two.

"Yes, dear," lady number one said with reassurance. "Valentine's Day is the one with the hearts."

"No," replied lady number two. "I mean the scarf. The scarf had hearts on it."

"Oh! Yes, I believe it did now that you mention it."

"Come on, Wood," Pete said as he stood up from his table.

"Where we goin'?" asked Wood. Following Pete's lead, he pushed himself away from his table and stood.

"We're going to . . ." Pete looked at the two sixty-something ladies at their table. He waited until Wood was standing beside him before completing his sentence.

"We're gonna talk to Mickey now before he hears about this," he said in a hushed tone.

"The store doesn't open for another ten minutes yet," said Wood, echoing Pete's hushed tone.

"We're police officers, Wood. God! We'll get them to let us in early."

"All right, but Mickey might not be there yet."

"Then we'll be there waiting for him when he gets there." Pete turned to Debbie Lynch. "Debbie, I gotta run. I'll pay you for the breakfast now."

Debbie stood and picked up her coffee pot. "But you didn't even eat it. You haven't even *seen* it."

"I'm sure it looks great but I'll have to skip it, Debbie. Sorry."

"Again?"

"Yeah. Leo, you can have my breakfast, okay?"

"Again?"

"Yes, again," replied Pete, searching his uniform pocket for some money.

"But, I had your breakfast yesterday, Pete," Leo replied with an ex-boxer's well-earned dismay.

"Well, you can have it again today," said Pete. "There's no law that says a person can't give away his breakfast two days in a row, is there?"

"Well, you should know," lady number two piped up. She then turned to lady number one. "Shouldn't he know?"

Pete ignored the interjection from the seniors' table. "Grace, I hope you have a nice day today. Leo, you show her a good time, okay? I'm counting on you." The officer set a five dollar bill on the table to pay for his breakfast order.

"I'll show her the best time, Pete," Leo responded confidently.

"I know you will," Pete gave Leo a firm pat on the shoulder and moved towards the front door. Wood was hot on his heels.

"Bobby?" Debbie, coffee pot still in her hand, moved quickly across the dining room to where her son stood. "You fight for her."

"What?"

"Jeannie," Debbie continued. "She loves you just as much as you love her. I can tell. I can see it. I'm a mother and mothers know these things. The both of you are just acting like a couple of damned idiots. That's all you're doing. Now, work this out, you hear? Don't let her get away. I'm thinking of my grandson now. That poor boy's suffering because his parents are giant assholes, pardon my French. Now, you work it out or so help me I'll take a yardstick to your hind end. And Jeannie's too. You hear me?"

" . . . . I hear ya." Wood was visibly taken aback by his mother's sudden outburst.

"Good. Now go and question Mickey Welton. Go on. Pete? Get him out of my sight."

Debbie turned on her heels and made a beeline for the kitchen. The kitchen's swinging door was now the only sound audible in the dining room, that was until ladies number one and two rewarded the now absent waitress with a smattering of applause.

"I think you'd better do what she says." said Pete.

"I think so," said Wood, still looking at the swinging kitchen door.

The two police officers spilled out of the dining room's front entrance and into the street, heading for Doug Petty's La-Z-Boy on the other side of town.

"I hope you find it," shouted lady number one as the door closed behind the officers.

"Find what?" asked lady number two.

"Roberta's scarf."

"Is that why they're in such a hurry?" asked lady number two.

"I think so."

"I thought they were going to question Mickey Welton at work," suggested lady number two.

"No, the store doesn't open for another ten minutes."

"Oh, right."

*

Officers Golliger and Lynch parked the police cruiser in the Rainbow police station parking lot. Doug Petty's La-Z-Boy was just up the street at the corner of Grandy and Main, and they thought it best not to draw any undue attention to their visit with Mickey Welton by parking the cruiser right in front of the store. As they strode past the front door of the police station, Pete opened the door and looked at Information Coordinator Lori Higgenson. He didn't say a word. He just stared.

"What?" said Lori innocently.

Pete remained silent as he pointed his finger at Lori with a warning he was certain she would understand.

"What?" Lori repeated.

Pete raised his eyebrows and nodded a 'you're in for it' nod, and letting go of the door he turned back toward the sidewalk.

"Pete?" Lori called just before the door closed shut.

Pete returned to the door and opened it. An apology would be a good place for his information coordinator to start, and Pete readied himself for it. He would not soften his angry boss demeanor though. He would make sure that Lori knew that he was pissed off at her, and that it would take him more than a short while or an insincere apology to get over it.

Lori held up her Tim Horton's coffee cup and shook it using only her wrist. "My coffee's gone. Are you boys goin' near the Tim Horton's?"

Pete's next stare lasted a good fifteen seconds.

"Yes? No? You're not?" Lori shook the coffee cup again as if this would hurry Pete's answer.

Pete let go of the door and turned once again for the sidewalk. Just before the door closed he heard Lori's plaintiff 'What?' squeak through the last crack and into the Rainbow air.

Pete and Wood needn't have worried about attracting attention with their police cruiser. Lori had apparently been very busy on the phone, and as they approached the front of Doug Petty's furniture store they were greeted by three of Rainbow's long time residents. Tudder Halliwell, Wood's high school football coach and the man who gave Wood his nickname, Doug Petty himself, the owner of the store, and Duffy Higgenson, the Parkinson's Disease-afflicted dentist and uncle of Information Coordinator Lori Higgenson.

"Morning, gentlemen," said Pete. He looked at Duffy. "Duffy, what's shakin'?"

"That never gets old, Pete." answered Duffy without a smile.

"Hey Wood," said Tudder, greeting his former player.

"Coach."

"Pete, did you fellas come to grill Mickey?" asked Doug.

"No, Doug, we're not grilling anybody. We just have a few questions for him, that's all."

"Duffy here told us he's your main suspect," said Tudder. "Ain't that right, Duffy?"

"That's right. I have it from a reliable source. I can't say who but it's very reliable."

"Oh, shit Duffy, we all know it's your niece," said Wood. "Christ, she couldn't keep a secret to save her life."

"Sorry. I can't say who it is," replied Duffy, and he locked his lips and threw the key over his shoulder.

"I wish your niece would do that sometime," said Pete.

"Mickey's not here yet, Pete," said Doug. "I don't know where he is."

"Well, you don't open for another five minutes yet, right?"

"Oh, but Mickey's always here early. Usually gets here at nine-thirty. Like clockwork. But not today."

"Uh-oh," muttered Wood. "Maybe he's in the wind."

"Maybe he's what?" said Pete.

"In the wind. You know, on the run. Splitsville."

Pete had used two quality stares on Lori, but he still had one good one left for Wood. "You have got to stop watching those crime shows."

"Here he comes," exclaimed Tudder pointing down Main Street.

The five men turned all at once and looked down Main Street to where Tudder was pointing. Mickey Welton was walking past Teeks, the antique store located next to The Frying Dutchman. He was looking down at the sidewalk in front of him as he walked, and as a result he failed to notice the greeting party that awaited him in front of Doug Petty's La-Z-Boy.

"Maybe we should hide," said Duffy.

"It's not a surprise party, Duffy," said Pete. "Jesus."

"Well, we don't want to spook him," replied the dentist. "He might run off."

"That's right. He'll be in the wind." Tudder nudged Wood with his elbow and smiled at his former tight end.

"Tudder, why don't you and Duffy move along now?" Pete suggested. "Doug, open the store, would ya' please?"

"But it's not ten o'clock," Doug replied.

"I don't mean open it for business. I mean open it so we can go inside and question Mickey."

"You wanna question him in here? In my store?"

"Yes."

"Why don't we question him at the station?" asked Wood.

"Yeah, right. In front of Lori? I don't think so." Pete looked at Tudder and Duffy. "You're still here."

"We're goin'. We're goin. Come on Duffy."

"Doug, open the door please," Pete implored the store owner.

"Right. Sure." Doug took his keys out of his pocket and unlocked the front door.

Coach Halliwell and Duffy moved slowly down the sidewalk in the direction of the police station. Pete and Wood turned their glances up Main Street. Mickey was now looking at the two officers who waited for him. He was at the northeast corner of Main and Grandy, only thirty or forty feet away from the officers who stood waiting at the northwest corner. As they watched Mickey step into the street and cross towards them, neither Pete nor Wood saw Tudder and Duffy enter the police station.

"Hi Mickey."

"Mr. Golliger. Wood. How ya' doin'?"

"Good, Mickey, good," replied Pete.

"Nice job on Jeopardy, Mick," said Wood with a friendly smile.

"Thanks," replied Mickey. He had reached his destination and he now stood outside the front door of the store with the three men.

"I'm surprised you didn't get the Vancouver Canucks question though," said Wood.

"Well, I knew the answer but she buzzed in first."

"The real estate woman," said Wood.

"Right."

"Yeah she was good."

"Can we talk to you for a minute, Mickey?" Pete appreciated Wood's amiable conversation with the Welton boy. It might put him at ease, if anything could, but now it was time to get down to business.

"Sure. What about?" asked Mickey. He smoothed his tie and shoved his hands into his pants pockets.

"Let's go inside," said Pete with a nod of his head towards the front door of the furniture store.

Doug Petty opened the front door and stood back holding it open as he stared at Mickey. Mickey looked at the three men, one by one. There were no smiles on any of their faces.

"I'd like to know what it's about first," said Mickey flashing a nervous smile. "Can't you tell me what it's about?"

This hesitation on Mickey's part was a red flag to Officer Lynch. He feigned kicking at a pebble on the sidewalk in order to take the two steps to his left which would put him behind Mickey. He was now in position just in case the young man decided to turn tail and make a run for it.

"We'll tell you inside," answered Pete

There was another small hesitation. Mickey looked behind him at Wood and then back to Officer Golliger. He finally said 'Okay' and the four men entered the store. Wood followed Mickey in and the two of them moved toward the far end of the establishment. Pete stayed back and as the door closed behind him he whispered to Doug Petty.

"Lock the door, will ya', Doug?"

"But, it's after ten now."

"What?"

"It's after ten. I'm open for business."

"I know but I don't want people coming in here during the interrogation," Pete explained.

"Is that what this is? An interrogation? I thought you were just going to ask him a few questions."

"That's what an interrogation is, Doug. It's questions."

"No, I think an interrogation is a lot more serious than that, Pete. An interrogation is browbeating and sweating and pounding the table and good cop bad cop, like that."

"I'll tell you what, Doug," said Pete trying to avoid a heavy sigh. His patience had been tested quite severely already this morning and it was now dangling from a very slender thread. "Maybe you should wait outside the store. That way if any customers come along, you can tell them that you'll be open shortly, and then you won't lose any business."

Doug thought about this for a second. "Good idea."

"Good."

"Just promise me one thing, Pete"

"What's that?"

"If you pound any tables during the interrogation, pound the tables that are marked down, okay?"

"Sure."

"The scratch and dent items."

"Got it."

"Thanks."

Doug stepped outside and planted himself in front of the door like a sentry. Pete shook his head and moved to the back of the store where Wood and Mickey waited.

"Pete knew all the Beatles questions," Wood said to Mickey. "Isn't that right, Pete?"

"Pardon me?" asked Pete. He had walked in on their conversation and didn't know exactly where that conversation sat at the moment.

"Henry Van Etten told me. You watched Mickey on Jeopardy with him at The Frying Dutchman, right? And he said you got all the Beatles questions right."

"Oh, right. Yeah, I guess I did."

"That's because he's older," Wood said with a wink to Mickey.

"Thanks, Wood."

Pete looked down at Mickey who was sitting in one of the display chairs. Wood sat opposite Mickey in another display chair. As good as those chairs were, Mickey did not look comfortable.

"So, Mickey," Pete began. "We need to talk to you about Bonnie Hoyt."

Pete paused and waited for a response from Mickey but none was forthcoming. The young man just sat there and stared up at the officer.

"Mickey? Did you hear what Pete said?" asked Wood.

"Uh-huh," Mickey replied, looking over at Wood.

"Well?" continued Wood. "Don't you have anything to say?"

"About what? You said you wanted to talk to me about it, but you haven't talked to me yet. What am I supposed to say?"

Wood looked up at Pete. "He's got a point, Pete. Technically we haven't started talking to him about it yet."

"All right, Mickey, look," Pete continued. "We know you were in Bonnie's back yard the night she was murdered. We know that much. You're not going to deny that, right?"

Mickey didn't answer. He looked across to Officer Lynch.

"Forensics matched your boots to footprints we found in the mud near Bonnie's back gate, Mickey," Wood explained. "That's how we know." Wood stood up from his display chair. He figured looking down on Mickey like Pete was would be a much stronger position to fire questions from. "And now what we want to know is, what were you doing there."

"Nothin'. I was just . . . . Miss Hoyt was coming over to watch Jeopardy at my house, that's all."

"Well, that doesn't explain why you were at her house, Mick," countered Wood.

"She was bringing some stuff over and I went to help her carry it."

"What stuff?"

"Champagne and stuff."

"Champagne."

"Yeah."

Wood looked over at Pete. Pete continued to stare down at Mickey. Both officers liked the Welton boy. He had excelled despite being from a severely dysfunctional home and they admired that. But they could both tell, this early in the interrogation, that Mickey was involved in the Bonnie Hoyt case somehow. They were hoping he would have a reasonable explanation for them, but so far, the smartest young man in Rainbow was coming up short in the smarts department.

"Come on Mickey," said Pete. "You went over to help Bonnie carry a bottle of champagne? Shit. Were you having sex with Bonnie? Was that it?"

"No", Mickey replied emphatically.

"We're you sneaking over to her place to get some before your show came on?"

"No! We weren't having sex! Miss Hoyt was a friend. Just a friend. She helped me get ready for the Jeopardy show. She was the best friend I had in this town."

"Why'd you come in through the back way, Mick?" Wood asked.

"I rode my bike over. I took the path in the field behind her house. It's faster."

Pete and Wood exchanged glances again. They both knew that it would have been faster to go right up Yarbro and onto Winston Street from Mickey's house. To get to the path in that field, Mickey would have to ride past Winston Street and then come back towards Bonnie's on the path.

"The fact is, Mickey," Pete began. "You went in the back way because you didn't want anybody to see you. Now do you want to tell us the real reason you went over there?"

Mickey looked at Pete and then at Wood. He ran his hand over the name tag on his shirt and sat forward in the big chair. He looked as though he was about to come clean, and then as if having a change of heart, he smoothed his tie and sat back. "I told you. I went over to help."

"So, why didn't you go in?"

"I knocked on the door but there was no answer."

"Did you look in the kitchen window to see if anyone was inside?"

"I don't remember."

"Did you try the back door to see if it was open?"

"I don't think so."

"Who was she having sex with?"

"I don't know."

"Aw Jesus Christ," Pete turned away and looked out towards the front door of the furniture store. There were now two or three people standing outside talking to Doug Petty. Pete reckoned they were customers and that this interrogation was holding up any completion of business the store might have. It didn't matter though. The questioning of Mickey Welton was far more important than a furniture sale. He turned back to Mickey with determination splashed across his face. "All right, here's what I think. Wood, you tell me if you agree with this or not," Pete spoke to Wood without taking his eyes off of Mickey. "Now, you were having intimate relations with Miss Hoyt."

"No, I wasn't."

"Well, I think you were. You two worked together all those months to get you ready for your appearance on Jeopardy and over time the relationship took a romantic turn even though she was much older than you. But, that's not unheard of. Happens all the time. So, on September the 21'st sometime between five-thirty and six you went over to her place. You came up to the back door and looked inside the kitchen window and you could see her in the hallway mirror. She was having sex on the floor with some other man."

"He could see that from the hallway mirror?" Wood interrupted.

"Yeah."

"How do you know that?"

"Because when we were investigating I was standing on the back porch and I looked in through the window and I could see Bonnie's body on the floor through the mirror."

"Oh."

"Now", Pete turned his attention back to Mickey. So you . . ."

"You didn't tell me that," continued Wood.

"What?"

"You didn't tell me you could see Bonnie in the mirror through the kitchen window."

"I thought I did", said Pete.

"No, I don't think you did."

"Well, I'm sorry."

"No, that's okay."

"I thought I did."

"No, that's fine."

"Can I continue now?"

"Yeah, sure. I just don't think you told me."

"Well, I thought I did."

"Well, I'm pretty sure you didn't."

"Fine. Then I guess I didn't. Fuck." Pete looked at Wood waiting for yet another intrusive response but there was none. He turned his attention to Mickey once again.

"I think I would have remembered if you told me", said Wood.

Pete stared at Mickey for a moment, ignoring Wood, and then finally he made an effort to continue. " . . . . Shit,. where was I?"

"Bonnie was having sex on the floor with some other man," Wood said.

"Right. Thanks."

"You saw it in the mirror."

"Right. Thank you. So, she was sitting on top of him and they were having sex. This made you very upset. It sent you into a rage. You couldn't think straight . . ."

"No," Mickey protested.

"Lemme finish."

"Yeah, let him finish," said Wood, very interested in hearing the rest of Pete's story at this point.

"You took a golf club out of the bag on the back porch and you went inside and you hit Bonnie with the golf club and you killed her. Then you ran out the back door again and went home. Later on, you remembered that you might have left fingerprints, so you went back to Bonnie's house and cleaned up. You ran the golf club under the kitchen tap. That's how the blood got down in the sink. And then you wiped off the golf club. That's why it was the only club in the golf bag that was dry. And that's why your boot print was in the back yard because you came back after the rainstorm. So, is that how it went down or not?"

Before Mickey could respond, Wood stood up and moved a few steps toward the front of the store. "Pete, can I see you for a second?"

"What?"

"Can I talk to you for a second?"

"What for?"

"Mickey, we'll be right back. Pete?"

"I'm at the climax of the questioning, Wood. You want to talk now??"

"Just take a second."

Pete moved to Wood and they took a few more steps toward the front door so that they could talk out of earshot of their suspect, for that was what he was now. A suspect.

"What are you doing? I think he was just about to break."

"When did you come up with this?"

"Come up with what?" asked Pete.

"This scenario you just presented. When did you come up with that?"

"On the way over here."

"On the way over here? What just now?"

"Yeah."

"In the squad car?"

"Well, it was what your mother said. She said you and Jeannie loved each other and that you should fight for her. It suddenly hit me that Mickey might be in love with Bonnie and that he could be the only one in town who could be jealous of Bonnie sleeping with somebody else. Everybody we asked said she wasn't seeing anyone. She wasn't dating. And her and Mickey were spending a lot of time together. I just thought maybe something sparked between them. And that's what started this whole thing. And her bathrobe was closed. Who else but a nice guy like Mickey would close the woman's bathrobe after he killed her? He was remorseful almost instantly. He saw her lying there with the robe open and she was naked underneath and so he closed the bathrobe for her."

" . . . . And you figured all that out on the way over here?"

"Yeah."

"It's a five minute drive."

"Well, that's when it came to me all right? God. So, does the story sound plausible to you?"

"Which one? The one about Mickey killing Bonnie or about you thinkin' it up on the way over?"

"Mickey killing Bonnie," Pete replied, putting his hands on his hips and grabbing his belt.

" . . . .Yeah. Yeah, I guess it does make sense."

"Good." Pete looked out the front door of the furniture store where there were now about ten people standing with Doug Petty. "There's a crowd gathering out there."

"Hmm?" Wood look toward the front door. "Boy, I'll say there is. Well, Doug's got good prices."

"Do you really think that's what it is?" asked Pete with a noticeable trace of derision, and he moved to the back of the store again and stood in front of Mickey.

Wood followed Pete and the two officers confronted the Welton boy once again, but before they could press Mickey for more information, the young man spoke up.

"That's not how it went down, Mr. Golliger," said Mickey.

"Well, how did it go down then, Mick?" asked Wood. "Have you got a better explanation?"

Mickey leaned forward and looked to the floor again. Surely this time he was going to come forth with the real story about that night. He clasped his hands and rubbed his thumbs together so hard that one would think he was trying to spark a campfire.

"Mickey?" said Pete softly in attempt to release the boy from his silence. "Tell us. What happened?"

Mickey unclasped his hands and put them on his hips. Leaning forward the way he was, it looked as though he was preparing to throw up. He took a deep breath. And then another deep breath as if to steel himself.

"I don't know what happened. I can't help you. I'm sorry."

Officers Golliger and Lynch looked down at Mickey Welton. There was a pause that hung in the air like a thick Saint John, New Brunswick fog.

"Well," Pete began, "I just wish you were denying it with a little more conviction, Mickey. I just wish you could give us that much." Pete looked at Wood. "We're gonna have to take him in."

"Yeah, I guess we are," agreed Wood.

"Shit." Pete turned away from Mickey, his frustration showing once again.

"Let's go, Mick," said Wood.

Mickey stood. "Are you sure you have enough proof?" he asked.

"What?" Pete looked at Mickey incredulously.

"Well, you don't have any proof, do you? All you know is that I was at Miss Hoyt's *after* she was killed. Everything else you have, you know, wiping off the golf club, seeing her having sex with somebody else, that's all conjecture, isn't it? You can't prove any of that. I mean I know that sometimes people get convicted based on circumstantial evidence but I don't even think you have enough of that."

"Too bad they didn't have any legal questions on Jeopardy. You might've won the fucking thing." Pete took Mickey by the arm. "Let's go."

As the officers and their suspect approached the front door of Doug Petty's La-Z-Boy they noticed what was now a throng of citizens gathered outside.

"What the hell?" muttered Wood. "What's going on here?"

"Well," surmised Pete, "My guess is that Duffy and Tudder went to see Lori and told her we were here with Mickey and then our Information Coordinator took it from there."

"Look at everybody," said Wood, scanning the crowd. "Glen Makarides, Jimmy Cane, George Fullmer, Wendy Norton. God, I haven't seen her in a long time. She looks good."

"Wood, let's just go, okay?"

Officer Lynch opened the door and Pete ushered Mickey outside.

"All right, stand back folks, okay?" said Wood. "Give us some room here."

"Did Mickey do it, Wood?" asked Doug.

"We're just taking him in for questioning, Doug. We don't have any answers yet."

"Did you do it, Mickey?!" came a voice from the crowd.

"Aw, come on folks. Leave him alone, all right?" Wood began backing his way down the sidewalk, quelling the crowd as he went.

Pete and Mickey were almost at the front door of the Rainbow Police station now.

"Hi, Wood," a woman's voice called out from somewhere inside the group of thirty or so citizens.

"Hi, Wendy," replied Wood with a wave. "How ya' been?"

"I got food poisoning last week in Moncton," came Wendy's reply. "But I'm okay now."

"Glad to hear that."

Pete and Mickey entered the police station. Wood was only a few seconds behind them and he turned back to look at the crowd as he stood in the police station doorway. The crowd stared back at the officer, not knowing what else to do. They appeared to be awaiting instructions.

"You can all go about your business now," Wood called back to everybody.

The citizens didn't seem to know how to react. Nobody ever got murdered in Rainbow. And now one of their favourite sons – the young man who appeared on Jeopardy only two nights before – was being taken into custody. They seemed numbed by the whole affair. They fell silent as a group and shuffled off slowly in different directions, like zombies from a nineteen-fifties B movie. They then went about their business as best they could.

-27-

Dan had placed a phone call to the Allemane Inn from Shiner's Truck Stop. The trucker ran back inside after Bryden had pulled out of the parking lot in his black BMW and headed north toward the border.

"Luanne, I need to use your phone."

"Is it a local call?" the waitress asked.

"No."

"Then I can't help you, Dan. Sorry."

"Luanne, it's an emergency. Please."

"Dan, if I let you make a long distance call I'll be in deep shit with Bill. He'll take it out of my pay."

Dan reached into his pocket and pulled out a twenty dollar bill.

"Here you can take it out of that and keep the change." He slapped the bill onto the counter.

"Done. Help yourself."

"This is your fault in the first place, you know? For shootin' your mouth off to that guy about Grace. This is all your fault."

Luanne shoved the twenty into her smock pocket. "You're still not gettin' any change back."

Dan called the Allemane at nine-thirty that morning and got a busy signal. He called right back and got the busy signal again.

"Goddamn it!" He slammed the phone down.

"Twenty dollars won't cover a broken phone, Dan," said Luanne from the other end of the counter.

Dan waited two more minutes and called again.

Kate Leger, the proprietress of the Allemane Inn was sitting at the front desk of the establishment. Last night had been a late night for Kate. Peggy Welton had stayed in the lounge right up until closing time. By the time Kate had cleaned up after everyone it was two in the morning, and she was up again at six-thirty this morning to prepare for the breakfast crowd. She sat at the desk and wearily flipped through this month's issue of Vogue Magazine. When the phone rang she sighed a highly-annoyed sigh. She had just gotten off the phone with her niece Wendy Norton. Wendy said she was heading over to Doug Petty's La-Z-Boy because she heard a rumour that the police were going to arrest Mickey Welton. Wendy wanted to know if Kate wanted to come with her. Kate had already heard the rumour about an hour earlier from Roberta Fry when Roberta called concerning a missing scarf. Kate declined Wendy's offer. She was not one to go traipsing along with a bunch of busybodies and poking her nose in where it didn't belong. In the course of the conversation Wendy told Kate about getting food poisoning in Moncton last week. Kate had already heard that story too from Wendy herself a few days earlier, but she listened politely to the salmonella update, and then Wendy said goodbye and hung up. Kate hoped this next call wasn't some other concerned citizen calling to spread the word about the impending arrest of Mickey Welton.

"Allemane Inn? Kate speaking."

"Hi. Could I speak with Grace please?"

There was a pause at the Allemane's end of the phone. Grace had told Kate that if somebody called for her, Kate should say there's no one there by that name. This was just between Kate and Grace. Even Officer Pete Golliger wasn't to know this. Kate had kept her word and not told anyone, proving that she was one of the few residents of Rainbow who could keep a secret.

"I'm sorry. There's no one by that name here."

"No, there is. Yes. I was in there last night with her. Is this the owner? Uhh . . . . shit . . . uh..Kate? Is this Kate?"

"Yes, this is Kate. That's why I said, 'Kate speaking' when I answered the phone."

"Right." Dan hadn't even heard anything after 'Allemane Inn', he was so anxious to get connected to Grace.

"Yeah, I don't often answer with 'Luther' speaking."

"Right. Well, I was in your place last night with Grace. My name is Dan. I'm a truck driver. We had a drink around nine o'clock. Remember? Some guy asked Grace to play Honey in some play he was doing. He called me swarthy. He asked me to take off my shirt."

There was no answer at the other end.

"Come on, Kate. You remember me. I know you do."

"I remember you," came Kate's voice at long last.

"Good. So can I speak to Grace please?"

There was another silence at the Allemane end of the phone. Grace's instructions to Kate were very clear. If somebody called, she wasn't here. She didn't say those instructions were to change if a truck driver named Dan called.

"Kate?"

"She's not here."

"Well, do you know where she is? Can you get hold of her?"

"I just know that she's not here."

"Okay, look, I think that Grace might be in trouble."

"In trouble how? What kind of trouble?"

Now it was Dan's turn to be careful concerning the dispensing of information. He knew that Grace wanted to keep her whereabouts a secret and he knew that by mentioning Bryden Downey's name, he might be saying more than Grace wanted anyone to know.

"I'm not sure exactly," Dan said.

"Can you hold on for a second please?"

Dan could hear the sound of a hand covering the mouthpiece of the phone at the other end. He used to hear that sound when he was talking to his former baseball agent during contract talks. More often than not, when the hand was taken off the phone and his agent came back on the line, Dan would get the news that he had been traded. The sound of a hand covering a phone was never a good harbinger for Dan.

At the Allemane's end of the phone, Debbie Lynch was just passing by the front desk on her way to the washroom. Kate put her hand over the phone and spoke in a hushed whisper to the waitress.

"Debbie? Debbie?"

Debbie didn't hear Kate and she continued towards the washroom..

"Debbie!" The hushed tone was no longer evident.

"Hmm? What?"

"Is Grace still in the dining room?"

"No, she left about ten minutes ago with Leo. They're going for a walk around town I think."

"Thanks." Kate removed her hand from the phone's mouthpiece. "Hello?"

"Yes? I'm here."

Kate was about to speak into the phone, but she noticed that Debbie had not moved. She was still standing there, listening. Kate covered the phone again with her hand. "Okay, that's all I need to know."

"That's it?" Asked Debbie.

"Uh-huh."

"Okay," replied Debbie and she moved off in the direction of her original destination.

"Uh . . . Grace isn't here."

"Yes, you already told me that," said Dan impatiently.

"I know, but this time it's the truth. She's not here."

"Well, can I leave a message for her then?"

There was yet another pause from the Allemane end of the phone. Kate's exhausted brain was working overtime, trying to think fast. If she said she would take a message for Grace, then that would mean that Grace would be there at some point later on. Did Grace want this man to know that? How did Kate know that this man wasn't a cause for concern for Grace. A threat. Sure they looked like they were enjoying each other's company last night, but a lot can happen in a matter of hours. Relationships can go sour in a matter of minutes.

"Jesus. Hello?" came the voice from the Shiner's Truck Stop end of the connection.

"Would you give me a minute please?" said the now irritated Kate. "I'm thinking!"

"Thinking about what? I just want to leave a message."

"Fine. You can leave a message. Fine! But I don't know if Grace will get it because I don't know if she's coming back. She might not come back. In fact, she probably won't come back. She might be gone. She might be far, far away from here now. But you can leave a message if you want, but she probably won't get it. What's the message?"

"Just tell her . . . ." Dan paused trying to formulate the message in his mind. He didn't want to give out too much information. He shouldn't mention Bryden Downey by name. Grace wouldn't want anyone in Rainbow to connect her with him. Of that, Dan was certain.

"Hello?" came the voice from the Allemane end.

"Hang on! I'm thinking!"

"Well, I haven't got all day, you know," said Kate. "I've got an inn to run." She turned a page in her Vogue Magazine. Jennifer Anniston was now staring up at her.

" . . . . Tell her there's a black BMW on the way to Rainbow."

"Come again?"

"There's a black BMW on the way to Rainbow."

"What do you mean a black BMW? You mean like the car?"

"Yes."

"A car."

"Yes."

"Is this like that car in Christine? An evil car with a mind of it's own or is someone driving the thing?"

"Would you just give her the message please?"

"Fine."

"Thank you."

"But, she probably won't get the message because she's probably not coming back so . . . ."

"I know. I know," Dan interrupted. "Just please give her the message after she probably doesn't come back, okay? Thank you."

Dan hung up the phone and turned towards the front door of Shiner's Truck Stop. As he did, he bumped into another trucker who was paying his bill at the cash register.

"Oh, sorry, Scotty," said Dan. He recognized the truck driver as one of many he had conversed with over the years at Shiner's.

'What's the rush, buddy?" said the trucker with a broad smile.

"Nothing. Excuse me."

Dan moved toward the front door but Scotty's next words stopped him cold.

"So, whatcha got goin' on with Bryden Downey?"

"What?"

"Bryden Downey. I saw you talkin' to him there a minute ago."

"Oh, nothing. Nothing. Just making conversation."

"Are you makin' time with his wife?"

"What?"

"That picture he was showin' around. That's his wife."

"Really?"

"Yeah. Shit, I recognized her right off. They're always showin' up in the society pages. They're the fuckin' Kennedys of Maine."

Luanne the waitress guffawed as she made change for Scotty. "You read the society pages?"

"The wife reads em'," said Scotty.

"Wow, Dan," said Luanne. "I guess you were riding with royalty the other day."

"What?" said Scotty.

"Yeah. Dan gave that lady a ride a couple of days ago. She was sitting in here for hours and then she left with Dan. Right, Dan?"

Dan didn't answer. He didn't even hear the last half of Luanne's sentence. He was out the front door and running towards his truck as fast as he could go.

*

The Trans-Canada Highway was a lonely stretch of road in this part of the country. It was only a single lane so it was slow going if you got behind a truck. There was talk that before long, the entire highway from Edmunston right through to Moncton would be turned into a two-lane divided highway. That couldn't happen soon enough for the New Brunswickers. They figured that better highways might improve their tourist trade somewhat. That wasn't true but it was something to chew about on a cold New Brunswick winter's night. The fact is that New Brunswick was not really a destination spot. As beautiful and as friendly as it was, it was merely the province that people drove through on their way to Nova Scotia.

Bryden couldn't help but notice the 'Watch For Moose' signs that dotted the highway. He passed eight of those signs before he came to a bigger green highway sign. It read 'Rainbow Business District, 1 Kilometer'. He looked at the clock on the dashboard. Eleven-nineteen. That was Maine time though. New Brunswick time was an hour ahead of Maine time. He would be pulling into the Rainbow Business District at the height of the lunch hour.

"Good," Bryden muttered. "Maybe I'll mingle with the lunch crowd and see what I can find out."

*

When Dan reached the border crossing in Houlton, he estimated he was now a good half hour behind Bryden Downey's BMW. Dan's plan was to drive straight to the Allemane Inn and see if Grace was there. If she wasn't, he would wait until she returned.

"Morning. Can I see your bill of lading please?"

Dan looked out his driver's side window at the smiling face of the female customs officer.

"Oh, I uh . . . I don't have my bill of lading because I'm not carrying anything. I came through here last night and now I'm just heading back on an urgent matter."

"Uh-huh?" Judy Winkley recognized the truck driver as the fellow who was giving Grace Downey a ride the day before yesterday. Judy's husband Ron had been talking to Bryden Downey earlier that morning, and during their break fifteen minutes ago, Ron had mentioned to Judy that the truck driver was Grace's drug addicted cousin and that Grace was looking after him. Keeping an eye on him was the exact quote from Bryden. And now this drug addicted trucker was in Judy's line at the border crossing, claiming to have no cargo and crossing the border for the third time in just over 36 hours.

"So can I go?" asked Dan anxious to move on through.

"No, sir, I don't believe you can go. Would you pull your truck into the second stall on your right please?"

"Pardon me?"

"Second stall on your right, sir."

"But, why? What's the problem?"

"Second stall on your right. An officer will be right with you."

"No, wait a minute."

"Thank you sir. Move along now please." Judy was sure that something was up with this guy. She would get her fellow officers to go through his truck with a fine tooth comb. If he was transporting drugs, they would find it, even if it took all day.

-28-

Leo Terrio didn't show Grace a whole lot that she hadn't already seen in her previous day's walk around Rainbow, but his running commentary on the sites of the town made up for the visual repetition she was experiencing. He talked about how the gym that he trained in when he was in his boxing heyday was one day going to be turned into an historical building to honour their storied resident. Right now it was home to Jillian Murdock's Pet Grooming Emporium, but Leo had been assured by many citizens that they were only weeks away from getting a petition started to set the historical building wheels in motion. Those assurances had been coming for at least five years, Leo observed, and mostly after a round of drinks at the Allemane's pub.

Walking by the Rainbow High School, Leo told Grace that he used to work there as boxing instructor for the school's boxing club. "They had to let me go because of financial cutbacks." Leo mouthed 'financial cutbacks' as if he had memorized the term but didn't really know what it meant. It was the reason Bonnie Hoyt had given him when she had to tell him he had been let go. She thought it unnecessary to inform Leo the real reason was that parents had complained about their children being instructed by a former boxer with diminished intellect.

Leo pointed out that Teeks, the antique shop on Main Street, used to be a barber shop owned by Slim Burgoyne. Whenever Leo had a boxing match, Slim would send the fighter a tube of hair cream. He told Leo to rub the cream all over his hair and face just before the fight. That way, his opponent's punches would slide right off of him. Leo's career record of seventy wins and fourteen losses would seem to indicate that on at least fourteen occasions, the opponent's blows didn't slide off as much as they landed flush.

Further down the street, Leo told Grace about a bar that used to occupy the site that was now a computer repair shop. This was the bar from which Marty

Lasalle emerged one night back in nineteen eighty, only to be run down by a hit and run driver. Leo said he knew Marty well but never liked the man. A bully, was how the boxer described him.

Leo talked a lot about his wife Marie during the walkabout, sometimes getting lost so deeply in his thoughts that Grace felt as tough she was eavesdropping on his memories. Marie was the love of Leo's life. He had never gotten over her loss. He said it made him realize that most men don't know how good they've got it. They take their wives for granted. They would be sorry if they ever lost them the way Leo lost Marie. Grace wondered if Bryden felt that way right now. She was fairly certain he did not.

When they walked past Doug Petty's La-Z-Boy Furniture Store, they passed a crowd of about ten or fifteen people standing outside on the sidewalk. Almost to person they said hello to Leo as he and Grace passed by. Leo commented to Grace that Doug must be having a sale and that's why a crowd was gathering. Grace knew better. She knew that Officers Golliger and Lynch were inside the furniture store questioning Mickey Welton.

At the end of Main Street, they came to Glen Makarides Esso station. Glen wasn't there. The mechanic on duty, Butch Pye, told Leo that Glen was down at Doug Petty's.

"Yeah, we just saw him," said Leo. "They're having a big sale down there I guess."

Leo and Grace spent the next hour sitting in two lawn chairs in service bay number one while Butch worked on a muffler in bay number two. As Butch banged and ripped and cursed at that muffler, Leo and Grace watched the world go by and Leo talked more about Marie.

"Marie used to make a lunch for me when I went to the gym," Leo smiled. "I never ate it because I was in training and you don't eat lunch when you're in training. You eat a big breakfast and a big supper. No lunch."

"Why no lunch?" asked Grace.

"You throw up. You start sparring and you take a shot to the stomach and you throw up."

Grace didn't ask for any further elaboration. Leo had put it very succinctly. She got the point.

"But I didn't tell Marie that because she liked making me that lunch. She was sending me off to work and she thought I should have a good lunch with me. She was happy that I was going to be eating well." Leo paused and thought for a moment, his mind going to a place where only he could visit. And then suddenly, he was back, picking at a loose piece of fabric on the arm of his lawn chair. "I used to give it to Shorty Visser. Shorty did odd jobs around the gym. Joe jobs, you know? Collecting towels, sweeping up. And he didn't have a wife who made him a lunch, so I gave him mine. He liked that."

"That was very kind of you, Leo," Grace observed.

"Well, some guys don't have wives, you know? For whatever reason. Maybe they've never found the right woman, or maybe they're too busy with careers and making money and such, or maybe they're just too ugly to attract any women. Shorty was too ugly. He died a couple of years ago. Still ugly. Still single."

Pete had told Grace about the accident that took Marie's life. Leo and Marie had been swimming off a rented houseboat on Grand Lake. Marie was about to dive in when she slipped. She banged her head on the side of the boat and went into the water unconscious. Leo's efforts to save her were in vain and her body wasn't found until the following day.

"Leo?" Grace began carefully. "Pete told me about what happened to Marie."

"Uh-huh," replied Leo, without looking at Grace. "Well, everybody knows about it. It was big news hereabouts. Big news."

Out on Koonary Road, a car passed by and honked its horn. Leo waved.

"That's Janice Simpson's boy Wayne. He's a good kid."

"I was just wondering if maybe you'd like to tell me about it. Is that something you'd like to do?"

Leo leaned his weight back in his lawn chair causing the front legs of the chair to lift off of the oily pavement beneath it. "Not much to tell," he said. "It happened pretty fast." Leo looked out onto Koonary Road, hoping that another car might pass by and serve as a distraction from the conversation that was about to take place, but there were no cars now. Only the sound of Butch Pye banging on the muffler. "I had just come out of the water and I was takin' a towel to myself because we were about to start making some dinner. Marie said she was going to take one last dive in and I said okay. I had the towel over my head and I was drying my hair and I heard a thump and I heard Marie groan a little bit and then I heard the splash. It wasn't the kind of quick splash sound that's made by someone diving in head first. You know how when they break the water with their hands first and it makes kind of a cutting into the water sound? It wasn't like that. It was an awkward splash sound. A flop kind of splash. Like somebody had dropped a big flat rock over the side and it went in flat side first. I didn't know what happened so I looked over the side of the boat to where she dived in but she didn't come up. I waited maybe five seconds and she still didn't come up. I knew right then that something was wrong because Marie didn't like to swim under water much. It hurt her ears you know, so she always just dove in and came right back up. So, when she didn't come back up right away I called to her. That was probably pretty stupid, right, because she couldn't hear me under the water but that's the first thing you do when you think something is wrong. You call out, right? But she didn't answer so I dove in to where I thought she dove in, but by the time I dove in, the boat had probably moved a few yards from where she dove in because we didn't have it anchored. We was just drifting. So, I probably dove in a few yards away from . . . you know . . . from where she did. If I was a little smarter I might have realized that I was in the wrong place, but I been hit a lot, you know? I'm not that smart to begin with and bein' hit a lot didn't help any. I looked for her in that water until I couldn't look no more. Until I was too tired to get out of the water myself. And then I just hung on to the side of the boat until I had enough strength to pull myself back up the ladder and in. That was the worst part. Hangin' on to the side of that boat, knowing that Marie was dead and that there was nothin' I could do about it. That was the worst part. Probably the worst moment of my life I guess."

Grace reached over and put her hand on Leo's. Meanwhile, in service bay number two, Butch was still banging on that muffler.

"How's the muffler comin', Butch?" Leo asked.

"Ah, she's right fucked, Leo," came the mechanic's reply. "She's right jeezlus fucked."

Leo leaned over to Grace. "Sorry about the salty language. Butch can't say a sentence without cursing."

"That's not a problem," Grace assured her tour guide. "It's not like I haven't heard the word before."

For the next few moments, Grace and Leo sat in silence, Grace's left hand still covering Leo's right. Finally Leo reached over with his other hand and patted Grace's hand gently.

"We should probably get some lunch," he said. "It's almost noon. Would you like to get some lunch?"

Grace wasn't particularly hungry, having eaten breakfast only three hours ago, but her companion was a big man with an even bigger appetite and so Grace agreed to Leo's lunch suggestion and the two new friends rose from their lawn chairs, Grace brushing the back of her jeans just in case the lawn chair had left some unwelcome residue.

"We'll see you later, Butch," Leo called over to bay number two. "Have a good day."

Butch put his hands on his hips and stared up at the muffler. "Yeah. Fuck."

The Frying Dutchman was close by and so Leo and Grace decided to make that establishment their lunch stop. They arrived at the front door ten minutes later, Leo quick-stepping ahead of Grace for the last couple of yards so that he could be in position to open the door for his dining companion.

"Thank you, Leo," Grace said, as she entered the restaurant. With her back turned towards Main Street now, she failed to notice the black BMW cruising slowly past The Dutchman.

As the restaurant door closed behind the boxer and his 'date', the black BMW moved on past Teeks to Grandy Street where it made a right hand turn. It continued on Grandy for a block and when it reached the corner of Grandy and Hawthorne, where the Rainbow Police Station was located, it made another right hand turn, and then at Yarbro another right hand turn. At Main Street, the BMW pulled into the Tim Horton's parking lot. The front window of the Tim Horton's afforded a paying customer a clear view of The Frying Dutchman, about eighty yards down the main drag.

"Good afternoon, Henry," Leo said with a hearty wave to the Frying Dutchman himself, Henry Van Etten.

Henry was standing behind the lunch counter about ten feet away, looking up at the Magnavox television, watching The Price Is Right. He turned his head slowly towards the voice and saw Leo Terrio and his 'date' standing, waiting just inside the front door of the establishment.

"Hey Leo. Ma'am." His warm greeting completed, Henry turned his attention back to the game show.

"Two for lunch," Leo continued. "Can you squeeze us in?"

Henry looked at the boxer for a moment, and then looked at the tables in his restaurant. All of the tables were empty except for a booth near the window where Wendy Norton sat by herself. Wendy had been one of the onlookers at Doug Petty's La-Z-Boy a while ago and she saw officers Golliger and Lynch take Mickey Welton into custody. The excitement was almost more than she could stand, so after the crowd had dispersed, Wendy wandered down to The Dutchman to get some deep fried ice cream. Deep fried ice cream always seemed to calm Wendy down.

"Just sit anywhere," said Henry. "I'll be right with you."

Leo looked around and pointed to a table near the back of the restaurant and he and Grace moved to it.

"This okay?" Leo asked.

"It's perfect," Grace replied.

Leo smiled and pulled out Grace's chair for her. As Grace sat, Leo pushed the chair back in ever so slightly so that her bottom hit the chair at exactly the right place. It was as if he had done this a thousand times before. Practiced it perhaps. Grace imagined that Leo had performed this exercise for his wife Marie on many occasions.

"Hi Leo," came a voice from across the room.

Leo looked towards the window of the establishment and saw Wendy Norton sitting in a booth by herself.

"Oh, hi Wendy," he said with a wave. "How are you?"

"I got food poisoning in Moncton last week. But I'm better now."

"Well, I'm glad to hear that. Well, I'm not glad to hear that you got food poisoning. I'm not glad to hear that. I'm glad to hear that you're better now. That's what I'm glad to hear."

"Thanks," replied Wendy, shoving a spoonful of deep fried ice-cream into her pretty face.

Henry Van Etten dropped two menus on the table in front of Leo and Grace. "Can we cut the talk about food poisoning please? This is my livelihood here. I don't need my customers talking about food poisoning."

"We weren't talking about getting food poisoning here," Leo assured the proprietor. "It was in Moncton. Where was it in Moncton, Wendy?"

"Where was what?" Wendy asked.

At that moment the front door of the Frying Dutchman opened and a woman entered, holding the hand of her young daughter.

"Where you got food poisoning?" Leo bellowed across the width of the room. "Where was that?"

"Oh, God, I don't even like to think about it," said Wendy through her mouthful of ice cream. "I was barfing for days. And that wasn't all I was doing if you know what I mean. Whew!"

The front door of The Frying Dutchman closed. Hearing the sound of the door latch catching, Henry, Leo, Grace and Wendy all turned and looked in the direction of the entrance. The woman and her daughter were gone. The swinging 'Closed' sign the solitary indication that anyone had been standing there seconds before.

"Great," muttered Henry and he turned and made his way back to his place behind the lunch counter.

"The fish and chips are good here," Leo said to Grace with an earnest smile. "That's what I usually get when I eat here. I don't eat here all that much because I try to stay loyal to Kate's Place, because she treats me nice over there and I'm the greeter over there and all, but whenever I do eat here I usually get the fish and chips." Leo opened his menu and looked at it for a very brief moment. He closed the menu again and set it down. "Yeah. Fish and chips."

"Well, I do like fish and chips." said Grace looking over the menu. "So, if you recommend them, then maybe that's what I'll have. But just a small order."

"You won't be disappointed," said Leo.

"So, did you hear about Mickey Welton?" came Wendy's voice from across the room.

"Hmm?" Leo turned towards Wendy. "Mickey Welton? Oh, right. Yeah. He lost by one dollar. I watched. He got some nice earthenware though."

"No, I don't mean the Jeopardy show. Although I still don't understand why he didn't get that Vancouver Canucks question. I knew the answer and I don't even follow hockey that much."

"The real estate woman buzzed in first," Henry chimed in from the lunch counter. "Mickey knew it. He just couldn't buzz in quick enough."

"Oh. Well, anyway, that's not what I'm talking about," Wendy turned her attention back to Leo. "I'm talking about Mickey being arrested."

"What?" Leo stared at Wendy as she loaded her spoon with another helping of deep fried ice cream. "What do you mean arrested?"

"A few minutes ago over at Doug Petty's. Wood Lynch and Pete took him into custody. Uh-huh." The 'uh-huh' was slightly muffled as the next spoonful of ice cream passed over Wendy's lips.

"What did they arrested him for? What did he do?"

Wendy held up her hand asking Leo to wait just a moment for her answer because she didn't like to talk with her mouth full.

"Bonnie Hoyt's murder," said Henry Van Etten without taking his eyes off of the Magnavox.

"What?"

"That's right," said Wendy, hot on the heels of a swallow. "I saw it myself. I saw them walk Mickey down to the police station in handcuffs."

"No, they didn't walk him down in handcuffs, Wendy," Henry said.

"Yes, they did. I saw it."

"I was there too, remember? And they didn't have no handcuffs on him at all. They just walked him down nice and peaceful-like. There wasn't much to it really."

"Well, they still arrested him. I know that much."

"For Miss Hoyt's murder?" Leo was still dumbfounded by this news.

"Uh-huh," Wendy replied.

"Mickey killed Miss Hoyt?"

"Now, we don't know that for sure, Leo," said Henry. He came out from behind the lunch counter and moved to the table where Leo and Grace were sitting. "He's just a person of interest."

"A what?" Leo needed clarification. He liked Bonnie Hoyt and was crushed to hear the news of her death. And now, to hear that a nice boy like Mickey Welton might be involved in the murder, well this latest news was turning Leo's world upside down.

"A person of interest. That's what the police call a suspect before they become an official suspect." Henry stood beside the table now and crossed his arms.

"Oh," Leo stared down at the table.

"So, fish and chips, Leo?" Henry picked up the two menus that rested on the table.

Leo continued to stare at the table top.

"Yes," said Grace. "We'll both have the fish and chips. A small order for me please."

Henry nodded, grunted, and disappeared through a swinging door that led to the kitchen. Grace looked at Leo who was now staring down the table top.

"Leo? Are you all right?"

"Hmm? Oh, yeah. I'm fine. I . . . . Mickey couldn't have done that to Miss Hoyt. Mickey's a good boy."

"I'm sure he didn't, Leo," Grace said, trying to allay her new friend's fears. "I'm sure they're just asking him some questions, that's all. That's what the police have to do. They have to ask everyone questions."

Leo didn't answer. He looked past Wendy Norton's window booth and out onto Main Street. A few people walked past the window but Leo didn't notice them. He was looking far beyond them, to a place he visited more and more these days. To a place where he stored his thoughts, good and bad.

"The one thing I don't understand about Miss Hoyt's murder," Leo began, still staring out onto Main Street, "Is how someone can do that to another human being. I made my living years ago by beatin' fellas up. I beat the hell out of em'. I never liked it all that much but it was all I knew how to do. And these were fellas who could defend themselves. Who knew what they was gettin' into when they stepped into the ring with me. People say that boxing is a brutal sport and it sure can be, but we all knew what we signed up for and when someone knocked us on our ass, we didn't say 'What'd ya' do that for? That was mean'. No ma'am. That's the nature of the sport. But outside of that ring, I never laid my hand on another person ever. I swear to God. And there was always some fella comin' up to me in a bar somewhere challengin' me to a fight, thinkin' he was gonna knock out this big time boxer and impress his girlfriend or his buddies, but I never bit. I never took him up on it. I always felt that fightin' in the ring was a sport. Fightin' anywhere else is just ugly and vicious and probably the darkest side of us humans. And to kill somebody? To kill somebody like Miss Hoyt? Well, we should all be sick to our stomachs over something like that. We should all just want to crawl into a hole and never come out again."

Grace didn't answer. She twirled a lock of her hair between her thumb and index finger and looked past Wendy Norton's window booth out onto Main Street. A few people walked past the window but Grace didn't notice them. She was looking far beyond them, to a place she visited more and more these days.

-29-

"Should we put him in a cell?"

It was a little past one o'clock now, about two hours since Pete and Wood had walked Mickey Welton into the Rainbow Police Station. They had tried to get more information out of Mickey about what had happened two nights before at Bonnie Hoyt's house, but Mickey kept claiming that he didn't know what happened. Information Coordinator Lori Higgenson was there too. She had even skipped her lunch because she did not want to miss a moment of the interrogation. Mickey sat in a chair across from Pete's Desk. Wood was sitting at his desk with his feet up, and Lori was sitting on top of her desk, her pretty legs shooting out of her short black skirt and dangling over the edge of the metal work station. This was about as casual an interrogation as you would find anywhere.

"A cell?" Pete asked.

"Yeah," Wood continued. "Should we put him in a cell or what should we do?"

"Well, if we put him in a cell that means he's under arrest, right?"

"Uh . . . I guess so. Yeah, I'm pretty sure that's what it means."

"Not necessarily," Mickey interjected. "You can hold a person in a cell for twenty-four hours I think without charging him. Just because he's in a cell doesn't mean he's under arrest."

"Is that right?" said Wood. "I didn't know that. Is that right, Pete?"

"I don't know," Pete replied. "Lori?"

"What?"

"Well, you're the information coordinator, aren't you? Can we hold Mickey without charging him?"

"Beats me," said Lori, crossing her legs. "Why don't you check the manual?"

"What manual?"

"The policeman's manual. Don't you have a policeman's manual?"

"No. There's no policeman's manual," Pete scoffed. "This isn't like being a hockey referee. This is a point of law we're talking about here."

"Well, then why don't you call that know-it-all RCMP guy and ask him? I'll bet he'd know."

"No," said Pete quickly.

"No," said Wood almost on top of Pete's no. "We don't want to get him involved. He might think we don't know what we're doing around here."

"Oh, yeah," Lori smiled. "We wouldn't want anyone to think that."

"You should ask me if I want a lawyer first," said Mickey.

"What?" Pete leaned back in his chair causing the wooden piece of furniture to creak like the hull of a pirate ship on a rolling sea.

"You should ask me if I want a lawyer," Mickey repeated.

"That's right," Lori piped up. "They always ask the criminal if he wants a lawyer present during the questioning."

"I'm not a criminal," said Mickey.

"And we've already questioned him," said Pete.

"Oops. That's not good." Lori put her hands on the desk and slid her rear off so that she was now standing in front of the desk. "That means that whatever information you got isn't admissible in court because he wasn't Mirandized."

"We didn't get any information," said Pete.

"Well, you should have asked me anyway," Mickey offered. "Lori's right."

Pete looked at Mickey for a moment, then at Lori and then at Wood who simply shrugged his shoulders.

"Fine," Pete began with a sigh of resignation. "Do you want a lawyer, Mickey?"

"No, thanks," said Mickey. "I don't think I need one. But thanks anyway."

"Well, then what the hell did you bring it up for?" asked Pete, his anger mounting.

"It's a point of law, that's all."

"How about a phone call?" said Wood as he brushed some dirt off of his boot which was perched on the edge of his desk.

Pete looked at Wood silently.

"Well, we're supposed to offer the criminal one phone call, right?" Wood continued defensively.

"I'm not a criminal," Mickey reiterated. "And Wood's right. I'm supposed to get a phone call when I'm in custody."

"You're not in custody," said Pete firmly.

"I'm not?"

"No."

"Oh." Mickey thought about this for a second. "Then can I go?"

"No."

"Then I must be in custody," surmised Mickey. "If you're holding me here and I can't go, well, that sounds like custody to me."

"He's right," said Wood.

"Uh-huh. Yep," added Lori as she moved to the front door and looked out.

There was yet another sizeable sigh from Officer Golliger. "Fine. Shit. Do you want to make a phone call, Mickey?"

"No thanks," replied the young man. "I don't wanna bother anyone with this."

"Jesus," Pete muttered under his breath.

"Well, maybe your mother would like to know what's going on," said Wood.

"Oh, she'll find out soon enough," said Mickey. "You know how fast news spreads in this town. She probably knows already. She's probably on her way over."

"She sure is," said Lori, looking at the blue Toyota which had just pulled into a parking spot across the street.

Turning as one, Pete, Wood and Mickey looked out the front window. Across the street, the driver side door of the blue Toyota opened and Myrna Welton stepped out. She clutched her purse in front of her with both hands, and without looking left or right, she started towards the police station. The four watchers in the police station heard the blast of a car horn off to the right and saw Myrna jump back against her car as another vehicle passed by, narrowly missing her.

"Christ," said Wood. "She did the same thing when she stopped in here yesterday."

As the four of them looked on, the passenger side door of the Toyota opened and a large, unwieldy mess of red hair appeared above the car roof.

"Oh, she's got your girlfriend with her, Wood," Lori observed.

"What?" Wood stood and moved to the front door and squeezed in beside Lori for a better look.

Across the street, Peggy Welton closed the passenger door and smoothed her tight jeans down the front of her thighs. Then she pulled the elastic bottom of her satin jacket down so that it fit snugly around her waist. The jacket was unzipped about halfway and Peggy's ample bosom, covered with a bright green turtleneck sweater, became the focal point of the ensemble. Having adjusted her look to suit her taste, Peggy moved around to the street side of the car and stood beside her mother.

"She's not my girlfriend, Lori. Knock that talk off, will ya?" Wood turned to Mickey. "Peggy's not my girlfriend, Mick. Lori's just having fun."

Mickey shrugged, leaned forward with his elbows on his knees and looked down at the floor. Whether or not his sister was Officer Lynch's girlfriend was the last thing on Mickey's mind at this moment in time.

"Lori, get away from the door," Pete said standing up from his chair. "Mrs. Welton doesn't need a welcoming committee waiting for her."

Lori moved away from the door and to her desk. She picked up a package of Clorets gum that was lying there, pushed a piece through it's aluminum packaging and popped it into her mouth. She then leaned against the wall behind her desk and began working the gum as if she were a nineteen-forties film noir broad. Myrna and Peggy had crossed the street at this point and were now stepping up onto the sidewalk in front of the police station. Myrna still clutched her purse in front of her as if she was expecting a purse-snatcher to come by at any moment. Peggy shoved her hands into her jacket pockets as if she didn't have a care in the world.

"Afternoon, Myrna," Wood said as he opened the door for the two women.

"Is my Mickey here?" Myrna asked nervously.

"He's right inside here, Myrna," Wood replied. "Come on in."

Myrna entered the police station and began to tremble as if the structure itself had suddenly given her a chill. Lori brushed past Wood and into the station without saying a word.

"Hey, Peggy," said Lori with a smile.

"Yeah, hi," Peggy answered coldly.

Wood let the door close behind the women and then he moved to his desk where he stood waiting for what he was sure would be a breakdown on Mrs. Welton's part.

"Hi, Myrna," said Pete, standing and placing his thumbs inside his belt. "I take it you've heard what's going on here."

"Yes, I've heard. I don't' know what to make of it though."

"Mom, it's okay. Everything's fine."

"Well, no I don't think it is, Mickey," Myrna continued. "I don't think everything's fine at all. I mean, here you are in the police station and folks all over town are saying you killed Miss Hoyt. That's what they're saying. Isn't that what they're saying, Peggy?" Myrna looked at Peggy, but she didn't give the girl a chance to reply. "Peggy heard it from a schoolmate. Called her right up not a half an hour ago and told her. Isn't that right, Peggy?" Myrna again looked at Peggy and once again gave her no time to respond. "And then Peggy told me and darned if I didn't drop my spoon right into the pancake batter. I didn't know whether to cry or wind my watch. My head was spinning. It's spinning this very minute. Mercy me."

"Would you like to sit down, Myrna?" asked Wood, pulling his chair out from behind his desk.

"Thank you, Wood. I think I'd better do just that before I fall down," Myrna took a seat in Wood's chair and looked across at Mickey.

"Myrna, here's the situation," Pete began. Knowing her fragile state at the best of times, he would break the news to Myrna as gently as he possibly could. "We got the forensics report back this morning and unfortunately it showed that it was Mickey's boots that left the imprint in Bonnie Hoyt's yard the night of her murder."

Myrna released her left hand from her purse and placed the shaking hand over her mouth to stifle a gasp. Her eyes began to fill with tears.

"Now, we've questioned Mickey about it," Pete continued, "But he denies having any knowledge of the crime. Says he doesn't know what happened. Well, to be honest Myrna, that doesn't really sit well with us. We think Mickey knows more than he's telling us. We think he knows a lot more. So, that's why he's here right now and I'm sorry to say that it looks like we're going to have to hold him for the time being."

Myrna let out a moan as her hand tightened on her face.

"Are you charging him?" asked Peggy.

"Well . . ." Pete hesitated as he looked at Peggy and then down at Mickey. "Based on the circumstantial evidence we've compiled – you know, the boot prints and all, and the time line, and his unwillingness to be forthcoming with what he knows – based on that, I think we're going to have to charge him with something. At the very least the charge will be impeding a police investigation. At the worst . . . well, it'll be the uh . . . it'll be the commission of the crime itself."

A silence filled the air. Myrna looked through her purse for a hanky. Peggy shifted her weight from her right foot to her left, hands still stuck in her satin jacket pockets. Wood stared down at the floor. Lori was glad she skipped her lunch because this was the single biggest moment in her five year tenure as Information Coordinator.

"I think you're going to have to get Mickey a lawyer, Myrna," Pete said, breaking the silence. "That's probably your next step because there's gonna be an arraignment, and then in all likelihood he'll be moved to Fredericton for his trial."

"Trial?" Myrna wiped away the tears with her hanky. "There's going to be a trial?"

"That's how it works, yes."

"But, I don't think I know any lawyers. Well, there's Maurice Leger, but I don't think he's a criminal lawyer, is he? Isn't he a real estate lawyer?"

"No. No, he got Kenny Farron off a few years ago," said Wood. "Remember that, Pete?"

"Kenny Farron was charged with mischief, Wood," Pete answered. "He took a pair of Lorna Yerxa's underwear off her clothesline one day."

"Maurice got him off though," countered Wood. "Lack of evidence because they couldn't find where Kenny hid the underwear. And then after the court appearance, Kenny told Maurice that he was wearing the underwear. Had em' on right there in the courtroom. Cheeky as all hell."

Pete turned his attention back to Myrna. "I wouldn't worry about finding a lawyer, Myrna. I'm sure they'll find you soon enough."

Myrna said nothing. She gathered herself and her motherly instincts kicked in. She stood and began to plan her next move out loud. "All right then, I should probably go and get you a change of clothes, Mickey. And a toothbrush and some toiletries. You don't want to neglect your hygiene just because you're in jail. And I'll have to call your father and tell him what's going on. He's doing a job over in Nackawic today so it might be hard to hold of him but that's all right. We'll get word to him soon enough. There's not much he can do right now anyway. And then, uh..well, I can make you a casserole of some sort for dinner tonight and bring that over to you."

"That won't be necessary, Myrna," Pete said, trying to comfort the woman. "We'll see to it that he eats right."

"No, that's fine Mr. Golliger. I know what my Mickey likes to eat and I want to be sure that he's as comfortable as he can be here. I mean, if you stray too far from what you're used to – from your routine – then it could upset your system, and I want Mickey to be as strong as he can for what lies ahead. And don't worry, I'll make enough for you and Wood and Miss Higgenson here too."

"That's very kind of you, ma'am," said Pete. "Thank you."

"So, I guess you'll be locking him up now, will you?"

"Not right this moment, no. There's no rush for that." Pete didn't want to lock Myrna's son in a cell with Myrna standing right there. "We're just gonna sit out here and talk for a while longer."

"I see. All right then . . . . uh . . . well, stand up, Mickey. Give me a hug. I've got to get busy with all of these things now. Honestly, sometimes I think they're aren't enough hours in a day for everything a person has to get done." The last few words of her sentence crackled through her tears.

Mickey stood as his mother moved toward him. She put her arms around the boy's neck and gave him a long hug, so long that it seemed that this might be a final good-bye between them. She then gave her son a kiss on the cheek, stood back and straightened his tie for him.

"Don't you give the officers here any trouble, you hear?"

Mickey said nothing. He simply nodded.

"That's my boy," said Myrna. She gave her son one last look and then turned to leave. "Take care of him for me, Wood." Myrna touched Wood on his left arm as she moved towards the door.

"I will Myrna. Don't you worry."

"All right, Peggy. Let's go, dear." Myrna opened the police station door and looked back at her daughter.

"I think I'll stay here for a while," Peggy replied.

"What for?" Myrna asked. "You'll only be in the way here. I'm sure the officers have lots to do and I don't want you getting in the way."

"She can stay, Myrna," said Pete. "She won't be a problem."

"Oh. Well, all right then," said Myrna with a smile that disappeared as quickly as it had come. "Thank you. Oh, do you any of you have any seafood allergies, because I think it'll be a seafood casserole."

The was another silence in the room. Myrna was breaking hearts, simply by standing there in her despair.

"Nope," said Lori.

"Nope," repeated Wood.

"Seafood's good, Myrna," said Pete.

Myrna stood in the doorway for a moment looking at everyone in the police station. The expression on her face gave the impression that she still had more to say. One final parting comment. She looked across the street to her car, not really knowing what to do, feeling lost. And then she looked back inside the police station again. After taking everything in, she nodded her head and was gone.

Wood uttered an involuntary comment on the moment. "Damn."

"Mickey, I guess we'd better get you into a cell," Pete said as he opened his desk drawer and began rifling through it to find the cell keys. "Wood, have you got the cell keys?"

"Nope. Not me," replied Wood. "I haven't used them in weeks."

"I've got them," Lori said, and she opened her desk drawer and pulled out a set of keys.

"What have you got them for?" asked Pete.

"No reason," Lori replied holding the keys out to Pete. It was obvious that she was hiding something. Pete didn't reach for the keys. He stood there waiting for a better explanation from the information coordinator.

That was all the coaxing Lori needed. She broke like a cardboard dam. "Roberta wanted to see what it would be like to be locked up so I locked her in a cell for an hour last week. All right? God."

Pete said nothing. He merely shook his head and took the keys from Lori. "Okay, Mickey, let's go."

Officer Golliger moved past Mickey Welton and headed towards the back of the station where the holding cells were located. He had only taken three steps when a calm voice broke the air.

"All right. I did it. I killed Bonnie Hoyt."

-30-

"You're not from around here, are you?"

This voice came from the table next to Bryden's at the Tim Horton's coffee shop. Bryden looked over to see an employee, a boy of about nineteen wiping off the table next to his.

"Uh..no I'm not. No."

"Yeah, I could tell."

"And how could you tell that?" asked Bryden, turning his attention back out the window and down Main Street.

"I saw your car pull in. The BMW. She's got Maine license plates."

Bryden thought of commenting on how sharp the lad's deductive powers were but he thought better of it. Best not to encourage any further conversation from this fellow. It might distract Bryden from the task of watching The Frying Dutchman's doors down the street. He simply smiled at the young man and continued his vigil. As it turned out, the young man did not need any encouragement in order to continue the conversation.

"Yeah, I see folks come and go all the time from this corner," he continued. "Well, like you're doing now. Watching. A person can learn a whole lot just by watching. You don't even have to speak or ask questions. The information comes to you like it's a fridge magnet and you're a . . . . well, a fridge. Like that. For instance I can tell you that Harvey Ludwick's son Justin is back in town again. I saw him walking down that very sidewalk yesterday morning. Looking pretty grim too. He's had a tough run. He's been out west trying to make a go of it in oil country but he's a puny sort and work like that is for a stronger man, you know what I'm saying? And Justin . . . well, Justin pictures himself as a cowboy type but he's about as much a cowboy as Bob Simms. You gotta know Bob. He's a puny type too and there are some who say he's a male chorus kind of fellow but that's okay with me so long as he doesn't come singing under my window. I think you know what I'm saying. So,

Justin's back now all broken down and defeated and looking like two thirds of a cup of crap. And he's not much older than I am. Probably twenty. Twenty-one. Looks like he's forty. He'll do all right though. Harvey owns a lumber yard here in town and I'm sure he'll find some office work that Justin can handle. So, there's Justin and there's a fellow who I don't know his name but he showed up here in the Tim's last week without a cent to his name and asked if we could part with a coffee and a donut gratis. On the house. And you know what? We did. Well, we're pretty good about that around here and it doesn't happen all that often that someone comes in asking for free stuff and the fella looked like he could use it so we give it to him. And wouldn't you know it, but Lyle Doyle was standing in line behind this fella and he sees what's going on and he asks the lad if he's looking for work. The fella says yessir and so Lyle gives him a few days work painting his house. Just enough to get the guy back on his feet you know? To give him some breathing room from the wolf that's beating down his door? And it works out for Lyle too because he gets his house painted at a good rate. They call that Karma. You do something good for someone in this life and it comes back to you, like getting your house painted cheap. And then there's the woman who blew into town in a transport truck the other night."

Bryden turned his head away from the street view and finally looked up at the verbose young man with renewed interest.

"A transport truck?"

"Yep. I was working that night. I saw the transport truck pull up out front of the Dutchman and this woman gets out with a suitcase and into the restaurant she goes. I don't know if she was a hitchhiker or what, but she goes into the Dutchman and then about a half an hour later, right after Jeopardy was done, she comes out with Pete Golliger, one of the policemen in town, and she gets into his cruiser with him. Now ordinarily I wouldn't have been able to see so much because I'm working you know, and my attentions would be divided because of my serving duties, but Mickey Welton was on Jeopardy that night and there wasn't one soul in here during the entire broadcast so we all just sat around and chewed the fat. Sat right here at this window and that's when I saw the truck. I don't know the woman's story but I know she took up residence at The Allemane Inn."

"How do you know that?" asked Bryden. He looked out the window again trying to appear disinterested even though his question betrayed that appearance.

"My sister Lori is the information coordinator over at the police station. She knows everything."

-31-

The five occupants of the Rainbow Police Station stood motionless. Lori had even stopped chewing her gum, and the small white wad could be seen sitting stock-still inside of her opened mouth.

"What did you say?" asked Pete.

"I did it. I killed her." Peggy looked at Pete with a dare on her face. "So, you can let Mickey go."

"Peggy, no," said Mickey. He looked at Pete. "She's lying. She's got nothing to do with this."

"Oh, Mickey, cut it out," Peggy said. "Shit, everyone knows that you couldn't do something like that. They would have figured out it was me eventually anyway. That's if they've got half a brain." At this early juncture in her confession, Peggy looked directly at Wood.

"You killed Bonnie?" Pete's disbelief could not be masked.

"Yeah."

"Bonnie Hoyt?"

"Well, what other Bonnie has been murdered here in the last couple of days? God. So, let Mickey go, would ya'?"

"I think you'd better start from the beginning Peggy," said Pete, moving towards the young woman. "We're not letting anyone go until you explain what you just said."

"She doesn't know anything," Mickey said, suddenly sounding desperate for someone to listen him. "She's just making this up to get me off."

"Mickey, shut up," said Pete. "You haven't told us one damned useful thing today so let's hear what your sister has to say. Go ahead, Peggy. What happened? And why on earth would you wanna kill Bonnie Hoyt?"

"Wait!" Lori moved to her desk, picked up the phone receiver and put the three phone lines on hold. Then she sat in her desk chair and looked at Peggy. "Okay, go ahead."

"This is gonna be the truth, right?" said Wood from his position near the front door.

"Yes, Wood, it's gonna be the truth. Jesus. Why don't you sit down? You make me nervous standing behind me. I feel like you're lookin' at my ass."

"I was not lookin' at your ass, Peggy. And you can't tell a police officer what to do in his own police station."

"Wood, sit down please," said Pete.

"What?"

"Sit down please. You're distracting me too."

"Fine. I'll sit for you but not for Peggy." Wood moved to his desk and sat.

"And for the record," added Lori. "I think you were lookin' at her ass."

"I was not!"

"Mickey, you sit down too," said Pete, looking at the young man who was soon to become his ex-prime suspect. "Let's all get comfortable and listen to what Peggy has to say."

As Pete moved around behind his desk and sat in his chair, Mickey took a seat in the chair he had recently risen from for his mother's hug,

"All right, Peggy. Let's have it," said Pete.

Peggy looked at the four faces staring at her. "Shoot. I feel like I'm putting on a show for you here."

"Well, I'm sorry about that," Pete replied.

"No, I didn't mean it was bad. Hell, I like being the centre of attention."

"Yes, we know that much about you, Peggy. Now please, tell us your story. Go ahead."

"Wait!" Wood exclaimed. "Shouldn't we Mirandize her first?"

"I don't think so," Pete replied. "I mean we're not arresting her. You don't have to Mirandize someone unless you're arresting them, right?"

"I don't know," said Wood.

"No, I think you're right, Pete," Lori chimed in. "It goes like, Peggy Welton, you're under arrest for the murder of Bonnie Hoyt. You have the right to remain silent, blah blah blah. That's when you're arresting them. When you're just questioning them, all you have to do is ask if they'd like a lawyer present."

"Jesus Christ." Pete leaned forward and put his head on his desk. He stretched his arms out in front of him so that his hands touched the far side of the desk, as if he was reaching for a life ring to save him from going under the waves of confusion.

"What's wrong?" asked Lori.

After a moment Pete raised his head and looked at Lori and then to Wood. "You know, I'll bet ten years ago nobody knew any of this shit except the police. But now you got shows like Law And Order all over the television and all of sudden everybody knows the fuckin' law. Sorry about my language, Peggy, but it's just been one of those days. Now, do you want a lawyer to be here when you tell us this story?"

"No," the young redhead replied as she unzipped her satin jacket.

"Good. All right. Are we all settled on this matter now?" Pete looked to Lori, then to Wood and then to Mickey.

"I'm good," replied Wood.

"Good to go here," said Lori.

"Shouldn't you record the interview?" Mickey asked quietly.

"Mickey, shut the hell up," came Pete's terse reply. "Peggy, go ahead."

Peggy Welton shifted her weight once more and slipped her hands into her jacket pockets. She looked down at the floor and kicked at a rogue paper clip that had no doubt fallen off of Lori's desk months before. Then she raised her head and through that mess of beautiful red hair, she looked Officer Golliger straight in the eye. "I've been sleeping with Tom Lasalle."

There was an audible gag from Information Coordinator Lori Higgenson as her Clorets chewing gum fell back into her throat.

"Holy shit," said Wood.

"That's a helluva beginning," observed Pete.

"Holy shit," Wood repeated.

"You certainly got our attention, Peggy," said Pete, "But what's that got to do with Bonnie Hoyt's murder?"

"I'm coming to that," Peggy continued. "You said you wanted me to start from the beginning, right? Well, that's the beginning. That's where it started. Tom Lasalle and I have sleeping together for a couple of months now."

"Ho-lee shit," Wood repeated his earlier remark yet again, not being one to stray from the mundane.

"Wood, do you mind?" said Pete. "Go ahead, Peggy."

"So," Peggy continued, "Last week he said we should break it off. He said it wasn't right. That I was too young for him."

"Not to mention the fact that he's married," added Lori, indignantly.

Peggy ignored the catty remark from the information coordinator and continued unfazed. "Well, I knew that my age wasn't the reason because why would he start up with me in the first place if he thought I was too young? I knew there had to be some other reason. So the other day I saw his car parked in the cemetery. I figured he was visiting his mother's grave and so I went in to talk to him, but he wasn't there. And then it hit me that Bonnie Hoyt's house is just across the field from the cemetery and I know that Tom and Bonnie used to be hot and heavy before Tom got married, and so I walked over to have a look. I went in through the back gate and I looked into the kitchen window and I could see them."

"Where were they?" asked Pete.

"They were on the living room floor."

"So, how could you see them on the living room floor if you were looking in the kitchen window? You can't see the living room from the kitchen window."

"I saw their reflection in the hall mirror."

This was the answer Pete was waiting for. "Okay, now I'm convinced that you're tellin' the truth. Go ahead."

"So, they were having sex there on the living room floor. Bonnie was sitting on top of Tom. She had a bathrobe on and Tom had his pants down and she was doing him like that. Riding him, you know? Back and forth?"

At this point, Mickey dropped his head into hands. His little sister's penchant for graphic description upset him almost as much as the deed she was about to describe.

"Well, I freaked out I guess," Peggy continued. "I wanted to hurt the bitch, and him too. Next thing I know I had a golf club in my hand. I'm not even sure where it came from. It just appeared there in my hands, you know? And I went in through the back door and into the living room and I hit Bonnie in the head with it. She fell onto Tom's chest and he rolled her off of him and I saw all of the blood on his shirt from Bonnie's head. I was gonna hit him too but he grabbed the club from me. We didn't say too much I don't think. I think he asked me what the fuck I was doing. I think he said that. And then I think I said 'fuck you' and then I turned around and left. I didn't even run. I remember walking out the back door and down the stairs and out the back gate. Then I went home. I was in kind of a daze I think because I remember it really started to rain hard but I didn't run or anything. I just walked through this pouring rainstorm like it wasn't raining at all. And when I got home I went up to my room and I guess I was sitting on the bed soaking wet and that's when Mickey saw me and asked me what was going on, and I told him what happened. And that's it. That's the story."

Lori's chewing gum was now getting a sizeable workout. Wood sat speechless behind his desk, staring at the emotionless young woman who stood before him. Pete looked at Mickey who was slumped forward in his chair, his head still in his hands.

"Actually, that's not the whole story," said Pete turning to look at Peggy's older brother. "Mickey? Do you want to finish it, or do you want me to finish it for you?"

Mickey didn't move. Officer Golliger waited for about ten seconds and then realizing that the Welton boy didn't have the stomach for the rest of the story, he proceeded to tell it for him.

"You went back to Bonnie's after Peggy told you what happened, right Mickey? You had two purposes in mind. First, to see if Bonnie was all right. Maybe she wasn't dead. Maybe you could still help her. And second, to cover up your sister's tracks in case Bonnie was dead. You looked in the kitchen window, into the hall mirror, and you saw her lying there on the living room floor. You went inside and determined that she was dead. Her bathrobe was open, right? And you're the one who closed it for her because you didn't want her to be found that way. Then you picked up the golf club and wiped it clean and put it back in the golf bag. That's why it was the only dry club in the bag when me and Wood got to the scene. Is that what happened?"

Mickey nodded his head and wiped the tears from his eyes with the fingers of both hands. Pete was moderately relieved that at least one of the Welton children was finally showing an inkling of remorse. Mickey leaned back in his chair, placed his arms on the arm rests, and stared up at the ceiling.

"And then you went back home and you and Peggy watched your little appearance on Jeopardy with your family and your snack food like nothing had even happened!" Pete shook his head slowly. "Christ. What the fuck?"

"Peggy?" Wood began, looking up at the young woman standing in the middle of the room, "You said that Tom grabbed the golf club from you, right?"

"Uh-huh."

Wood looked at Pete. "Then why wouldn't Tom have wiped the club off? His fingerprints would have been on it too."

"Maybe he did," Pete replied. "But Mickey didn't know that, so Mickey wiped it clean again."

"Wow." Lori let out her first breath in over a minute. "So, if Mickey didn't go back to Bonnie's after the murder, you wouldn't have found his boot prints, and if Tom did wipe off the golf club, we might still be looking for the killer."

"Life sure takes some strange turns sometimes, doesn't it?" said Wood. "Some strange goddamned turns."

"You know this makes you an accessory, Mickey? said Pete. "You know that, right?"

"Well, what else was I supposed to do?" Mickey replied on the brink of a sob. "She's my sister."

Pete looked at Mickey and then to Peggy. His thoughts flashed to their mother, Myrna Welton, one of the nicest, most innocent women in the entire town. He thought about how this news was going to affect her. Later that evening, Myrna would deliver her seafood casserole as promised, this time for her daughter, and not her son, and Pete Golliger would have a short conversation with the distraught woman about her daughter's inexplicable behaviour.

"What kind of girl have I raised?" Myrna would ask tearfully. "She sat with us and watched Mickey on Jeopardy. She was laughing and cheering him on. And the whole time she knew that Miss Hoyt was lying dead. Lying dead, alone in her house. What kind of girl does that? What kind of girl could be so callous?"

"Some things can't be explained Myrna," Pete would reply compassionately. "They just are."

"But what kind of mother does that make me? I raised Peggy. I'm the one who taught her right from wrong. I taught her as best I could, Pete. I really did." Myrna's sobbing would be nearly uncontrollable.

"Myrna, this isn't your fault. Some people . . . some people have got different chemical make-ups, that's all it is. They're wired differently from the day they're born. Peggy's just wired different from most of us."

That was the conversation that Pete would have with the girl's mother in just a few short hours, but right now, on that cool September afternoon in the Rainbow Police Station, there was a long pause as Pete stared at Peggy, still standing in the middle of the room, hands in her satin jacket pockets. The thought crossed his mind that this girl really was wired differently. She stood there and confessed to a murder as if she was ordering take out from a fast food joint. Officer Golliger ran his hand slowly back and forth across his desktop for a few seconds as he thought about what should happen next. He then stood up, stuck his thumbs into his belt, and looked at the young woman with the bright red hair. "Peggy Welton, you're under arrest for the murder of Bonnie Hoyt. You have the right to remain silent . . ."

-32-

Tom Lasalle's two o'clock golf lesson on the afternoon of September the twenty-third was Cindy Keller. Cindy had called Tom earlier in the day to move her lesson up. She was originally scheduled to be his last lesson of the day, but Cindy's best girlfriends, Charlotte Gaines and Wendy Norton had called to invite Cindy to meet them for a drink at The Allemane at five that afternoon. No doubt, after Wendy had talked at length about her food poisoning experience in Moncton, the three women would then spend the remainder of their time together pouring over the details of the Bonnie Hoyt murder and the subsequent questioning of Mickey Welton. Some details would be based in fact, others in speculation which they would insist was factual. And so, at two-thirty in the afternoon, at The Rainbow Golf and Country Club, Cindy Keller in her yellow shorts, was showing the usual generous amount of leg even though on this day, the temperature was slightly cooler than it had been on previous days. But Cindy was very aware of her most admirable attributes and she chose to show them off whenever possible.

Tom and Cindy were about half way through the lesson on the driving range of the course when from behind them, they heard the sound of a car approaching. This was unexpected because the golf club parking lot was about fifty yards on the other side of the clubhouse, and there was no access road for vehicles on the driving range side where Tom and Cindy now stood. The two golfers turned towards the sound of the approaching vehicle and were surprised to see a Rainbow Police cruiser kicking up dirt and dust as it roared across the browning grass towards them.

"What the hell?" Tom muttered.

The cruiser moved as if it was aimed straight for the pair, the front end pitching up and down as each little gully was traversed, giving the vehicle the appearance of a living, menacing predator bearing down on its prey. When the driver finally slammed on the brakes of the cruiser, it fish-tailed slightly and came to a stop about fifteen yards from the stunned couple. The driver-side door opened and Officer Pete Golliger climbed out of the vehicle and without stopping to close the car door behind him, he moved with long, measured steps towards Tom and Cindy.

"I don't know what the hell you think you're doing, Pete," said Tom, leaning his left hand on his driver and crossing his left foot over his right in a relaxed golfer's stance. "But cars aren't allowed over here at anytime. I don't care if you're a cop or . . ."

The last few words of Tom's sentence would not be uttered. Officer Golliger's fist saw to that. The punch sent Tom Lasalle sprawling backwards into the dirt and grass of the torn up tee box.

Pete was breathing hard, more out of anger than physical exertion. He turned to the pretty golf student who now had her hand covering her mouth in shock. "Hi Cindy."

Cindy did not uncover her mouth, but instead, gave a muffled reply through her hand. "Hi Pete."

"Lesson's over."

"Kay," came Cindy's meek reply.

Pete then pulled a pair of handcuffs from the back of his belt and looked down to the ground at Tom. "Tom Lasalle," He began. "You're under arrest for impeding a police investigation. You have the right to remain silent . . ."

-33-

Kate Leger was not at her usual post at the front desk of The Allemane Inn when Grace Downey and Leo Terrio returned from their tour of the town on the afternoon of September the twenty-third. If she had been, she surely would have given Grace the ominous phone message from the distressed trucker about a black BMW on its way to Rainbow. Instead, Kate was in the lounge, Kate's Place, setting up for the evening crowd that would certainly begin arriving now that the work day was over. It was five o'clock and there were always some regulars who stopped in for a quick one before heading home. And some, like amateur thespian Louis Little, who stopped in for more than just a quick one, whiling away the evening hours with spirited conversation over three or four long ones.

After their lunch at The Dutchman, Grace and Leo walked some more, this time to the east end of the town, where they sat on a bench in Moran Park and talked more about Leo's life in the ring. Grace found this gentle giant to be a fascinating man and she was happy that Officer Pete Golliger has suggested the two spend the day together. Through all of their conversation though, the topic of Grace's life was readily avoided. When Leo would ask Grace a question about her home life, she would side-step the query by asking Leo another question about his life, and off he would go, happy to reflect upon past and present triumphs and failures.

Arriving back at The Allemane at five o'clock, Grace thanked Leo and offered to buy him dinner in the Inn's dining room to show her appreciation for the day. Having a woman buy his dinner was not something that Leo's old school background was accustomed to, and he politely declined the offer, but Grace was persistent, and eventually, Leo acquiesced and the two agreed to meet downstairs in the dining room at six. This would give Grace time to freshen up and Leo time to grab a quick nap, which he needed badly after his day of walking and talking. The two new friends parted ways in the second floor hallway, Grace going to her room, The A.R. Wetmore room, and Leo to his, The Charles La Tour room, two doors down the hall from Grace's.

Once inside her room, Grace removed her shoes, sat on the edge of her bed and rubbed her feet for a couple of minutes. In her haste to leave her husband and the state of Maine in her wake two days ago, Grace had not taken the time to pack her best pair of walking shoes. This might be a mission for tomorrow. Buy a pair of comfortable shoes. She let her hands fall to her sides and then lay back on the bed, covering two thirds of the width of it with her torso as she did. She looked up to the ceiling and breathed a long sigh. Then she turned her head slightly to the left and looked at the clock on the bedside table. Five oh seven. "I can shower in a few minutes," she thought. "I'll just lie here and close my eyes for a while first." And she did. This day, like the last two, had taken a lot out Grace, and before she knew it, the closing of the eyes had led to her drifting off to sleep.

The soft knocking on the door is what finally brought Grace out of her slumber. For only a few seconds she didn't know where she was, whose bed she was lying on, or what ceiling she was now gazing up at. She continued to stare up until her sleep-interrupted brain filled in the details for her, and then she turned her head slightly to the left. Five fifty-one. "Five fifty-one," Grace thought. "Five fifty-one. That time is significant, but why?"

There were another five soft raps on her door. "Leo!" she thought. "I have to meet Leo at six for dinner." She sat up on the edge of the bed and ran her hands through her hair to push it none-too-gently away from her face. "Shit. Coming!" It must be Leo Terrio knocking on her door, coming to escort her down to the dining room for their dinner date. And she hadn't even showered yet. She hadn't changed her clothes. And she was still half-asleep. She stood up and moved down the two steps into the sunken living area. Four steps later she reached the door to her room. She put her hand on the door knob but then stopped after she had given it a half turn. She looked at the door, her not-fully-alert mind trying to process information. "We agreed to *meet downstairs*," she thought. "There was no mention of his coming to my room to get me first." She let go of the doorknob and it took back the half turn. "Who is it?" she called out. For exactly three seconds there was no response from the other side of the door. One thousand one. One thousand two. One thousand three. In the next instant – the instant before the fourth second – the door exploded in Grace's face and she found herself lying on the floor at the other side of her sunken living area. She quickly propped herself up on her elbows and looked at the figure standing in the doorway.

"Hello, Grace." Bryden Downey closed the door behind him and stood towering over his confused wife. "Miss me?"

Grace got to her feet quickly and backed up the two steps to where her bed was, but Bryden was on her in no time and he pushed her down onto the bed. Her backwards momentum was so strong that her knees came up this time and she kicked at the man standing before her. Bryden smiled condescendingly, pushed her legs aside and put his left knee on the bed. He then put both hands on Grace's shoulders to pin her there, preventing any further movement from the cornered woman.

"Hel..!" Graced called out.

Bryden swiftly moved his right hand from Grace's left shoulder and covered her mouth, preventing the 'P' in 'Help' from being heard. "Shhhh. It's okay, Grace. I'm not going to hurt you. I mean, I thought of hurting you. I thought of it all the way up to this Godforsaken place, but in the end, I decided against it. You know why?"

With Bryden's hand covering her mouth, Grace was in no danger of answering his question. She stared up at him with eyes not frightened, but angry.

"You don't know why?" Bryden continued tauntingly. "Well, let me tell you why. Because it would be so much easier for the two of us to simply go back home and continue on as if nothing had ever happened. As if this silly situation was nothing more than a misunderstanding. You can see your way clear to do that, can't you, Grace?"

Grace squirmed beneath the pressure of Bryden's arms, trying to free herself, but her movement was kept to a minimum by his force.

"Sure you can. Because the alternative would be so unpleasant. Not just for you, but for the both of us. Well, it would be far more unpleasant for you of course, but it would be a lot of work for me. Explaining, covering my tracks. I've got more important things on my plate right now. A distraction like that would set my progress back immeasurably, and I want this train to keep moving forward. All the way to Washington in due time. You understand that, don't you, Grace? Of course you do. So, I'm going to take my hand away from your pretty mouth now, and you'll pack whatever belongings you've got here in this little hovel and we'll head home. Okay?"

Grace continued to stare up at Bryden angrily. His right hand was covering her mouth, and his right elbow was on her left shoulder, but her left arm was now free. She couldn't turn her in head in that direction, but she knew that the clock on the bedside table to her left was within her reach. She moved her left hand towards the clock, but Bryden slid his elbow down so that it now sat firmly on her bicep, preventing any further movement.

"Maybe you didn't hear me, Grace. I said the alternative would be unpleasant. Did you not understand that?"

Bryden was now in an awkward position on top his wife, left knee on the bed, right foot still on the floor, left hand on her shoulder and right hand on her mouth. He started to bring his right leg up so that he could straddle the woman beneath him and be in a much more favourable and dominant position above her. His leg was halfway to its destination when Grace brought her right knee up and caught him squarely between his designer dress pants. Bryden grunted as if all of the wind had left his lungs, and he slid off of the bed and landed with his knees on the floor, grabbing his crotch as he did. "You fucking bitch!" Those words used up the last of his wind and he began gasping for air, his head still leaning against the edge of the bed.

Grace reached over for the clock and yanked it, pulling the plug violently out of the wall. She raised the clock high over her head and as hard as she could, she brought it down towards her husband of ten years. If she could knock him out, she thought, or at least daze him, she could then run for help. The clock failed to reach its target. Bryden's hand shot up from between his legs and latched onto Grace's wrist, forcing it to stop sharply, and the clock to be released from her grip and go smashing onto the floor. Bryden, still on his knees and still holding onto Grace's wrist, flung the woman in a whipping motion across his body, causing her to go crashing into the chest of drawers on the other side of the room.

"All right," he said, getting to his feet shakily and still trying to catch his breath. "I guess this means . . . you've chosen . . . . the alternative."

"I need some air," Officer Golliger said to Wood Lynch and Lori Higgenson as he pushed open the front door of the Rainbow Police Station. He didn't wait for a reply before stepping out into the brisk September air.

Peggy Welton was in one of the three holding cells located in the rear of the station. Tom Lasalle, his nose bloodied and both eyes blackened, occupied the other cell. Peggy's bother Mickey Welton had been sent home with instructions to stay close. The affairs of this day had left Pete Golliger wondering what in the hell the world was coming to. A pretty young redhead, with no prior inclination towards violence, had beaten another woman to death in cold blood. He felt a twinge of relief knowing that this policing job would end in a few short days. He didn't know what was next for him in this life but he was fairly certain it would not be another stint in the law enforcement field. It was dinner time but he had no appetite. He stepped outside of the police station with no real destination in mind. He stood with his hands on his hips and looked down Grandy Street towards Main Street. If he walked down that way, he would almost certainly be stopped by inquisitive citizens wanting to know what the latest news was on the Bonnie Hoyt murder case. He looked in the other direction towards Hawthorne Street. It was a quieter street but in all likelihood someone would find him there too. Small towns are like that. There is nowhere to hide amidst a population of nine thousand. He dropped his head and stared down the length of his six foot frame and his eyes came to rest on his shiny black policeman's boots. He recalled the first time he put the uniform on eleven years ago. He instantly felt authoritative. He felt responsible, something he had rarely felt in his carefree life up until that point. He knew that he now had to set a good example, especially for the children of the town because their parents were telling them that the police are their friends. The police are there to protect them. You can trust the police. Look up to them. One of those children eleven years ago would have been eight year-old Peggy Welton, and now she sat in a cell on her way to a jail sentence that would almost certainly see her into her late thirties and perhaps beyond. Pete suddenly felt as though he was as much to blame for Peggy's fall from grace as anyone else. "It takes a village, right?" he thought.

Out on Main Street, the blast of a semi's air horn shattered Pete's moment of self-examination. The officer looked to his right towards the town's main drag. There was another horn blast. Judging by the sound, the vehicle was approaching from the east end of Main Street. As the third blast of the horn shot through the evening air, a Kenworth eighteen wheeler roared past the corner of Main and Grandy and as soon as it's rear wheels had cleared the intersection and disappeared from Pete's view, the officer heard the air brakes wheeze and whine and the tires screech and yelp. "Jesus Christ!" Pete ran towards the corner that had seconds ago been violated by the big rig. Reaching the intersection he looked west and on the next block up he saw the Kenworth turning left onto Mary Street. The truck took the corner at such a speed that Pete held his breath momentarily thinking it would surely jackknife or just plain tip right over. It didn't. Instead it gave one more air horn blast and continued angrily up Mary Street.

Officer Golliger turned and ran back towards the police station. As he did, he saw Wood and Lori emerge via the front door of the station and train their gaze on him.

"What the hell was that?" asked Wood.

"I don't know," Pete replied, running past his law enforcement mate. "Let's go find out!"

The two officers ran to the small parking lot beside the station and climbed into one of two police cruisers which were parked there in the gravel lot. Pete, was about to put the key into the ignition when he stopped abruptly.

"What the hell is that smell?"

"Peggy threw up in the back seat last night."

"Aw, Christ." Pete lurched out of the cruiser and slammed the door.

Wood exited the vehicle and slammed the passenger side door. The two officers sprinted towards the other cruiser.

"Jesus Christ, Wood!"

"And I did not have sex with her!"

"Shut up!"

Pete and Wood climbed into the second cruiser. Behind the wheel, Pete turned the car on and gunned the engine but he didn't bother backing out of the parking spot and exiting the lot through the driveway as he normally would. Instead, he put the car into drive and shooting gravel from his rear wheels he proceeded right over the curb and onto Grandy Street. He swung the car to its right and roared towards Main Street. Lori Higgenson watched from the sidewalk, mouth agape yet again. This was without a shadow of a doubt, the biggest goddamned day in her entire professional life.

Bryden managed to get to his feet before Grace, who lay in a heap in front of the chest of drawers that had just broken her forward motion. She had hit the piece of furniture with such force that the face of the top drawer had buckled and caved in. And now she felt Bryden's hand on the top of her head as he grabbed her by the hair and pulled her to her feet. She now stood face to face with Bryden. The look of condescension that he wore when he arrived had disappeared and had been replaced with a look of rage. Grace felt something metallic pressing up under her chin. It caused her head to push back so that she now had to strain to look at Bryden through the bottoms of her eye sockets. It also prevented her from calling out. She could barely open her mouth now, let alone scream for help. He pushed her up against the chest of drawers and held her there. His left leg was between her legs and his right leg wrapped around her left leg so there was no chance of a repeat of Grace's last self-defense move.

"I can't believe you would pull a gun on me," said Bryden in a low, growling, maniacal voice. "But that's what you did. That's right. I came here to try and talk my wife, the woman I love, into coming back home with me and getting the help she so desperately needs. But her bi-polarism or her Cyclothymia or her Capgras Syndrome or whatever the fuck the mental illness of the month is these days, got the best of her, and she pulled a gun on me. I don't know where she got the gun, officer. I swear. We were talking – I was pleading with her to come back with me – when all of a sudden she had a gun in her hand. I tried to take it away from her. I know that was a stupid thing to do. I know you should never do that, but I thought for sure she was going to kill me, so I moved toward her and reached out for the gun. but then she did something completely unexpected. She put the gun under her own chin, pulled the trigger, and blew the top of her head off. It happened so fast, I couldn't stop her."

Grace was now fully aware of what was pushing up from under her chin. This would be her final moment on this earth. Her last breath was only seconds away. She felt sad that the last voice she would hear in her life would be that of this man she once loved and now, so despised. There would be no one holding her hand gently and telling her in a soothing voice that it was okay to go to sleep. That they loved her but it was time to let go. This was how she had always pictured her death. Lying in her own bed at home with a son or daughter or both at her bedside. Grandchildren waiting in the other room. A long life lived to the fullest, and a family she was so very proud of there to see her off. There might even be an angel in the room. Grace was not overly religious, but she did have high hopes that angels existed and that one would be on hand to escort her to her next destination, whatever that might be. But there were no angels in this small room, in this inn, in this town she didn't know all that well. There was just a man she loathed pressing his body up against hers so hard that she could feel the metal knob of the second drawer digging into her back. And under her chin, a gun.

*

Dan the trucker, was held up for a good five hours at the U.S.-Canada border in Houlton, Maine while the suspicious customs inspectors went through his truck. He was questioned in an office by two other inspectors, even though he pleaded with them to let him go. He explained the situation. There was a woman in trouble in a small town called Rainbow and he had to get there as quickly as possible. But, the inspectors had heard every story in the book over the years, and had never yielded to verbal flights of fancy from a suspect. And so he sat and waited in a cold sweat, until finally, finding nothing untoward in his vehicle or on his person, the inspectors let him pass. And now here he was, racing up a side street in this small New Brunswick town, his big rig steaming and snorting towards the inn where he had last seen Grace Downey. He didn't even notice the black BMW parked two blocks down from the inn as he roared past. He parked the truck as close to the front door of the inn as he could, almost taking out the covered entryway in the process. He jumped down from the cab and in a matter of seven or eight strides, found himself in the lobby of The Allemane.

"Help you?" the vivacious brunette behind the check-in desk asked.

"Grace. Grace Downey. What room is she in?"

"You can't leave your truck out there," the woman replied, looking past Dan towards the front door.

"What?"

"Your truck. It's blocking the wheel chair access. How are my wheel chair customers supposed to get in?"

"I don't give a shit how they get in! Where's Grace Downey?"

Kate Leger swept her jet black hair away from both shoulders with her hand right and steeled herself. She had as much fight in her as the next person and she did not take kindly to being spoken to in such a bold and gruff manner. Over the years she had thrown many a drunken patron out of her lounge all by herself. The situation did not exist that Kate could not handle.

"Listen, dipstick," she began. "Move your damn truck, and then come back in here with a brand new fucking attitude and talk to me nicely. Okay?"

Dan took a moment to gather himself as the woman in the Spanish style dress looked him straight in the eye. "I'm sorry," he said. "But, Grace Downey is in danger and I have to see her right now."

Kate paused, then spoke as if a light had just been turned on. "You're that guy who called about the black BMW."

"Yes, that's me."

"The mystery car, right?"

"Right. That was me."

"The Stephen King Christine car."

"Look, can we just forget about the car for a minute please?"

"Well, it seemed pretty important when you called. And now you want to forget it?"

"I just need to talk to Grace. That's all I want."

"Are you stalking her?"

"No."

"Because that would explain why she showed in town all by herself and is hiding out here. A woman doesn't do something like that unless she's getting grief from some jerk, dildo, Chuck Norris-loving man."

"I am not stalking her. I'm the one who drove her here. Remember? We had a drink in the lounge last night."

"Do you expect me to remember everyone who comes into my bar?"

"There were only FOUR people here! I was one of them! Christ! You're Kate. I'm Dan. Remember?"

There was a long silence as Dan and Kate stared each other down.

"I remember you. I remembered you right off. But just because you had a drink in the bar with Grace doesn't mean you're not stalking her."

"Oh, Sweet Jesus." Dan put both hands on the counter and dropped his head in frustration.

"Look, Grace hasn't come back yet so I couldn't give her your message and besides I haven't seen a black BMW."

"She didn't come back?"

"Not yet."

"Are you sure?"

"Positive . . . . Well, unless she came back while I was in the lounge and I missed her."

" . . . . So you could have missed her?"

"Isn't that what I just said?"

"What in the hell is your hurry, mister?" Pete's voice came from behind Dan.

The truck driver turned to see Officers Golliger and Lynch standing just inside the front door of the inn.

"That's a quiet neighbourhood street you were driving on. Kids play on that street. You could have killed someone."

"Officer, look," Dan began. "You've got to help me here. There's a woman in danger and I have to get to her now."

"What woman?" asked Pete.

"Her name is Grace Downey. I dropped her off in town a couple of nights ago and now her husband is on his way up here for I don't know what reason exactly but I know it's not good. He must be here already because he had a real good head start on me and I just got here."

"He the one driving the black BMW?" Kate asked.

"Yes," Dan replied, giving Kate a quick look and then turning back to the officers.

"Yeah, well, I haven't seen a black BMW," said Pete. "And a black BMW would be hard to miss in a have not town like this one."

"We passed a black BMW up the street," said Wood.

"What?" Dan looked at the officer.

"Yeah, a block or two back. Parked on the street."

"Are you sure, Wood?" Pete asked.

"Pete, it was a black BMW. I notice these things. And like you say, there's nobody in Rainbow drives a BMW as far as I know."

The sharp snapping sound of the gunshot from the second floor of The Allemane Inn abruptly ended the four way conversation in the lobby.

*

The large meaty hand was on the wrist of his gun hand a split second after Bryden heard the door to the A.R. Wetmore room swing open. In the next instant, Bryden was spun around and the thundering punch sent the jawbone of Penobscot County's front-running District Attorney candidate up into his brain and he was dead before he hit the hardwood floor. The crushing blow also caused Bryden's index finger to flex tightly on the trigger of the handgun, resulting in a loud discharge into the stomach of his assailant. Leo Terrio, rocked by the bullet, took two unsteady steps back, but like the true boxing warrior he was, he did not go down. He pressed his right hand to the wound and saw the blood seep out slowly from between his fingers. He looked at Grace, who was still leaning against the chest of drawers. He spoke to the woman. His friend. "Are you all right?"

-Epilogue-

Wood Lynch stood in the driveway of the small house he once shared with his wife Jeannie and their son Evan. Jeannie's car, its back seat loaded down with all belongings it could hold, and now towing a U-Haul trailer, sat idling on the inexpensive blacktop covering of the driveway. She and Evan would probably make it as far as Montreal today, stay there overnight and then continue on to Kingston, their final destination, the next morning.

"Call me when you get to Montreal," Wood said to his estranged wife, the woman he still loved so very much.

"I will. Don't worry."

"Don't tell me not to worry, Jeannie. I'll be worrying from now until I get that phone call. You know that."

"Yeah, I know."

There was a pause as Wood looked to the front lawn where his son Evan was kicking at a soccer ball. Out of every three attempts, Evan's foot would only connect with the ball once if lucky. The boy had inherited his father's questionable athletic skills.

"So, what are you gonna do, Bobby? Do you know yet?" Jeannie had never liked the nickname 'Wood'. She always called her husband Bobby. That's what he was known as when she met him all those years ago in high school and that's how she knew him to this day.

"Nope. Haven't decided."

"Well, you're gonna have to find work. Today's your last day as a cop here."

"I know."

"I still think Charlottetown is your best bet."

Wood looked at Evan on the lawn. Another missed kick. "Nice try, Ev. Eye on the ball now."

"You won't go to Charlottetown, will you?"

"Probably not," came Wood's reply.

"Yeah, I figured."

"I still love you." Wood said the words without taking his eyes off of Evan. "I've never stopped loving you, Jeannie."

"Bobby . . . . I still love you too. You know that, but I can't live with a man who won't give me any room. You smother me. Shit. I can't breathe the way you smother me."

"Maybe I could change."

" . . . . You? Change?"

"I could try. I really could."

Jeannie thought about it for a moment. If Wood could change there really might be a chance for the two of them. She would much rather have a family unit in place for her son than be a single mother any day. And she did love Wood. She really did. She loved him more than she would ever love another man, and she knew it. " . . . . Bobby, we've gotta go. If we don't leave now we won't get to Montreal until it's dark."

"I don't want you driving in the dark in a strange city, Jeannie."

"Jesus Christ, Wood. Jesus Christ! What did I just say? There you go smothering me again."

"I'm sorry."

"Shit."

"I'm sorry."

Jeannie opened the driver's side door and turned to her son on the lawn. "Time to go, Evan."

"Can I come to visit?" Wood asked.

"Of course you can come to visit. You can come anytime you like."

"When?"

"Anytime."

"Soon?"

"Yes, soon. Anytime."

"I could help you get set up in your new place."

"That soon?"

"Why not? I'm out of a job."

Evan threw his soccer ball into the back seat of the car. As he did, Wood, swept him up and put the boy on his hip. "You be a good boy for Mommy, huh Ev?"

"I will."

"Promise?"

"I promise."

"I'm gonna miss you, you know that?"

"Uh-huh." Evan was looking inside the car to see where his soccer ball had come to rest.

"I'm gonna miss you a lot." Wood kissed Evan on the cheek. He fought back a tear in an attempt to prevent this moment from being an unpleasant one for his son. He wanted to make the boy think that this was just one more good-bye. The kind of good-bye the two had said many times over the past two years when Wood would drop Evan off at home after an ice cream, or after a game of catch at Moran Park or after a weekend stay at Wood's sparsely-furnished apartment. "How much does Daddy love you, Ev?"

Evan looked at his father. The two had performed this good-bye ritual with each parting since the separation. "Bigger than . . . the moon?!"

" . . . Way bigger," Wood said, his voice breaking. "Way bigger than the moon." Wood kissed Evan's cheek again, set the boy down, and watched him scramble into the driver's side front seat and then across to the passenger side.

"Bye, Bobby." Jeannie gave Wood a kiss on the lips. She wiped away the tear that Wood had let flow since setting his son down. "As soon as you like, you come visit. Okay?" And a tear flowed from her eye as well. "My God. Dammit. I love you so much, you . . . you idiot!" Jeannie put her head into Wood's chest and cried.

"I don't suppose you're ready for a date yet, huh?"

"Well, Dan, my husband died four days ago. I don't know if a four day mourning period is quite suitable."

The truck driver stood at the bottom of Grace's front porch, his left foot perched on the first of the three steps that led up to her door. He had dropped her off here two days ago and he had stopped in on this day to see how his passenger was making out. After her husband's death, Grace stayed in Rainbow, New Brunswick for one more day, and then decided to come back and face the Maine press who would have an endless round of questions for her about Bryden Downey's demise. Dan stayed over in Rainbow for one more day as well. He didn't want Grace to have to make the trip back home all alone and so he stayed on so he could drive her back himself. On the way home in the big rig, Grace told Dan that she had decided to sell the house that she and Bryden had shared and then she would move down to Boston to try and find work in public relations, the career she had been fairly successful at before giving it up to aid in her husband's quest for a prominent spot on the American political landscape.

"All right, then how a bout' a coffee sometime? That's not a date. That's just coffee."

"Coffee's not a date?" Grace smiled wryly.

"Hell, no. Coffee is just coffee. Well, unless you get one of those fancy giant coffees with the whipped cream on top. You know the kind of coffee they make with a machine that makes all that noise? That's pretty fancy so that might be a date coffee."

"Don't play the hick with me, Dan. I think I know you a little better than that."

"Yeah, I guess you do." Dan slipped his hands into his back pockets and looked down at the step where his left foot rested. " . . . . Remember at Shiner's Truck stop when you asked me how come I didn't have a woman in my life and I said because I never found a woman tall enough?"

"Yes."

Dan looked up at Grace. "How tall are you?"

"Five ten."

"Hmm. Five ten. That's pretty tall."

"It is, isn't it?"

"Damn right it is." Dan looked down the sidewalk for no other reason than he thought that if he continued to stare into Grace's eyes, he might surely melt right there at the bottom of the stoop. "Well, I'll guess I'll get going then." His gaze drifted back to Grace and he fumbled for something clever and Dan-like to say. "I'll be back though. I'll give you a little more mourning time and then I'll be back. How's tomorrow sound?"

Grace continued to smile at Dan but didn't answer.

"Right. Maybe not tomorrow then. But you'll be seeing me sometime. I can guarantee you that much. I'm a pretty determined fella."

"I'm counting on that," Grace replied.

Dan turned and walked down the pavement towards his truck which was rumbling in place on this well-to-do street. He stopped halfway down the walk and turned back to the beautiful woman standing in the archway of her front door. "You okay, Grace?"

Grace looked at the man who had been so kind to her during this past week. The look on his face was one of genuine concern and right now she appreciated that more than anything else he could have offered. " . . . . I'm getting there."

*

"All right, Lori, gimme a hug."

Information Coordinator Lori Higgenson moved to Pete Golliger and nestled her head into his chest. "I can't believe you're really leaving, Pete."

"Well, there's nothing here for me now, is there?"

"You've got friends here. Lots of friends." Lori looked up at Pete without letting go as the two of them stood on the sidewalk in front of The Rainbow Police Station

"Yeah, I know, but years ago I got this wanderlust in me and I put it on hold when I took the police job. I think maybe it's time to re-visit it."

Lori stepped back and took hold of Pete's hands with hers. "I'll miss ya', Pete."

"I'll miss you too, Darlin'. I hope I wasn't too rough on you these past few years."

"Naw. Whenever you were rough on me, I deserved it anyway."

"Yeah, I know you did." Pete smiled and turned to the big man in the RCMP uniform standing beside him. "Sergeant McCaffrey, you take care of this young woman you hear? She's invaluable."

"I will. And good luck, Mr. Golliger," the Sergeant replied holding out his hand.

"Thanks." Pete reached out and shook McCaffrey's hand.

"And by the way, officer. Good job on the Hoyt case. Real good job."

"Well, we didn't do too much. The girl up and confessed. That's how the case got solved. It wasn't police work that did it."

"You fellas put the pieces together. That's why she confessed. She had no choice. No, that was some damn fine police work if you ask me."

"Thank you. I appreciate that." Pete looked down the sidewalk towards Main Street and the citizens who were passing there. "Look after this town for me, okay? These are good folks here. The very best."

"I'll do that."

Pete nodded to the RCMP officer and then walked around to the driver's side of his Pontiac Grand Am. Having use of the police cruiser over the past eleven years, Pete hadn't driven his old car maybe more than a couple of hundred miles in that whole time. As he put his hand on his car door, he spoke across the top of the vehicle to the RCMP officer on the sidewalk. "Oh, about Leo Terrio. You'll see him through this thing all right, will you?"

"Nothing to worry about, sir," the Sergeant replied. "I doubt if there will even be any charges. Once he's released from the hospital he can go right back to living how he was."

"You think so?"

"He's got a bullet hole in his stomach, sir. If that isn't self-defense, I don't know what is."

"Thank you, Sergeant."

Pete heard a ringing coming from his pants pocket. "Shit . . . what the?" He fumbled in his pocket and pulled out a cell phone. Pete had never owned a cell phone before but Lori Higgenson had finally talked him into buying one because he might need it on the road and the RCMP might need to get hold of him if they have any questions about their new surroundings. What Lori really wanted was someone else she could call up at all hours and spread the town gossip to.

"Hello?" Pete yelled into the phone.

"You don't have to yell, Pete," Lori said from her position on the sidewalk. "It's like a real phone. It amplifies your voice and everything." Her sarcasm was not lost of Pete.

"Hello?" Pete said in a softer voice.

"Pete?" came the voice from the other end of the phone. "It's Wood."

"Wood? Hey, guess what? You're the first person to call me on my new cell phone."

Pete looked to Lori and she gave him a faux-enthusiastic thumbs up.

"Pete, listen . . . ."

"Did you hear me, Wood? Did you hear what I just said or do I need to yell?"

"I heard you. I don't care that I'm the first person to call your stupid phone, okay? I don't care. Now, listen, I haven't got much time. I'm calling you from a pay phone in Edmunston."

"Edmunston? What are you doin' in Edmunston?"

Edmunston was a town near the New Brunswick/Quebec border. It was the last real good stop for food, gas and the use of facilities before a traveler got to Quebec City three hours later.

"I'll explain that some other time. Listen, Pete, how much would one of our police cruisers run a fella?"

"What do you mean, Wood?"

"I mean, how much would one of our police cruisers cost?"

"Cost? Shit, I don't know," Pete replied. "Probably fifty or sixty grand."

"That much huh? Damn. Well, I've got the cruiser with me here and I'm on my way to Kingston, so, uh . . . ."

"Wood, hang on a second, okay?" Pete tossed the cell phone over the roof of the Pontiac Grand Am to Sergeant McCaffrey. "It's for you." Pete smiled, climbed into his car and drove off in the direction of Main Street where he made a left turn. He drove down Main Street slowly, taking in the view as he went. The Frying Dutchman, elm tree, the hardware store, elm tree, Tim Horton's, elm tree. "Nice," he thought. At Moran park the road bent to the right and before long Pete found himself sitting at the entrance to the Trans-Canada Highway. Take the highway west and he would travel through Quebec and back to his home province of Ontario. Take it east, and he would go to Prince Edward Island or Nova Scotia. Pete tapped his fingers on the steering wheel. He had plenty of time to think about this before now. He knew he would be leaving town on this day and yet here he sat, still undecided about which direction to travel.

*

Pete Golliger moved to the third stool in from the front door of The Frying Dutchman – his favourite stool – and sat down.

"Hi Pete," said Henry Van Etten with a nod. He then turned his gaze back to the twenty inch Magnavox that sat on a jarry-rigged shelf above the microwave.

"Hey, Henry."

"I thought you was leavin' town today."

"Changed my mind."

"Uh-huh? What can I get ya'?"

"How about a piece of that famous raspberry pie?"

"You got it." Henry pointed up to the television set. "Is that too green?"

"Hmm?"

"The colour? Is it too green? It looks too green to me. And the Price Is Right is comin' on." Henry moved down to the end of the counter and took the plastic lid off of one his famous raspberry pies.

Pete looked up at the television set. "I think it needs more red."

"Well, then it's too green. That's what I'm sayin'. How big a piece?"

"Hmm?"

"The pie. How big a piece?"

"What do you mean? You mean I have a say in how big a piece I get?"

"Hey, for the man who's done everything you've done for this town all these years, you're damn right you have a say."

Pete looked at the Dutchman. For a moment the former police officer didn't speak. He cleared his throat and looked at the pie that Henry held on a tray. He looked back to Henry. "No kiddin'? . . . . Uh . . . . All right then, well . . . just a regular size piece, Henry. Thanks." Pete turned to his right to look out the window onto Main Street where the town was going about its business. He recalled that he was sitting on this very same stool seven days ago when Mickey Welton made his appearance on Jeopardy. This was the first time that Pete had been back to The Frying Dutchman since that eventful night.

"Henry?"

"Yeah?"

"Nobody we know is gonna be on The Price Is Right today, are they?"

"Don't think so."

"Good."

END

CPSIA information can be obtained at www.ICGtesting.com
Printed in the USA
LVOW070420140513

333577LV00002B/40/P